RYANN FLETCHER

Imperfect Shot

First edition

ISBN: 978-1-9163750-3-1

This book was professionally typeset on Reedsy.
Find out more at reedsy.com

To all the women who look at the night sky with wonder.
The stars are yours.

Contents

CHAPTER ONE

Evie scrubbed at a sticky patch on the worn wooden bar, watching the slight sheen of the dried ale disappear. She rubbed her shoulder, prodding at the knot in the muscle from a long day of hefting heavy boxes of ale, whiskey, and wine all the way from the port back to the Purple Pig Tavern where she had worked for the better part of five years.

She didn't mind the work, but preferred it when people left her alone to do her job, instead of drunkenly spilling out their sad stories, most of which were brought on by their own bad behavior. Pull a pint, serve the liquor, wipe the bar. Her boss, Tansy, was trusting her to make fair trades, goods for booze, and log it all at the end of her shift.

The gold clock on the wall ticked slowly, in spite of the glare she gave it. She could swear it was moving backwards. Her girlfriend was coming back from a month long salvage mission today, after three weeks drifting in the Near Systems looking for scrap they could sell at a profit.

Holly was the most beautiful woman Evie had ever seen, tall and curvy with long, wavy locks of brunette hair and eyes so deep and blue, you could almost see straight into space when you looked into them. In fact, Evie wasn't sure how she managed to end up with someone as perfect as Holly, not with her dead-end job. When she met Holly in the Purple Pig six months ago, her heart nearly pounded out of her chest. She'd almost choked on the dregs of her ale when Holly gently caressed her cheek and asked her on a date.

"Hello Babes!" Holly shouted as she burst through the swinging doors of the tavern. She swung her long, shapely legs over a bronze stool and leaned seductively over the bar in front of Evie. "Did you miss me?"

"Of *course* I missed you," Evie said, unable to contain her enthusiasm. "I've been counting the days until you came back."

"I'll bet you have," Holly said with a wink. "When are you off? I have a surprise for you!"

"A surprise?" Evie hadn't been expecting a gift. Just seeing Holly's perfect face was gift enough for her. She'd missed her desperately, and being in Holly's presence was like raising your face to the sun after a long, cold night.

"Mhmm," Holly nodded absent-mindedly. "So when are you finished?"

"Another few minutes yet," Evie admitted, a sullen, petulant tone to her voice. She couldn't leave until her replacement, Gabe, arrived, and he was never early. Even if he was, she doubted he'd let her leave even a few seconds before the end of her scheduled shift. "Why don't you grab a seat and some food, and I'll join you when I'm finished?"

Holly wrinkled her nose. "I don't want to eat *here*."

Before Evie could argue, a group of scrappers wandered in, laughing and shoving each other playfully. Holly waved to them and grinned, her pearl white teeth nearly blinding in the relaxed, dim light of the tavern. "Hey!" she shouted, beckoning to them loudly over the din of the other tavern patrons. She turned back to Evie. "Babes, say hi to my team." Her sparkling eyes glimmered and melted Evie's heart. How could one person be so beautiful, so intelligent and perfect, and be interested in her? Evie gazed at Holly's face, and couldn't wait to feel the weight of the woman in her arms. "Babes?" Holly prompted.

Evie waved and squeaked out a quiet "Hello" before they, and Holly, left the bar to crowd around a table in the center of the room, but not before placing a sizable drinks order. She bustled about, preparing their drinks. Two pints of ale, seven shots of whiskey, four glasses of fortified red wine so strong it would eat through the lush purple velvet that covered the walls. The group was chatty and loud, and Evie watched their interactions with interest. Holly had told her that the crew had all known each other for years, hopping from ship to ship to get the most lucrative salvage missions, but the way they all looked at her told Evie they were just as dazzled by Holly's presence as she was.

"Hey, Holly," said a sultry voice from the entrance. When Evie turned, a tall, broad-shouldered woman with features almost more striking than Holly's sauntered in. She was dressed in the same navy blue jumpsuits as the others, with their salvage team name represented by an embroidered gold snake on the collar. The woman glided over to the table and leaned gracefully on the back of Holly's chair. "I looked everywhere for you at the port, I didn't realize you'd be coming here."

Holly beamed up at the woman with wide, innocent eyes. "I just assumed you'd head up this way, Babes," she said sweetly, and Evie flushed with jealousy. "Anyway, you're here now, but we aren't staying long, the food here sucks."

"We have a new cook since you were last here," Evie interjected helpfully, and punctuated her suggestion with a nervous cough. Holly's team intimidated her; they were brazen, successful salvagers with plenty of credits to spend and none of the insecurities that plagued Evie.

"Oh, don't worry Babes, we have plans to eat at that new place on the other side of the port."

This was the first Evie was hearing about it, and in fact she had assumed that she and Holly would go back to her room and have a quiet night in. Maybe Holly wanted her to become more friendly with her team? "Oh, okay, I'll run home and change my clothes," Evie said, untying the strings of her dirty, ale soaked apron. Gabe came in through the back door of the tavern, and the clock finally proved that her shift was over.

"Oh, Babes..." Holly said, looking guilty. She walked to the bar and leaned over it to kiss Evie on the cheek. "We only got reservations for team members." She made an apologetic face that made Evie giggle. "I can't wait to tell you about your surprise, though... meet you later, at yours?"

"Mine?" Evie nodded enthusiastically. "Of course." Holly had never been to her place before, and it felt like they were taking their relationship to the next level. Maybe she'd have a key made for her, as a token of how much she trusted her.

"We're heading off, Babes," Holly called from the table. "I'll see you later, yeah?"

"Yeah, see you later," Evie agreed, though she couldn't quite swallow back the bitter pill that she wasn't going with them. At least she had time to go back home and get cleaned up before Holly came over; she hated the way that Evie's clothes smelled after working a shift. Grease, booze, and on particularly unfortunate days, vomit.

She watched the group gather their things and leave half-empty glasses on their table, waving over their shoulders as they piled out onto the cobblestone street. It would have been nice if they had returned their dirty cups to her at the bar, but it was okay, they had reservations at the swanky place across town. She collected the dishes and piled them on top of a sticky tray, and glanced up just in time to see the new woman drape an arm around Holly's shoulder. Jealousy burned in her stomach, but she took a swig of ale to try to quench it. She was just being silly.

A woman dressed in black pushed her way past Holly's group into the tavern, rolling her eyes. She sat down at the bar and pushed a wide, heavy hood off her head. It flopped onto her shoulders and she looked up at Evie through thick lashes. "Rum. Make it a double." She had a confident, disarming smile that Evie liked, even though she'd never seen the woman before, and definitely not in the Purple Pig.

"Sure thing, coming right up," Evie said, pouring thick, amber liquid into a small glass. "I've not seen you in here before," she offered, setting the glass in front of the woman. Something about her made Evie curious enough to make small talk, which she usually despised.

"I'm finishing up an assignment," the woman said bluntly. "I've been in here once or twice before, though."

Evie glanced over her shoulder into the kitchen area of the tavern, but she still couldn't see Gabe. Odd, but she shrugged it off. "Well, welcome back, then," Evie said, trying to put the thought of Holly and her attractive crew mate out of her mind. "Staying long?"

"No," the woman replied. "My line of work is extremely fast paced."

"And what do you do for work?" Evie asked, but before the woman could answer, Gabe stumbled into the bar.

"Evie," he said in a pleading voice. "Can you take my shift? I'm a little, uh—"

"Hungover?" Evie interjected. "I can tell. You look like you're about to keel over." She sighed angrily. "Gabe, I told you, Holly is back tonight, I can't work late. She's been gone for weeks, and once she gets back from dinner with her team, I—"

"She went to dinner without you?" the woman asked. "After weeks away?"

Evie stared. "Yes, but it's for work. She had no choice."

The woman shrugged. "Sounds like bullshit to me."

Evie turned back to Gabe, deciding to ignore the woman. "Gabe, are you sure you can't just suck it up and work the shift?"

He covered his mouth and retched. "No, Evie, I don't think I can. Can't Tansy cover for me?"

"I don't know, did you ask her?"

Gabe shook his head but wandered away to drag himself up the stairs to Tansy's apartment over the tavern, where she lived ever since she bought the Purple Pig over a decade earlier. Tansy had spent a decade slinging illegal alcohol in the pirate port of Bradach, where the Purple Pig sat high on the hill, overlooking the docks. She'd gotten injured on an illegal salvage mission over ten years ago, and dumped her life savings into the tavern when she realized she couldn't go on salvage missions forever. She'd turned the tavern from a grubby, dank hole into a borderline opulent tavern for pirates and scavengers of all kinds to have a drink and a meal before they set off into space again.

"Did you want anything else?" Evie asked the woman in a steely tone, turning back to face her.

"Another."

"It's not her choice, you know," Evie explained as she poured rum into the glass, regretting letting her curiosity get the better of her. This is exactly why she hated talking to strangers. "If Holly had her say, I'd be eating dinner with the rest of them tonight. Or we'd be at my place, and I'd make her dinner. She's beautiful, and kind, and she cares about me."

The woman stared at her for a moment before taking a sip of the rum. "Are you trying to convince me, or yourself?" she asked.

"You!" Evie said, a little louder than she had intended. She felt flustered that this stranger could just insert herself into her life and make assumptions about her relationship. "It's actually pretty damn rude for you to say these things, and I— "

The woman put her hands up to silence Evie. "Look, lady, what's your name again?"

"Evie."

She smirked. "Look, Evie, I'm not trying to make waves for you and your girl, alright?" She drained her glass and set it down noisily on the bar. "I'm just saying, it seems real inconsiderate. If some asshole said I couldn't bring my girl to dinner, I'd sock him one, right in the nose." She winked at Evie and slammed down a chunk of metal on the bar that looked like a part for an appliance or a ship. "This enough to get me another?"

"I don't know what that is."

"It's some kind of rare ship part, I don't know, some mechanic gave it to me."

Rolling the part around in her palm, Evie examined the piece of metal. It was cold and smooth, a long empty cylinder with jagged edges that suggested it had, until recently, been attached to something. "I don't know, my boss..." Evie mumbled, wishing the woman had something normal to trade for her drinks. Some gold, or stolen scrap metal, or even outdated tech would be preferable to hunks of common metal.

"Come on, Blue, I promise it's worth more credits than you get paid in a month." The woman leaned forward across the bar. "Nice hair, by the way."

Evie pushed a stray tuft of blue hair off her forehead and huffed. "Don't call me that," Evie said. Something about the woman's unapologetic confidence and charm was disarming, and made her feel off balance and irritated. She sighed again and logged the odd part into the trade book under the counter before pouring the woman another glass of rum.

"Thank you," the woman said, running her fingers around the rim of the glass. "It's much appreciated, and your kindness won't go unrewarded."

Evie snorted a laugh. "Oh yeah? What are you going to do, waltz in here in a few months and dump a pile of rare ore into my lap?"

The woman shrugged. "Maybe. Or maybe your luck will improve, and you'll end up an heir to some mining fortune." She held the rum close to her face and inhaled the scent of the amber liquid. "Maybe your girl will take you out for dinner at that fancy restaurant next time." Before Evie could reply, the woman squinted at her and leaned over onto the bar. "You know, I never could see why anyone would want a restaurant like that in a port like this. Pirates, scavengers, nobility, Coalition, it doesn't matter. Give someone a little money and all of a sudden they think they're better than anyone else."

"Mm," Evie nodded, aware that the rum was loosening the woman's tongue. "Yes, I agree. But there's no feasible alternative, not while the Coalition still holds most of the Near Systems in its grip."

"See, there's where you're wrong, Evie," the woman said, pointing at her. "Sometimes, you just gotta pry up some planks and see what's underneath. If it's rotten, it's rotten. And rot needs to be gotten rid of, don't ya think?"

"I think you should take a breather on that rum," Evie laughed, taking the empty glass from the woman. "What are you in here running from, anyway?"

The woman stared for a moment. "Nah. Nothin'. Just wanted a good time."

Evie turned to serve another patron of the tavern and paused to wipe down the bar again. Where the hell was Gabe? The clock chimed, and Evie just wanted to bolt from the tavern and whisk Holly to her room. On a night like tonight, there weren't enough credits in the Near Systems to keep her at work with a smile on her face. Tansy paid her a fair wage, but there were limits to her generosity. Bradach assured that every citizen had shelter, food, and care, but Evie had always wanted more for herself than to stay where she'd been planted, infamous pirate port or no. What else was out there for her? Maybe nothing. Maybe an adventure, or at least an experience to remember that wasn't the same old routine of working at the tavern, and going home to her small room in a shared house.

"Gabe?" she called up the winding staircase, her voice lost among the noise of the tavern. "Gabe, come on!" she said, getting frustrated. She turned back to the bar and cleared the empty glasses, setting them noisily into a damp wooden crate.

"You should stop being a doormat," the woman said, her head propped up on one hand.

"I'm not a doormat," Evie replied, her tone with more of an edge than she had intended. "What else am I supposed to do, just leave?"

The woman laughed. "You could do that. You could also march up those stairs and drag his hungover ass back down to the bar and leave him to nurse his headache and his sore stomach while you go home to the girlfriend who definitely respects you enough to not get cuddly with her new recruit right in front of your place of work." She tilted her head to the side in an appraising way as she looked at Evie. "But that's just me."

"You know, I'm surprised you've not been thrown out of more taverns with this kind of attitude. Most barkeeps wouldn't tolerate it, you're lucky I'm nice."

"Alright, prove me wrong. Throw me out, then." The woman raised an eyebrow and sat up straight, like she was challenging Evie to toss her out of the tavern for her comments about Holly. The deep hood fell over one side of her bronzed cheeks, the tail of a long, dark braid peeking out from beneath her cloak.

Evie rolled her eyes and went back to wiping the bar. It wasn't the first time a drunk on a barstool had too much to say.

"That's what I thought," the woman said, a smile playing at her lips.

"Hey, Evie," Tansy said apologetically as she descended the stairs outside her office. "Gabe's not in good shape. Definitely not in any condition to work tonight." Tansy's tweed shorts brushed against dark skin and alloy; her time as a scavenger had left her with one top of the line, expertly crafted cybernetic prosthetic leg that she was proud of showing off. "If you could just stay on for another couple of hours..."

"I told Gabe that I have plans tonight," Evie complained. "Holly is back, and I was going to spend time with her."

"Holly, who went to dinner *without* her," the woman snorted.

Evie whirled around and glared at the woman. "Keep out of this," she hissed.

"Let's just take a breath, Evie," Tansy said, stepping behind the bar and tying an apron around her waist. "I'll cover for Gabe until the next shift starts. Go see your girl. I'll see you back here tomorrow."

"Thank you," Evie said, heaving a sigh of relief. "You don't know how much this means to me." She wiped her hands off on her worn canvas dungarees and lifted the bar counter to slide out from behind it. "I'll be here for my shift, don't worry."

"Yeah, you'd better be," Tansy laughed. "Next time I'll be the one with plans. Don't let me down like Gabe did tonight."

Evie rolled her eyes. "Definitely not." She yanked her cap from a hook on the wall and gestured towards the woman at the bar. "And no more for her, she's had enough." She smirked at the woman's incredulous face and clapped her on the back. "Not so much a doormat as you thought, am I?" she said, low enough so only the woman could hear.

* * *

Evie straightened the thin grey blanket on top of her tiny bed and tried to ignore the nervous tension that hung heavy in the air. Holly would arrive any moment, and it would be the first time she'd see where Evie lived. They had spent all the other times at Holly's room in the last ship she worked on, which was a top grade salvage craft with en suite bathrooms and vast beds with soft mattresses. Now that her contract had ended, she would have nowhere to stay until her team signed on for their next assignment.

She looked around the room with a critical eye, unable to ignore the patch of black mold in the corner near the window, or how the curtains were slightly too short to keep out the bright sunlight, or the lopsided, overstuffed chair in the corner next to a pile of notebooks neatly stacked against a wall covered in peeling, floral wallpaper. Bradach was a prosperous town, and though Evie's living quarters weren't the best, they were light years above what poorer people living in Coalition tenements had to endure.

Someday she'd save enough to leave Bradach for good, and travel to Gamma-3 or Delta-4 where the largest cities were, where she could take on an apprenticeship in research, digging through dusty old tomes searching for the answers to all the problems of the universe. Her brothers had left Bradach years earlier after cashing in on a huge illegal scrap salvage. Evie was the only one left on Bradach of her family after her mother left to join her brothers on a scrapper settlement near the boundary of the Near Systems. Money there went further, but living could be harder, and Evie wanted to give herself a real chance of making it on her own.

"Babes?" There was a soft knock at the door, and Evie leapt up to open it. Holly stood there, beautiful as ever, now wearing a corseted vest and skin-tight pants, having changed out of her team coveralls. Her long brunette hair tumbled in perfect waves down her back, and she leaned on the door frame with an impatient look on her face.

"What's wrong?" Evie asked, worried she'd forgotten something important.

"I thought you were going to send a palan-carriage for me," Holly pouted, sticking out her full lower lip. "I had to walk all the way here, it took me ages!"

"Oh, you didn't say..." Evie said apologetically. But the truth was that even if Holly had asked, she couldn't afford the cost of a cross town palan-carriage this week, not after splurging on a stack of new encyclopedias. Guilt settled in her stomach like a rock. "I'm really sorry, Holly."

"I hate this place, it's bad enough that they don't allow steamcars, but trying to flag down a palan-carriage at this hour is impossible. The only way to get one is if someone sends one for you." She sighed heavily and pulled at one of her bronze curls.

"They're expensive," Evie mumbled. Paying two people to wheel a carriage across the city was never going to be cheap.

Holly flopped onto the lumpy bed and kicked her shoes off, casting a judgmental eye over the room with a frown. "I can't believe you live in a place like this. Evie, you have to *share a bathroom* with three other people!"

"It's not so bad, the others are clean enough, and rarely home long enough to annoy me."

"It's practically a hovel!" Holly pulled at some of the peeling wallpaper and cringed. "If you'd only just join a salvage team, you wouldn't have to live like this. Like a pauper."

The guilt in Evie's stomach turned to shame in an instant. "I told you, I don't want to join a salvage team. I wouldn't fit in. I wouldn't be of any use to them."

"And struggling to get by working as a part-time barkeep does?" Holly asked, draping herself over the bed to take one of the notebooks from the pile. "And what's this?"

Evie tried to snatch the notebook away, but Holly held it tight and out of her grasp as she thumbed through the pages. "These are cute," she said, examining each page. "What's this, some kind of bird?" Holly asked.

"Something like that," Evie said, and managed to grab the notebook back and set it back on top of the pile. "It's for research." She sat down next to Holly on the bed and rubbed her shoulders thoughtfully. "So how was the dinner meeting?"

"Huh? Oh, that, yeah, fine."

"When do you head out again?"

"In a week or so."

Evie swelled with love for her girlfriend, and the knowledge that they'd have a whole week together made her heart flutter with excitement. "That's great!" she said, a little too eager. "We can finally spend a little time with each other."

Holly rolled over and reached up to caress Evie's face with the tips of her uncallused fingers. "I was actually thinking we could take a trip together off-world?" she said softly. "It's planned and everything, all you have to do is say yes."

"Yes!" Evie nearly shouted. A trip away from Bradach with the love of her life? What more could she possibly ask for? "Uh, yeah, that sounds good," she said sheepishly, embarrassed by her outburst. "When do we leave?"

"Well," Holly said with a bright grin, kneeling on the bed, "we have to leave tomorrow, it's the last ship out for ten days." She took Evie's hands in her own and caressed them gently. "I know you're disappointed you couldn't come tonight, and I wanted to make it up to you."

"Tomorrow..." Evie mumbled. She'd promised Tansy she wouldn't skip her next shift. The pay at the Purple Pig wasn't wouldn't put her in the penthouse, but it was reliable, and Tansy was a kind boss. The last thing Evie wanted to do was let her down. "I have to work tomorrow."

Holly frowned and sat back on her haunches. "Babes, I thought this was what you wanted."

"It is, it is what I want. I just promised Tansy I wouldn't skip my shift tomorrow."

"Who cares about Tansy?" Holly said, pouting again. "You can find a new dead-end job when we get back."

Evie turned away, stung by Holly's words. "I like this job."

"Really?" Holly asked, disgusted. "It's just a tavern. You're just a barkeep. This could be something really nice for us, and I'm doing it for you, but you'd rather scrub vomit off the floor than take a trip with me to celebrate six months together."

"No, it's not that," Evie pleaded. "I just don't want to leave Tansy in a lurch, not after she covered Gabe's shift for me tonight."

"Sounds like it should be Gabe who owes her, not you." Holly leaned forward and gently pulled Evie's face to hers. "You deserve this, Babes."

Evie always felt like putty in Holly's hands, but especially when they kissed. She still couldn't believe someone so stunningly beautiful would want anything to do with her, a plain, broke bartender with broken dreams. She felt her stomach flip with excitement as Holly deepened the kiss, and she thought her skull might explode from the thrill of it. Holly made her knees go weak and all rationality disintegrate like a papier mâché sculpture in a rainstorm. Holly pulled away from the kiss and wiped her mouth with the back of her hand.

"So what do you say, Babes?" she asked in a husky voice that made Evie shiver with excitement. "Feel like taking a week off to travel the stars with me?"

"Where are we going?"

"It's a surprise, silly."

"I don't have any travel documents," Evie said.

"Don't worry, I've got it covered."

Evie wound a lock of Holly's hair around her finger, relishing the bouncy smoothness of it. "What about Tansy?"

Holly pushed Evie back onto her pillow and climbed on top of her, gently rotating her hips. "What *about* Tansy?" she asked mischievously. She arched her back and ran her hands over the scratchy fabric of Evie's dungarees, fresh from the laundry but still smelling faintly of grease and ale.

"Uh," Evie said, trying to remember what her objection had been in the first place. Though she and Holly had been together for months, they'd never slept together before. Holly said the ship where they used to meet was too crowded, too likely to send sound through the vents, and she had to maintain her professionalism, after all. Maybe tonight was the night. Evie reached up and caressed Holly's thigh hungrily, a tightness spreading inside her.

"So will you?" Holly pressed again, arching an impeccably shaped eyebrow.

"Of course," Evie sighed happily, her only thoughts being of the beautiful woman on top of her. "How could I say no?"

"You alway know how to make me happy," she said, running her fingers through Evie's short hair. "As much as I would adore spending the night here, I think we should wait until tomorrow, yeah?"

Evie's eyes flew open. "Stay," she said, still breathless from the kiss.

"Listen, Babes, I'm going to stay with Erica at her pod tonight, you wouldn't believe it but it's loads bigger, and she has a spare sofa." She slipped her feet back into her short, ankle height boots and pulled a piece of paper from inside her corset. "Here's the information about the port, we leave at noon tomorrow."

"Wait," Evie begged. She reached out for Holly's hand, but she pulled away, leaving Evie with nothing more than the slip of paper. "Holly, there's plenty of room here, I could even sleep on the floor," she offered hopefully.

"Don't be silly," Holly said, and leaned forward to kiss Evie on the forehead.

"We'll have plenty of time for all that on the trip. You know what they say, absence makes the heart grow fonder," she added with a wink.

And with that, Evie was left alone in her room to pack for the trip. Tonight wasn't the night.

CHAPTER TWO

Larkin stumbled out of the Purple Pig tavern into the streets of Bradach, one of the places she liked least in all the Near Systems. On Coalition planets and moons, people tended to mind their own goddamned business. But not here - no, here everyone was friendly, asking "what's your name" and "haven't I seen you somewhere before?" Couldn't an assassin for hire be left alone to drunkenly celebrate the completion of her latest contract in peace? *Goddamn pirates*, Larkin thought.

The road was uneven, with missing cobblestones creating holes just wide enough to trip on and leave you sprawling like an inebriated fool. She'd forgotten how much stronger the rum here was, compared to the bootleg stuff most places had. Bradach was the only place your booze was unlikely to be watered down until it was barely drinkable, and the three doubles she'd just finished in that tavern had her legs feeling wobbly underneath her. She blinked furiously to try to stop the city from spinning around her, and suddenly she felt sick. Maybe she should have ordered some food, too - but the strange hunk of polished metal she'd stolen from some mechanic on the docks was only good for so much trade, and it would be days before the contract actually completed and left a large sum of credits in her name.

She relished her solitude at times like these, when she was wandering aimlessly, looking for the next job. Bradach was usually a good place to find an easy contract, with pirates aiming to bump off their competition, or their ex-lover, or some asshole who'd welched on a deal and screwed them out of what was rightfully theirs. If she hung around in enough taverns, she'd eventually overhear something, and convince some drunk fool to pay her half her fee, which would be enough for a couple weeks' rent for a room and some decent food. She never stayed anywhere long; her illustrious, accomplished career of murdering people who deserved it kept her on the move.

"Hey," a tall, burly man said when she bumped into him. "Watch where you're going!"

She looked up at him and squinted, trying to see through the haze that the rum had brought on. "Hey yourself," she replied. "Know where I can get some decent grub around here?"

The man rolled his eyes and jerked his thumb towards the center of town. "Some vendors selling hot meals over that way, if you've got credit."

"Got a couple credits you could spare?" she winked. She'd blown the last of her money in a back-alley cards tournament, and had the pants beaten off of her by some chirpy medic in a pink sequined coat and matching combat boots. Until her payment came through, she was broke.

"Piss off," the man grunted, and shoved his way past.

"You sure you don't need anyone murdered?" she called after him cheerfully. She'd never be so bold and brazen in a Coalition settlement, but Bradach was a hive of less than legal dealings, assassinations included. She wasn't the only killer for hire. There were dozens of people running around the Near Systems with blood lust. The man responded with a rude hand gesture, and Larkin couldn't help but laugh. The city's clear separation from Coalition control made for a much more colorful nightlife.

She headed in the direction the man had pointed in, and was grateful when the broken cobblestones turned into a dirt path that led to the center of a small park, with food vendors dotted over the grassy field. Pirates and scrappers alike were spread out beneath towering trees that were in bloom, with pink and white petals drifting gently in the breeze. Terraforming machines controlled the seasons here, keeping the city closely tuned to a Gamma-3 year. It turned out that humans were innately attuned to Gamma-3's day and lunar cycles; recreating them even on far settlements like this one helped early space explorers adapt.

A host of smells slammed into Larkin, awakening her stomach and tempting it into a loud growl. She hadn't eaten a proper meal since before she began her last job; she'd been living on those disgusting Coalition protein ration bars that tasted like sawdust and cane sugar, with a side of cardboard.

Meal replacement bar, her ass. She needed some real food, but without access to her account, she didn't have anything else to barter with. She cursed herself for using the odd ship part on rum instead of food back at the Purple Pig, and swore softly when her stomach grumbled again. She stood at the entrance to the park and stared, growing hungrier by the second. She might be an assassin, but she'd never steal food from one of these vendors. The preparing of food for another was something sacred, and should never be disrespected by petty thievery.

"Larkin?" someone shouted from across the field. She squinted in the bright light of the long day here on Bradach, and could just about make out the face of a man she thought she'd seen the last of. Her heart squeezed in on itself, the result of years of swallowed guilt and grief.

"José?" she shouted back. It couldn't be, not after this many years. Not after everything that had happened.

"Oh my gods, Larkin!" the man cried, his voice thick with emotion. He darted out from behind one of the food stalls and sprinted across the field towards her. He was older now, his hair greying at his temples and deep lines etched into his face. He took Larkin's hands in his own, leathered from years of minor burns from stoves and ovens back on Gamma-3. "I thought I'd never see you again," he said softly, a tear leaking from each of his deep brown eyes.

"José, what are you doing here?" Larkin managed to choke out, trying desperately to swallow back her own shock. The sudden riptide of emotion threatened to sweep her out to sea, and it was a feeling she'd worked hard to avoid for over a decade.

"I've been on the run for years, ever since... well, you know. Ever since then. I came here, and the city welcomed me with open arms, so I pay them back with the best paella in the Near Systems." He laughed quietly. "And the credit isn't bad, either. I do pretty good. A much better life than the

Coalition could give." He wrapped Larkin in a warm embrace, but her arms lay stiff at her sides. It was the first human touch she'd had in weeks, after hiding in a dusty ship cupboard waiting for her opportunity to make good on the contract. "Come on, mija," he said gently, leading her across the grassy field with a heavy hand on her shoulder. "You look hungry." He cast a concerned sideways glance at her. "Have you been drinking?"

"No," she lied. The rush of emotions continued to wash over her like a tidal wave, threatening to drown her under its weight. Her head was still fuzzy from the rum, and she wasn't prepared to deal with running into the last person who knew her then and would still speak to her. What was left of her family had written her out of their history books years ago. "I am hungry, actually."

"Good, good," José said, patting her hand gently as he pulled her through the market, past stands overflowing with grilled dumplings, fresh, juicy tomatoes ripening on the vine, steaming bowls of rice topped with savory sauces and soft fried eggs. Bradach had managed to crack the sometimes complicated code of agriculture under a terraformed atmosphere, and the proof was in the mounds of fresh produce nestled into wood crates at the sides of the food stalls. Terraformed agriculture didn't always work. Some early colonies had been abandoned because the crops just wouldn't grow, despite all correct specifications being achieved. Maybe the plants knew something they didn't.

José's stand had two huge pans of paella simmering beside stacks of freshly washed, ivory white bowls that dripped water onto the table, which then streamed onto the floor in a thin rivulet. The smell of garlic, peppers, and saffron hit Larkin like a steamcar, awakening memories she thought she'd long since locked away. "This smells amazing," she said in awe. She'd never learned to cook, not well anyway, and the act of creating a masterpiece like this felt like a precious ancient magic to her.

"Here, eat up," he said, thrusting a bowl heaped with rice and vegetables, finished with a squeeze of fresh lemon. The peppers were nestled within yellowy orange sticky rice and heaps of tomatoes, with smoky crushed garlic throughout.

She took a bite and chewed with her eyes closed, savoring the flavor and texture of the food. It would probably be months before she ate this well again, and she wanted to remember it in its entirety, to pretend she was eating this instead of the inevitable ration bars as she hid in some poor asshole's cargo hold, waiting to pounce. She didn't mind her job, and she was good at it, but the food options while on a contract were seriously lacking. "José, this is phenomenal," she said between bites.

He nodded proudly and topped off her bowl with another heaping spoon of the paella. "I think I've perfected it now." He laughed and stirred one of the pans, folding more peppers into the rice. "It only took me ten years." His eyes fell on the shining pendant that hung from Larkin's neck. "You still have it. I'm glad."

Larkin stuffed the necklace back under her shirt. "Yeah." Eager to shift the conversation, she shoved another forkful of paella into her mouth. "I could eat this every day and not get bored."

José looked at her seriously. "You could, you know."

She nearly choked on her food. "What?"

"You could leave..." he waved his arms at her, gesturing at her head to toe black clothing and hood wide enough to obscure her face from prying eyes, "all this behind. You could stay here with me, help me run the stand, be safe for once."

Larkin barked out a laugh, spraying grains of rice onto the grass. "José, you know I can't cook."

He set down the wooden spoon and wiped his hands on his grease stained apron. "I'll teach you."

"I'd burn your stand down."

"Larkin," he sighed, staring at her with concerned eyes. "I never thought I'd see you again. I thought you'd gone into hiding."

She shuffled her boots on the grass. "I did."

"And?"

"And then I had to get on with it, change my last name, officially. No one knows who I am or what happened, and they never will. I'm fine. I'm safe. I'm damn good at my job, and I don't mind the solitude. Most of the time, anyway."

"I promised them I'd look after you."

"And you did!" She gestured at her now empty bowl. "And you are!" She set the bowl on the damp plywood counter and put her hands on the man's shoulders. "I'm grown now, and I can take care of myself, I promise." She smiled broadly, trying to convince him, and maybe herself too, that it was the truth. "Seeing you here means I'll come back to Bradach more often, I promise," she lied. "It won't be so long next time, just you wait and see."

"Larkin, wait," José said. "Where are you staying tonight? I have a spare room you could have as long as you want!"

She waved and took another step backward. "I have to drum up my next contract. I promise I'll come see you before I leave Bradach!" She couldn't face the guilt, or the shame of what happened. Every nerve ending in her body screamed at her to get away or she'd drown in it.

"Please..." he said softly as she turned and walked away. She heard him, but couldn't risk him seeing the tears welling up in her eyes. Emotions like this were dangerous, and they'd get her killed if she wasn't careful.

* * *

The Bronze Bell tavern was at the end of an alley that stank of piss and vomit, the visual remnants of which were splashed up the walls and crusted into the grout of the brick. Larkin held her nose as she gingerly stepped over a pile of someone's half digested dinner and pulled the heavy door open with the sticky brass handle. The tavern inside was dark and damp, with mold growing on the old rugs that were laid out underneath the tables. She found herself missing the plush home comforts of the Purple Pig, but she suspected that the Bronze Bell was more likely to host the more recklessly monied members of Bradach society, and she was here to scare up some work. Rum wasn't going to buy itself.

She sat on a wobbly stool in the corner and observed the patrons from underneath the wide hood of her tailored black jacket. It wouldn't hurt to be as anonymous as possible in a place like this. Some people were pirates to stick it to the Coalition, to protest their iron fisted, fascist, violent rule of the Near Systems that only benefited the already-rich members of their society. Some people were pirates, because they were just lawless, indecent assholes. The Bronze Bell was said to cater to the latter, and those kinds of people were far more likely to be interested in hiring an assassin to take out their competition.

While Larkin usually liked to be more judicious with her contracts, losing her savings to that card shark after her last job meant she was scraping the barrel until payment came in, and that wouldn't happen until the kill was confirmed. Given how she had killed her mark, it would be at least a few days before their body was discovered, probably by their second in command.

A pair of women whispered at a table on the other side of the tavern, but judging by their body language, it was far more likely that they were having an affair, rather than a heist or an extra-judicial killing of someone who wronged them. Larkin's gaze shifted to another table, crowded with men cheering on an arm-wrestling competition. *What a ridiculous display of bravado*, she thought to herself, *it's not as though anyone was ever arm-wrestled to death.* The next table was promising: a pair of pirates huddled over what looked like a map of a derelict, abandoned Coalition station. The blueprints were obvious, the yellow and purple Coalition seal in each corner like a beacon.

It was illegal to scrap or salvage any Coalition ships or equipment, of course, with punishment ranging from years in a work camp to death for repeat offenders. She'd seen an ex-Coalition scientist executed on public broadcast just last week for leaking plans of some new technological marvel. The report hadn't specified what the marvel was, but it was probably a weapon. It was always a weapon.

She watched the pair closely as they scrawled over the map with blue chalk, charting possible approaches, entries, and exits that would avoid the gaze of the ever present surveillance drones, which stayed in service long after a site had been evacuated. The Coalition wouldn't even spare one rusty nail to a civilian, not even if their family was starving and the scrap money would put some three-day-old, stale as shit bread on the table.

This pair didn't look like they were starving, though, not in their carefully tailored waistcoats, made to conceal blades from pat down searches. She employed that clever design herself as a great insurance policy against fights where the odds were stacked against her. She ran her hands over her waist, where a large curved blade rested between boned layers of fabric. She would be surprised if the same tailor hadn't made theirs, too.

They spoke in muttered tones too soft and garbled for Larkin to hear, so she flagged down the barkeep to give her an excuse to readjust her position closer to them after ordering a pint of ale. If she was right about the situation, and she was almost always right about contracts, she'd have plenty of coin to barter with by the time this pair left the tavern. The barkeep set the pint of cloudy ale on the sticky high top table, and Larkin shifted closer to the pair and strained her ears to hear their conversation.

"If we can take out that drone on the north side of the settlement, we could get in and out without being seen," said one of them, who was wearing large gold hoop earrings in each ear and a thick, ropey braid that fell to her waist.

"Getting anywhere near that drone is going to trigger an alarm, you fool," the other said, combing a full beard dotted with crystals that sparkled in the dim light.

"Yeah, well there's no other way in or out for the ship to manage with that kind of cargo weight, and you know it," Gold Earrings argued. "And besides, I bet we could get someone to take care of the drone."

Larkin's ears perked up. She was no tech expert, but she definitely had a knack for solving problems for people in unorthodox ways. Scrapping old settlements was dangerous, but astoundingly lucrative, and could set her up for at least another year without having to take on more jobs. Maybe she'd even meet a nice pirate and settle down, at least until the credit ran out. She smirked to herself, knowing it was far more likely that she would piss it all away on rum and cards.

"We don't have much time to get this done, the whole settlement is scheduled for demolition in ten days' time. Whatever we decide, it needs to be decided fast. Soon there won't be anything left to salvage," said Crystal Beard. He sighed and stroked his beard for a moment. "I don't want to let this opportunity get away from us."

The pair sat in silence as they studied their map, and Larkin bided her time in speaking up. They had to be just desperate enough to decide to raise the stakes and cut in a third on their little enterprise, but not so panicked that they would sell her out to keep all the scrap for themselves. She cleared her throat softly. "I might have a solution to your problems," she said in a hushed voice from beneath her hood.

"Piss off!" Gold Earrings said, yanking the map from the sticky table and rolling it up. "We found it, it's our score!"

"Calm down," Larkin said easily, tracing the rim of her glass with her index finger. "I don't want to steal your score. I merely want to help."

Gold Earrings stared at her suspiciously. "Go on."

"As your friend so astutely noted, getting anywhere near that drone will set off a security alarm. Once an alarm is triggered, you'll have less than an hour to salvage, load, and get off the settlement with enough distance that they won't be able to track you." She leaned back on the stool and folded her hands together neatly to show that she was serious. "We all know that's not nearly enough time. You'll need to evade detection for at least seven hours if you want to make enough to have this all be worth your while."

"And how are you going to do that, you some kind of security expert or something? An ex-Coalition data processor who can hack into the security feeds?" Crystal Beard asked in an openly hostile tone.

"No," Larkin said, raising her head so they would see her face beneath the hood. Convincing people that they needed her services was almost an art, and Larkin was a grand master. "But if you remove the one watching the drone feeds, then the drones don't matter. No trigger, no alarm."

Crystal Beard recoiled in his seat. "We're not trying to kill anyone." He nudged his partner and hissed, "Let's go."

"It's your loss," Larkin said coolly. "I was just trying to help."

The one with the earrings squinted at Larkin and leaned over the table. "What's in it for you? You got some kinda grudge against the security watch?"

Larkin shrugged. "No. Just looking for some work. Thought I might find some here, I heard the clientele at this tavern was made of sterner stuff." She stared across the table and slid the pint of ale away from her. "But I guess not." She swung a leg over the stool, hearing the buckle on her boot clink against the iron of the base. If she was clever, she wouldn't fall on her ass on her way out. The room was starting to spin around her, which was annoying as hell. *Fucking Bradach booze*, she thought.

"Wait— " Gold Earrings said, holding up her hand to stop Larkin from leaving. "What did you have in mind?"

"I'm not saying anything until you agree to cut me in on a third of the profits," Larkin said with a confident smirk. "I don't want you stealing my ideas just to get some other hack to do my job for less of the credit."

"No way," Crystal Beard said, shaking his head. "We've been working on this plan for almost an entire year. You think we'll just agree to give up a third of the spoils to some stranger in a tavern, just like that? This drone is the last thing standing in the way of a huge score."

"Without a way of avoiding that security drone, your masterful plan is basically useless," Larkin challenged, now leaning across the table and speaking in a hushed whisper. Places like this had a way of leaking information. It wasn't just the walls that had ears, it was every greedy pirate in the room, looking for an easy job that would line their pockets for the foreseeable future. At least she had the fortitude to look for her own jobs. "Admit it. You need me." She sat back on the stool and raised an eyebrow at the pair, waiting for their response.

"I mean, maybe we should..." Gold Earrings suggested. "Like you said, we don't have much time to get it done before it's scheduled for demolition. After that, there won't be anything worth salvaging, anyway."

Crystal Beard sighed. "Sam, I really don't know about this. Adding murder to the list of charges is awfully risky."

Gold Earrings, or rather, Sam, poked him in the ribs. "Don't use my real name in here!"

"There are no Coalition spies in here," Larkin laughed. "What is this, your first time in Bradach?" She was kidding, but she also needed to know if she was going to be working with rookies. Pirates new to the salvage and scrap trade could be too jumpy for her liking, too likely to back out at the last minute and leave her holding the bag, and likely, the prison sentence.

"No," Sam said defensively. "I just try to keep a low profile. You know, to avoid making any enemies."

"Well, to answer your concerns, erm, what was your name again?" Larkin asked, gesturing towards Crystal Beard.

He stared back for a moment before answering, "You can call me MJ."

Larkin raised an eyebrow. "MJ, okay. Clearly not your given name."

"And yours?" MJ needled.

"Sandy," Larkin answered. She sure as hell wasn't about to give them her name until she knew they were rock solid. "To answer your question, MJ, we don't necessarily have to kill the security manager. We can just incapacitate them for a while." She had no qualms about offing Coalition management drones who worked to enrich the assholes at the top of the food chain, especially the ones who spent their working hours snitching on pirates just doing salvage missions, dooming them to rot away in a prison camp or be publicly executed to make an example of them. It was just metal, for gods' sakes.

This pair was unsure if they were ready to commit to the Big M for murder yet, so she'd play along as long as she could. Incapacitating the security manager was a surefire way to get caught the second they woke up and raised the alarm. Dead bodies could do no such thing, and so long as none of them got caught, Larkin knew from experience that they wouldn't give a single shit about her methods once they had a cargo bay full of loot.

The pair whispered behind their hands, before each extending one across the grime encrusted table. "Do we have an accord?" MJ asked seriously.

"Aye," Larkin said, shaking each of their hands enthusiastically and signaling the barkeep to bring her another pint. "I think we do."

CHAPTER THREE

"Ready, Babes?" Holly asked with a wide, sparkling grin.

Evie nodded, staring up at The Delilah, a moderately sized luxury ship made for traveling across the Near Systems in lavish comfort. The ship's name was painted in metallic gold paint, nearly blinding in the light. "I'm ready," she finally said.

Holly interlaced her fingers with hers, and Evie's heart skipped a beat. She would never love anyone as much as she loved Holly. Beautiful, successful, strikingly intelligent, and she wanted *her*. Evie could barely believe her luck landing Holly on most days, but today most of all. The interior of the ship was pristine, with scarlet plush lined walls and gilded mirrors along every corridor, reflecting their visages back at them, Evie's eyes wide with wonder. She barely heard the captain as she showed them around the ship, taking pains to focus on the generously sized dining hall and private chef. Evie was hungry just thinking about the food she could request, but she was even hungrier for Holly's touch. She squeezed her girlfriend's hand gently and wrapped an arm around her waist.

"Where is everyone else?" she asked.

"It's just us," Holly replied, kissing her on the forehead. "All this is just for us, to celebrate six months together."

"Wow," Evie breathed. Flying a ship this size with so few passengers would be considered wasteful by Bradach standards, in the light of recent fuel shortages, now that the Coalition had banned the waste incinerators that made fuel economical and easy to come by. But it was all for her, and she basked in it, knowing it would be difficult to return home to her shabby rented room when their trip was over.

"I'm so sorry about dinner last night," Holly said, pulling her into their shared suite and closing the door behind them. "If there was any way to get around it, I would have."

"It's okay, really." Evie sat on the bed, a huge four poster piled high with thick velvet blankets and fluffy pillows that made gentle crunching sounds when she poked them. "It's so opulent," she said in awe. "I've never seen anything like it."

"You deserve it. And besides, your first trip into space should be one to remember." Holly took her hand and laid back on the bed with a laugh. "I'm so glad you finally decided to come with me. I don't know what I would have done all by myself on this big ship."

Evie felt a pang of guilt when she thought about Tansy, and how she was going to skip out on her shift after promising not to. She just hoped she would have a job to come back to when this trip was over. "Of course I came with you. I love you."

Holly blinked her huge blue eyes at her and tilted her head. "Oh, Evie." She patted the bed and propped herself up on an elbow. "Why don't you lay down next to me? We can talk about whatever's on your mind, I feel like I've been gone for ages."

"You *were* gone for ages," Evie laughed, sinking down into a pile of pillows. "It seems like whenever I see you, it's only for a night or two and then you're off on another job." When Holly frowned, Evie rushed to correct herself: "I just mean, I miss you is all. Your work is important, I know that. How else would you be able to afford to spoil me like this?"

"You know, darling, it wasn't cheap reserving this vessel for just the two of us. Had to call in a few favors, too."

"I just... I ache for you when you're away," Evie said, lightly trailing her fingertips over Holly's exposed forearm. "I wish we could just have a normal life together."

"What's normal?" Holly laughed. "These days, the abnormal is normal. Everyone has an angle, a desire to exploit and conquer."

"I don't think that's true. I think people are good, inherently. They just get caught up in corrupt systems."

"Oh, Evie," Holly repeated with a sigh. "You can't know how things are off-world. Outside Bradach, things are sharper, more dangerous. Lethal, sometimes." She tousled Evie's cerulean hair gently, leaving a lock out of place over her eye.

"I worry when you're away."

"I know, Babes, but you shouldn't. I'm tough stuff."

Evie stretched out her legs on the bed, feeling herself sink into the softness of the mattress. "Where are we going, anyway?"

"It's a surprise!" Holly scolded her playfully. "You'll see when we get there. You're going to absolutely love it, I just know it."

"I'll love anywhere I go with you," Evie whispered, staring up at her girlfriend with misty eyes. "I love you."

"Would you do anything for me?"

Evie nodded. "Of course."

"You're too sweet, Babes." Holly kissed the tip of Evie's nose and lingered near her lips. "You know, we are the only ones on the ship," she whispered. "We've waited so long for this."

"Yes," Evie said, her voice cracking from the excitement building in her chest. "Yes, we've waited such a long time."

Holly leaned over Evie, her dark chestnut hair cascading down around Evie's face and tumbling over the pillows. "Evie, sweet, kind Evie," she uttered in a voice barely above a whisper. She bent and kissed Evie's neck slowly, tracing her lips across the delicate skin, hovering where Evie's quickened pulse pounded through the artery in her throat. Holly bit gently, and Evie gasped with equal surprise and excitement, which coursed through her veins like electricity.

The lighting in the room dimmed for a moment as the boilers began to power the thrusters of the ship with a slight shudder. "We're cleared for takeoff, stand by," the loudspeaker in the corridor outside their room called in a robotic voice. "Feel free to move about the ship once we are through the atmosphere."

CHAPTER THREE

Evie lay amid the piles of cushions and blankets, with the most beautiful woman in the world draped across her. Life, for her, would never get any better than this moment. She closed her eyes and breathed deep the scent of the jasmine oil Holly dabbed behind her ears every morning, savoring the moment and committing it to memory. When she was at the end of her days, and death was coming for her, this is the moment she would recall. She felt the ship move underneath them, ascending into the sky and carrying her further from Bradach than she had ever been. This must be what bliss felt like.

The kisses that Holly laid over Evie's neck and collarbone sent shivers up her spine and scrambled any rational thought. Her breath grew shallow and quick with anticipation, and she reached for Holly's waist with nervous, quaking hands. She slid her arms around Holly, pulling her closer and crushing Holly against her chest with a closeness she dreamed about whenever Holly was away on a job, far from her reach and frequently out of contact. "I love you," Evie murmured into Holly's hair. "I really, really do."

Holly responded by silencing her with a kiss, biting Evie's lower lip and tugging on it gently. She ran her hands over Evie's hips and up her short, wide torso as she kissed her deeply, the pair silent except for the sounds of their mouths on each other's. The ship rumbled softly as it passed through the atmosphere, the softly rumbling boilers sending them out into the stars.

Evie tentatively tugged on the toggles of Holly's waistcoat, letting it open and flop to the side. She reached for the buttons on the blouse below, releasing them one by one to reveal Holly's white lace bra underneath. Evie felt like she might explode from the pent up excitement and yearning built over half a year with Holly. She traced her fingers over the delicate lace, surprised by how soft it was. A soft moan escaped from her lips as Holly leaned forward and shrugged out of it, freeing her perky breasts.

"Do you like this?" Holly asked, running her hands over Evie's shirt.

"Mmhmm," Evie responded, unable to remember any words.

With a swift, graceful movement, Holly straddled Evie with her back arched, gathering her hair on top of her head but missing one loose curl that framed her perfect face and twisted downward to rest on her bare breast.

"What next?" she whispered seductively.

Evie reached forward and pulled at the waistband of Holly's tight-fitting trousers. She pulled herself up and wrapped her arms around Holly's bare skin, drowning in the softness. Holly released her handfuls of hair, letting it tumble down her back, and rested her arms on Evie's shoulders with her hands entwined into Evie's short, unruly locks.

"I like this," Holly said, running her fingers through Evie's hair. "You're very cute, you know."

With that, Evie dragged Holly back down to the bed and laid her there, topless and perfect. She knelt at the edge of the bed and kissed across Holly's flat stomach, hesitating where the trousers met her hips in a satisfyingly snug way. She fumbled with the button fly, hearing each button make a thrilling little pop as they released. Evie tugged gently at the trousers, and Holly lifted her hips to shimmy out of them, leaving her in nothing more than a bit of white lace between her thighs.

Evie's heart pounded with excitement and her vision narrowed to include only Holly as she ran her hands over her girlfriend's smooth thighs. She reached to pull the bit of lace aside when there was an insistent knock at the door.

"You've got to be kidding me," she hissed.

Holly looked at her with apologetic eyes. "What if it's an emergency?"

Evie shook her head and mouthed *NO* at her girlfriend.

"Uh, we're busy," Holly called through the door with a laugh, and waited for a response. There was an awkward shuffling on the other side of the door, and then a deep, authoritative voice.

"I'm afraid it's a matter of utmost importance," the voice said. "We've been hailed by a Coalition vessel that was stealthed beyond our radar's capability. We are to land at the nearest Coalition trading beacon for inspection of crew and passengers, and then we'll be on our way."

Holly's eyes widened in fear, and Evie sucked in a breath. "They can't just do that, can they? Demand to inspect a civilian vessel?" Evie asked, panic tearing at the edges of her voice. There were stories of ships being commandeered by the Coalition, but she was desperate for even a pretty lie from Holly. "You have my travel papers, right? The fake identification and the permit?"

"We'll be right there," Holly called through the door, and reached for her trousers and blouse. When the heavy footsteps faded, Holly burst into tears. "Oh gods, Evie, this is it for me isn't it? They're going to throw me into a prison camp for the rest of my life!" she sobbed, fumbling with the buttons on her shirt. She covered her face with her hands, and Evie's heart broke in two.

"Maybe they're just checking the ship for contraband," she said soothingly, reaching out to deal with the buttons. "In fact, I'm sure that's what it is. I bet they won't even look at us twice, they're far too busy looking for violent offenders. Besides, you said last night that our papers are all in order." But even as she brushed a wet curl from Holly's tear-stained cheek, her own stomach tied itself into knots. They were both in terrible danger, a heartbeat away from consequences no one ever wanted to pay. She swallowed hard and put on a brave face. "Let's get you dressed and see to these officials, and I just know we'll be picking up where we left off." She gave Holly a cheeky grin, and her girlfriend choked out a laugh.

"You're right," Holly said shakily, tucking in her shirt. "I'm sure it's nothing."

And yet, Evie couldn't help wondering what the hell a top of the line stealthed ship was doing in these parts, so close to Bradach. Officially, the Coalition wasn't aware of the pirate settlement, but she suspected there had been some back room agreements to protect financial assets of the powerful. That's what it always came down to, after all. Had the ship been waiting for them, or were they just flexing their military muscle out of boredom? She supposed only time would tell.

The ship's engines stuttered for a moment as they locked onto the small trading beacon, a place where ships of all sizes could refuel with the expensive petroleum based fuel. The decision to outlaw the more efficient steam engines for fear of "intermittent explosions" had devastated small traders, but made the fuel beacons filthy rich in an incredibly short span of time. The actual station was tiny, room only for the operators and one medical tech in case of emergency, so the Coalition inspectors would likely be boarding the Delilah from a small shuttle, and wearing protective space suits.

"All hands, all hands, report to loading bay one. All passengers please convene in loading bay two," the loudspeaker announced in a wobbly voice that betrayed the captain's worry and desperation.

The pair closed their door behind them and walked along the carpeted corridors which muffled their steps. As they approached the loading bays, tense whispers from the few crew members on board echoed into the hall. Evie wondered how many of them were hiding secrets too.

"Never should have signed up for this job," one of them muttered as he stalked past them into the bay. "Goddamn Coalition owns every goddamn thing these days."

Loading bay two was empty, except for Holly and Evie. Being the only passengers on board at the start of the journey was exciting and important, but now made Evie feel incredibly vulnerable and scared. She shuffled her feet against the scuffed rubberized flooring, a far cry from the manicured creature comforts from the rest of the ship. The ground quaked beneath their feet, a sign that the Coalition inspection vessel had locked into the trading beacon as well. It wouldn't be long, now, until they boarded.

Holly cried fat tears that slid down her high cheekbones and splashed onto her shirt, darkening patches of the fabric with wetness. "Do you think we could escape?" she whispered in a shaky voice. "What if we stole a shuttle and went back to Bradach?"

Evie shook her head. "They'd see us and pursue. Anyone trying to enter Bradach airspace can't be tailing a Coalition vessel, or it will be denied landing privilege, you know that." She rubbed her girlfriend gently on the small of her back. "No, it's best to play by the rules." She couldn't see any shuttles in this loading bay, anyway. Maybe there weren't any on a ship like this, or perhaps they were all locked away and inaccessible without a crew identification chip.

The boilers cooled, leaving the Delilah motionless as it drifted through dark space attached to the trading beacon. Even the angry sighs and muttering from loading bay one had ceased, as the entire crew braced themselves for boarding. It was an open secret that Coalition inspection agents were rarely fair, and frequently thieves. But as long as the Coalition bank vault got its share of credits, higher ups didn't care what their drones got up to. "I bet it's just routine," Holly finally agreed, just before the airlocks engaged.

Sound from the other loading bay was muffled, but Evie could hear enough to know that tensions were high. The crew was being questioned about something, where their supplies had originated. One of them shouted, "You can't do that!" and then a soft grunt and the unmistakable sound of a body sliding to the floor. Bile rose at the back of her throat and she squeezed Holly's hand gently.

"They probably just knocked him out," she said quietly, but turned to see Holly's face as white as a sheet. Anxiety and fear crawled up her spine one vertebra at a time, seeping into her nervous system and infecting her with the sickness of worry. Even if they got out of this, she didn't want to stay on the Delilah. She just wanted to go home to Bradach, to her shabby little rented room and the security of a boring job at the Purple Pig. She scoffed at her past self's dream of being an adventurous researcher, unraveling the mysteries of the universe. What an utter fool she had been. She'd give anything to be back home.

Boots snapped sharply on the tiled floor between the two bays, and Evie steeled herself for whatever came next. She hadn't technically done anything wrong, and Holly had their Coalition identification and travel papers. They would be fine.

"Passengers Holly Ambrosia and Evie Anderson, I presume?" one of the inspectors asked, reading their names from the ship's manifest log.

Evie nodded. "Yes, that's us."

The man scowled. "Identification?"

Her stomach leapt into her throat as she pretended to search her pockets. Holly handed her own ID over, along with travel papers, and the man examined it for a moment before nodding at her. "And you?" he asked, gesturing at Evie.

"Holly?" she asked, desperation clawing at the back of her throat. "You have my papers too?"

Her girlfriend stared at her, brows knitted together. "Why would I have your papers, Babes?"

Evie felt her heart pounding against her rib cage. Traveling without papers was an offense punishable by prison time, and it wouldn't take them long to discover that there was no record of her in the Coalition database anywhere, on account of being Bradach born and raised. "Oh, I uh... I guess I forgot mine," she said apologetically. "Maybe it fell out of my pocket on the dock!"

"Where did this ship last make berth?"

She certainly couldn't say Bradach, but didn't know where the ship's official logs said they'd been picked up. She didn't know the answer, so she kept quiet. The man looked down at his navy blue clipboard and made a note with a gold pen so ornate, it would cost the average Bradach citizen a year's salary.

He stared from Holly, to Evie, and back again. "Holly," he said, tapping the pen against the side of the clipboard. "Looks like you've been in some trouble in the past?"

Holly blanched, her eyes filling with tears again. "It was never anything serious," she protested quietly. "I was young, and—"

"I would hardly suggest that armed robbery of a Coalition officer was a minor offense."

Evie whipped her head around to look at Holly. *What the hell*, she thought. This was the first she was hearing about a prior record, or an armed robbery, for that matter. And why hadn't Holly used her fake ID to book the ship, and on the passenger manifest? She was smarter than that, surely.

"I was never convicted of that," Holly said with a sniffle. "I just wanted to take my girlfriend on a trip, and—"

The officer slowly turned away from Holly, putting a hand up to stop her pleading. "Evie, was it?" he asked in a cold, monotone voice. Her stomach felt like it would catapult out of her mouth at any moment, and she lightly pressed her hands to her torso in a bid to calm her roiling guts.

"Yes."

"We don't have any official Coalition record of an Evie Anderson. Why might that be?"

"Database error?" Evie said, and tried for a laugh. It came out more like a strangled sob.

"Do you want to know what I think?" the man asked. Evie didn't say anything, or even dare to move. "I think that you're a filthy pirate using a piss poor fake name to cover up for all the laws you've broken." He laughed, and the sound sent shivers down Evie's spine. "What's your real name?"

"That is my real name."

He sighed and stared at the pair, his steely gaze moving from one to the other as he continued to tap against the clipboard with the pen. "You see, we're here on an anonymous tip," he said, his face blank and unreadable. "We were told, or rather, our regional dispatcher was told, that the filthy pirate responsible for hijacking and scrapping the C.S. Sparrowhawk was aboard this vessel."

"It was her," Holly said quickly, jabbing her thumb at Evie. "She admitted it to me in confidence, and I'll formally attest to that."

"Holly, what the hell!" Evie shouted, and one of the silent guards with the inspector stepped forward with a large gun in his hands. She raised her hands to show she was no threat and turned back to her girlfriend. "Holly, you know I didn't do that!"

"Evie, don't argue with them. Just go quietly and serve your time. It's what's right for the Coalition."

Heat rose in her face as she sputtered to get the right words out. "I — I never — You —" Emotions swirled in her mind and blocked all rational thought. It wasn't lost on her that in some extreme cases, the penalty for this crime was execution for treason. "Holly, *why*?" she finally managed to spit out.

Holly folded her hands in front of her as though she were praying, tears spilling over and dampening the crisply starched lapel of her shirt. "Evie, I care for you so desperately, but you know that I cannot abide someone who endangers the welfare of the Near Systems with such treachery."

Evie's jaw hung open at her girlfriend's inexplicable betrayal. This made no sense at all, and she'd gone from worrying about an identification document to facing a death sentence in just a few wild moments. "I didn't do it!" Evie yelled, and the guard with the gun, their face obscured by the tinted visor, stepped forward again.

"Miss, I'm going to need you to calm down," the guard said in a muffled voice. "I don't want to sedate you, but I will if I have to."

"Just do what they say, Babes," Holly said, resting a hand on Evie's arm. "I don't want to see you get hurt."

"Why are you doing this?" Evie asked, hot tears of rage gathering at the corners of her eyes and making her vision swim. "*Why*?"

"Miss." The guard stepped forward and gestured for Evie to offer her hands to be cuffed.

Evie lifted her hands and watched in astonishment as the guard snapped the cuffs closed around her wrists. "I didn't do it," she said again, quietly this time as the shame and resignation washed over her like a tidal wave.

The inspector unclipped a bulky radio from the belt around the hips of the space suit and raised it to his lips. "Sector Four, we have the suspect in custody. Stand by for booking and please arrange transport to the nearest prison camp at your earliest convenience."

"Roger that, Inspector, over and out," the radio crackled.

"You'll have to serve your debt to society now," the inspector said to Evie with an expressionless face. "But I should warn you that the prison camps are not kind. You'll have to work off your debt... that is, if they don't see it fit to charge you with treason, instead." He leaned in close, so close that Evie could smell the stale coffee on his breath. "Did you know that those poor Coalition soldiers were adrift for days before they got picked up? I can't even imagine the horror, can you?" He stepped back again and tapped the clipboard. "It would be a real shame if something happened to you at the prison camp. A real shame, indeed."

Holly cleared her throat. "Inspector? Could I just have a moment with her before you take her?" She gestured at the heavy plastic cuffs around Evie's wrists. "It's not like she's going anywhere." She batted her eyelashes and bit her lip, and the inspector grunted an affirmative before waving the guards out of the room. When they were gone, Evie burst into tears, sobbing and choking on her own snot.

"Holly, why? Why would you do this?"

"Didn't you say you'd do anything for me?" Holly asked, patting Evie's arm gently. "You know I wouldn't survive in a prison camp."

"What about me?" Evie asked, trying in vain to wipe her face on her own shoulder.

"I'll do the best I can to help you," Holly said with a parting kiss on Evie's cheek, before she walked off the loading bay.

Evie was on her own.

CHAPTER FOUR

When Larkin stepped off the transport ship, she was swiftly reminded what Skelm smelled like: melting plastic, hot metal, and the sickly sweet scent of whatever was in the clouds of grey emanating from factory smokestacks. A tall poster glued to the brick read "NO JAYWALKING. BY ORDER OF GOVERNOR RALPH BAKER." Larkin snorted a laugh - *how very Coalition,* she thought. All concerned about petty crimes while people starved in the streets.

That governor had appeared out of nowhere several years back, too - no one had questioned it, not when he had the backing of the public broadcasts, but one look at the man's file proved something strange was going on with him. Probably an up-jumped pretty boy from a wealthy family who did something stupid in his youth, something that would put anyone else in a work camp for life, but he got promoted, instead. A tale as old as time.

She coughed as the fumes burned the back of her throat, her eyes watering in protest after the leafy, crisp air on Bradach. Her fellow passengers pulled fabric scarves from their pockets to tie around their faces for protection, and Larkin followed suit.

The city was bustling this time of day, with people rushing to and from space transport vehicles on the dock, and dock workers loading huge Coalition trading barges with pallets of goods. Produce, nutrition bars, spare parts, and suspiciously unmarked boxes were all being loaded onto the ships. As she tied a black silk scarf around her face, she watched the captain of a ship scream at a cowering dock worker until he was red in the face. *Asshole,*

Larkin thought.

She knew where the security building was here on Skelm, she'd been inside of it before on another job a while back. Larkin tapped the vial inside the deep pocket of her jacket, just to be sure it was still there. She had a backup in her boot, and another one tucked into her hair's tight braid, and one more sewn into the lining of her waistcoat. But an assassin couldn't be too careful. Waste not, want not, or whatever the saying was.

Passengers and dock workers streamed around her as though she was a boulder in a river, shuffling past on their way to work, or home, or maybe to a lover's house for an affair. Larkin was here to kill a man.

The security manager in question was a man called Robert, a man with no family who spent most of his time writing angry letters to anyone who would listen. There were public records of his diatribes to minor celebrities who offended his delicate tastes, to a woman who had dumped him fifteen years ago, to local city officials about the disgusting stench of the city, though Larkin couldn't blame him on that last count. Robert was a man who thrived on anger, and who didn't add much to society.

In all her years of working as a killer for hire, she'd never once killed someone and regretted it.

Skelm was a moderately sized city, grown up from the small settlement it had started as nearly fifty years prior. It grew up and out quickly, attracting people from all over the Near Systems with promises of work in the factories and newly built buildings furnished with all the home comforts you could want. Of course, only the higher ups got the home comforts; people who arrived on transports looking for work were stacked on top of each other in a labyrinth of bunk beds, all shoved into a drafty warehouse.

A few left, returned to their homes. But the overwhelming majority of desperate people arriving on Skelm had spent their last credits to pay for the transport. They had no choice but to sign up to live in warehouses and get sick with illness after illness, working to pay their rent to the Coalition who owned the barracks with their underpaid jobs as laborers. Most went hungry and became desperate. Hungry people aren't able to cause dissent or organize their efforts for better conditions. They were expendable, anyway.

Plenty of starving people in the Near Systems looking for a better life.

Not Robert, though. Larkin's research on the man had been very insightful. He got to live in one of the nice furnished homes that had been advertised. He got paid a decent wage, despite his mediocre work reviews and being written up by his superiors for showing up late and harassing his coworkers.

She'd seen enough men like Robert to know the score. She climbed over the razor-wire fence surrounding his building and easily picked the lock open. She'd be screwed when people decided on digital locks in favor of the old school ones; her hacking was good enough to dig up dirt on a careless asshole like Robert, but the digital clamp locks still eluded her and almost every other petty thief and assassin in the Near Systems. At least they were mostly only used in high level Coalition bases, for now.

Inside, she eased open the door to Robert's apartment. The cleaner wasn't due until tomorrow, which she had learned from infiltrating one of the Coalition's physical databases and checking the man's calendar, and she instantly felt a deep sadness for whoever the poor person was. Robert had dirty clothes strewn all over the floor, and the smell of stale body odor and urine hung in the air. Larkin preferred the smell of the industrial waste outside to this man's home. She tugged on the scarf to tighten the knot, desperate to block out more of the smell.

With a delicate step over a pair of underpants near the couch, Larkin picked up a pile of post and shuffled through it. Letters from his bank, with his annual yields, form letters from the local elected officials, and a commendation from the Coalition. "What the hell has this prick done to earn a commendation?" Larkin wondered aloud. She didn't bother to steam the envelope open, or hold it to the light, she just ripped it open. Robert would probably be dead before he realized her snooping. He'd be dead before he was in any kind of condition to report it.

The commendation letter listed his achievements, which were, in Larkin's opinion, not very impressive. According to the letter, he had prevented dozens of crimes with his work as a security manager, and had never missed a day of work, despite showing up late at least once a week. Crimes like salvaging long abandoned equipment, probably. With her thoughts focused on the task at hand, she opened the man's icebox. A plate of spaghetti was covered in a fine fuzz of mold, untouched food rotting away while people outside the razor-wire fence starved. It was disgusting, and the injustice burned in her stomach.

She gave some quick glances into the man's bedroom, study, and bathroom, and found nothing out of the ordinary. Robert was just an average Coalition stooge, and today, he was going to die for his sins of mediocrity and casual cruelty. Sometimes, Larkin would pocket trinkets from her marks, but Robert repulsed her so much that the thought of taking something from the man's home made her feel ill.

Now, she just had to decide where the vial needed to go. She examined the rest of the kitchen, analyzing Robert's habits. It was clear that he didn't like leftovers, hence the fuzzy spaghetti in the icebox. She yanked on a handle for the main pantry, and potatoes that had begun to sprout tumbled out. More wasted food, she imagined, but she couldn't figure out why he was hoarding so much food that he wasn't eating.

The potatoes back in their container, Larkin opened each drawer to examine the contents. Silverware, made of real silver, and she reconsidered her vow to not take anything from this man's home before replacing several spoons back in their drawer. Plates, squeaky clean, probably kept in good form by the cleaner. Tea mugs that looked like they'd never been touched, covered in a layer of dust at the back of a cupboard. *There must be something reliable here to use*, she mused as she poked and prodded through the man's belongings.

She went back to the bedroom again and frowned at the grey rug. That color could hide a multitude of sins, and she didn't want to think about what Robert got up to by himself in his room. The man's closet was basically empty, except for one spare brown waistcoat made in an uninspiring canvas material, and one pair of faded black trousers. His trunk was full of moth eaten socks and stained underwear, but beneath the pile of his unmentionables, the glimmer of a glass bottle caught her eye.

Using one of the empty hangers from the closet, she freed the bottle from its hiding place. Robert did have a secret, and it was a love of black market booze. The homemade rum was cloudy in the bottle, with sediment coating the bottom of the glass. Rummaging in the trunk, she spotted something unusual in the corner: a false bottom.Grimacing, she pried up the false bottom and found quite the cache, with dozens of small bottles of rum lining the bottom of the trunk. So Robert wasn't just a casual drinker, he was someone who drank swill so often he had to stockpile it under his underwear.

Larkin smirked and pulled the vial from the pocket of her jacket as she crouched on the floor. The cork came free with a satisfying pop, and Larkin dumped it into the open bottle of rum and swirled it around. If the presence of all the bottles were any indication, Robert would be dead by midnight. She carefully replaced the false bottom and the rum with the additive, and closed the trunk with a clunk. A job well done, and now her irritating partners in crime would be able to get in, get out, and sell the scrap before anyone noticed. After all, their good friend Robert wouldn't be around tomorrow morning to take his shift staring glassy-eyed at dozens of security feeds. His frequent lateness would buy them a few extra hours, which was a nice bonus.

Yes, someone would probably figure it out eventually, when Robert missed his shift, and the reviewed footage showed figures in masks carrying off chunks of the derelict equipment, but by then they'd be long gone, and Larkin would be enjoying her spoils like a queen.

Of course, the other two didn't know she was going to kill Robert. A security manager who awoke from sedation tied into a chair was a security manager that could scream for help and get them all killed. No, Robert had to die. Earrings and Beard wouldn't care, they'd forget her methods as soon as the credits started pouring in. Larkin frowned, looking at the rum. It was unlikely to have as high an alcohol content as the stuff on Bradach, but it would still slow his digestive enzymes, which were needed to turn the amygdalin into a lethal dose of cyanide.

"Better safe than sorry," she muttered as she dumped another vial into the bottle. It was a shame, really, that her source for castor beans had dried up with the Coalition's crackdown on piracy. She could make ricin from the beans, a poison thousands of times more effective than cyanide, and difficult to trace. An autopsy might reveal the source of Robert's death, but she would be long gone by then, a faint, untraceable shadow on Skelm's security drones, covered in the thick scarf and wide hood. Even if they wanted to find her, she was untraceable, impossible to track. She'd been a ghost for years.

Some would say that poison is a coward's way to deal death, and maybe that was true. But Larkin didn't think that Robert deserved to see the face of his killer. His mediocre, toxic existence didn't merit an honorable or interesting death. He would keel over, alone in his bedroom, wearing grey underwear and a stained undershirt. If he was lucky, someone would find his corpse before he started to stink. She didn't wish any inconvenience on his neighbors, after all. They might be Coalition bootlickers, but at least they weren't *him*.

She knew better than to stick around and wait for the inevitable, that was the quickest way to get caught. She wasn't the only assassin in the Near Systems, and she had seen some of her colleagues make some devastatingly unwise choices that led to their capture and inevitable death. Larkin checked the trunk again and backed out of the room, checking to be sure she hadn't left any evidence of her presence. Though there was no official record of her, she would rather be safe than sorry, and she didn't want to have to sleep with that information processor again to convince her to delete some footage a security manager had gotten of her poking around the boundary of a Coalition base back on Gamma-3. It was an effective way to control information, but a messy one.

The door to Robert's apartment clicked closed behind her, and she silently swept down the hall, the tails of her black jacket swirling behind her. She checked her pockets again, making sure she had taken the empty vials with her. She had; they were safe and ready to be refilled the next time she had a few barrels of apples and some time to kill.

She pushed the thought to the back of her mind and slipped out the building and back over the razor wire fence. Now she just had to find a cheap tavern and a cheaper bed to sleep in until morning, and she'd report back that her team was clear to strip the settlement and pack it out to a fence who would sell it on for them. Most fences dealt in scrap these days, now that the

Coalition had taken ownership of every steel factory, junk yard, and mining operation all across the Near Systems. If you needed anything, you had to go through the Coalition to get it, which meant registering your ship and all of the crew on board. Obviously, not a good choice for a pirate.

They'd cracked down after an embarrassing debacle a year previous, where a rag-tag group in a busted up ship lured a Coalition barge to an abandoned base, blew it up, and left all the crew members and military staff stranded for a week before an anonymous report came in from a trading beacon on the other side of the Near Systems. Every broadcast got wind of it, and in their embarrassment, the Coalition punished everyone with stricter controls on goods and a more robust registration and licensing system. They also took control of all the public broadcasts. She was glad that she wasn't responsible for a ship and a crew, only herself, and that was exactly how she liked it. No strings, no responsibilities.

There was a quiet place on the other side of the city where she could have a hot drink and some mediocre food in exchange for a few credits, and wait for Robert to clock off and go home to his disgusting apartment and poisoned rum. Part of her regretted not taking some of the rum to put into her tea. It would have taken the edge off while she waited, at least. But black market booze on Coalition settlements was notoriously unreliable. Watered down, tainted with gods knew what, or just plain sub-par, and Robert was the sort of man who was more concerned with quantity over quality. If she was lucky, he'd down the rest of the open bottle in one swig and be stone cold by evening, plenty of time for the others to scrap and sell everything from the derelict site the second he didn't show up for his shift.

She slid into an uncomfortable booth at the tiny bistro and smiled at the server. She was cute, tall and broad shouldered with hundreds of tiny braids tied up into a thick bun. Larkin gave her a winning smile and a wink, but the server slid a menu across the table without so much as a passing glance, clearly uninterested.

"Well, fine then," Larkin said under her breath, scanning the menu for something that would be at least mostly edible. With nearly all the fresh produce either being sent off world or reserved for the upper echelon of

Coalition enthusiasts, pickings were slim and relied mostly on canned goods or nutritional substitutes. "Can I get a black tea and three nutritional bars?" she asked the server, who was dressed in a wrinkled white shirt under a simple black pinafore that swept the floor and was frayed at the edges.

"Of course," the server said, making a note on a pad of paper. "I'll be back in just a moment."

Larkin watched the broadcast feed flicker across a tiny screen in the corner. More news of pirate executions, but that was nothing new. The Higher Council of the Coalition, the ones who made all the decisions, were in talks about expanding to the Outer Rim, establishing new Coalition outposts for strip mining ore and coal from moons and asteroids. Just like all the others, they'd leave the sites derelict when they were done with them. Such waste. Such greed.

The server slid the tea and the pre-packaged nutrition supplements across the table along with the bill. Larkin drank the tea quickly, feeling the warmth spread throughout her body, out to her fingers and toes, which had been colder than she'd realized. She pocketed the supplements and paid her tab on credit, signing a fake name that was attached to her very real account. At least she had a little credit now, having demanded half payment before she boarded the transport to Skelm. It wasn't the most she'd ever made. She was still waiting for that payment to come through. Larkin frowned, aware that it was now past due. She hated having to chase clients for payment, and they rarely enjoyed the experience themselves.

She glanced quickly down the road, and on seeing no steamcars or trams, she crossed the street, her mind on where she wanted to spend the next few hours before she could radio her team and let them know the coast was clear.

"Hey, you," a sharply dressed man shouted from an alley.

It was an MPO, a military police officer, and Larkin wanted nothing to do with him. They were almost always up to no good, but ignoring him would only make things worse.

"Yes?" she responded, perhaps a little too sweetly. If she was lucky, he would just want to ask her on a date. She'd say no, she was married, apologize, and leave.

"You were jaywalking."

Larkin looked back across the street. There were no designated pedestrian crossings here, probably because steamcars and trams rarely came this way down the dead end road. She restrained a sigh, and smiled instead. "Oh dear me, you're right, officer! I promise I won't ever do it again."

The MPO's face hardened, and Larkin knew she was in for some trouble. "Jaywalking is a class E fine, miss."

Larkin bristled, but swallowed her pride for the sake of the mission and her own safety. "Well, I will just pay that and be on my way, then," she said.

He held out a pad for her to sign, illuminated at the top where she had to sign her name for the credit transfer. She gasped at the amount listed. "But sir, this is far too much for a class E!"

"Fines have gone up," he said flatly. "Now can you pay, or not?"

It was everything left in her account, every last credit. Her identity might be fake, but failure to pay a fine on the spot would see you dragged to prison where you'd work it off instead. That process took years, even for smaller amounts. "I'll pay," she said through gritted teeth, signing the name Mabel Masterson in the illuminated box. Her stomach dropped, realizing she'd now have to wait for them to sell the scrap and pay her the other half before she'd be able to afford transport off Skelm. *Fucking MPOs*, she thought, smiling broadly at the officer.

"Masterson," he read from the pad. "I went to school with a Masterson."

"Oh you know, we're everywhere!" Larkin tried to chime, feeling dread prickle at the back of her neck.

"He was a real asshole."

She stared for a moment, unsure of what she should do, before she gave a wave and turned to go.

"Miss, you have to pay your fine," he said with a steely voice.

Larkin turned back to the MPO and saw him holding a different pad now, this one more weather-worn and beaten up, with the official Coalition crest adorning the top. Fucking asshole had gotten her to transfer her credits to his personal account, and now he was extorting her for more. "I paid my fine just now," she said, preparing to run. It would be difficult to lose him in a Coalition city like this, but she could probably do it. "I just signed there, on your pad."

"Oh, see, that was a gift for me, you said so yourself," he sneered. "A present for being such an honorable MPO, risking life and limb to keep the citizens of Skelm safe from pirates and brigands." He edged closer and held out the pad again. "I reckon you know what happens to people who can't pay their fines."

She turned and prepared to sprint back in the direction of the cafe, where there was a confusing system of alleyways resulting from the quick expansion of Skelm, disorganized and nonsensical. She began to run across the street when she got smacked in the side by a slow moving MPO steamcar, sending her sprawling across the pavement. Pain shot through her shoulder, which was probably dislocated. Her trousers were torn at the knees and the skin was split, leaving an angry, raw mass of tissue oozing with blood. Larkin moaned, and even the act of breathing caused sharp pains in her side. A broken rib too, then, and she was in danger of puncturing a lung. She dragged herself to the side of the road, and two more MPOs got out of their vehicle. The first one stood over her with a fake smile.

"That's why we don't allow jaywalking," he said in a saccharine voice, as he pulled a pair of heavy steel handcuffs from his jacket.

CHAPTER FIVE

"Here," a short, angry looking MPO said, shoving a pile of raggedy grey coveralls through the wide bars of the prison cell. "Change into these. Someone will be along in a while to take your old clothes."

"Do I have to?" Evie asked, wondering what would happen to her clothes once they were taken.

"Yes, you fucking have to," the military police officer said dryly. "And you better be changed by the time someone comes by to collect your stuff, or there will be hell to pay." The MPO smirked and rested his hand against a large gun on his hip. "You don't want to see what that looks like."

Evie sank to the ground, too overwhelmed and distressed to even cry. This must be what shock felt like, and she tried to calculate how long it might last. How long it *would* last. Proving her innocence would be nearly impossible without a Coalition identity, and having been born and raised on a pirate settlement that didn't officially exist, she had no real defense. Not that she could afford a lawyer anyway, especially with her measly amount of credits locked away in a Bradach bank that wasn't recognized anywhere the Coalition controlled, which was basically everywhere else.

The grey jumpsuit was itchy and ill-fitting, and the legs so long that Evie kept tripping over them as she tried to yank them over her hips. The toggles to close the front of the jumpsuit strained at the fabric, and bit into her flesh no matter how she pulled at them. She was in a cold, damp prison cell waiting for her inevitable sentence, and the clothes she'd been given were hardly fit for purpose. She hugged herself around the middle, part for comfort, and part to conceal the bare skin that peeked through the toggles. She shivered from the cold, and watched as her skin rose in goose bumps across her wrists and the bits of belly that poked through the jumpsuit.

"Inmate EA72, pass your belongings through the bars," an MPO wearing a full suit of protective gear said through their visor. "And hurry up."

She pushed her trousers, shirt, and suspenders through the bars of the cell, and watched as the MPO shoved them into a large bag marked "incinerator."

"The boots, too," the officer said, gesturing at Evie's feet.

"But they didn't give me anything else," she protested.

"Do I look like I give a shit?" the officer laughed, the sound muffled in the helmet. "Off. Now."

Evie unlaced her boots one at a time and handed them to the officer through the bars of her cell. "Is there a blanket? It's cold."

The officer slammed a baton against the cell bars, and the sound of the impact rang in Evie's ears. "EA72, you're going to learn that your pirate bullshit isn't going to fly in here. You'll take what you're given and be grateful for it." Evie watched her hard-earned boots disappear into another bag, one marked "MPOs only." She wondered if taking boots was even standard procedure, or if the MPO just wanted to add something to their spoils. The officer disappeared down a long, brightly lit corridor, washed in the yellow light of bare light bulbs. Evie was left alone in her cell, with the adjoining cell empty, too.

She had to believe that Holly was hard at work trying to secure her release, maybe hiring a lawyer right this minute to defend Evie in front of a judge. Maybe she was making calculated bribes to some of the more ethically flexible military police officers at the prison to allow her to escape, and then Holly would be there waiting with a rescue ship. Maybe this was all just part of the story they'd tell people when they were old and grey together, living a quiet life on Bradach. Strange, that she'd been so desperate to leave the place she'd known her whole life, and now the only thing she wanted was to be back there.

She sat on the bed, which was shoved against a brick wall covered in crisp white paint. The only other thing in the cell was a bucket, presumably for human waste. With a hesitant glance over the side of the bucket, Evie was at least glad someone had dumped it out after the cell's last occupant, but there was still a suspicious smudge at the bottom. Her stomach lurched, and she used the tip of her foot, now clad only in a thin sock, to push it to the far side of the cell.

Nothing in there could be considered comfortable, or even the bare minimum of human needs, not really. She hadn't expected much from the Coalition, having grown up around tales of their misdeeds and their underhanded successes during the last rebellion years ago, but this was worse than she had anticipated. They had no proof other than Holly's statement, and yet she was facing almost certain conviction and indefinite imprisonment on one of the prison camp bases. Until Holly got her out, anyway.

Evie laid back on the bed and reminisced about the first time she saw Holly, who had sauntered into the Purple Pig six months prior in her jumpsuit undone to her hips, the arms knotted to keep the rest of it up, with a tight fitting white undershirt that hugged her breasts and small waist. She glowed in the dim light of the tavern, and she shined brighter than the gold leaf accents on the walls. Her laugh was infectious, and Evie had been immediately entranced. She'd never seen a woman so beautiful in her whole life, and now a goddess was sitting at a table just a few feet away. Drawn in by Holly's charm and magnetism, Evie had brought her and her team a round of drinks, "on the house," even though Evie ended up paying for that round out of her own paycheck. Holly had smiled and thanked her, and Evie nearly melted on the spot.

She asked Evie how long she'd lived in Bradach (forever), where her family was (long gone away), and where she'd visited off Bradach (nowhere). At closing time, when Evie apologetically explained that she had to lock the doors, Holly had leaned across the bar and kissed her on the cheek, apologizing she couldn't stay longer.

The springs under the mattress jabbed Evie in the ribs, bringing her back to reality. As much as she loved Holly, and trusted her, she'd still been the reason Evie had ended up here in this cell. Maybe someday they'd laugh at the whole thing. "Remember that time Evie was in a prison cell, shivering in the freezing temperature to save Holly from a worse fate? Wasn't that funny?" they'd say at parties, surrounded by people who found their partnership impressive, a thing to aspire to. Still, it didn't change the fact that she'd definitely end up with a bruise from this awful bed. She'd always hated her narrow, cheaply made bed back home, but she longed for the comfort of the threadbare blankets now. She rubbed her hands vigorously over her arms, trying to generate some warmth with friction. If she could only warm up a little, maybe she could sleep through the process. Maybe when she woke up, Holly would be standing over her, having infiltrated the prison and locked all the officers into a supply closet.

"Prisoner EA72, it's time for your sentencing," the short officer barked through the cell bars.

"Isn't there supposed to be a trial?" Evie asked, a hint of defiance in her voice. The Coalition was known for forcing people to sign confessions under duress, or denying trials, but they would sometimes demur if challenged.

The officer laughed. "No trials for treasonous rats like you," he spat.

Evie's stomach twisted into a knot. They weren't charging her with the lesser charges of unlawful salvage or piracy, she was a traitor, and traitors didn't get trials, or lawyers, or mercy of any kind. No wonder they'd denied her even a blanket and taken her boots. These officers thought she was responsible for their peers drifting in space for a week, terrified and alone. "I didn't do it," she said, panic rising in her chest. "It wasn't me."

"That's what they all say," the guard said, unlocking the cell door with some kind of digital keypad and swinging open the heavy iron door. "Let's go, scum."

She briefly daydreamed how she would escape if she managed to take the officer's gun. She would sneak out of the prison and then...and then what? There's no way she'd be able to get off world without detection. This was one of the most highly watched settlements, due to the prison. The guard slapped a pair of heavy handcuffs around her wide wrists, and she shuffled behind him down the hallway.

* * *

Evie had been waiting in the small, windowless room for hours, with nothing more than a glass of room temperature water that she had long since drained, leaving grains of sediment at the bottom. After the short guard had shoved her into the room and closed the door with a loud clunk, she'd been left on her own to sit at the steel table with only her thoughts to occupy her.

The chair she sat in was too small for most adults, much less one her size, and the sides cut into her hips. She kept her arms folded over her stomach to hide the bare skin that peeked through the toggles, and lamented that they hadn't at least given her an undershirt to wear under the standard prison jumpsuit. She supposed that the cruelty was the point, especially as they were all convinced of her treason.

The word still felt foreign in her mind, treason. A traitor. Fear nested in her gut with every delicate tick from the clock on the wall, every second bringing her closer to her sentencing. Would it be public execution, or a lifetime of hard labor?

Finally, a dapper woman entered the room and closed the door softly behind her. She was wearing a three piece suit, with the bronze chain of a pocket watch glinting from beneath her unbuttoned jacket. She took off her black felt top hat, which sported bronze goggles at the rim, and set it onto the table. She smiled warmly at Evie and perched at the edge of the only other chair in the room, a thick folder in her hands. "Evie Anderson, I presume?"

"Yes."

"If that's your real name?" the woman said sweetly.

"Yes."

"Ms. Anderson, I am Inspector Allemande, and I deal with situations like yours."

Evie wasn't sure what to say, so she remained silent, squeezing her arms tight to her side, despite the sweat pooling under her armpits.

"Ms. Anderson, I have here some very incriminating evidence placing you at the hijacking of the C.S. Sparrowhawk, is that correct?"

"No."

"Ms. Anderson, let me repeat myself, I have very convincing evidence that you were the mastermind behind the hijacking and subsequent unlawful seizure and salvaging of the Coalition Ship Sparrowhawk. Let me remind you that denial in the face of such overwhelming evidence can only hurt your case, and in some cases will suggest to the assigned judge that you are not penitent for your treason. Now, is this correct?"

"No," Evie repeated, shifting uncomfortably.

The inspector sighed and shuffled some papers around, perfectly poised at the edge of her seat with her ankles crossed. "Ms. Anderson, the Coalition has no record of you. Not your birth, nor your education, or employment, not even a family history. Let's start from the beginning, shall we? Where are you from?"

If there was one thing that was drilled into them in Bradach schools, it was to never mention the settlement, no matter what. To admit that Bradach existed would be to endanger every single one of the residents, and doom the entire city to Coalition destruction, and then control. Images of people she cared about on Bradach flashed through her mind's eye: her friends at the Purple Pig, the vendors in the market, and Holly, if she'd made it back there. "I don't remember," Evie answered.

"I find that very difficult to believe, Ms. Anderson," the inspector said, her warm smile turning to steel. "I will ask you again, where are you from?"

"I was... an orphan," Evie choked out, staring at the ceiling. She'd never been much good at lying, so stammered out one of the ready-baked alibis they'd been taught as children. "I was found on an abandoned floating base near Delta-4, just by chance. The Coalition military unit who found me took me to Gamma-3, where I was raised in a group home." She'd never been to Gamma-3, or anywhere off Bradach. Right that moment in the prison was the furthest from home she'd ever been.

"We keep extensive records on orphans in the Coalition, Ms. Anderson, and we have no record of you." She dipped her fountain pen into a tiny well of ink and scratched something on the back of the file.

"The group home I was in didn't keep very accurate records, they... they were closed down in the end." Evie racked her memory. She was sure she'd read something about Coalition orphanages being closed due to neglect, or children going missing, but she couldn't quite remember.

Inspector Allemande looked surprised, maybe even slightly taken aback. "The group home in Sector 7?" she asked, her pen poised over the paper.

"Yes, that's it," Evie said cautiously. Maybe her lie had worked.

"Well, that's very unfortunate for you," the inspector said, pity in her eyes. "It's no wonder you turned to a life of crime."

"Inspector Allemande, I didn't have anything to do with the C.S. Sparrowhawk. Someone set me up, though I don't know why."

"We have a sworn eyewitness account that puts you on the C.S. Sparrowhawk at the time it was hijacked by your crew, a civilian passenger on her way to military intake."

"That's impossible."

The inspector raised an eyebrow and lifted a monocle to her eye. "A Ms. Holly Ambrosia?"

Evie choked down a gasp. It couldn't be. Why would Holly go so far as to act as a witness? Why would she pretend that she had been there, that she had masterminded the seizure and scrap of a Coalition vessel? Was it possible that she'd been arrested, too, and forced to give them false information? "Why would she say that?" she asked quietly, a sob threatening the back of her throat.

"Well, Ms. Anderson, perhaps because it's the truth? Our Coalition tracking data puts her on the ship as a civilian at the time of the takeover, which validates her claim that she was there. You, however, don't have a chip, and therefore your location cannot be verified. And why would you remove your chip, unless you were planning subterfuge?"

The truth was that Evie had never received a chip. No one born and raised on Bradach had. But if Holly had been on the C.S. Sparrowhawk, then maybe she had been the one to scrap it and was now using Evie to take the fall for it. Tears welled up in her eyes and her shoulders slumped with the realization of the complete and total betrayal. She didn't even want to believe it. It couldn't be true, her Holly couldn't do this, could she?

"Confess, Ms. Anderson. We have you dead to rights."

There was something about the way that Inspector Allemande had emphasized the word "dead" that chilled Evie to her bones, despite the humid, stuffy interrogation room. A possible sentence for treason was death, and Evie sensed her own impending doom.

"If you confess, we will be more lenient. Your history at the group home is a pitiable story which will no doubt influence the judge's decision. Confess."

Evie said nothing, her thoughts and words jumbled at the back of her throat in an increasingly threatening, choking sob that threatened to escape at any moment. She was afraid that if she opened her mouth to deny the allegation, everything would pour out in an uncontrollable wave of truths about her family, Holly, and Bradach. To keep them all safe, she stifled back the tears.

The inspector's glare grew angry again. "Confess!" she hissed, her knuckles white with strain around the gilded pen. When Evie again said nothing, Inspector Allemande calmly dipped the pen into the ink, made a note on the file, and then leaned across the table, and stabbed Evie in the back of her hand, sending a jet of sticky red blood and thick black ink spurting across the table.

Evie screamed through the searing pain in her hand, pressing her palm flat against the flat steel table, which was now decorated with flecks of crimson and black, mixing together in a viscous black cherry mess. Tears welled up in her eyes and splashed down her cheeks, diluting the pools of black inky blood. "Why did you do that?" she sobbed, now totally undone, yanking at the pen lodged in her hand. It wouldn't come free, and every pull on it made pain wash freshly over her.

Inspector Allemande tilted her head and examined Evie quizzically. "Ms. Anderson, dear, I can see that you're distressed, but there was no need for that kind of violent display," she said kindly, and pulled the pen free from Evie's hand. She took a scarlet handkerchief from her pocket, perfectly creased into a triangle. The pen dripped black and red onto the fabric for a moment before the inspector carefully cleaned the blood and ink from the nib, and placed the pen back into the small well of ink, drawing it out carefully and making a note in the file. "Suspect stabbed herself with the pen in a wild plea for pity and mercy."

Evie's jaw hung open. She pulled her hands to her chest, watching the blood spread across the thinly woven fabric of her coveralls. Tears continued to cascade down her cheeks, making the skin on her face feel salty and raw, while sobs choked her throat with every intake of breath.

"Oh, Ms. Anderson," the inspector said pitifully, "you poor dear lamb. You must be so frightened. Who could blame you for your actions, after the no doubt horrific upbringing you experienced?" She opened her briefcase and pulled out gauze bandages and a small vial of iodine. "Here, why don't you let me clean that for you? I'd hate to think that you faced a terribly debilitating infection after harming yourself rather than confessing."

Inspector Allemande couldn't be trusted, that much was true. But Evie also didn't want to end up sickly in this prison, because she had a strong suspicion that medicating their prisoners, especially treasonous ones, wasn't on the Coalition's agenda. She also wanted very much to stop bleeding all over herself, in fact she wanted to stop bleeding, period. She extended her hand across the table with trepidation, laying her palm flat on the cool, smooth surface.

"There, that's a good girl," the inspector said, dabbing at the wound filled with blood and ink. She carefully cleaned Evie's hand, gently applying the iodine and filling the room with its pungent odor. She snipped the gauze with some tiny scissors and wrapped it tightly around the puncture, securing it with a knot near the thumb. "Now that's done," she said quietly, tightly gripping Evie's wrist with one hand, "and given we both know there was never a group home in Sector 7," she continued, dipping the pen into the inkwell with the other, "shall we try this again?"

CHAPTER SIX

Larkin stepped off the Coalition transport, prodded in the back by a bored looking MPO. Her hands were cuffed in front of her with a set of heavy iron cuffs, held together with a chain of links that had been expertly welded closed.

She grimaced against the sharp pain of what she suspected was a broken rib, which felt like someone was stabbing her in the chest every time she breathed. Luckily, the shithead MPO had popped her shoulder back into its socket so he could more effectively cuff her. Asshole.

If only her last job had paid her what she was owed, none of this would have happened. She'd be out some extra credits, of course, but that was easily rectifiable. But now she was being pushed along a fenced in concourse towards one of the most heavily guarded prisons in the Near Systems. Pure terrible luck that it was the closest one to Skelm, and thus the one she had ended up at.

Poor old Robert was probably busy starting to decay on his bedroom floor now, his rigid, filthy corpse just waiting for his cleaner to find him. The odd piratical pair was probably still waiting in their ship for the all-clear, just out of range of the surveillance drones on the abandoned base. They'd be thinking that she'd taken the up front half of the money and run with it, cursing her name and vowing revenge.

By the time they found out, if they found out, that Robert had been dealt with, it would be too late to complete the job. The Coalition would have someone else filling that position in no time, probably less than a full shift after Robert was reported dead. Even then, they'd assign the feed to some other overworked manager until they got a permanent replacement. The Coalition was no stranger to replacing humans like cattle.

"Hurry up, Prisoner," the bored MPO said, pushing her further along the narrow walkway, lined on either side with ten foot high concrete walls and topped with an abundance of razor-wire. Even Larkin couldn't scale something that high, not without climbing equipment, or at least a rope. She shuffled along, just fast enough to avoid the MPO's impatient prods with his baton. They came to the door of the prison, a digitally locked door pressurized by a dedicated boiler. The officer waved a badge at a surveillance drone, and the door hissed and popped as the seal opened to reveal a processing area. It was empty of other prisoners but full with plenty of MPOs, ready to book in everyone who'd arrived on the prison transport.

"They'll log you here and take you to your assigned cell. Once a judge signs off on your sentence, you'll be assigned to a work camp somewhere on this base, or maybe another. Depends on where we need workers, and how long your sentence is." The MPO gave a mock salute to a short guard with a cropped haircut. "See you, Miller," he said as he backed out of the prison door. "I'm back on shift in two days."

"Enjoy your shore leave, asshole," the woman he'd called Miller shouted after him, before grumbling something about favoritism and scheduling. She turned to Larkin and scowled, as if her presence had reminded her that she was stuck here in the prison too, and not free to spend the next two days cavorting at the nearest Coalition pleasure base. They only existed unofficially, in the margins of accountant's log books and at the bottom of Coalition slush funds.

"Name?" Miller barked, waving a clipboard at Larkin.

"Mabel Masterson."

Miller checked the name against a yellowed registry on the desk and frowned. "Never been arrested before?"

"No."

"Right then, you need to be booked. More work for me, fantastic. It's not as if I've already been dealing with booking in the Sparrowhawk treason prisoner today."

"You could always just let me go," Larkin said hopefully, though she was at least passingly curious about the treason case. Traitors could be useful allies under the right circumstances.

"Shut up!" Miller shouted, pointing in Larkin's face. She grabbed Larkin's arm roughly and scanned the underside of her bicep with a small device that made irritatingly chipper beeps as it confirmed Larkin's identity. "Stand over there. Face the circle on the wall. Don't smile, you idiot."

Larkin did as she was told, grateful that at least her fake identification chip had held up this long. Feigning ignorance was easier when you had an official past as boring and uneventful as hers was.

"Turn, face the other side. Hands at your sides."

"So, a traitor, eh?" Larkin said, probing the guard for information. "Not every day you get one of those, is it?"

"Near enough," Miller replied. "Sign here." The guard held out a pad for Larkin to sign with her finger.

Larkin signed her fake name with a flourish and looked expectantly at the guard. "Are they going to execute the traitor?" she asked hopefully. Desperate traitors were even better allies.

"None of your business," Miller growled. "Empty your pockets."

She plunged her hands into her pockets and felt the empty vials clink gently together, suddenly very glad that she had decided to use two on Robert instead of the customary one vial. Of course, there was another vial in her boot, but she doubted that would be found; it was embedded deep into the sole of the rubber and wrapped in several layers of fabric. She set the empty vials on the table next to the guard.

"What are these for?" Miller asked suspiciously, eyeing the vials as she held them up to the light.

"Drugs," Larkin said without hesitation. Better to have an added sentence for a prohibited substance than an added sentence for murders. It was unlikely that someone would link her to more than one murder, even if caught in the act, but better to be safe than executed by gleeful MPOs in a live broadcast to deter piracy and assassinating.

"You bottom feeders are all the same," Miller sneered. "Drugs, booze, thieving. You couldn't be a productive member of society if your life depended on it." The guard tossed the empty vials into a waste incinerator, satisfied with Larkin's answer. "If you don't wise up, you'll end up in a work camp until your dying breath."

It was fascinating to Larkin how common it was for MPOs and Coalition employees to condescend to others who used drugs and alcohol, given the incredible usage among their own ranks. One rule for them, and another for everyone else. Everyone knew that the rich top dogs of the Coalition used more drugs than whole settlements, but somehow it didn't matter, because they were rich. Escapism was only allowed if you'd spent your life exploiting people.

"That way," the guard said, nodding at a corridor. All the way at the end."

Larkin nodded and shuffled along, trying to memorize each twist and turn down the hallway. She had no intention of spending even one week in a prison, and examining the building for oversights and weaknesses was how she'd escape as soon as she had a chance. She just hoped that they wouldn't find the very large knife hidden between layers in her waistcoat. If she was lucky, she could stash it in the mattress for when she escaped. If she was very unlucky, they'd find it and send her straight to a work camp.

"Move it!" Miller said sharply, and jabbed Larkin in the back. "I don't have time to spend all day taking a lazy stroll through the prison with you, thief."

"For the record, I didn't steal anything," Larkin said over her shoulder.

"You stole from the Coalition when you couldn't pay the fine for your infraction, and now you're going to pay off that theft with hard labor. Keep it up, and I'll make sure you're recommended for the hazardous waste containment crew."

Larkin swallowed back her pithy retort and shuffled faster down the corridor. Escape wouldn't matter if she was assigned to that crew, it was more or less a death sentence. It was where troublesome prisoners were sent to die, when they hadn't been handed an execution order. Death by slow acting, corrosive poison. Even Larkin wasn't that inhumane; her poisons were fast acting, or relatively, anyway. The ricin she preferred could be a little bit messy.

Miller held her arm up to a small pad on the wall and the cell door sprang open. *Goddamn digital locks*, Larkin thought. There went her idea of picking the lock to escape once she had seduced or blackmailed an MPO into smuggling her onto a military transport ship off-world. Hers was the second to last cell in the corridor, with no one else around. If nothing else, her time here would be incredibly, painfully boring, and that was punishment enough.

"Here's your uniform," Miller said, stuffing an ugly grey set of coveralls through the bars. "Be changed by the time I get back, or else."

Larkin didn't want to find out what "or else" meant, so she quickly shimmied out of her trousers and jacket as soon as the guard's footsteps faded down the hallway. The pendant under her tongue was starting to chafe, so she clasped it around her neck again, arranging her hair to hide the chain.

Her whole left side was bruised and scraped from the collision with the steamcar, and she wasn't looking forward to seeing how fucked up her ribs were. Those steamcars looked flimsy, but they damn well packed a punch, even when moving at a low speed. When steel met flesh, it was rarely a pretty sight.

It wasn't her first time in a prison, but she hoped it would be her last. The whole charade was growing boring. She unbuttoned her waistcoat carefully to keep the knife concealed, and gasped quietly from the pain in her ribs. Maybe it was only a fracture, and not a full break, though the dramatic deep purple bruising spread under her arm suggested otherwise.

"Slow, shallow breaths," Larkin said quietly to the empty cell, her eyes watering from the pain. Goddamnit. She didn't want to alert the guards, knowing how they loved to use any weaknesses against you.

The large, silver knife with the curved blade was still concealed between the stiff layers of the waistcoat, and she ripped at the stitches with her fingers, snapping them one by one. Listening for footsteps and hearing none, she slid it from its fabric sheath and sliced a clean opening into the mattress, and hid the knife within. Might come in handy.

Miller stomped back down the corridor after making her rounds, and collected the pile of Larkin's clothes that she had set neatly outside her cell, after shoving it through the cell bars. She watched hopefully as the guard picked up the pile with an unassuming swipe, and then her jaw fell open as Miller tossed the entire pile into a large black bag marked "incinerator."

"Hey, you can't do that!" she shouted before thinking better of drawing attention to herself. She liked her clothes, and this asshole was just going to burn them?

"I can do whatever I like," Miller said, laughing. "It's not like you're going to be needing them, anyway. From what I hear, there are some vacancies in the waste containment unit."

Though it was likely an empty threat, used to keep low-grade criminals like her in check, Larkin knew when to stop pressing her luck. She watched as the guard disappeared down the corridor, probably to set all of her clothes on fire in an incinerator.

Miller didn't seem like the kind of guard that could be manipulated, certainly not by seduction, or at least not by her. Maybe blackmail was the answer, or maybe it was best to avoid Miller entirely and focus on whatever guard had the next shift. She was growing increasingly uneasy in this prison, and she wanted out.

"Fucking asshole," Larkin muttered under her breath, and sat gingerly at the edge of the sterile, thin mattress. She wouldn't be recommending this prison to any of her friends, that was for sure, not with these shitty beds. If a punctured lung didn't kill her, sleeping on that fabric covered steel might. There was nothing else in the cell except a bucket, and she quickly decided to ignore that until absolutely necessary. Nothing to entertain her other than challenging herself to recall the exact route she had taken through the prison, memorizing each twist and turn so that in the unlikely event the doors sprung open and the guards all vaporized, she'd know how to escape. Fat chance of that happening, though. It was probably the most aggressively guarded prison in the Near Systems.

This place was covered in unpickable digital locks. The only way you'd get that door open without an activated MPO chip would be to use dynamite, or some other exceptionally entertaining explosive device.

Larkin chuckled to herself, remembering the time she used C-4 to blow open a safe she'd found on a job. She regretted laughing when a sharp pain spread across her back, and felt like her lungs were going to explode. Breaking ribs was her least favorite risk of any job, but unavoidable, especially when getting run over by a steamcar.

"Fucking traitor!" Larkin heard Miller shout down the hallway, a cold mirth in the guard's voice that sent a shiver down her spine. She heard someone crying softly. A door slammed and MPOs jeered the prisoner, whoever they were. They laughed and cursed, asking if the prisoner had "had enough yet," and it made Larkin's blood run cold. She'd been in the business of killing for a long time now, and there was nothing more cruel than those in power using their position to hurt others. When she killed, she did it for a reason, but she'd learned that much of the Coalition's cruelty was just for sport. The cruelty was the point.

The jeers and cackling grew louder, and Larkin felt her muscles stiffen in response. She felt the adrenaline swim freely in her veins, preparing her for a fight or a run for her life, neither of which was likely to happen right now. She took a deep breath and winced, and tried to make a mental note that breathing deeply was not on the menu of calming techniques right now. Stupid fucking fragile ribs. Stupid mortal fleshy body. She envied the heavy machinery used for strip mining asteroids, huge and clunky but impervious to pain.

"I hope they execute you on public broadcast," Miller sneered at the prisoner as the small crowd came into view. "I hope the Coalition officers you left adrift for weeks in dark space will finally have some peace, you... sewer rat."

Larkin smirked. Not the most potent insult she'd ever heard in a prison, but it got the point across. She craned her neck to see through the bars, curious about the treasonous rat. The prisoner was surrounded on all sides by the on-duty MPOs, and so it was impossible to see their face. The other MPOs smeared food, at least she hoped it was food, over the prisoner's grey jumpsuit, and laughed and pushed at the prisoner's back, causing them to stumble and fall. Miller jerked her foot back and sent it flying into the prisoner's side, and Larkin flinched instinctively. She could hear the boot connect with the prisoner's soft flesh, a *whump* sound, but thankfully not a crunch. Whoever this poor asshole was, they'd been through enough.

The prisoner was shoved into the cell next to Larkin's, the cell door slammed shut and held in place until the digital steam locks engaged. Whoever they were, they were locked up same as her, with the same likelihood of escape. Though perhaps a high powered traitor would have high powered friends, the kind of friends who would stage a dangerous prison break to save you from imminent doom. Valuable friends.

Larkin sidled up to the bars that separated their cells, gently holding her side to dim the pain that came with every breath. "Hey," she hissed, once the cheering crowd's noise had faded to a dull roar across the prison. The prisoner's face was hidden as they faced the solid brick wall, laying on the disgusting mattress, but Larkin could hear the soft sobs. "Hey," she said again, more gently this time.

No response. The prisoner's arms were tightly bandages from shoulders to wrists, and blood was visible beneath the thick layers of sterile white gauze. Whatever they'd done to this poor asshole to coerce a confession, it had been bad.

"What are you in for?" she asked, hoping her light tone would inspire a conversation.

The prisoner rolled towards Larkin, her face tear-stained, her expression broken. "Leave me alone," she said softly, and rolled back to face the wall.

Larkin gasped softly. "Hey, it's you! The girl from the tavern!"

CHAPTER SEVEN

Larkin grasped the bars of the cell and pressed her face to them as far as it could go. "Well, aren't you a sight for sore eyes?" It wasn't untrue, even in her current condition. She'd taken her for a townie, a Bradach native with a quiet, safe life. Definitely not a traitor, and never as someone capable of hijacking, stripping, and scrapping the C.S. Sparrowhawk.

"It is you, isn't it? Wow, I just can't believe that, what are the odds?" she mused aloud. "Well, how in the hell did you end up here?" When there was no answer, she responded to her own question: "Well, I suppose you hijacked and ripped apart their ship." Larkin raised an eyebrow, even though Evie was facing the wall. "Nicely done."

"I didn't do it," Evie said flatly, and Larkin wondered how many times she'd said that before she signed the Coalition's confession. "I was set up. Or I took the fall for it, whatever."

Larkin slowly sank down to the cold tile floor next to the bars, holding her ribs. She didn't want to be shouting about treason across two cells, she had enough to deal with without getting tied up in whatever this was. Still, her curiosity was piqued. "What do you mean, set up?"

Evie sighed softy. "Leave me alone," she repeated, a note of hopelessness apparent in her voice. The poor woman had obviously been tortured, her spirit broken. Though Larkin was fuzzy on the details, the brownish red patches of blood across the gauze on her arms gave some indication. There was a thick, antiseptic smell of iodine, and she could see the telltale sticky yellow substance seep out from under the tight bandages. She was surprised the Coalition had treated the wounds they'd inflicted on her at all, rather than leave her to develop an infection, and then likely, sepsis. Perhaps they wanted to keep Evie alive long enough to endure further punishment, more torture, a public execution. With that thought, Larkin's heart broke for Evie, and even though she was almost a total stranger, she wished the bars separating them were wide enough for her to slip through, just for a moment to give her a comforting touch.

She lowered her voice to a whisper. "My real name is Larkin, by the way. I never told you before."

There was no response from the other cell, but Larkin could tell that Evie was listening. She could see the woman's body rise and fall with each pained breath, which weren't deep or even enough to indicate sleep. "I'm here on an investigation." A lie, but she didn't know if she could trust Evie with more personal information. If she really was a traitor, then she might be playing Larkin like a cheap fiddle. "I set myself up on a bogus charge, waited to be arrested so I can report back on the conditions here."

She stretched her legs out in front of her, enjoying the feeling of straining the muscles in her calves. Though her left leg was bruised all down the left side, there didn't seem to be any real damage, and for that she was grateful. She covered her mouth with her hand to muffle the sound. "These MPO fucks are always trying to get away with shit." Larkin had surprised herself with the bit about being an investigator, though she supposed it would suit her natural talents of observation and finding an answer to a question with only half the information. Maybe in another life she'd have been an inspector for the Coalition, instead of being very good at murder.

"Do you want to tell me what they did to you?" Maybe if she could endear Evie to her, then she would tell her how she'd been set up, if that was the truth. Larkin suspected it was: after all, she was an excellent judge of character, and Evie didn't seem like the treasonous type.

"No."

"Hmm," Larkin mumbled, pointing her booted toes at the cell door. Evie only wore holey socks, with calloused heels poking out. Callouses, the mark of physical labor. "Hey, where are your shoes?"

"Gone." Evie shifted slightly on her bunk, the thin mattress practically invisible wherever any weight rested on it. "They took them."

"Fuck," Larkin said softly. She didn't want to imagine her bare feet on this cold, damp floor. It was practically a guarantee for pneumonia.

Long-buried guilt threatened to seep into the forefront of her mind, and she shook her head violently to push it back down. Maybe if she helped Evie escape, she could finally escape the shame that always lived just under the surface. "Hey," she whispered through the cell bars. "I'm sorry. For what they did to you. Whatever you did or didn't do, you don't deserve this. It's inhumane."

Evie rolled onto her back, and Larkin could see tears glistening in the woman's eyes. "They made me confess. They said I'll likely be executed publicly, in order to discourage piracy across the Near Systems." She sniffled, and the tears spilled down her cheeks, soaking the thin white sheet over the mattress. "Even if you are a rebel reporter, it won't matter. I'll be dead long before you get out of here. You'll probably end up dead, too."

"We might get out," she said, but heard the uncertainty in her own voice, the slight waver that gave away her anxiety.

"We won't get out," Evie said flatly, and turned back to the wall.

Larkin stared at the wall, pristine white bricks freshly painted. She wondered what the fresh paint was hiding, and then decided maybe she didn't want to know after all. She turned her gaze to the bed, memorizing every nick in the steel frame, every loose thread that stuck out from below the sheet. Wall. Bed. Bucket. Bars. It didn't take long to fully memorize the entire room, to recall in her mind every insignificant detail when she closed her eyes, to walk the corridors out of the prison if she could just get out of this cell. It felt like it had been hours since Evie last spoke, but there was no way to know. The yellow, buzzing overhead lights were on all the time, twenty-four hours a day without stop. It's easier to manipulate people if you starve them of sleep. It's easier to coerce confessions from desperate, confused people.

Though she had always been a loner, a detached killer for hire, she felt a strange want to protect Evie, borne of a decade old sin she could never take back, the mortal transgression of causing the death of an innocent. But how could she protect anyone locked in this cell? She didn't even know her, she wasn't a lawyer, didn't even have legal representation. She had no way of contacting anyone, not that she knew anyone powerful enough and foolish enough to risk storming a highly guarded Coalition base.

Footsteps grew closer, the sharp, piercing clicks of Coalition uniform boots. Larkin sat up and stifled a moan that escaped her lips when the pain in her ribs shot through her center as though she'd been shot. Rib injuries sucked. She leaned nonchalantly against the bars that separated the cells, with one leg stretched out and the other folded up neatly, the sole of her boot resting against the opposite thigh.

"No, thank you, I will take it from here," a voice said firmly, and a tall, coiffed woman came into view, holding a briefcase and wearing an impeccably tailored suit with a black top hat and matching gloves. Larkin peered into Evie's cell, the woman's eyes squeezed shut, silent tears streaming from her face as she looped her arms around her legs, the cuffs still holding her wrists, as though she was trying to take up as little room as possible.

"Evie, my dear," the woman said, and something about her made the hairs on the back of Larkin's neck stand on end. "I think we should discuss your sentence."

Larkin looked from one to another, from broken to breaker, from innocent to guilty. Evie didn't even move, the terror etched plainly on her face, crushing herself against the back wall as though if she tried hard enough, she might fuse right through to freedom, or else become part of the wall itself, brick and impermeable to pain.

"Ms. Anderson, don't make me come in there," the woman said gently, her threateningly white smile glittering in the yellow lights like a wolf's in the moonlight. "I know you'd prefer to be left alone, but you need to be officially informed of your sentence."

Evie still didn't move, but trembled at the sight of the sharply dressed woman. An inspector, probably, Larkin thought. They were the ones to coerce confessions out of innocent people, using any means necessary, at any cost. The Coalition had to be protected, and that meant finding a suitable scapegoat for every crime, but especially high profile ones like the C.S. Sparrowhawk. How the hell did the woman sleep at night, after torturing people into false admissions of guilt? The inspector was a husk. An empty, duplicitous husk.

"You there," the woman said sweetly to a guard at the end of the corridor. "Won't you open this cell for me?"

"Of course, Inspector Allemande," the guard replied, and Larkin heard the telltale hiss of the door's lock beginning to de-pressurize. Larkin felt panic tighten the muscles in her shoulder blades, the dull ache of her bruised shoulder becoming sharper. She had to think fast to buy Evie some time, anything to keep her out of that interrogation room.

"Hey lady!" Larkin shouted loudly at the inspector, who jumped at the sound. "What's your name, huh?"

"My name is Inspector Allemande," the woman replied, clearly ruffled from Larkin's outburst. "And I shall thank you very much to stop shouting. It's wholly inappropriate." She smoothed the hem of her tailored jacket and stepped to Larkin's cell door. "And you are?"

"Mabel."

"And you are here because?"

Larkin's mind raced, looking for some way to throw the woman off balance, to shift her attentions away from Evie. She raised an eyebrow at the woman and smirked, her face perfectly hiding her uncertainty. "I'm in prison because I've been very bad." She stood and pressed herself against the cell door, grasping the bars so that she was as close to the inspector as she could get. "Don't you think?"

Inspector Allemande stared back. "I think that you are a criminal, and that makes you a traitor to the Coalition. Perhaps there's some crime, some malfeasance you've yet to confess to? Perhaps we should have a meeting to discuss your sins against the glorious empire?"

"Oh, *Inspector*," Larkin said, draping herself across the cell bars suggestively, "I bet you would like that, wouldn't you?" She heard the guard down the corridor snicker, and then stifle a louder laugh.

A blush spread quickly across Allemande's face. "No, I don't — you — I, " the inspector stammered, as the guard down the hall lost control of themselves and burst out laughing.

"I bet you get all the naughty girls to mend their ways, don't you, Inspector Allemande?" Larkin said, pressing her breasts gently against the bars. "Maybe you could mend *my* ways, too? Oh yes, *please*, Inspector, help me *mend* my *ways*!"

"That is enough!" Allemande said, clearly flustered. "This kind of behavior is unacceptable here, and your actions will be reported to the head MPO on duty and noted in your file for punitive actions."

"Will you be the one to deliver my punishment?" Larkin asked suggestively, flipping open the top two toggles of the jumpsuit. "Please tell me that you'll be the one to punish me, Inspector. I'm so *bad*."

"I will make sure that Miller hears of this!" Allemande shouted, her face pink with embarrassment, running the tips of her fingers over the silver pen in her breast pocket. "Perhaps there's a space on the hazardous waste crew that needs to be filled, what do you think?"

"I know of a space you could fill," Larkin said, wiggling her eyebrows. At this, the guard down the hall completely lost their composure, busting out with a loud guffaw and ensuing laughter that kept them from breathing.

"Ms. Anderson, I will be back tomorrow to discuss your sentence!" Allemande said sharply, pulling her hand away from the pen. "As for you," she said, looking at Larkin, "I'm going to make *sure* you face punishment for this little sordid display. I'm going to go and file the paperwork to make *sure* you are immediately reassigned, we can't have *your kind* getting away with this behavior." Inspector Allemande stalked off down the corridor, and Larkin heard a sharp slap of skin on skin, and then a quiet whimper as the guard went quiet. Though it had probably earned her a spot on that doomed crew, at least she'd taken the focus from Evie, at least for a moment. The woman in the cell next to hers was still crouched on the bed, with a look of total and complete confusion on her face.

"Well that got rid of her, at least for a while," Larkin said, releasing the cell door bars and closing up her jumpsuit.

"Why would you do that?" Evie asked quietly, still hugging herself tightly.

"She did that to you, right?" Larkin replied, gesturing at the blood spotted, iodine soaked bandages that covered Evie's arms from shoulder to wrist, and on one arm, her palm was bandaged, too.

Evie nodded.

"Well then, let's just say I wanted some peace and quiet." She sat on the edge of the bed and stretched her arms over her head. "Hard to sleep when someone is screaming for mercy and begging to confess." She paused a moment, watching Evie fidget in the iron cuffs, trying to rearrange the fabric on her forearms. "How is all that feeling?"

"Hurts. Burns."

"Yeah, I'll bet."

"It doesn't matter, they'll just kill me off in a few days anyway."

"Well, maybe this at least bought you a few hours of reprieve from that monster and the evil overlords she works for. More time to hope for a rescue, anyway."

The hazel color of Evie's eyes flicked from one side to the other. "A rescue isn't going to come. The person that set me up, she... she acted as witness. I don't know why."

"Was it that girl? The one from the tavern?" When Evie didn't respond, Larkin continued, "I knew she was bad news. I hate to say that I told you so, but— "

"Leave me alone." Evie laid back on her too-small bed and faced the wall.

"Aw Evie, come on, I'm just... " Larkin stopped. She'd spent so long on her own, so long without real friends or people that cared about her, that she was rusty on her people skills. Manipulation, seduction, coercion, all came as easily as breathing to her, regularly practiced and performed in her art of killing.

Affection and empathy, well, they were harder to come by for an assassin. Larkin took a deep breath and tried again.

"I'm sorry, I didn't mean that.

"Yes, you did," Evie replied, her voice muffled by the wall.

"Well, I shouldn't have said it. I'm... sorry."

"You were right though," Evie said, turning her face towards Larkin. "She was selfish, she framed me. She probably never even loved me. I was probably just some gullible, foolish mark." She squeezed her eyes shut, and a tear leaked out, criss-crossing the already existing tear stains on her cheeks. "She was just so beautiful, and talented, and she chose me, and I was a fool."

Larkin tilted her head at the woman. "You're beautiful too," she said, and meant it. Evie didn't open her eyes or respond, so Larkin thought maybe she hadn't heard her. Still, she felt like she was on a cliff edge with this conversation, trying not to fall into a swirling void of saying the wrong thing. She couldn't quite figure out why she felt so drawn to, and protective of Evie. She was just some girl in a tavern who served her too much rum once, and was now coincidentally in the cell next door. Was she so starved for real human connection, or panicked deep down about her own imprisonment, that she was attaching herself to the first recognizable human? Or perhaps seeing José again after all these years had shaken something loose inside of her, making her feel off balance and vulnerable.

She cleared her throat and then sat against the bars separating their cells. "Maybe I can find us a way out of here," she said quietly, not wanting to alert the guard at the end of the hall who would probably be grateful for any reason to take out their slap on Larkin. "Though it's safe to say that seduction didn't work its magic this time around."

Evie cracked a tiny smile, which made Larkin grin widely. "You know," Evie whispered, sitting down on the opposite side of the bars, "I bet it definitely would have worked if she hadn't had an audience busting a gut laughing."

"Yeah, you know, I've seduced loads of inspectors and guards, I don't know, maybe this jumpsuit just isn't working for me."

Evie snorted a laugh, and Larkin suddenly felt like the sun was shining on her face. She didn't know why, but making Evie laugh felt more powerful than killing dozens of high level Coalition assholes. She raised an eyebrow and grasped the bars. "Oh *please*, Inspector, won't you *take me*?" she said, mimicking her own ridiculous display.

"Yeah, I think she was into it," Evie laughed, and then sobered. "She's sadistic enough to abuse power like that." She dragged her forearms back and forth over the rough coveralls, the gauze catching on the dried blood beneath and making a soft ripping noise as the scabs broke open.

"Hey, don't do that," Larkin said gently, and reached through the bars to catch Evie's hand. "Let it heal."

"It itches, and it burns," Evie said, dropping her hands back in her lap. "But thank you." She rubbed her thumb over the top of Larkin's hand. "At least she won't be back again today."

Larkin's face warmed at the contact with Evie, but she didn't turn away. She held the woman's hand, and for a moment they were comrades in arms, giving each other a little bit of comfort before enduring whatever horrors the Coalition had in store for them. "I doubt that act will work twice," she said softly. "I worry they'll transfer me somewhere else, to a hazardous waste containment facility or something."

"Why are you *really* here?" Evie asked.

"Jaywalking, bogus fine," Larkin responded. She sighed heavily and pulled her hand away gently, her thoughts too mired in her own grisly future. "I just have to hope they don't tack on other charges." She smoothed some flyaway hairs from her forehead. "Have to hope they don't find that knife I smuggled in my waistcoat. I hid it in the mattress."

"A knife in your waistcoat? What are you, some kind of assassin?" Evie laughed.

Larkin stared at her for a moment, not how to respond. "Yes." Something compelled her to be honest with Evie, despite their situation.

The smile disappeared from Evie's face as she searched Larkin's. "What? No. That's impossible."

"It's true. I'm one of the best assassins in the Near Systems."

"Not that good if you still ended up in a Coalition prison."

Larkin smirked. "I was careless. Impatient." She flipped open the top toggles of her jumpsuit again, this time pulling it down over her left shoulder to show Evie the bruises, her skin breaking out in goosebumps where bare skin met the cold, damp air. "Got hit by a steamcar as I was trying to get away." She pulled the jumpsuit back on and stretched her legs out along the length of the wall of bars separating them, tucking the silver chain back into her bra.

Evie squinted, as if trying to discern truth from fiction. "Sure," she said suspiciously, and it was clear she didn't believe her. It was just as well, really. It didn't matter right now unless somehow the Coalition managed to figure out who she was and put together all the pieces of that puzzle, but that would be impossible.

CHAPTER EIGHT

Larkin was a strange but welcome presence, as far as Evie was concerned. With no hope of escape and nothing to go back to even if she did. She appreciated the company of the woman who was just barely more than a stranger.

Bradach may as well have been a lifetime away, such was the improbability of ever making it back there. She had so much to mourn, her relationship, her job, her freedom, and soon, her life. There was no way the Coalition would let her live, but even if they did, it would be no life worth having, living out an abbreviated existence on one of the hazardous waste containment colonies, a necessary addendum to the business of strip mining asteroids and small moons of their value, cleaning up the mess, and blowing the rest of it up.

Amid all the chaos, there was this boisterous, challenging woman in the cell next to her, who risked her own freedom and prison sentence. Evie's arms burned beneath the tightly wrapped gauze, but she dared not remove the bandages for fear of infection. She had enough to worry about without a high fever on top of it.

Evie sighed and rolled over in the bed, if you could even call it that, desperate to get some sleep. Her body was exhausted, her eyes dry and her eyelids heavy, but it was nearly impossible to sleep with the bright yellow lights always on, and constant muffled noise and chatter from the guards at the end of the corridor. Every twenty minutes, or at least, it felt like that much, a guard would walk past their cells and "accidentally" bang their batons against the cell bars, waking them up if they'd been lucky enough to find some sleep.

Unfortunately, Evie's history according to the Coalition was too murky for blackmail, and she wasn't important enough to be afforded that luxury anyway. Bribery was out of the question, because with a crime this public, they needed someone to take the blame, and Evie didn't have any family she needed to protect. Her mother and brothers had long left Bradach with fake identities that were unconnected to her in any way. So Evie got torture, with Allemande pinning her arms to the desk in that tiny, windowless room, screaming with every cut into her flesh.

Not being the kind of person to come up with cunning plans for escape, or the kind with friends in the right places, Evie was increasingly resigned to her fate. At least once they killed her, she wouldn't have to endure more sessions with Inspector Allemande. The smallest of mercies, and yet, a mercy nonetheless.

Evie found herself pacing the cell, counting the number of bricks in the wall, and then the numbers of pock marks in each brick to pass the time.

She'd give almost anything for a good book. Even a bad book would suffice. Most had been outlawed during the last rebellion, and most of the remaining copies were on Bradach, in disorganized piles stacked atop market stalls, available for sale or trade. The other copies were probably in the collections of upper-echelon Coalition members, those who were above the law. Most people knew that a law being punishable by a fine just meant it was legal for the rich. Banned books, jaywalking, medical experimentation, all was legal to those with enough power and credit.

The metal frame of the bed dug into Evie's back and hips, and scraped at her skin every time she turned over or moved at all. She was coming to realize that the discomfort of the bed was part of the punishment, too. She'd already had to piss in the designated bucket, which now wafted the hot scent of stale urine. At least she'd been able to hold her bladder until Larkin fell asleep; no one wanted to have to squat almost naked over a bucket in front of a stranger, friendly or not.

"Hey, asshole, wake up," Evie heard Miller shout at the other guard, probably prodding him with her baton, because he yelped in response. "Your shift is over. Though it doesn't seem like you've done any actual work tonight, have you? What's all this paperwork?"

The other guard mumbled something about Inspector Allemande, and Evie strained her ears to hear.

"I don't care what the bitch said, protocol is protocol. If she wants to pull shit like that, then she can do her own goddamned paperwork." There was the sound of keys scraping against the fake wood veneer of the duty desk, and one of the guards sleepily shuffling down the hallway. Evie heard Miller sink into the chair and sigh heavily, muffled by the sound of rustling paperwork.

"Fucking inspectors," Miller said angrily, and Evie's interest piqued at what Allemande might have left on the desk. Was it her sentence information, or maybe a recommendation that Larkin be sent to a hazardous waste crew? Maybe it was nothing important at all, but that was unlikely. Evie wanted to know what the paperwork said, wanted to pore over the pages and let them reveal her own grim future. Public execution, or a slow, tortured death cleaning up toxic chemicals that would eat away at her skin and overtax her immune system until her mind was dragged under by a current of minor illnesses, rendered confused, sick, and in pain?

Evie cleared her throat and grasped the bars of the cell door. "Um, excuse me?" she said carefully. "Miller, is it?"

Miller threw down the paperwork and glared at Evie from the end of the hallway. "The fuck do you want, traitor?"

"I was just... wondering if that was my sentence paperwork on your desk there."

"So?"

"So I was wondering if you could let me see it?"

"Allemande can clean up her own goddamned messes," Miller growled. "I'm not her servant, and I'm certainly not yours. Pipe down or I'll make sure she pays you an extra early visit tomorrow morning, and she can take her paperwork with her."

"She mentioned something about my sentence, I just thought maybe if you told me now, then that's less work for you later, and—"

"Didn't I make myself clear?" Miller snapped, stacking the disorganized papers. She looked down at one of the pages and back at Evie. "Ah yes, here we go: you're to be released in a field of frolicking bunny rabbits and given a castle to live out the rest of your life with a whole team of personal chefs, gardeners, and cleaners. Is that suitable for you, Your Highness?" she asked.

"Uh... yeah. Sure. Thanks," Evie said, and sat back on her bed. She'd just have to wait until Allemande got back to read her the official sentence, which would probably come with a side of cutting and torture again. Maybe if she knew it was coming, she'd be able to mentally prepare for it, brace herself against the pain. It would still be pain, regardless, though, and Allemande was more satisfied when Evie had begged for mercy. She never imagined the torture would continue *after* she confessed, but that was how things worked here, or at least with the inspector. Thinking about the slices in her arms made them hurt more, so Evie went back to counting, this time, the cracks in the grey, unpainted concrete floor. So far, she'd counted fourteen.

She sighed and laid back on the hard bed, and tried not to think about the oozing cuts under the bandages. The burning sensation was getting worse, and more difficult to ignore. What was the bigger challenge to distract herself from? The pain from the cuts, or the hunger pangs that were growing steadily more insistent as her stomach's growls echoed around the empty cell? When was the last time she'd even eaten? It was impossible to tell here, with no way to tell night from day, or track the time. Maybe it had been a day, maybe it had been a week, though she suspected she'd be much worse for the wear if it was the latter. Larkin was still sleeping, sprawled out on her bed with a leg hanging off the side, snoring softly. At least one of them was getting some rest.

"Here," Miller said, and it made Evie jump. She'd been so lost in her own thoughts she hadn't heard the guard approach. Miller slid a tray under the bars, along with a metal capsule she suspected had water in it. Miller banged on Larkin's cell with her baton. "Hey! Wake up! Get your pirate ass out of that bed if you want food."

"Not a pirate," Larkin mumbled, but sat up and rubbed her eyes anyway.

Miller stomped back down the hallway, and Evie heard her sit heavily on the chair at the desk. Evie greedily snatched up the tray, her stomach roiling from hunger. She stifled a sob when the tray's contents were revealed: moldy bread, covered in a greenish-blue fur, some kind of indistinguishable slop, and half a brown banana, which was more slime than fruit. Larkin was also poking at the slop suspiciously.

"Well, at least it's something, I guess," Evie said sadly, unscrewing the lid of the capsule. Inside was indeed water, but it smelled like it had been in the metal capsule for weeks, and tasted of iron. She had to bite back the reflex to spit the water back out, knowing that she'd be in even worse shape if she didn't keep her strength up.

"The bread isn't so bad once you scrape the mold off," Larkin mused, using her fingernails to remove what she could of the fuzz. "I'm surprised they even feed us in here, rather than let us DIE!" She yelled the last part loud enough for Miller to hear, but there was no response from the guard. "How's yours, Evie?"

"The same, I guess," she responded, tearing the bread in half to eat the center. It was stale, and tasted strange, a side effect of the mold, she supposed. "I wish the water was rum, to be honest."

Larkin gave a wry smile and a mock toast with the capsule. "To better times, eh?"

"Yeah. To better times." Evie returned the toast and choked down another sip of the water, holding her nose to avoid tasting it as much. She'd taken so much for granted on Bradach. Her heart ached.

* * *

Allemande's sharp footsteps yanked Evie from the light drowse she'd finally managed to achieve, and her stomach leapt into her throat. She felt an anxious sweat prickle at the back of her neck and under her armpits, and suddenly it was as though her lungs didn't want to function. Breathe in, breathe out. It felt like there was a vice around her ribs that was slowly crushing the life from her, a painful suffocation.

"Ms. Anderson."

Evie struggled to remember how to breathe, and her vision swam in front of her. "Inspector Allemande," she said, choking on her clumsy tongue.

"Ms. Anderson, I do apologize for the delay after yesterday's... antics." The inspector looked sideways into Larkin's cell, but Larkin was pretending to be asleep. Evie could tell she wasn't asleep, her body was too stiff, too rigid, and her breathing uneven and shallow. There was only so much someone could risk for another, and that was becoming obvious. "Ms. Anderson, the judge has deliberated your case, taking your confession into account, and I'm afraid we've uncovered something unpleasant about your past activities."

"Oh?"

Inspector Allemande sneered, pulling Evie's file from her brown leather briefcase, unlatching the brass toggles and clearing her throat, as though she was about to deliver an important speech on public broadcast about the state of the Near Systems. Evie held her breath, her mind racing in the seconds she waited for the inspector to begin speaking, imagining hundreds of scenarios in the amount of time it took the inspector to flip open the cream colored folder.

"The judge, in his wisdom, realized that what happened on the C.S. Sparrowhawk was markedly similar to how other Coalition vessels have been hijacked and scrapped in the past."

Evie stared, barely able to comprehend what was happening.

The inspector took a pair of small, rectangular eyeglasses from her breast pocket, the one with the red handkerchief, and set them primly on her nose to read from the file. "Last year, a Coalition shuttle was stolen from a trading vessel and never seen again, presumed scrapped. I suppose you have no knowledge of this?"

"What? No!"

"Six months ago, the C.S. Wasp, a small military ship used to investigate rebel bases and reports of piracy, was dismantled while the crew was on shore leave, the parts sold to a black market trader who couldn't be located. The judge has determined that this, too, was your doing, Ms. Anderson."

"I've never even heard of that ship!" Evie protested, and began to feel her heart race in her chest.

"Four years ago, an exploration vessel, the C.S. Lupine, hijacked, stripped of parts, and abandoned." Inspector Allemande looked at Evie over the tops of her glasses, her eyes emotionless and void of any compassion or mercy. "In that instance, the crew were set adrift in their flight suits and abandoned. No distress signal was ever sent from their position, likely because the navigation panel had been deactivated by the scrappers." She snapped the file shut and glared at Evie, boring into her with those watery green eyes. "Ms. Anderson, that entire crew died out there."

Evie's mouth opened and closed like a fish gasping for air, but no words came.

"You shoved an entire crew, member by member, through the airlock of the ship, watching them scream in their flight suits for mercy. It's reprehensible. It's monstrous, Ms. Anderson."

She couldn't even kill a spider, much less another person. She didn't even wish harm on Holly, even after everything she'd done.

"Ms. Anderson, what do you have to say for yourself?" Allemande demanded.

"It wasn't me!" Evie shouted, desperate tears spilling out onto her cheeks. "I've never even heard of these ships, how would I have known where they'd be, or how to take them apart? Was I meant to have done all this by myself, as one rogue actor? How could one person overpower an entire crew?"

"I think you'll agree that every crew needs a leader, Ms. Anderson, and with the C.S. Sparrowhawk, you proved yourself more than capable of these heinous acts."

"What about the rest of my supposed crew?" Evie asked bitterly.

"A crew is nothing without their leader, and we have their leader safely in custody. Still, crime cannot go unpunished, and investigations will continue." Inspector Allemande folded up her glasses and put them back into her pocket.

She continued in a warmer, kinder voice: "Ms. Anderson, I will do everything in my power to make sure that you are given exactly the treatment that you deserve. As for your crew, well, the judge in his wisdom has ruled that as you were the ringleader, you smart girl, you likely coerced the others with lies and promises of wealth, blackmailing the rest. Even if we find them, it's unlikely they will be convicted. It's you that's the problem, not them. You're the one we have to root out, like a poison, like a weed, before your toxic nonsense spreads to other innocent Coalition citizens."

"Who is this judge?" Evie demanded. Even with the iron grip of control that the Coalition had over the Near Systems, this had to be in breach of some kind of law or intergalactic agreement.

"That is none of your concern, Ms. Anderson. The judge has served the Coalition faithfully for decades and has never once been wrong about a case. Now, if you confess, you will enjoy the same leniency I have offered you with the C.S. Sparrowhawk case." The inspector lovingly stroked the fountain pen in her other breast pocket. "Confession is the first step to serving your sentence to the Coalition."

"Fine. I confess."

"What?" Allemande asked, jerking her hand away from the pen. "What do you mean, you confess?"

"I did it, the whole thing," Evie said defiantly, pleased to be taking Allemande's pleasure away. She also wasn't fond of the idea of having more parts of her sliced up. She was already going to die, probably, and this would just expedite the whole charade. "I did all of the things you said, and I am willing to sign my name to the confessions I'm sure you have prepared in your folder." She held her hands out expectantly, the cuffs clanging against the metal bars, and watched as disappointment clouded the inspector's face.

"Well, given your obstinate attitude upon your arrival here, I did not anticipate that you would acquiesce so easily." She shuffled papers in the file, and closed it again, setting it back into her briefcase. "I will have to draw up the confession agreement before the judge can pass sentence, in order to offer you any leniency the Coalition can offer you for your...cooperation."

Evie let her hands drop. "Oh, that's a shame," she said as sarcastically as she could without raising the inspector's ire, "I had such a change of heart after our session the other day."

"Yes, well, good," Inspector Allemande sniffed. She snapped the briefcase toggles closed, and a sneer spread across her face. "Although, the judge might decide, in his wisdom, that perhaps the names of your crew should be given up, as part of your confession. And I'm sure he will want those names to be vetted and confirmed, else..." her fingers brushed against the fountain pen in her pocket. "Else your confession will need to be confirmed in other ways."

Even after everything that had happened, Evie still didn't want to implicate Holly. She couldn't bear to think of her rotting away in a prison like this, though she probably deserved it for what she had done. If she was responsible for the other ships as well, she had done enough.

Evie didn't even know the other names of Holly's crew, or not their legal names, names that would attach them to the crimes, anyway. She'd never be able to give Inspector Allemande the names she asked for; though Evie was suspecting that indulging in her sadistic tendencies was what the inspector really wanted. "I'm afraid I don't have any names for you, Inspector, and you can tell the judge that if you wish. I confess to the crimes you have brought before me, but I did each of them alone, without the help of any crew. It's a good thing I was caught, isn't it, Inspector? Being that dangerous, who knows what vessel I might have targeted next."

"Ms. Anderson, I think you will find that the judge is not fond of silly games, and neither am I."

Evie shrugged and smiled. "No games. I confessed to the crimes, and I want it recorded in the Coalition log books that I, Evie Anderson, carried out these heinous acts by myself with acts of sheer treachery, using blackmail, bribes, and coercion to achieve my wretched goals. Splash your victory across the public broadcasts, Inspector, you're a hero."

Allemande narrowed her eyes. "We'll see about that."

"Inspector, we have a problem," Miller called from the desk, her voice thick with worry. "It's urgent."

"Perhaps it's my crew coming to break me out," Evie said darkly. "After all, I'm the most dangerous woman you've ever met."

"Enough!" Allemande shouted, unsettled by Miller's announcement. She glanced from Evie to the guard station and back, hesitant. She thrust her hands through the bars and snatched at Evie's arm, yanking it forward and reaching for the silver pen in her breast pocket.

"You're an excellent candidate for public reeducation, Ms. Anderson, a real prime example to deter the other miscreants—"

"Inspector!" Miller shouted.

Evie forced a smirk across her face, despite her heart racing inside her chest. If Larkin could bluff, so could she. Allemande released her grip on Evie and walked quickly and poised to the desk, where she spoke in hushed tones with the guard so quiet and frantic, Evie couldn't hear a word of what they were saying.

As she suspected, Larkin had not been sleeping. She was now sat bolt upright on the bed, leaning as far forward as she could to try to hear. She nodded at Evie, and it made her feel like she had an ally, the kind of partner in crime she'd have needed to accomplish everything she'd been accused of. Someone whip-smart and cunning who could tell lies without blinking. Maybe in another life, they'd have been partners in crime, traveling the Near Systems and taking swipes at the Coalition. A few days ago, Evie had never even been outside Bradach, and here she was fantasizing about an unattainable life with a woman she barely knew, dreaming up ways to make the Coalition pay for their misdeeds.

"Go, then! Don't just sit there staring at me!" Allemande shouted, Miller took off running down the hallway, her Coalition issued boots skidding on the smooth concrete surface. Their uniforms were sharp, but impractical. Fools. Evie stole a glance at Larkin, and was surprised to find the woman staring intensely at her, perched at the edge of the bed. She made a motion to suggest that Evie shouldn't make any noise or speak out loud, drawing her index finger in the shape of an X over her lips.

Evie nodded, though she wasn't sure what was really going on. Larkin stood and silently moved towards the door of her cell, craning her neck from side to side to see as far down the corridor as she could. Evie watched as she wrapped her hands around a pipe that hung from the ceiling, rusty and fragile, probably unused for at least a decade. Larkin pulled herself up, pain etched on her face.

Evie wanted to tell her to stop, to let go if it was causing her pain. It wasn't worth being able to see a few extra feet down the hallway. But she remained silent, not wanting to give Larkin's plan, whatever it was, away to the inspector, who was noisily pacing behind the guard desk. Whatever was happening, it must be big. Had someone broken out of the prison? If so, then maybe it wasn't as impenetrable as they'd thought. Maybe there was a way out. Or if the rebels were attacking the base, a bold, possibly suicidal move, then some prisoners might be able to escape in the chaos, though it was possible that the rebels weren't interested in freeing people like Evie and Larkin, only their own falsely imprisoned people.

Muffled shouts and angry voices drifted through the corridors, and Evie became nervous. What if it was Coalition higher ups, come to make sure the prisoners were being treated as unfairly as possible? She scanned the cell, looking for something to defend herself with if necessary, but there was nothing, not unless she was going to swing a bucket of urine at someone. Larkin was back on the ground of her cell, holding her left side, her breathing labored. Evie wanted to ask if she was alright, tell her to sit down, but she couldn't, not until they knew what was going on.

The voices grew louder with every passing moment, and Evie's heart raced in her chest. An escape, rebels, or Coalition? The scenarios played out and rewound in her head dozens of times, each with a different outcome. She dared not hope for escape for herself. She was learning that hope was a dangerous drug in Coalition prisons. Hope could get you killed, or it could keep you alive just long enough to endure more torture at the hands of people like Inspector Allemande. Both outcomes were frightening.

Electrical pops echoed down the corridor, and the lights went out, leaving them encased in darkness. Her eyes were slow to adjust, and she stumbled over her own feet in a desperate bid to locate a light source. There was a dim glow, far past the guard station, past Allemande, and it looked like the glow of a kinetic torch. With the power out, she had to assume it was a breakout, a long-planned, detailed schematic of escape from other prisoners that she'd not been invited to. Larkin shifted in the cell next to her, and knew she was looking at the light, too. Allemande was fumbling in the dark and hadn't seen it yet.

A figure emerged from the darkness, a small woman draped in a flowing black cape who leapt from shadow to shadow, even as she held the light source herself. She was followed by two more figures, another small woman in a close fitting waistcoat, and a tall, broad woman with long silver braids wearing a green set of coveralls. The woman in the cape motioned for them to be silent, but Allemande whirled around and spotted them.

"You can't be in here!" Allemande sputtered, reaching for her radio.

"I wouldn't do that if I were you," the cloaked woman said, holding up a small droid. "These are set to target those with activated Coalition chips, the kind that unlock these cell doors. If you don't comply, it will send enough electricity to stop your heart."

"You filthy pirates, you treasonous rats—"

"Kady, don't bother, just zap her like the rest of them," the woman in the waistcoat said in a voice as smooth as fresh honey. There was a small pop, and Inspector Allemande collapsed to the ground in a heap. The tall woman sighed and dragged her body to the side before shining a torch into the cells.

"Are you Larkin?" the tall woman asked, shining the light on Evie's face.

Evie shielded her eyes from the light and shook her head. "No, she's Larkin," she said.

The woman shined the torch into Larkin's cell. "Are you the Larkin who assassinated Lionel Cabot?"

There was a moment of tense silence before Larkin swallowed audibly and answered, "Yes."

CHAPTER NINE

Evie tried to stifle a gasp, but failed: "You killed Lionel Cabot?" One of the most renowned Higher Council members, murdered in the Capitol on Gamma-3 years ago, a notorious case where everyone knew the accused had been stitched up by informants. No one knew who really killed him - at least, that's what she had thought until a second previous.

"Yes," Larkin replied without emotion. "I killed him."

"You don't look old enough to have killed Cabot," the cloaked woman they'd called Kady said. "That was over ten years ago, and you barely look as old as me."

Larkin shrugged. "I was young."

"This can't be her," the tall woman whispered to the woman in the waistcoat. "She would have been almost a child when he was killed."

"I know, Alice, but it must be her. All the research led us here," the waistcoated woman said. She rubbed her temples for a brief second. "We don't have time to debate this, no doubt reinforcements are already on the way. Just get her on the ship and we'll sort it all out later." She extended her hand through the bars. "I'm Captain Violet of the Cricket pirate ship. Can I offer you a place on my crew in exchange for your freedom? We don't have much time, you'll have to make a decision now."

"You have to take her, too," Larkin said, gesturing at Evie's cell.

Kady shifted uncomfortably and checked a bronze pocket watch that glinted in the light of the torch. "Captain, we can't just take anyone with us, what if she's a spy, or a plant?"

"She's not," Larkin interjected.

"Captain?" Kady prompted, while Alice smacked a valve noisily with a wrench.

Captain Violet hesitated, looking from Larkin to Evie and back again.

"She's a crack shot," Larkin offered. "I once saw her shoot the badge of an officer's uniform."

Evie whipped her head around in shock. Her, a crack shot? She'd never even held a weapon, much less fired one. What kind of stunt was Larkin trying to pull, why was she lying to these strangers? Still, she kept her mouth shut, desperate to be out of this prison by the time the Coalition landed with an almighty cavalry and no one to take out their rage on but her.

"My good friend Evie would be an asset on your crew, of what ship did you say, the Cricket?"

Kady looked at the captain and shook her head.

"I'm not going anywhere without her," Larkin said, and folded her arms defiantly.

The captain nodded. "Alright then, Alice, bust them both out."

"Aye," Alice said, and a piece of pipe went flying down the corridor followed by a jet of steam that quickly dissipated. The cell doors hissed as they depressurized, released by the broken piping with an eerie low creak before the locks popped open and the cell doors swung outward. "Alright, let's get the hell out of here," Alice said, retrieving her wrench from the floor where it lay in a pool of rusty water. "We've got about five minutes before the lights come back on." She turned towards the cells, loose silver hairs matted against a patch over her eye. "Let's go!"

Evie scrambled out of the cell, her hands still bound by the iron cuffs. Allemande's body gave her an odd sense of triumph, before bending and snatching the pen from the inspector's pocket. Larkin pulled on her arm and motioned for her to follow the group through a labyrinth of corridors that were even more confusing in the darkness.

"Which way?" Captain Violet asked. "Kady, come on! Which way?"

"Er..." Kady stammered, looking from one corridor to the next. "It's like a damn labyrinth in here, maybe—"

"Left here," Larkin said confidently, and stepped into the lead, taking a kinetic torch from Alice's hand. "I memorized the layout when they brought us in, and recited it backwards and forwards until I could see the whole place in my head."

Violet and Alice exchanged an approving look, while Kady scowled behind them. Evie decided that her best move right now would be to keep her mouth shut and follow the group, and hope that she made it out of this mess alive. Everything was happening so fast, she could barely process it all

Larkin hadn't been lying when she said she was an assassin. Anyone who was responsible for killing Lionel Cabot had to be a skilled mercenary, able to infiltrate layers of Coalition security and emerge unscathed. They'd tortured workers for weeks, threatening their families with starvation to try to coerce a confession. People died, the public broadcasts screamed about sedition, but they never got an admission of guilt. The chain that held Evie's wrists rattled quietly, and she pinched herself to see if she would wake up from this dream of escape.

"Another left, and then a right at that fork up ahead," Larkin said, handing the torch off to Alice and dropping back to squeeze Evie's shoulder. "You okay?" she asked quietly.

"Why did you do that?" Evie replied, slightly out of breath from the speed they were hightailing it through the prison. "They could have left us both here!"

"Shhh, not now," Larkin hissed. "We'll talk later." Then she smirked, a mischievous look in her eyes: "I told you I'd get us out of here, didn't I?"

Evie nodded and followed the group down one long corridor and then another, before it dumped out into the main area she'd been processed in. Bodies of guards littered the floor like forgotten rag dolls, collapsed in heaps. Evie's stomach churned with the thought of so much death, so much destruction just to save them from the Coalition. The idea that so many had been sacrificed twisted her insides, the guilt settling noisily in her chest before one of them snored loudly, making her jump. "They're... not dead?" she whispered.

"Of course they're not dead!" Captain Violet said incredulously. "What do you think we are, animals?" The captain paused for a moment as she read through a clipboard on the main desk. "Though even animals aren't as cruel as the Coalition can be. Here, Kady, look at this." She handed the papers to Kady, whose face blanched.

"Gods, they're using outlawed interrogation techniques here." Kady handed it back and shook her head. "Shred it," she said. "And I'll wipe their data here, just to make sure they're even a little bit delayed in getting back on schedule. Alice?"

"On it," Alice said, twirling a large wrench through her fingers. "I'll go disable their ships. Violet, tell Ned I'll only be a few minutes. Won't take long to put a few holes in their boilers." The captain nodded and picked up a large, clunky radio that was attached to her belt. "Cricket this is Captain Violet. Ned, ready the ship for transit. We have the package." She paused for a second, looking Evie over. "We also have a second package. Over."

"A second package? Aye, Boss," came the gruff reply.

"What about the other prisoners?" Evie asked. She couldn't bear the thought of other innocents being held here and possibly tortured. It wouldn't take Allemande long to find another victim for her sadistic bullshit. She felt even stranger now knowing that Allemande was not, in fact, dead, and would wake up in a manner of minutes, full of rage and a desperate need to take it out on someone. Evie worried for the others trapped in here, whose cells had not been sprung. What would happen to them, once the Coalition got wind of their escape?

"We can't vouch for them," Kady said firmly. "We can vouch for Larkin, or at least, she's why we're here. We agreed to take you, too, but our ship can't hold everyone."

"But that's not fair!" Evie shouted, the burning sensation under her bandages reminding her what would become of the other inmates.

"Some of the others here aren't charged with treason or piracy." Kady sighed. "Captain?"

"We can't take them with us," Captain Violet said. "The ship will struggle with the weight of that many extra bodies." She eyed a locked room marked GUARDS ONLY. "But in the interest of equality, we could spring their cells and be very foolish indeed, leaving this door open to whoever wishes to get access to its contents." She bent and yanked on a guard's key ring, which snapped off their belt. Captain Violet opened a door which swung open to reveal walls of heat guns, pistols, and ammunition enough to protect the base from a hundred years of pirate attacks. "Kady, use the override to spring the cells five minutes after we set off. Don't do it now or we'll be swarmed, and that won't help anyone. And make sure you put a lock over that override, or these numbskulls will just lock it back down the second they wake up," Violet said, kicking the boot of a knocked out guard. "Satisfied?"

"Y — yes," Evie stuttered, shocked that her outburst had changed the outcome of something with people who didn't even know her.

Captain Violet clapped a hand on Evie's shoulder. "Let's get you on the ship, shall we?"

* * *

The interior of the Cricket was dated, with vaguely rusty grate floors and paint on the walls that peeled in the corners. Evie suspected it had been liberated from a scrap yard, but given the state of it, not recently. Coalition ships were routinely destroyed, decommissioned and scrapped to make way for the newer, sleeker vessels that lined the pockets of Coalition higher ups. She was following the tall, broad woman, Alice, down into the depths of the ship, towards the boiler room.

"We're going to get those cuffs off, okay?" she said, gesturing for Evie to descend some stairs into the messy, unkempt room. There were piles of parts everywhere, though there were hints of order in the chaos. The workshop was warm, with the boilers heating to maximum to give the ship maximum speed. She felt sweat prickle on her forehead, and the heavy cuffs rubbed against the raw patch on the inside of her wrist.

"So how long have you been a mechanic?" she asked, hoping to fill the awkward silence.

"Since forever," Alice replied with a smirk. "But I've been a pirate less than a year."

"How's that?"

"It's a long story," Alice said, dragging a rusted circular saw from behind the workbench. "Captain Violet helped me realize what really mattered to me."

"Oh," Evie said, and couldn't help but notice the broad smile that spread over Alice's face when she talked about the captain. They seemed close. Alice was a large woman, at least a head taller than Evie, with broad shoulders and wide hips that strained the fabric of the green coveralls she wore.

"Put your hands here on the table," Alice said, clearing a wide space. "Pull the chain taut, and I'll saw through it. It might take some time to get rid of the cuffs themselves, though. The lock is beyond my ability for lock picking."

"Are you sure?" Evie asked, gesturing clumsily at Alice's eye patch.

"Ha! Of course I'm sure. I still have excellent depth perception. You ready?"

Evie nodded, straining at the chain as Alice sawed through the thick iron links that held the cuffs together. The noise was deeply unpleasant, the sound of metal on metal scraping at her already shredded nerves. Sparks flew from the links, but Alice was quick with a wet rag, dampening them as soon as they appeared.

"Where are you from?" Alice asked, her voice raised over the noise of the sawing.

If this was some kind of test, she had to make up a lie to be allowed to stay on the ship - but was she too exhausted for fabrications now? "I was born and raised in Bradach."

Alice stopped sawing and raised her eyebrows. "Bradach, really? Fascinating," she said, pushing the saw at the iron links again. If it was a test, Evie had passed, at least for now. "Where did you learn to shoot?"

This was a question that Evie definitely did not have an answer for, and she let it hang in the air while her stomach clenched. "Oh, you know, just around," she said finally in a noncommittal way. "I think it might have been a friend's mother at first, before the formal instructors." The lie stuck in her throat, threatening to choke her. The boilers grew louder, and the ship shuddered and shook with the vibrations from the thrusters. Alice stopped sawing and gestured to some seats near the stairs.

"Sit over there until we're through the atmosphere!" she yelled over the boilers.

Alice strapped her into the seat, the cuffs preventing Evie from doing it herself. The ship quieted after the artificial atmosphere had been breached, but the boilers continued to roar. She looked down at the cuffs, only a thin thread of metal still connecting her hands together. With a heaving yank, she strained against the cuffs, and the last bit of the dull grey link snapped. "I guess that's it, then," she said, forcing a smile. She was so tired, and so hungry, and scared of whatever was about to come next. It wouldn't take the crew of the Cricket long to discover her secret.

"You know, it's strange," Alice said, tilting her head. "You look so familiar."

"Er," Evie started, her heart beating in her throat, "I just have one of those faces."

"Ha! You're probably right," Alice laughed, and slapped Evie gently on the arm, and even the bandages and sleeve of the ill-fitting coveralls didn't dull the pain.

Evie flinched away from the slap, a fiery sting reigniting and radiating out from where Alice had touched her. She tried to stand and wobbled on her feet, her legs swaying and the room spun around her.

"Whoa, there," Alice said, catching her. She pulled a radio from her belt and called, "Hyun, I'm bringing one of the new ones up to you. Looks like she's in rough shape."

"Okay!" came the chirpy reply.

Alice wrapped one arm around Evie's waist and supported her weight carefully, all the way across the ship to the medical bay. Evie was now very aware of the burning sensation under the bandages, and feeling weak from the lack of sleep and proper food wasn't helping. She wanted to cry, but couldn't even muster the energy to squeeze the tears from her eyes. Alice led her to an old adjustable medical bed covered in a crisp white cotton sheet, which was in stark contrast to the rusted wheels at the base. The mechanic nodded at a short woman in a long white jacket and ornate braids piled on top of her head, before backing out of the room quietly.

"Hello, I'm Hyun," the woman said warmly, with a smile so earnest and kind that Evie wanted to stay in the medical bay forever. "Tell me what's wrong."

"My arms, the bandages, it feels like burning," Evie squeaked out.

Hyun closed the heavy door of the medical bay and pulled a fresh folder, identical to the one Allemande had. "Get out of that jumpsuit so I can see properly, the fabric is too tight."

Evie flinched at the sight of the folder, but steeled herself enough to peel the fabric away from her skin, sticky from sweat, grit, blood and iodine that had seeped through the tight bandages, which were now a sickly looking muddy color, the dried brown blood and thick yellow iodine mixed together in a disgusting concrete that stiffened the bandage.

"Alright, let's see what's going on," Hyun said, sitting next to the bed perched on a stool that looked like it belonged in the Purple Pig, not a medical bay. "What happened to you? Why the bandages?" she asked, pulling a pencil from the pocket of her jacket. "Any lingering pain? Do you have any known allergies, so that I can note them in your chart?"

"Are you a doctor?"

Hyun tilted her head slightly. "No. But I assure you, I know what I am doing." She tapped the pencil against the folder, waiting for replies to her questions.

"I was imprisoned for something I didn't do, and they wanted a confession."

"Ah," Hyun said knowingly, and grimaced. "That explains the bandages. Tell me how long you've felt like this."

"The pain has only gotten worse since it happened a few days ago, it burns, and itches. I've been too afraid to look under the bandages, I didn't want to end up with an infection."

"Smart. May I?" Hyun asked, gesturing at the bandages. Evie nodded, and winced when Hyun tugged at the gauze, which had fused itself to her wounds. Underneath the blood-soaked bandages, her skin was red raw and blistered, and looked more like someone had taken a heat gun to her arms than a sharper than usual fountain pen. Hyun gasped softly. "You poor thing." She snipped away the rest of the gauze before removing her gloves and pulling a large, rattling bottle from one of the cupboards. "They used iodine, it prevents infection, but it also burns when used incorrectly." She poured some colorless crystals into a glass and dissolved them in water from the tap, stirring the solution with a glass rod. "I doubt it was an oversight on their part, let's just be clear about that. They burned you on purpose."

Evie grit her teeth against the pain that washed over her skin anew, now exposed to air and released from its tight bandages. "Somehow that doesn't surprise me."

Hyun nodded grimly and doused pristine white rags in the solution. "Any allergies, before I start?"

"No. Or at least, none that I know of."

"Excellent. Now, this may sting a little, but I promise it will help." She laid the wet rags on Evie's skin gently, being careful not to apply too much pressure or scrape against the blisters and burned areas of the skin. "You'll need to stay here for a little while at least, if that's okay with you?" Hyun asked, opening a cupboard filled with wool blankets that had fed many moths by the looks of them.

"Yes." Evie's skin was prickled and tingling as the treatment worked to soothe the burns and prevent any more damage. She shivered in the cold air of the medical bay, sitting in only her underwear and sweat stained bra on the frigid bed.

"Here." Hyun laid a thick green blanket over Evie's legs and adjusted the angle of the bed so that she could lean back on it comfortably. "How is that?"

Before Evie could answer, there was a commotion at the door, muffled sounds of protesting and a boot kicking the heavy metal. "Hyun, open up!" a gruff voice said through the steel. "I've got the other one!"

Hyun rushed to the door and pulled it open, just as a huge burly man and Larkin barged through. He was carrying her, but she looked more annoyed than grateful. In fact, the look on her face was almost murderous.

"Hyun, I was showing this one to her room, and—"

"Larkin."

The man looked bemused, but started again. "I was showing *Larkin* to her room, and I noticed she had some labored breathing. She didn't want to come on her own, so I... convinced her."

"You picked me up and carried me here, it's not like I had a choice," Larkin muttered.

"Ned..." Hyun chastised the man, laughing. "You shouldn't be carrying injured crew members, not with that leg of yours." Insulted, Ned huffed and set Larkin down on the other medical bed.

"I'm fine," Larkin protested, and went to get up off the bed.

"I think I'll be the judge of that," Hyun said firmly, gesturing for Ned to sit in the chair near the door. "Now, what's going on?"

"Take care of her first," Larkin said, nodding at Evie. "She's worse off than me."

"I'm fine," Evie interjected quickly, noticing the odd rattle in Larkin's breathing. It was labored, and sounded painful. "I've already been seen to." She leaned back on the bed, her arms resting on the blanket over her legs. "See? Fine."

Larkin tried for an irritated sigh, but halfway through her face contorted in pain and she held her palm to her side, squeezing her eyes shut and tensing every muscle in her face. "Alright, doc, listen, I got hit by a steamcar and—"

Hyun rushed forward and pulled an accordion folded privacy screen between Larkin and the rest of the room. "You *what?*" she asked, incredulous. "And you weren't going to say anything to anyone?"

"It wasn't going that fast!" Larkin deflected. "I've seen myself through worse, and besides, I wanted to make sure Evie was okay."

Evie smiled at that, and the happiness felt foreign and strange. It was foolish to rely on Larkin, but it was the first act of selflessness anyone had ever given her.

"And when were you planning on letting me know that you had been hit by a steamcar, then? Before, or after your injuries caused major complications that could potentially put the rest of the crew at risk? I know you've only just met us, Larkin, but on the Cricket we take care of each other and ourselves. Your health is paramount for what we have planned."

"And what do we have planned?" Larkin pressed, pain evident in her voice.

"You'll have to talk to the captain about that," Hyun said, making a note on a clipboard. "Let me help you take off your jumpsuit so I can see what's going on, okay?"

Larkin didn't reply. Fabric rustled and dropped to the ground, Hyun sucked in a breath.

"You've broken a rib, Larkin."

"I know, it's not the first time."

"This can be very serious if left untreated."

"I know."

Hyun sighed and snapped on a fresh pair of gloves. "I'm going to give you an injection for the pain, okay? You need to be able to breathe properly or you'll end up with pneumonia."

"Anything else?"

"You'll have to stay here in the medical bay tonight so that I can monitor your condition and make sure you don't have a punctured lung. And I'll get you an ice pack to reduce the swelling in the tissue around the broken rib. Do you have any other injuries you think you should tell me about? How about that shoulder, it looks like it was dislocated."

"Yeah, it was — hey, wait," Larkin said, the suspicion evident in her tone. "You look familiar, Doc."

"I don't recognize you."

"Wait, you were at the Banríon tournament a couple weeks back!" Larkin accused. "You're the reason I was in that cell, I didn't have the funds to pay a fine!"

"I don't recall forcing you to go all in on that match," Hyun replied, raising an eyebrow.

Ned burst out in a deep, gut-bursting laugh, slapping his knees and shaking his head. "Hey, Larkin," he laughed, "that's the first rule here on the Cricket. Never, ever play Hyun at Banríon. She'll rinse you for everything you've got. She's got no mercy outside of this medical bay, I'm telling ya."

"Yeah, that much is becoming crystal clear," Larkin said wryly. "A card shark and a doctor, that's not something you see every day in the Near

Systems. I'll need a rematch once I build my deck back up."

"I'm not a doctor," Hyun said. "Keep this ice pack on your side for a few hours, and that injection should kick in soon. Your shoulder seems okay, but come see me if you feel like it needs a sling, and definitely say something if you feel like the swelling is getting worse, or the pain doesn't subside."

"Thanks, Doc."

Hyun reappeared from behind the privacy screen with a hint of a smile and tossed her gloves into the trash. "I'll be back to check on you in a while, I have a meeting with Captain Violet to discuss medical supply needs. Get some rest, both of you."

Ned followed her out of the medical bay, closing the door behind him with a soft click as it latched close.

"Evie?" Larkin said softly.

"Yeah?"

"Would it be okay if we got rid of this screen?"

"Yeah."

Larkin lowered herself carefully to the floor and pushed the screen back to its storage nook between the beds. She had the arms of her jumpsuit flopping at her hips, holding a large bag of ice against her side. She sat at the edge of Evie's bed and sighed quietly. "Listen, I'm sorry about all that. I just - I wanted to get us out of there."

"So you lied? You didn't kill Lionel Cabot?"

"It's complicated, Evie. I am an assassin. A killer for hire. A mercenary."

The weight of Larkin's words landed heavily on Evie's mind. "Okay."

"That doesn't bother you?"

It did, but Evie shrugged. "It doesn't seem to matter just this minute. We're free. I just... I want to enjoy it for as long as it lasts." She turned her head to look Larkin in the eye. "Though it probably won't last long for me, once they know I'm not, in fact, a highly skilled sharpshooter."

Larkin grimaced. "Sorry, I panicked." She stretched a leg out across the bed in the empty space. "We'll get you some lessons, how about that?" She went to pat Evie's hand, and noticed the cuffs still around her wrists. "Hmm."

"Yeah, Alice, the engineer, said that the lock was too difficult. She was able to snap the chain, but I'm stuck with the cuffs until we can find a better locksmith."

"Lucky for you, Evie Anderson, I am an excellent thief as well as being an assassin." She tugged a long hooked pin from inside her long dark braid and thrust it into the lock. "We'll get you out of these in a flash." She wiggled her eyebrows and Evie laughed, despite the pain under the wet packs, which felt worse now that she knew the ugly blisters were there under the bandages.

"Hmm," Larkin said, pulling the lock pick back. "These are more advanced cuffs than any I've ever worn." She raised an eyebrow at Evie and smirked, jiggling the cuffs around her wrists. "I guess they give the super strength cuffs to the real criminals, eh? Oh, don't make that face at me Evie, I'll get them off, I just need to feel out the lock a bit more. There's something else going on in there, it's not just a regular tumbler knocking around."

Evie hadn't even realized she was making a face. They were heavier than they looked, and clunky, and rubbing her wrists raw. "I don't suppose you could just leave them, I might start a new fashion trend that will take the Near Systems by storm."

"Ha!" Larkin guffawed and threw her head back in a laugh. "You're funny, Evie."

It had been a long time since someone had sincerely complimented her on something other than her work ethic, when she was jumping in on an extra shift when Gabe was sick, or late, or just didn't feel like going into work that day. Gabe was probably picking up her shifts now. If he was, it was at least some payback for all the times he'd left her high and dry. "Heh. Thanks."

"Here, hold this," Larkin said, and pushed Evie's palm to the bag of ice that was against her bruised ribs. "I can use both hands on this cuff now." She bent over Evie's other hand, her face set with concentration. "Hmm, strange, very strange..." she mumbled.

"Uh..." Evie said, suddenly very aware that she was sitting in just her bra, stained from days of sweat and anxiety in the prison. "It's cold."

"Mhmm, you'll live," Larkin said, her brow furrowed as she examined the lock. "There seems to be some kind of gate blocking me from the tumbler.

Do you have a hair pin, or something?"

"Do I look like someone who needs a hair pin?" Evie asked, shaking her head so that the turquoise coif on top of her head waved gently from side to side. "I don't have much hair to pin, Larkin."

"Fair point. Hmm." Hunting for a hair pin, Larkin grimaced when she twisted her torso too quickly. "Stupid fucking rib," she grunted.

"Hey, be careful," Evie said, and without thinking, pulled the bag of ice away to gently trace her fingers over the purpled skin. "At least the swelling is starting to go down." She readjusted the ice to lay flat and laid it against Larkin's rib again. Realizing what she had done, she felt the heat of a blush crawl up her neck and flood into her cheeks. "Oh gods, I'm sorry, I—"

"It's fine, Evie," Larkin interrupted, tugging another pin from her thick black braid. "Forgot I had this." Without another word, she returned to her work on the lock, with a pick and a bent pin, which had both been hidden in her hair. "Come on, you bastard," she hissed at the cuff, and then the metal made a soft pop as the cuff released and fell to the floor. She grinned triumphantly and waved the pins in the air. "Victory! Now the other one."

"That was fast." Evie twisted around in the bed to hold the ice with her free hand, setting the other cuffed wrist in Larkin's lap.

"Yeah, well, I've spent enough time practicing this shit, I'd better be good at it. Remember, Evie Anderson, the art of lock picking is all in the wrist." She bent over the cuff, a piece of hair dislodged from her braid when she'd pulled the pin out, draped over her sharp cheekbones to frame her dark eyes.

"I don't even know what I'm good at," Evie admitted, and then immediately regretted saying anything. It was the truth, but a painful one. Most of the time, she just felt kind of lost.

Larkin looked up as the cuff popped open and fell to the bed with a soft thud. "I bet you're good at tons of stuff," she said. "I mean, you're an expert markswoman, for one thing," she added with a laugh. "That's good for something, isn't it?"

"Shhh, they might hear you!"

Larkin rolled her eyes dramatically as if to prove a point, and then held a hand to her stomach. "Goddamn, I am hungry. You hungry?"

Evie's stomach rumbled loudly. "Yeah, you could say that."

"What do you say we go rustle up some grub?"

"I, uh..." Evie trailed off. She only had the prison jumpsuit, ill fitting and dirty, and sleeves too tight for her wet packs.

"Ah, right," Larkin said. "Well, how about I go rustle some up for the both of us?"

"How about neither of you go anywhere?" Hyun said, reentering the medical bay with two trays of food. "I ordered you both to rest, did I not?" She was joking, but with that distinct no-nonsense undertone that Evie was growing to like. "Here, I brought you some food from the kitchens. You're lucky, Ned cooked tonight, and last week we raided a Coalition trading beacon that was stuffed with fresh produce. He used what was left after we delivered drops to the rebel camps." She set the trays on the bed and looked at them expectantly. "Well, eat! You have to keep your strength up!"

Evie tore the lid off a tray, and the room filled with steam and the savory aroma of potatoes and vegetables roasted in butter and herbs. "Oh, my gods," she whispered, inhaling the scent of garlic.

"A little better than what you'd get in a Coalition prison, I'd imagine," Hyun laughed. "Eat up, and then you're both to get a full night's rest on my orders. Tomorrow the others will want to talk about why we went through the trouble of breaking you out of that hellhole, and you will want to be sharp for that. Captain Violet doesn't tolerate lateness or dishonesty."

Evie swallowed hard. "Noted."

"I'm leaving a radio here for you both if you need me; I'm just down the hall. Normally I'd stay in the medical bay with a patient, but you're both stable and not in any danger." She pointed at Larkin and frowned. "You, Larkin, don't let me catch you doing anything that could puncture a lung. I mean it."

"Got it, Doc."

"Not a doctor," Hyun said over her shoulder, before closing the door behind her.

Without another word, Evie and Larkin shoveled the food into their mouths as fast as they could chew.

CHAPTER TEN

Larkin leaned against the wall on the bridge, and waited for the others to arrive. She was grateful to have been sprung from that hellhole, especially since she didn't actually have any feasible plans for escaping, but she was apprehensive about their reasoning. Sure, they were a rag-tag, do-gooder type pirate crew with a healthy dose of a hero complex, but they wouldn't go through the trouble of planning and executing a high level extraction from a nearly impenetrable Coalition prison for nothing.

No, they must need her for something. And given their first question to her about how she'd killed Lionel Cabot, she was pretty sure she knew what it was. They needed her to kill someone for them.

She was still wearing the gross prison jumpsuit, and mourned the loss of her clothes those assholes had incinerated. She wanted to sneak into Miller's barracks and torch everything she loved, watch it burn on the horizon as she boarded a ship bound for anywhere other than there. But no, instead, she'd been busted out by this surprisingly bold crew, and now would have to pay back that kindness with a favor.

Being indebted to someone was not something Larkin was a fan of: it meant attachment, responsibility, emotional ties that ground further into her skin than the simple exchange of credits for her services that she preferred.

The dusty clock on the wall suggested that she was early, but it was still strange to find the bridge of a ship empty. No captain, no pilot, no navigator, and it was unlikely that a ship of this advanced age would have the newer auto-piloting systems available. Maybe it was a test to see what she would do, if she would attempt to take the controls or adjust the flight path towards a more favorable location than wherever they were all headed. That would be foolish and suicidal, and besides, she wanted to see what this was all about.

It wasn't every day that an assassin in prison for a jaywalking charge was sprung from her cell by an ex-Coalition mechanic and a band of rebels, or pirates, she couldn't decide which just yet. She'd never met a crew that was both. It was obvious that Alice was ex-Coalition; it was practically written on her face in permanent ink. She walked like someone raised in Coalition settlements, like someone who'd spent her entire adult life in service to the grand fascist empire, just another cog in the machine. The story of how she ended up here was probably a fascinating one, though.

People were something Larkin could understand and read easily, after a lifetime of watching quietly from the shadows. Most people had simple aims: find money, love, and power. Usually people found one and stopped looking. She couldn't blame them, not with monsters like Holly floating around. She'd known from the first glance that she was bad news. Holly had strutted past her at the Purple Pig with a sneer and her hand firmly on the ass of the lean, muscled looking girl next to her, immediately after blowing off Evie for some fancy dinner. Evie didn't deserve to be treated like that; Evie deserved better, and she'd have her work cut out steering this crew's attentions away from her. If they could just get to the next drop, or wherever they were headed, Evie could easily slip out unnoticed and start a new life in a rebel camp. It was better than rotting away in a Coalition prison, anyway.

"Morning," Captain Violet said as she stepped onto the bridge with calm authority and an underlying curiosity. "Sleep well?"

"Yes," Larkin replied simply. In situations like these, it was always better to be brief and to the point. Never give an unknown party with unknown ultimate aims any more information than necessary, or it would be used against you as blackmail later on. She was a stranger to these chirpy, friendly tactics, so she closed her mouth in a tight-lipped smile.

"Excellent."

The other officers shuffled in: the big burly guy who'd caught her wheezing the night before and taken her to the med bay, Ned, was it? Alice strode onto the bridge with the easy confidence only someone screwing the captain of the ship would have, in her jet black eye patch and emerald green coveralls, stained with grease at the elbows and knees. And Hyun, the not-doctor doctor wandered in along with the quiet, stern woman with a jacket that Larkin felt very envious of. The ugly, tattered prison jumpsuit now felt even more hideous than before, and she folded up the sleeves in a desperate bid to look like something more than a common criminal, even though that's exactly what she was, even if not so common. The criminal aspect was accurate. Captain Violet cleared her throat softly.

"Friends, we are here to discuss the next phase of the plan, now that we have successfully extracted Larkin from the high security prison— and a job very well done that was. Everything went to plan, though we did decide to leave things at the prison in slightly more disarray than we'd planned." She clasped her hands behind her back and paced near the captain's chair at the front of the ship. "We are ready now to do what we've been planning since the run in with the Stronghold, what we decided as a crew needed to be our focus moving forward."

Larkin rolled her eyes and sighed. The theatrics of this were tiring, and she wasn't interested in whatever plan they had to pillage and scrap some old, burned out Coalition base, which was likely what they were after. Either that, or revenge against a rival ship, or maybe they had it in their heads to do something a little bolder and hijack a vessel. It had been done by a few crews, but even fewer had succeeded. Still, they'd managed to break her out, so maybe they were up to the challenge after all. She wished that Evie was here to crack a joke or ask the questions Larkin couldn't ask, but she'd told her to stay in the medical bay. The less the crew saw of her, the less likely they'd be to discover the lie.

"Once we create the plan and study it, we will take the central Armory."

"You *what*?" Larkin laughed,and nearly choked on her own saliva. "Are you out of your minds? I mean, you must be to entertain something that will definitely be a suicide mission. Do you have any idea how fortified the Armory is, how much over-armored Coalition military is on that base, protecting it?"

"We did just break you out of a high security prison, did we not?" Captain Violet asked. "Don't underestimate us, Larkin. We can handle ourselves."

"Don't get me wrong, what you did was impressive, and I'm grateful, but this is on a completely different level. I've seen the security feeds at that place, and there are so many surveillance drones flying around that you can barely move." She pushed herself away from the wall to stand straight, and grimaced at the pain in her side. *Fucking rib.* "You'll never get close enough to even land your ship, much less take the armory. There's got to be at least six or seven concurrent security managers watching those feeds."

"Five, actually," Violet said, pulling a lever which pushed a wide table up from the floor. She spread papers out over the surface, blueprints of the armory, detailed lists of security managers and their shift times, schematics for some kind of droid that looked like it was supposed to disable security drones. "This isn't our first rodeo, and we've become skilled at being a thorn in the Coalition's side. We do more than loot ships, we disable trading beacons, we provide food and medical supplies to rebel camps under siege, and after our run in with the Stronghold last year, we decided that it was no longer enough to just be a thorn in their side. Besides," she said, gesturing at the petite woman with the grouchy face, "Kady has been hard at work improving our tech."

"We can handle everything except the security managers," said Kady, the woman in the excellent jacket. Larkin quietly seethed with envy again. "We have droids in development that would be able to at least temporarily cut the surveillance feeds, and with our study of the base's schematics we're confident that we can strategically place some charges to disable the base."

"And then what?" Larkin asked, stifling the laughter that would make her rib cage sear in pain. "As soon as you leave, the second the rubble stops falling, they'll be all hands on deck to rebuild bigger and better and more fortified than ever and you'll never get back in there, not ever. And if you think they won't come after you with the force of ten thousand suns, then—"

"The point isn't to disable the base, not really," Violet interjected. "We want them to think that's what we want to do. But really, we'll be focusing our attack on destroying their weapons research lab."

"Okay, sure, but all that information is backed up in hundreds of servers already, it would be like stamping on one cockroach when there are thousands under the floorboards."

"We will also steal their prototypes."

Larkin exhaled heavily. "And do what with them?"

Violet and Alice exchanged a hesitant glance, but then the captain nodded. "We have a lab here on the ship," Alice said. "It's not big or fancy, but we've managed to innovate some incredible things in a relatively short amount of time."

"Who's 'we'?"

"Me, I am the head engineer here, and Kady, who is a gifted scientist and programmer."

"So you want to break into this base, bust everything up, make them think that you only wanted to disable the base permanently, which is impossible, as a cover to destroy their lab and steal their research for your own, I assume, reckless do-gooder ventures? Have I got that right?"

The captain nodded. "More or less."

"You're all out of your minds, do you know that? This plan is ludicrous. It's suicidal. You're all going to end up killed." She snorted back a laugh and shook her head. "And I suppose you need me, the infamous killer of Lionel Cabot, to get rid of the five security managers for you, in order to execute this absolute disaster of a plan."

"We would never ask you to kill for us," Ned said gruffly. "You just need to make sure they're nowhere near their stations when the attack begins, so we can disable their drones and replace the live footage with a loop, so that they won't be able to radio in any backup support. We will be approaching from the far side of the base, and so we will have the aid of darkness, at least."

"Killing them is easier."

"Let us be clear, then," Captain Violet said firmly, "we don't want any bloodshed if it can be avoided. I don't know how you do things, Larkin, but we try to keep our body count to a minimum. There are ways, I am sure, that you can incapacitate these managers without killing them and devastating their families."

"You realize that my own personal body count is the only reason you came to me for help, don't you?" Larkin asked, her voice edged with annoyance. "You sprung me, a known assassin, from a high security prison in order to help you attack the largest arsenal in the Near Systems to steal some technology, but you don't want me to kill anyone. I suppose I'll just wander into their building, shall I, and ask them politely to step away from their desks for a few moments so that my friends can do something real quick? Do you have any idea how ridiculous that sounds? And why do you care about Coalition families, anyway? Aren't you all out here flying around, sworn to disrupt and destabilize the Coalition anyway?"

"Because some of those Coalition employees didn't have much of a choice, and some of them have children. Why should we punish children for their parents' deeds?" Alice asked. "It's likely my family were Coalition military, should I be punished for that?"

Larkin narrowed her eyes at the mechanic, and knew she was being lied to. No one with Coalition generals for parents, who spendtdecades fixing Coalition equipment, leaves a cushy pension to jump on an old, broken down ship unless there was something else there. "Other people's children aren't my problem," Larkin said flatly. "I don't have a team, I don't prioritize other people's health and well being above my own. I take a job, I do the job, I get paid, I move on to the next thing." She didn't want to mention that her last contract hadn't paid her, and that she'd end up making a visit to the asshole that stiffed her. *Prick.*

"I told you this wasn't going to work," Kady muttered.

Captain Violet put her hand up to silence Kady,and stepped close to Larkin. "We risked a lot to spring you from that cell, Larkin."

"No one asked you to."

"If you refuse our offer, then we will drop you on the nearest planet or settlement, and that will be that."

"And I suppose you'd call in an anonymous tip, telling the Coalition exactly where to find me, yes?" Larkin spat. "I don't really get much choice in the matter here, do I?"

"We know you're broke. Level with us," Violet said calmly. "We know that if we drop you somewhere, you're going to end up right back where we found you. You know as well as we do that trying to survive without credit on any Coalition controlled base or settlement is impossible. You were in that prison not because you got caught doing a job, but because you couldn't pay a fine. You're no stranger to the malice and fraud of the Coalition, so why not help us make a dent in it?"

Larkin sighed again. "Yeah, well, what's in it for me? It's not like I have any use for cutting edge weaponry. My methods are more... traditional."

"You will be paid very well for your efforts. Name your price, and we will see that it happens." Violet squinted at her, and added, "Within reason, of course."

"You can't afford me."

"We are very good at what we do, and I can assure you that we can."

"Alright, well...why me, then? There are plenty of people like me for hire that aren't locked away in prisons. You could have just met with one in a tavern on some backwater base, instead of going through the efforts to break me out of that hellhole." She wrestled with how much to tell these strangers; for all she knew, they could be waiting to dump her corpse on a derelict beacon and call it finished, once she's completed the job. "And don't get me wrong, I am grateful, but it doesn't seem like the most efficient use of your resources, including your crew's time and welfare."

"*You killed Lionel Cabot*," Alice laughed. "Only someone with extremely developed skills would be able to pull that off and escape, and we don't have very much wiggle room with this plan. We needed the best of the best for this job, the most elite, the— "

Larkin blinked at her. "Yeah, yeah, I get it. My reputation precedes me." She'd been coasting on her infamy her entire adult life, getting lucrative jobs after subtly suggesting it may have been her who'd killed the high standing Coalition man, the man with four different security teams and enough surveillance to deter even the most foolish of thieves and brigands. Tell someone you killed Lionel goddamned Cabot ,and the world was your oyster.

"I can't guarantee there won't be deaths." She couldn't guarantee that, because she had no intention of doing anything except what she always did: remove the risk entirely. She had no desire to end up back in a Coalition cell, especially not now that they had her accurate biometric data. It would be harder to hide under false identities, now. People didn't complain about her methods because they never got caught.

Violet nodded. "I understand. But I will say that our terms will contain caveats. Every death will reduce your pay, and we won't be paying at all if you fail at the job you've been assigned. Let me be clear, Larkin," the captain said with a steely glare emanating from her dark eyes. "If we even suspect that you're planning on turning in any member of this crew to the Coalition, or causing discord in any way, we will terminate the contract and make sure you are well taken care of."

Larkin's blood ran cold at the captain's words. It was clear that this bitch didn't mess around, so she prepared a convincing lie. "I wouldn't do that. Ever. It's against everything I stand for." As soon as she could get her and Evie away from this ship safely, she'd do it in a heartbeat.

"Funny, I didn't think you really stood for anything," Kady muttered under her breath.

"I may not be someone of high morals, but I respect the sanctity of a contract," Larkin shot back. "I know you can't trust me, and I can't trust you either, but we can complete this job together." Larkin put her hand out to shake the captain's hand. "I want enough credits to pay for a new identity for me and for Evie, and to spend a year somewhere quiet, where I can fly under the radar and, I don't know, learn to paint or some shit."

"Agreed," Violet said, and shook her hand firmly. "And we will need Evie's talents too, of course, to cover us at the armory. I trust you will relay the plans to her?"

Larkin swallowed hard. "Of course."

* * *

"So? How did it go? What did they say?" Evie asked eagerly, her deep hazel eyes bright with curiosity, and Larkin decided she liked that about her.

"Oh, you know, it's what I suspected," Larkin replied, desperately trying to downplay the significance of what the crew of the Cricket had asked.

"Well? What is it they want to do?"

"They, uh, want to raid the Armory."

All the color drained from Evie's face, leaving her pallid and sick looking. "The Armory? But that's suicide. Larkin, you can't!"

Larkin sat at the edge of Evie's bed and readjusted the cold, wet patches on the woman's skin. "Nah, it will be a piece of cake," she lied, feeling her own panic creep up her spine and settle right at the base of her neck. "All we have to do is make sure the Cricket crew makes it in and out alive, and we'll be swimming in more money than you've ever seen. Enough to buy new identities, whatever you want."

"What do you mean, *we*?"

"Well, you see," Larkin said, keeping her voice light and even, "they want you to use your skills as a sharpshooter to help cover them during the job, and watch out for them if anything kicks off."

"Oh, no. Oh, gods," Evie moaned, burying her face in her hands. The wet packs on her arms slid off, landing on the metal grate floor with a soft squelch and splattering the clear liquid up the wall. "Larkin, I can't believe you didn't tell them I can't shoot," she said, her voice becoming louder and more panicked.

"Shh, it's alright." Larkin worried she would see one of the crew members lurking in the doorway. She kicked the heavy door shut with a slam that echoed around the medical bay, desperate for more privacy than they'd been given so far. Perhaps that was on purpose, so the crew could keep a closer watch on them. "They didn't give me much of a choice in the matter, Evie. Our faces will be all over the public broadcasts now after that breakout, and we need credit to get a new identity, or at least somewhere to hide out to let it all blow over."

"I never should have left Bradach," Evie sobbed, her voice strangled from snot and tears. "They're going to throw us out into space once they find out you lied!"

"I won't let that happen, okay?" Larkin wrapped an arm around Evie's shaking shoulders and hugged her tightly until she stopped shaking. It wasn't surprising that Evie was breaking down, not after all she'd been through in less than a week. "I have a plan," she whispered. "I think we can get you to be a good enough shot that you'll fool them, and then after this job is over you'll have enough money to live out the rest of your years on Bradach in luxury."

"But how will I practice without them noticing? I don't even have a gun!" Evie sniffled.

"I'll get us a gun, okay? And we can practice in the loading bay when no one else is around. It will all be okay."

Evie glared at her with red, puffy eyes. "I can't believe you told them I was a sharpshooter. Couldn't you have said something else? Like that I was a political prisoner, a high ranking rebel from a base at the edge of the Near Systems, or something? Why did you have to tell them I can shoot?"

The guilt started to creep in again, and Larkin bit the inside of her cheek to chase away visions of Evie's corpse floating through space. "I'm not great at improvising."

"Yeah, well, that's an understatement." Evie muttered, picking at a scab on her arm. "Why can't we just come clean and tell them you were wrong? What's the worst that can happen?"

"I can think of a lot of bad things that could happen." Larkin puffed out her cheeks and rubbed her temples, which were beginning to throb. "I need for this to go well. *We* need for this to go well, okay? We're out of options, Evie. We need credit, we need new identities, we need to get this done and then get as far away as possible."

How strange that Evie had gone from a stranger in a tavern, to the only friend she had in all the Near Systems in just a few days. Granted, Larkin didn't usually have friends at all, but she could at least rely on favors owed to her by desperate people she'd done jobs for, even though they didn't have the credit to pay her with. Desperate favors came in handy, and she liked to stockpile them. And now, she was fresh out of any favors that could really help her.

"Evie, please," she said earnestly, half begging as she knelt on the hard floor and felt the metal grate bite at her skin through the thin fabric of the jumpsuit. "We can still get out of this alive, but you have to work with me."

Evie pushed Larkin's hands away. "I didn't want this. I just wanted to go home."

"And you will, just not right now," Larkin promised. "Please, Evie."

"You can stop asking, it's not like I have a choice, do I?" Evie snapped. "Things just keep getting worse and worse, the further I get from home. And to think, not so long ago I was desperate to leave Bradach, I couldn't wait to do something more exciting than wash dishes at the Purple Pig," she laughed wryly. "Just leave me alone. I'm tired."

Larkin stood up and moved to her own bed, setting the privacy screen between them. She pulled her knees to her chest, and cried silent tears in a way she hadn't since Lionel Cabot died.

CHAPTER ELEVEN

Evie sat staring at the wall, counting the rivets in the steel and contemplating the irony that she felt as trapped here as she had in the prison. At least no one was trying to torture her here, not yet anyway, but she could only imagine what they'd do when they discovered the lie that she was a sharpshooter. Stupid, stupid, stupid.

She'd been a fool to think she could leave Bradach, and now she was paying the price. Sure, she'd been rescued from the prison, but now she was no more than a hostage, though well-fed, at least. The rations in the Coalition prison had no right to even be called food.

The iodine burns on her arms had begun to scab over, and whatever Hyun had used in the medicine had lessened the burning, too. She poked at one of the larger scabs and winced at the pain. It would be weeks before the skin underneath was no longer tender and sore, and she'd probably have scars for the rest of her life. The urge to pick at them was almost irresistible.

She knew that Larkin had been crying, but she hadn't said anything. She was angry that Larkin had given that explanation, and put her into more danger, and made this whole thing even more terrifying. She'd give almost anything to just be a passenger on the Cricket, or trade menial labor for food and shelter until they went back to Bradach. Then she'd beg to get her job back from Tansy and continue scraping by, lonely and miserable, but alive. Maybe she'd even get the opportunity to see Holly again, and tell her to go to hell. Even then, Evie would probably just mop up the spilled ale Holly's friends would leave, and be grateful for it.

"How are you doing?" Hyun asked as she quietly eased open the heavy door. She looked at the wet packs on the ground and tilted her head. "Did you fall asleep?"

"Er, yeah," Evie lied. "Sorry."

"They have a room for you, if you'd prefer it to staying here in the med bay. You'll just have to catch me in the galley at breakfast for more wet packs for those burns."

Evie nodded. "Okay." She could hear Larkin's calm, measured breathing through the thin privacy curtain, and gestured with her thumb. "What about her?"

"I'll come back for her later. Let her sleep a while, it seems like she needs it." Hyun looked over the scabs on her arms and frowned. "This is still looking very swollen, Evie. Those lacerations must have been deep."

She nodded. The pen she'd stolen from Allemande was still in her pocket. A defense weapon, maybe, if it ever came to that, but the Cricket crew all had guns, as least as far as she could tell. A pointy pen wouldn't do much against a bullet or the business end of a heat gun. Still, having it made her feel safer, somehow.

"Come on then," Hyun said softly, and led her down a series of long corridors until they reached a dead end with three doors. "Yours is on the right, there. It used to be Alice's room when she first joined us."

If it wasn't Alice's room anymore, then maybe there was something wrong with it. "Thank you." She pushed open the door with a creak of metal on metal as the hinges dragged across each other, and led into a simple room with a bed, a desk, and a small bathroom. Her eyes grew huge at the sight of the cramped bath and immediately wanted to strip off her grubby prison uniform and soak beneath soap bubbles. It was just a shame she'd have to put it back on again when she was done. "There aren't any, uh, spare clothes or anything, are there? It's just that this jumpsuit is filthy, and..."

Hyun smiled and tapped the knob. "I'll see what I can do."

Evie closed the door and felt a relief when the lock latched closed. At least now she had some space to breathe, to sort through her tangled emotions and figure out what was next. Without a moment's hesitation more, she stripped off the dirty, ill-fitting jumpsuit and dropped it in a heap on the threadbare carpet that ran from the bed to the doorway of the bathroom. She peeled off her underthings and left them with the uniform as she bent to fill the small tub with water. She sank into the hot water with a soft groan.

What the hell was she going to do if the crew discovered her lie? Evie had spent her whole life around pirates, and she knew how ruthless they could be, especially when a newcomer threatened their fellow crew mates. She was in danger. Lathering up a fresh bar of soap that had been perched at the side of the tub, she felt grateful at least to have a chance to be clean. The soap was pink with yellow flecks, and smelled of lemons and pomegranates fresh from the trees in Bradach.

She groaned with the satisfaction of washing away the days of grit and grime that had accumulated on her skin, being careful to keep her newly formed scabs out of the water. Suds scraped over her legs and stomach, and she used the soap to wash the mess of hair on her head, too. Evie had never felt happier to be clean, even cramped in a tub that was too small, on a pirate vessel drifting through space on its way to the biggest weapons depot in the Near Systems. Bubbles dripped silently from her earlobes into the water, and she sighed a deep, long sigh. She should be grateful to Larkin, really, for bargaining with the Cricket crew to get her released. She sighed again and watched bubbles dance across the surface of the water.

"Evie?" there was a soft but insistent knock at the door in an unfamiliar voice.

"Uh, hang on," Evie replied, irritated at her bath being interrupted. The bubbles skimmed the surface of the hot, steaming water as she wrapped herself in a fluffy green towel that had been folded atop the sink. It was huge and plush, and nicer than any linens she had back in Bradach by far. She dripped onto the warped wooden parquet floor tiny puddles of water and soap, and left wet footprints on the thin carpet. "Yes?" she said through the locked door, still hesitant to interrupt her first moment alone in days.

"Hyun sent me, she said that you needed some things. Can you open the door?"

Evie grumbled under her breath and unlatched the door, pulling it open just wide enough to see a young girl with a shock of green hair peeking out from under her cap and a huge, infectious grin. "I'm Ivy, I work with Alice mostly." She thrust her hands out, and stacked on top was a pile of clothes, sundries, and oh yes, thank the gods, a pair of well-worn boots.

"Oh, thank you," Evie replied, taking the stack of textiles and struggling to keep her towel from falling down. "It was getting tough to not have any boots. The metal grates on the floor are hell to walk on otherwise."

Ivy nodded. "Don't I know it!" she said, and laughed. "I don't want to interrupt you, I just wanted to drop this off for you. I think this is some of Alice's stuff, so it will probably be a little long on you, but it's better than putting that grubby old prison uniform back on, doncha think?"

"Definitely," Evie agreed. "Well, thanks, I guess I'll see you later in the mess hall."

The girl nodded again with a huge smile and practically skipped down the corridor with a lightness in her step that Evie had never once in her life experienced. If this girl was so happy here, then maybe it wasn't such a bad place after all. She was well looked after, and her rosy cheeks showed she didn't want for much. She couldn't be much older than eighteen or nineteen, and already an apprentice on a renowned pirate vessel.

Now that she was mostly dry, and the steamy water growing tepid, the allure of the bath had lost its charm. Evie pulled up the plug and watched the sudsy, pink tinted water circle the drain and disappear. She dragged the towel over her legs, the terrycloth wicking away what moisture was left on her skin.

Her blistered, burned arms were sensitive to even the lightest touch, so she shrugged on the coveralls gently and with extreme caution. The clothes that Ivy had brought were definitely too long for her, made for a woman at least two heads taller than she was, with shoulder seams that sagged over her biceps and a crotch that hung nearly to her knees. Still, the fabric was fresh and crisp, recently cleaned, and smelled far better than her prison uniform, caked in blood, sweat, and grit.

She was grateful for the bagginess of the coveralls, which gave the skin on her arms gentle, floating protection. The boots, however, fit like a charm and were perfectly worn in, the soft malleable leather like a hug for her blistered, sore feet. Evie sighed with relief and lay back on the bed in her too-big clothes that made her look like a small child playing dress up. It didn't matter, she was safe from the Coalition, at least for now, and far from Allemande's reach.

She had Larkin to thank for that. A fresh wave of guilt washed over her and left a tightness in her chest that she didn't appreciate. Larkin had saved her life, even if she'd done so in a clumsy, haphazard way that now put her into a different kind of danger. Maybe she would turn out to be a natural at markswomanship, a crack shot with a keen inclination for weaponry that would prove useful enough to captain Violet to get the job done and get her back home to Bradach. Without Larkin vouching for her, she'd still be in that cell of the prison, awaiting Allemande's next visit with increasing dread, feeling sweat drip down her brow and melt into the collar of her prison jumpsuit, adding to the sickly yellow sweat stains that graced it. Instead, she was plotting to pull the wool over the eyes of a pirate crew, and hope it was good enough to fool them.

Captain Violet didn't seem like a fool; she was canny and quick, otherwise she wouldn't be leading one of the most infamous pirate ships in the Near Systems. It would be an incredible feat of deception to convince her that she was a gifted sharpshooter, and not just a barkeep at a tavern. She held her arms out in front of her, as though she was shooting a gun like the ones she saw on Bradach, big, hulking revolvers with mother of pearl handles and obscenely long barrels. Her fingers trained over the imaginary trigger, she imagined how it might feel to shoot someone, to take a life with no remorse. She wasn't so sure she could do it, if she was being honest with herself.

Larkin was a stone-cold killer, an assassin, a murderer for hire, and she seemed... normal. There was no hint of sociopathy, at least not on the surface, and she'd put her own life on the line to vouch for Evie with the crew of the Cricket. She needed to apologize to Larkin for being so dismissive and angry. With a heavy sigh, she hauled herself up, determined to go back to the medical bay and comfort Larkin.

The door creaked loudly as she yanked it open, and then let it slam behind her. There was no key, at least not one she'd been given, but what was someone going to steal, her grubby old prison rags? There wasn't even anything decent to snoop through, not a notebook or anything at all. She turned and ran smack into Larkin, her hands connecting with the woman's hips in a most awkward manner.

"Oh!" Evie exclaimed, surprised but a little bit delighted. "I was just coming to look for you."

"Were you really? I've spent ages looking for your room, I swear this place has more corridors than that goddamned prison. Wish I'd known you were just across the hall from me."

"Heh," Evie laughed lightly, but detected the slightest of smiles playing at the corners of Larkin's lips. "Wait, you're not... angry?"

Larkin made a face. "Why would I be?"

"Well, because I... never mind."

"Anyway, I think I found a good spot for us to practice later. Like I said, the loading bay is far enough from everything else I don't think they'll hear us. And it's not like they're following us, and my room isn't bugged, I checked."

Evie suddenly felt very paranoid about her own room. She pushed open the door and squinted up into the corners. Cobwebs, or tiny wires? A bit of chipped paint, or a hole where a pinhole camera was hiding? "Well, how do you know they didn't bug my room?"

Larkin sat at the edge of the bed and stretched her legs out in front of her. "Nah, they'd never have planned to have you on board, remember? I'm honestly surprised that they had a room for you at all, it's not like this is some huge passenger vessel or anything. Ships like this, they were only ever meant to be for crew and goods transport. There's a sizable cargo hold, but a pretty restrictive weight limit, at least for boats this age."

"Yeah, okay, but we spent a night in the medical bay, they could have bugged my room then, couldn't they?"

Larkin raised an eyebrow. "Evie, you could be on to something. Better safe than sorry, no?" She leapt off the bed and began to run her hands over the pockmarked walls that had been painted over at least a dozen times. "Check the lights, sometimes it's easier to hide bugs in the fixtures."

"How do you know all this?" Evie asked, and then immediately felt ridiculous for asking. It was obvious why Larkin, an assassin, would know how to bug a room.

"Would you believe it if I told you that I once studied under the most highly respected Coalition agent, and that I was his prime student, being groomed to take his place when he retired? Basking in the tutelage of his genius, studying day and night before I turned against them and faked my own death?"

"No."

"Well good, because it's a lie. You're becoming an excellent judge of character, Evie, a welcome development after that girlfriend of yours."

Evie rankled at the mention of Holly again. It was like Larkin was incapable of leaving well enough alone, and had to keep picking at the scab of her broken relationship. That scar was going to take even longer to heal than the nasty, yellowing scabs over her arms. She couldn't think of anything to say, so kept her mouth shut.

"What? Too soon?" Larkin pressed. "You know, the sooner you accept that she was a rancid pile of rot as a person, the better off you'll be."

Evie gritted her teeth and ran her finger around the base of a small lamp on the bedside table. There was nothing unusual there.

"You're too good for her, Evie. She used you, she set you up to take the fall for all her bullshit. Have you even considered that all that other stuff was probably her and her crew, too? How do you think a small scrap team had the credits or trades to eat at fancy restaurants, if not for turning in huge piles of lucrative tech?"

"Can you please just leave it?" Evie said quietly, trying desperately to swallow back the anger and hurt at the back of her throat.

Larkin scowled, her ear to the wall. "Yeah, alright then." Her irritation oozed from her tone, annoyed that Evie wasn't ready to hold a funeral service for her relationship with Holly just yet. Yes, she had betrayed her, but maybe if they could just talk for a few moments, Evie could find out why Holly had done it. Was it desperation, or just a callous act from a hard-hearted woman with an agenda? Whatever the answer, she wasn't going to be able to let it go until she knew for sure, and that meant sucking it up until she got back to Bradach, whenever that was.

"I didn't find anything," Evie said, and Larkin nodded in agreement.

"No, I didn't either. I think we're all good here." She flopped back on the bed and leaned back onto Evie's pillow. "Interesting, though, because if I were them I would absolutely be bugging the rooms. I'd want to make one hundred percent certain that the assholes I just broke out of prison were exactly who they said they were, and not con artists or... or something else."

"Why should we bug your rooms, when you openly and loudly talk about whatever you're up to?" came a voice from the other side of the door.

Evie bounded to the door and wrenched the door open to find Captain Violet standing on the other side of it, a sly smirk pulling at the edges of her lips.

"We believe that we should trust those we bring on board, and not bugging your rooms or throwing you in the brig until we're sure of your moral character is a good way to show that. Now, Evie, Larkin, we need to discuss what's next. The other officers have already been brought up to speed, so I dropped by to debrief you...and discovered you ransacking the room looking for recording devices." She sighed and leaned against the door frame, resting a petite hand on the bronze doorknob. "We aren't yet ready to do the job we brought you here for, and certainly won't be until we can all trust each other, savvy?"

Evie nodded, and Larkin rolled her eyes.

"The best way for us all to learn to work together, is to actually do the work, wouldn't you agree?"

Evie nodded again, and Larkin huffed quietly.

"I'm gonna have to bill you for this one, Cap," Larkin said, her eyes narrowed as though she were scanning Captain Violet's every expression.

"Yes, of course," Violet said, returning the glare. "And Evie, you will be paid as well, your usual rates."

"Oh, well you don't have to pay me, I—" Evie started, before Larkin rammed an elbow into her ribs. She swallowed the last of the sentence, and stood staring. "Uh, yes, that sounds agreeable," she finally managed to mumble.

"We're going to do something similar to our plan for the Armory, but on a much smaller scale. We're going to attack the data center in Skelm."

Larkin burst out laughing. "Skelm? *Why?*"

Annoyance flashed across the captain's face. "If you were as adept and knowledgeable as the others say you are, then you'd know that Skelm is a major data center. It stores much of the data from this quadrant, including that of the Armory, not to mention the archives in their Administration Building. If we can destabilize their infrastructure, then we have a better chance of knocking out additional surveillance feeds as and when we need to. But I suppose you already knew all of that."

Evie turned her head to Larkin in just enough time to watch her shrink almost imperceptibly. "Of course I knew that," Larkin mumbled, and then cleared her throat and straightened. "Of course I knew that, Captain, I just wondered if Skelm is the best use of our collective skill set, especially considering that's where I got picked up for jaywalking. It would be a shame if I ran into that same MPO and you had to break me out all over again."

Captain Violet's face hardened. "We're going to Skelm, and you will do your goddamned best to not run into that MPO again." She glared at Larkin a moment, and then sighed quietly. "I know you won't let me down, not after all we did to free you."

* * *

Evie crept through the corridors of the Cricket, grateful for the boots she'd inherited, the leather soft and broken in after years of use. They were so worn, they barely made a sound as she passed door after door, with no way of knowing which was a utility closet full of dusty mops and which had a member of the crew up late at their desks, just waiting to be disturbed from noise outside. She found the gentle hum of the ship's engines a comfort, a low drone that muffled her steps as well as the troubled thoughts in her head. Where could she even begin to unravel the tangled mess of emotions causing unwieldy chaos in her mind? It was easier to think about the low buzz of the ship and the quiet hiss of the boilers, and learning to shoot.

Pushing open the door to the loading bay, she found it curious that there had been no airlock to unlock, just a door that easily gave way. The thick glass of the airlock hung suspended over the door by a large pulley that dangled from the ceiling. Larkin was sprawled out over several large wooden crates with lettering so faded no one would ever be able to determine where they'd originally come from. She had one leg dangling over a box and swinging lazily, scraping against the worn wood and peeled paint of the letters.

"About time you got here," Larkin said, and hopped easily off the crates onto the ground. "I was beginning to think that you changed your mind, that you weren't coming after all." She had shed her filthy prison jumpsuit for a tight fitting black jacket with equally form fitting trousers that disappeared into her own boots, the ones she'd been allowed to keep in the Coalition prison.

Evie shrugged her shoulders. "What else was I going to do?"

"Something stupid, like admit to the captain that I lied. I don't know if you caught all that earlier, but it really feels like Captain Violet is not a particularly large fan of mine."

"Well, you don't make it easy, scoffing at everything she says."

"Makes me wonder why they even bothered busting me - us - out, if they don't have any faith in my abilities. Also makes me wonder why she allowed it, if she's so sure I'm some kind of good-for-nothing grifter with an agenda and ham fisted methods."

"Maybe you're a last shot, or they just want to make things that much more sure and safe for the other crew members."

"I dunno."

"Where are the clothes from?" Evie asked, keen to change the subject.

"That Kady girl, we're a similar size it seems. Though she was definitely not happy about handing them over, and demanded I return them in exactly the same condition they were given to me, the exact second I have something else to wear."

Evie stifled a laugh. "Well, if I had clothes like that, I'd probably say the same thing." She tugged at her oversized coveralls that would have dragged on the floor if she hadn't tucked them into the boots, and the comically large collar that flopped back and forth at the base of her neck. "I'm glad to have something clean, but it's not exactly flattering."

"Ah who cares about flattering, when it's what's underneath that counts?" Larkin said with a nonchalant smirk, and Evie felt an odd flush wash over her cheeks.

"Er — sure," she stammered, and held her hand out. "So where's this gun?"

Larkin produced a comically large pistol with a worn, dirty wooden handle that was in some serious need of an oiling, and a long, wide barrel that almost looked bent in the middle, as though something very large and heavy had rolled over it. The end of the barrel was coated in a thick black dust, and where it met the wood, there were spots of obvious rust that hungrily ate into the metal. "Voila!" she said proudly, brandishing it around.

"What the hell," Evie said, horrified, "is that."

"A gun! I told you I would find you one to practice with."

"Where did you find it, on the body of some dead goon two hundred years ago?"

"Under some dusty crates marked VIOLET, actually."

"So you stole it. From the captain who already isn't very sure about us being here." Evie sighed and buried her head in her hands. "Perfect."

"It's not like she was using it, that much is obvious, isn't it," Larkin said, and wobbled the gun as she dangled it by the hammer. "Anyway, it's not like we're really stealing it, just borrowing it. Wouldn't get much for it anyway, even if we did want to shift it." She noticed Evie's stricken face and added quickly, "Which we don't, obviously."

Evie took the gun and held it in her hands, memorizing the surprising weight of it and feeling vaguely unsettled that she was holding something whose only purpose was to kill another person. She examined the gun, the sticky layer of grease and grime over the wood handle, the wide base of it laying flat against her small hands. She held her hands out in front of her, as though she were really going to shoot, and closed one eye as she looked through the iron sights mounted to the barrel.

"Okay, first lesson," Larkin said, taking the gun back. "Don't close your eyes. You'll be more accurate with both. Second lesson, never have your finger on the trigger unless you mean to fire the gun. And third, never fire it unless you're okay with killing whoever is at the other end of that barrel." She mimed a shooting stance, her shoulders square and both hands on the pistol. "Fourth, don't shoot from the hip. It's amateur."

Evie nodded, taking it all in. "Anything else?"

"Yeah," Larkin said, handing the gun over. "Don't miss."

She tried to copy Larkin's stance, but her body felt unfamiliar and unwieldy, like her limbs weren't her own. With a deep breath in, she aimed at a barrel in the corner that Larkin had nailed a paper target to, a big red X painted over it. The barrel was filled with bags of wet sand, used as ballast on the ship when it was empty, like it was now. She imagined what it would be like in this loading bay when it was stuffed full with stolen crates of produce, tech, and weapons. At least then all the goods would muffle their sound more, instead of their voices bouncing around the rafters in chattering echos. She pulled at the trigger, and much to her surprise the gun jerked back with an explosion, sending the bullet in a wild ricochet over Larkin's head and slicing through the rope that held the airlock suspended in the air. It came crashing down, the heavy panes of glass with spider-webbed cracks all across the surface.

"Gods, Evie!" Larkin chastised. "What the hell!"

"I only did what you told me to!" Evie yelled back, embarrassed and a little afraid of the damage one bullet had done. "You didn't say it was loaded!"

"What?! Of course it was loaded!"

"I thought I'd get a practice shot!"

"Well great, we're stuck in here now," Larkin said with acid on her tongue. "I can't pick the lock from the wrong side of the glass. We're going to have to wait until someone sees us stuck in here, and opens it from out there." She sat heavily on a crate and swore under her breath. "And let's hope it's not Captain Violet, or she might decide to just open the loading bay doors and let our frozen, brittle corpses be sucked out into space."

Not a moment later, Alice's face appeared on the other side of the glass, looking alarmed and confused. "Larkin! Hide the gun!" Evie hissed. With a nod, she wedged the gun between two slats of the empty crates, and turned it on its side so it wasn't visible unless you already knew where it was.

The airlock hissed and cracked, and the door popped open just as Alice strode in. "What the hell are you two doing out here?" she demanded. "And what the hell did you do to the door?" she asked, gesturing at the cracked glass.

"We, uh, er..." Evie stammered.

"We were just familiarizing ourselves with the ship, when the rope splintered and sent the airlock crashing down, isn't that terrible? Imagine if someone had been inside when it happened!" Larkin said convincingly.

Alice craned her neck to look at the broken rope, shielding her eye against the dim yellow lighting that hung from the ceiling of the loading bay. "Odd, we only replaced that a few months ago." She squinted at the pair and tilted her head. "Don't let Violet know you've been sneaking around her ship, she doesn't take kindly to that kind of nonsense, especially when expensive mistakes happen as a result." Alice turned and tapped on the cracked glass lightly with a hammer. "The cracks didn't go all the way through, you're lucky for that," she said sternly. "I don't know what is actually going on here, but the both of you had better get back to your rooms and thank your lucky stars that it was me who heard this ungodly loud noise, and not Violet, or Kady, for that matter." She sighed loudly. "I know being new here is tough, especially when no one trusts you. But do you think maybe you can both avoid causing major damages wherever you happen to be sneaking around?"

Evie nodded vigorously and noticed that Larkin had joined her. With abrupt, nervous good nights, they backed out of the loading bay and left Alice to repair the severed rope which had caused all the damage. Evie just hoped that the mechanic wouldn't find the bullet wedged in a rafter up there and put the pieces of the puzzle together. If she did, their lie would meet the steely glare of one Captain Violet.

CHAPTER TWELVE

Alice's warning to stop wandering through the ship at night had no impact on Larkin's sense of curiosity. She wanted to memorize the ship's layout, and besides, she couldn't sleep. She had tried to sleep, of course, laying on the slightly lumpy mattress and turning from one side to another, every minute feeling like an hour had passed.

So that's how she came to be wandering the halls, against the mechanic's advice, and without Evie. No, Evie had gone straight to her room after the loading bay debacle and stayed there. Larkin hoped that she wasn't too upset or angry, but was annoyed at how much she cared what Evie thought about her, and it pulled at the back of her mind with a low hum of persistence.

She shook her head fiercely to clear her thoughts, her long thick braid swinging wildly behind her. She was memorizing the corridors of the Cricket, something she always did. It meant that in an emergency, her instincts would take over. Memorizing the layout of a building was paramount to a successful job, knowing every decommissioned elevator shaft and laundry chute exponentially increased the odds of success. Larkin smirked, remembering the time she had perfectly timed her escape, throwing herself down a garbage chute and landing in the steamtruck that carried her and all the refuse away from the scene of the crime. A brilliantly calculated plan, and it went off without a hitch.

Five doors down every corridor, some that intersected with others which led to the main areas of the ship. What the hell did they need so many goddamned doors for, anyway? It's not like it was a very big crew, and their storage needs were simple and isolated to the loading bay. Larkin stretched her arms over her head, feeling the painful twinge of her ribs pull at her core. "Stupid fucking ribs," she muttered under her breath. She deeply resented that there was nothing she could do to speed the healing of a broken or fractured rib. Nothing other than rest and remaining immobile, anyway. Her arms fell back to her sides and hung limply from her shoulders.

Larkin closed her eyes to imprint the layout of the ship on her memory, when something else floated up to the forefront of her mind. She still hadn't been fucking paid. That's what had orchestrated this whole mess, hadn't it? It landed her in the Coalition prison because she couldn't pay a fine, and now it left her shackled to the Cricket until they decided to pay her. *Goddamned good-for-nothing clients*, she thought angrily. It was rare that she had to chase up payment, because most people were too afraid of her to try to stiff her. They imagined her sneaking into their homes at night and slitting their throats while they slept, but she was never one for the gory methods of killing. Too messy, too easy to get caught, and who wanted to be confronted with a reminder of their own mortality, anyway? Killer or mark, they were all made of the same stuff, meat that was vulnerable to disease and disaster alike.

Not only had she not been paid by the benefactors of her last assignment, but the quick job in Skelm with that weird pair she'd found on Bradach remained incomplete. Oh, Robert was dead, alright, she'd seen it on the public broadcast as she lurked in the doorway of the bridge while it played. They said he'd died of alcohol poisoning, she suspected, as a way to discourage people from seeking out illicit swill. They also said that after he died, the inspectors investigating his death found masses of conspiratorial materials stacked in his bedroom on how to blow up buildings and overthrow the government. That part was obviously a lie, but the Coalition always lied. She just couldn't figure out why they'd lied about that specifically.

And yet, no news of a derelict base being stripped and scrapped. It was true that the Coalition rarely shared their failings as a government, but there were still usually some whispers you could detect. Signal failures due to a broken satellite usually indicated an attack on a base, increased security protocols in certain quadrants usually meant that a derelict base had been attacked for scrap.

The pair was jumpy, nervous, they hadn't even really wanted to hire her to secure the job, so she wouldn't be surprised if they had opted to ditch the job when they didn't hear from her that it was all clear for them, with Robert slowly expiring into the filthy carpet of his apartment. He had all but died for nothing, but his waste of a life wasn't much worth preserving anyway. Most Coalition middle management wasn't good for too much, having lived a life away from any kind of real trials or hardship, secured into a safe little bubble of privilege and dull day-to-day activities.

She stopped at a junction in the corridor and committed it to memory, the same way you would memorize a route to work, or the layout of your home. It became second nature to her, as though she'd spent years walking the halls of the Cricket, absent-mindedly going about her work. It was something she found soothing and important, knowing the exact layout of where you were. If you always had an idea of what could be around the corner, no one would be able to back you into one. Left led to the dining hall, right, to the boiler room where Alice and Ivy worked to optimize the old ship's systems. But now, Alice was probably still in the loading bay, repairing the ballast for the airlock, and Ivy was likely asleep in her room, an excellent opportunity to examine the boilers for herself. She turned right down the hall, her steps soft on the harsh metal grates.

Everything felt too loud, too bright, too much information for her to process. Skelm, prison, Evie, Cricket, Violet. She hadn't felt so out of control of her own situation in years, not since... well. Not since everything fell apart last time. Not since Cabot. Fucking Cabot.

"Hey," a gruff voice said softly, and Larkin flinched in surprise. It was Ned, the navigator, the one who caught her poking around last time and dragged her to the medical bay, ignoring all of her protests that she didn't need any medical attention.

"Hey," she repeated back to him. "Up late?"

He shrugged. "Someone's got to keep an eye on the Cricket while the rest of you are getting your beauty sleep. It's why I'm so haggard and troll-like,

I rarely get any sleep for myself." Larkin laughed and covered her mouth with her hand to muffle the sound and keep it from echoing down the long corridor. "What are you doing wandering around?" he asked, without a hint of suspicion, only genuine curiosity.

"Just... getting my bearings, I guess," she admitted. "I like to know where I am. I like to know the layout of a situation, you know?"

"Mm," Ned nodded. "I'm a navigator, so I know what you mean. It's nice to know where all the secret trap doors and trouble spots are."

"Yeah."

"Want me to show you my favorite one on the ship?" he asked, a twinkle in his pale blue eyes.

"Sure," Larkin said nonchalantly, but she was secretly pleased. Even if no one else on the ship trusted her, including Evie, it seemed like Ned at least understood a little part of her, the part desperate to know where she stood in the universe, even if that happened to be at the intersection of two corridors aboard the Cricket, hurtling full force toward Skelm in the middle of dark space.

"Well then, follow me!" he said happily, and led the way down a series of winding corridors that Larkin had only half mapped in her mind, and so she struggled to keep up with where her position was aboard the vessel.

"Not easy to find then, I assume?" she asked as they climbed over a stack of overturned crates at the end of a corridor.

"Why do you think it's one of the best-kept secrets aboard this ship?" Ned asked, wrenching up a trap door in the floor. "I don't even think Alice knows this is here." He snorted and added, "Nah, she definitely knows it's here. She's just too busy in the boiler room to spend her time wandering around the ship."

Larkin followed him down a rickety ladder into a dark room with a ceiling so low that she had to duck. Ned was practically bent in half in the space, huge man that he was. "What is this place?" she asked, and sneezed into her sleeve as a cloud of dust rose from the ground.

"It used to be a captain's hideout, in case the ship was hijacked. They don't have these on the newer models. Captains are expected to fight to the death for the glory of the Coalition." He wiped a thick layer of grime from a padded chair in the corner. "They'd hide in here and direct their crew with radios to hopefully fend off the attackers. In the event the hijacking was successful, the captain would hide until they had an opportunity to either take the ship back, or self-destruct the whole thing." He was quiet for a moment. "It was usually the latter."

"Wow."

"But, once we pirates figured out where they were hiding these safe rooms, they were of no use anymore. Someone leaked the plans of every ship in their fleet into a database, so they retired every single one of them and replaced them with new stock, with better weapons, more stealth capabilities, and more military staff on board." He patted a box, sending a cloud of dust into the air. "Of course, they've been out of use nearly two decades now. Most people don't even think about these rooms anymore."

"Huh. So what's it used for now?"

He kicked a box in the corner, and it released a soft rattle. "Storage, mostly. Not really much. Not big enough for gala banquets."

Larkin snorted. "Oh, you mean you can't fit twenty crew members in here with enormous trays of food?"

"Nah, we tried it once but once half the crew knocked themselves out on the low ceiling, we declared it a bust."

"Only half?"

"Yeah, we like to put safety first here on the Cricket," Ned replied, and they both broke into giggles. "Listen, Larkin," he said earnestly, "I know it's been a whirlwind few days, and things probably feel unstable right now. I get it. The Boss wasn't sure about taking you on, but that's because she's a good captain who always puts her crew first and foremost in her mind. She doesn't like to take undue risks or put any of us into danger we can't handle. Hell, she even spent ages ignoring her affection for Alice because she thought it would negatively impact the crew, or lead to problems later on. She's fiercely loyal, and if you earn that loyalty, it'll be the biggest achievement you've had this decade."

Larkin dragged her boot across the floor, drawing wobbly lines in the dust.

"Sure."

"Just keep your chin up, things will all start to make sense soon. Not long until we get to Skelm, anyway."

"Ugh, Skelm."

"Tell me about it," Ned said, rolling his eyes. "Greyest, most lifeless place I've ever been to. The first time I saw how they do things there, how people are basically forced into indentured servitude, I was so angry I wanted to blow up the Administration Building there myself."

"Why didn't you?"

"I'd have gotten caught, obviously. I'm not stealthy, and I'm not a munitions expert. I'm a navigator." He slapped his thigh. "And with the leg now, I'd be unlikely to be able to make a hasty exit if need be."

"How'd that happen?"

"Rival pirate crew shot me in the leg. Heh. But we got them in the end."

Larkin headed back toward the ladder leading out of the hidden hatch. "And what does that mean?"

"Boss killed their captain when he threatened her crew. And when they came back for more, we were agile enough to escape, thanks to Alice, and they got cornered by the same Coalition turncoats they were working with. Probably rotting away in some work camp, now." He scratched his bushy ginger beard thoughtfully. "Serves them right."

"Seems harsh."

"They'd have kept coming for us. Boss offered an olive branch back in Bradach with their new captain, who'd been the second in command until the boss gave him some lead right between the eyes, but she wasn't interested. Told her to go fuck herself, if memory serves."

Larkin could see why the rivals weren't interested in niceties. Who would be after watching their captain get blown away during an attempted hijacking? True, she was no expert on manners in piracy, but what did Captain Violet expect, for her rivals to bow down at her feet and declare her the one true pirate captain of the Near Systems? It was bullshit. She frowned at the floor, examining the squiggles in the dust made by the toe of her boot, wondering why anyone even bothered to be a pirate anyway. Seemed like a hell of a lot of work if you asked her, which obviously no one had. "Mm," she mumbled in a noncommittal way.

"Well, do you want something to eat? Got leftovers in the kitchen if you're interested. Not often I have company on the night shift, that's for sure."

"Sure." She wasn't hungry, but maybe a slice of bread would help to soak up the nervous bile building in her stomach. She wasn't used to feeling this out of sorts, so emotional, and it unnerved her. Usually she felt perfectly balanced, like a watch or a set of scales, but the past few days she was feeling more like a house of cards on a slick surface.

They climbed out of the hatch, Larkin leading the way with pained pulls up the vertical ladder, and Ned lingering behind, focusing on using his uninjured leg to push his considerable size out of the hatch. He stood and carefully rearranged the boxes atop the secret entrance and gave Larkin a conspiratorial grin that made her feel a little bit more like herself.

The halls of the Cricket were silent, except for the constant hum of the engines, the soft leather of their boots on the metal grate floors, and the distant, almost imperceptible snores of their crew mates as they slept soundly in their rooms. The mess hall was dark and abandoned, with not even a crumb left on the tables.

"It's almost spooky," Larkin whispered, and Ned smiled wryly.

"You get used to it. Besides, there are no ghosts in space." He busied himself with some bread and bits in the kitchen, humming to himself softly while Larkin waited at a table, her boots resting on top of a table, her eyelids heavy and difficult to prop open.

In fact, she started to doze off, and caught her head as it drooped to her chest. All the sleep she hadn't had the past few days was catching up with her. She'd pretended to be asleep in the infirmary earlier so that she wouldn't have to talk to Evie when she was upset, and it had worked a charm. Evie left to find her new room, and Larkin was left to cry and hurt in peace. She understood why Evie was angry, but even so, she'd risked her skin to get her freed from that shithole. Who cared if the lie she made up wasn't exactly accurate? It still worked, and that's what was important.

"Here," Ned said, setting a basket of lightly toasted chunks of bread next to her boot. "Don't let the boss see you with your feet on the tables, she'll skin you alive." He also set down a dish of hummus, liberally sprinkled with something Larkin recognized as a smoked spice from one of the settlements. Not particularly rare, not outside the Coalition anyway, but it was delicious and warming nonetheless. She dragged her boots off the table and let them thud heavily to the floor.

"Yeah, I've been warned about Violet's temper by more than one crew member," she muttered, digging into the pile of warm, crunchy bread. "At this rate, I'll be surprised if I make it off this ship alive."

Ned sighed, chewing his mouthful of food thoughtfully. "It's not easy being a captain, you know."

"I never said it was."

"I'm just saying, you're new here and you'll have to earn her trust, that's all. Once you've got it, you'll have it for life, unless you do something monumentally stupid."

"Yeah, well, I have been known for doing monumentally stupid things," she replied. She'd put Evie in danger with her lie about sharpshooting, and shoving a huge chunk of bread into her mouth as a distraction from her own intrusive thoughts wasn't helping.

"Uh, hey," Evie said from the doorway, and Larkin stopped chewing in surprise. Evie was disheveled from sleep, the swirl of cerulean hair on top of her head flattened and sticking out in all directions like she'd been dragged through a forest of brambles. In spite of all that, she was cute and sleepy, rubbing at her eyes with one hand and covering a yawn with the other.

Larkin swallowed the huge mouthful of bread and blinked. "Hey, yourself."

"Where did you go?" Evie asked, leaning against the door frame. "I knocked on your door but there was no answer. I wandered until I heard voices."

"Oh, uh, just couldn't sleep, I guess."

"Yeah."

Ned looked from one woman to the other and smirked knowingly. "Well, would you look at the time" he said, checking a nonexistent pocket watch.

"Here, Evie, take my seat, I'm going to head to the bridge, where I'm unable to hear anything from anywhere else in the ship." He winked and pushed himself off the chair with his cane, a beautiful piece of woodwork made from the roots of olive trees, with dozens of different tones all woven together and polished to a high shine. It was both practical and ostentatious, just like its owner.

"Oh, no Ned, you should stay," Evie protested, backing out of the room. "I was just..." she trailed off.

"Please, I insist," he said, gesturing at the now empty chair. "I was about to leave Larkin on her own, anyway." He winked again and squeezed Evie's shoulder on the way out of the room. "Just make sure you clean up after yourselves, the boss doesn't like mess."

Larkin rolled her eyes, but brushed crumbs off the table into her hand before depositing them back into the basket of bread. "Message received, officer."

The uneven beat of Ned's footsteps faded down the corridor until there was no sound other than the deep hum of the ship and the sound of Larkin crunching on the crispy, toasted chunks of bread. Evie sat down at the table, perched at the edge of the seat Ned had just vacated, as though she was unsure how long she would be staying.

"Here," Larkin said, pushing the basket of bread and the bowl of hummus towards her, "have some."

"Thanks, I was getting kind of hungry, I guess."

"So, couldn't sleep, huh?"

Evie swallowed. "Neither could you."

"Just felt unsettled, I guess." The truth was that she'd felt guilty about what had happened in the loading bay, and couldn't stop thinking about how upset Evie had been. The truth felt a little too close to the bone, however, so she settled on 'unsettled.'

"Yeah." Evie dragged a piece of bread through the hummus lazily and watched it pile on top of the bread in messy blobs that spilled over the sides where the crust was slightly charred. "Larkin, I —" she stopped herself and dropped the bread into the hummus, staring earnestly across the table.

"Never mind."

"No, what is it?"

"Nothing, don't worry about it," Evie said with a forced smile. She dug the bread out of the hummus with a fork and shoved it into her mouth. "It's good though, right?" she said around a mouthful.

"Yeah, lush. Nice of Ned to set it out anyways." Larkin speared a piece of bread with her knife and dunked it under the surface of the hummus, pushing the smoked red spice under where it disappeared into the spread. She sighed heavily and left her knife, and the bread heavy with hummus, balanced across the bowl. "Evie, I'm sorry, I shouldn't have pushed you into that so fast."

"No, you shouldn't have," Evie agreed, looking down at the table. "What if that bullet had ricocheted and hit you? Gods, I'd never forgive myself."

Larkin was taken aback by the admission, and blinked in confusion. That was the reason Evie was upset, because the bullet may have ricocheted? Not out of embarrassment that the airlock glass had nearly shattered and Alice showed up, or frustration that the first shooting lesson hadn't gone well, or fear that their lie would be found out, but because Larkin could have gotten hurt. She wasn't used to people caring about her welfare, that was for sure. "Oh," she said in a quiet voice. "I... didn't realize."

"Just because you take your own life for granted, Larkin, doesn't mean everyone else does. You're my friend, right?"

"Friend." A smile spread across Larkin's face and she reached across the table to squeeze Evie's hand gently. "Yeah."

"So next time, we'll be more prepared. I'll do as much research as I can without getting caught. There's got to be at least a few books about shooting on this ship, don't you think?"

"Books? Evie, you don't learn this kind of thing with *books*."

"Weapons manuals, then," Evie shrugged.

Larkin snorted back a laugh. "You really think you can learn how to shoot from reading about it?"

"Well it can't hurt," Evie said stubbornly. "Better than shooting more holes in the loading bay, don't you think?"

"Yes, it's probably best if we keep holes to a minimum, you're right about that." She moved to retrieve her abandoned chunk of bread when Evie darted across the table with her fork and snatched it.

"You snooze, you lose," she said laughing, and stuffed her stolen prize into her mouth triumphantly.

Larkin's jaw dropped open in mock surprise. "I can't believe you just did that," she said seriously. "You'd steal food from a starving mercenary?" She draped herself over the back of the chair as though she'd passed out, and Evie stole another chunk of bread. "Evie, honestly, I did not expect this callous behavior from you," Larkin said from her faked unconscious position. "I'm really surprised at you."

Evie held the stolen bread in front of her mouth and breathed heavily on it. "I breathed on it, it's mine now, those are the rules."

Larkin sat up and snatched the bread from Evie's fingers, stuffing it into her own mouth. "I don't play by the rules," she said with an eyebrow raised, and they both broke down into giggles.

* * *

Larkin lay in bed on her back, staring up at the ceiling of her small but comfortable quarters. Sleep still wouldn't come. It may have been the dull pain in her ribs that throbbed angrily at irritatingly regular intervals, or her mind buzzing, or a million other things.

None of that mattered; what mattered is that she was exhausted but unable to rest. Every time she closed her eyes, something angrily poked at the paper-thin veneer of calm she was desperately trying to embody. There were thirteen places on the ceiling where the paint was beginning to chip away and reveal the iron beneath.

She rolled to her left side and faced the little table next to the bed, kicking at the covers that tangled themselves around her legs. Sleeping in clothing was the worst, and she hated it — but she didn't know these people well enough to trust them, and without trust there was fear of the unknown. The last thing she wanted was to be caught with her pants down, literally. It was hard to defend yourself while naked.

Her late-night snack with Evie had ended, and they walked each other back to the dead-end corridor where their rooms sat across from each other. Right now, Evie was probably drifting into a deep sleep in her bed, or at least, Larkin hoped that she was.

Larkin thrashed onto her other side and tore off the covers, throwing them onto the floor. She wasn't cold enough to need them, anyway, and they were just irritating her. Light pooled out under the bathroom door, but not enough to cast shadows behind her worn leather boots, their tan color blue in the dim light. She'd kept the light on as a kind of comfort, an assurance that nothing could sneak up on her even in these unfamiliar surroundings. It's not that she was afraid of the dark, per se, more so that her biggest fear was to be caught unawares, to be caught off-guard and unbalanced, vulnerable as a child or to be honest, the average adult without having trained as an assassin.

Seconds ticked by like hours, and she grew more frustrated with every passing moment. Sleep was usually something easily attained for her, regardless of locale or environment. It was a learned skill, necessary for her line of work. If you couldn't sleep while folded in half in a tiny cupboard under a maintenance duct, well, then, you wouldn't sleep at all. Yet here she was, sprawled out atop a soft bed with a feathery pillow, the deadbolt clicked into place on the door to her comfortable quarters, and yet she was more on edge than she'd be on a job.

There would be no more wandering tonight. She didn't want to risk waking Evie in the room opposite, or risk running into Captain Violet, who was ready to stuff Larkin unceremoniously into the airlock and blow her into space without a second thought.

Larkin growled softly and sat up in the bed, pressing down into the rough, worn carpet beneath the soles of her feet. She gripped the edge of the metal bed frame, relishing the stabilizing feeling she got when the metal lightly bit into her palms. The air was still, despite being constantly cycled through a large grate high on the wall to remove carbon dioxide and impurities they might bring in on their boots.

There was a soft knock at the door, and Larkin nearly jumped a mile. "Who's there?" she asked.

"It's me, Evie."

Larkin flipped the door's deadbolt with a satisfying snap and eased the door open, wincing at the loud squeak that announced their conversation. "What are you doing up? You should be asleep," she whispered, gesturing for Evie to come inside.

"Did I wake you?"

"No, I couldn't sleep either."

"I'm sorry, I know this is strange for me to show up in the middle of the night like this," Evie apologized.

"No stranger than the situation we're already in," Larkin responded, quietly engaging the deadbolt again.

"I just wanted to see a friendly face. Everything feels so..."

"Yeah."

"And I just...it's strange, but you're the only one I can trust. After Holly, I feel so off balance, like I realized how bad my character judgment must be."

Larkin smirked. "Thanks."

"Oh stop, you know what I mean," Evie said, smacking her lightly with the pillow. "I just trusted her so implicitly and she—"

"People are assholes."

"Yeah."

"Honestly, Evie, I've met maybe three decent people in my life, and you're one of them."

"You barely know me."

"Yeah, but unlike you, I am a fantastic judge of character," Larkin teased. "And most people suck. Most people are just out for whatever they can steal, or manipulate from you, or hoard for themselves. It's the human condition."

"That's a bleak way of looking at things."

"It's true. Just look around at the society we've built. The assholes at the top get all the goods and keep them, everyone else is just a sucker propping up the system until they die, and the rich assholes with all the stuff dance on their graves until the next generation shows up to fight for their shitty job,"

Larkin said, perching at the edge of the bed. "The cycle just goes round and round, and will until the sun blows up and kills us all."

Evie looked at her with her head cocked to the side, her brow furrowed in thought.

"What?" Larkin asked.

"Nothing, it's just interesting to hear different perspectives. Before last week, I'd never been off of Bradach. It was all I knew. Sure, there's some inequality, but no one starves. No one sleeps on the streets unless they want to."

"There's no such thing as a utopia, Evie."

"Don't patronize me, I didn't say there was. I'm not much use to anyone except as a bartender in the Purple Pig. I can tell one rum from the next and keep the tavern clean, but I'm no navigator, or scientist, or mechanic." She paused a moment and then continued, "Or assassin."

"That doesn't matter," Larkin scoffed. "You have other qualities that are... desirable." She frowned as the word left her mouth and wondered why she'd said it in the first place. Exhaustion was making her mind feel fuzzy and manic at the same time.

"I just mean that maybe there are more than three people in the Near Systems deserving of friendship and empathy," Evie challenged.

"How can you say that, after what happened? How can you still have that much faith in people?"

Evie shrugged. "Holly is just one person. Her crew is just one crew. I can't base my opinion of the entire human race on one selfish asshole." She sighed noisily and laid back on the bed. "Just lay back on the pillow and let's talk, at least it will make the time pass quicker."

Larkin did as she said, after floating the blanket over the other woman and straightening the edges. She laid on top of the blanket with her hands behind her head, staring at the peeling paint on the ceiling. "Evie?"

"Mm?" the other woman said sleepily.

"Nah, never mind."

"Okay," Evie mumbled.

Larkin listened to Evie's breath steady and slow as she fell into a deep sleep on her bed. Without even the slightest hesitation, Larkin draped an arm over her protectively, and promptly fell asleep to the rhythm of her breathing.

CHAPTER THIRTEEN

"Alright folks, listen up. We got some intel about a Coalition trade vessel, ripe for the picking. We're very close to the drop zone for this job, so let's make sure we all know our assignments, shall we?" Captain Violet said, standing in front of the curved glass window at the front of the ship. "Ned, you're here on the ship with Hyun, Ivy, and Kady. Alice, Evie, and Larkin will pile into the shuttle transport first, followed by myself and Jasper. Everyone clear?"

The officers on the bridge all nodded confidently, this being the sort of thing the crew of the Cricket did on a regular basis. To them, the hijacking and pillaging of a Coalition trade vessel was as normal as a morning cup of coffee. For Evie, though, it was possibly the most terrifying idea she'd ever heard.

"Larkin, you and Evie will be first to drop onto the ship. We're counting on you both to make this as quiet and seamless as possible. The fewer eyes on this, the better," Violet continued, her intense stare boring into them both. "Larkin, do *not* kill anyone. This mission should be easy enough, no extra security patrols on the ship, and our shuttle still reads as a Coalition vessel to their radar, so you shouldn't raise any alarms when you pull in. Alice will return to the Cricket and wait for your signal. If everything goes to plan, we won't need more than two trips in. We won't be able to see what's going on, we'll be too far out of line of sight, so we're relying on the encrypted radio channels for comms."

Evie felt her chest tighten with anxiety. Here she was, expected to be a markswoman covering Larkin, and the only time she'd fired a weapon she'd nearly destroyed the ship's airlock. It was time to come clean to the captain and her crew, and just hope they weren't angry enough to shoot her corpse out into space. She gathered herself and took a deep breath. "Um, Captain?" she started.

"Yes, Evie, of course," Captain Violet said, pulling a long-barreled pistol with a large cartridge at the back from the holster on her thigh. "Here is your weapon for now, we'll get you something more to your taste and specifications when we reach Bradach."

Evie's heart jumped at the mention of her home settlement. "When are we going to Bradach?"

"After this mission, to offload whatever we manage to steal. Best black market in the Near Systems for rapscallions like us," the captain laughed, and set the weapon into Evie's outstretched hands. "I'm sure you've used something similar before, but this is a newly developed weapon, it fires rubber bullets coated in a concentrated dose of a heavy sedative. Best if you hit skin, don't aim for the temple or the impact might kill them anyway."

"Uh, sure," Evie said, swallowing hard. She had to come clean now, before anyone got hurt. "You know, Captain, I've never— "

Larkin elbowed her hard in the ribs and coughed loudly to cover Evie's pained squeak. "She's never left a mark alive," Larkin said loudly. "She told me in the prison."

Captain Violet looked over them both suspiciously and narrowed her eyes. "Of course," she said in a measured tone, "I understand that Evie's tactics in the past differ from our own, but I would expect that on this ship, she abides by the plan agreed upon by the officers."

Evie cleared her throat and aimed for a wide smile that probably looked more like a shocked grimace than anything else. "I was just saying, Captain, I've never, uh, been part of a crew before. I usually work alone."

"Well, you'll have to get used to it, because we work together as a team on this ship," Violet said sharply. Had she managed to convince the captain, or not? Now that the moment of truth had been lost, it would take her ages to build up the courage again. Why was Larkin so hell bent on maintaining this charade?

"Of course, Captain," Evie agreed, and turned the weapon over in her hands. It had been recently cleaned, that she knew for sure; the sweetly acrid scent of the concentrated solvent still lingered on the brightly polished silver. It was much heavier than the gun they'd practiced with in the loading bay, and though the bullets were rubber, somehow felt more immediately dangerous. The cartridge held the sedative, and Evie assumed that when the trigger was pulled, it would release it into the firing chamber to be carried with the bullet. Curious how the heat of the explosion in the barrel didn't affect the compound of the sedative, especially when fired at a distance. She'd read a pamphlet on the dangers of heat based reactions in medications, once, while waiting to see a doctor for a nasty burn she'd gotten at the Purple Pig, one that left her with a thick, shiny scar on her forearm that still shone in the light.

Captain Violet turned to the ship's officers. "Everyone understand what we need to accomplish today? Ned? Kady?" She paused for a moment. "Alice?"

"We just want whatever we can carry in the transport, right?" Alice asked. "Not much room in there, especially after the modifications we did to fit an extra person."

"Correct. No produce other than what fits in your own pockets. We're after data and tech, specifically the micro-droids we think they've been passing around to all the Coalition bases. We'll need to figure that into our plan anyway, but it's nice to know what we'll start facing as a regular occurrence when we do jobs like this."

Alice nodded and smiled at Violet, who raised an eyebrow and smirked back. "Excellent. Ned, park us in the drop zone and we'll get this job over and done with. Then we can all head to Bradach for a much deserved shore leave, eh?"

The officers nodded, and Ned clapped a huge hand on Hyun's shoulder. "We on for some of that amazing bibimbap?" he whispered gruffly.

"You bet," Hyun winked, grabbing her clipboard from the desk and heading out the door and back to the medical bay, or at least, Evie assumed that's where she was headed.

"Let's get this over with," Larkin sighed, and nudged Evie gently towards the doorway of the bridge. "The sooner we're out of here, the better," she grumbled under her breath.

* * *

The tiny transport shuttle docked neatly onto the C.S. Blackwall, a moderately sized merchant vessel on its way to a trading beacon to shift its wares and pick up fuel and supplies for its crew. Evie sat crammed between Larkin and Alice in the transport, the gun laying heavily in her lap, its weight pressing down into the soft woven cotton of Alice's hand-me-down jumpsuit, with the hem of the legs cuffed four times so they wouldn't drag on the ground. She could barely breathe, partly to do with the very small space, but mostly because Captain Violet and her crew expected her to flawlessly execute this job, using a weapon they all assumed she was a crack shot with.

"Well, here we are," Alice said. "Here's a keypass to get you through the loading bay doors, it uses a fake identification number. We've got an hour before the servers reset and it's purged from the logs, but that should be plenty of time, as long as no one sees you." She handed a small rectangular card to Larkin and turned back to the navigation panel. "I'm going back for Violet and Jasper, radio if you need me, it should reach far enough." She grinned widely. "Good luck, though I'm sure you don't need it."

Evie and Larkin climbed out of the transport and into the huge loading bay piled high with cardboard boxes and wooden crates, stacks of data servers due to be transferred to the trading beacon, their disconnected wires hanging in a tangled mess behind them.

Alice started the engine of the transport, and the sound reverberated off the high metal ceiling. They tapped their air masks to show Alice it was safe for her to engage the airlock, and strapped themselves to the wall with heavy woven belts that ended in large bronze clasps that clicked into place. Without any hesitation, Alice pulled the transport out of the lock and thrust it back towards the Cricket as the air lock automatically sealed itself again.

"Give me that gun," Larkin said, pulling off her mask. "I know you don't want to be carrying it around."

"It's not as though you're some sharpshooter, either," Evie mumbled, but handed the gun over to Larkin, who slid it into a makeshift holster on her hip made from two leather belts criss-crossed around each other. Obviously she had planned for this in a way Evie definitely hadn't.

"Yeah, but at least I know how to shoot one," Larkin said with a snort. "Anyway I'd rather not have to use it at all, I just want to get what we need and get out. Once we get to Bradach you can leave, just disappear back into the city."

"And what about you?"

A dark look fell over Larkin's face that made Evie feel uncomfortable. "I have some business to attend to."

"Right." Evie poked a box with the toe of her foot, producing the soft rattle of metal on metal. She bent to open it, sliding the cardboard flaps away from each other to reveal what looked like a box of junk. Random bits of bronze and aluminum that didn't even look like ship parts, more like some kind of strange art installation that had been dismantled and put into storage.

"Scrap. Not what we want," Larkin said, opening another box. "More scrap here."

"What about these?" Evie asked and gestured at the stacks of data servers. "Could be useful?"

"I doubt it, they'll have wiped all classified information from them before storing them here in the loading bay like that. Probably just blank servers to set up on a new ship, or they've got useless public information on them, like the public broadcasts, maybe."

Evie frowned at the servers and turned to another pile of boxes, only to find more random bits of bronze and lead. "I'm not seeing anything that looks like a micro-droid, just a bunch of useless crap."

"Yeah, this is definitely abnormal. I know security measures have tightened up recently, but you'd think having a ship like this trading in random scrap was a bit pointless, really." She opened another box and sighed. "I feel like we're missing something here."

"Maybe whatever we're looking for is hiding in plain sight," Evie said thoughtfully, stepping back to survey the room for any kind of clue. She'd read enough mystery novels to spot things that seemed out of place. Maybe there was a trap door somewhere, or a crate of classified bots hidden amongst loose cabbages and potatoes harvested from one of the terraformed colonies. She peered into a large crate filled with onions and dug her hand into it, feeling around for anything that didn't feel organic, but all she found was a couple of small, bent gears at the bottom, probably from whatever the crate had housed last.

"Some droids here, but they're all older models, decommissioned," Larkin said. She tossed one back into the box with a loud clank. "Damn it."

"Do you think their intel was wrong? Maybe this ship doesn't have what they're looking for."

"They don't strike me as the kind of crew that flies by the seats of their pants, or trusts dodgy information from dark sources." Larkin sighed heavily. "No, we must be missing something. I wanted to find whatever it is before Alice gets back with the shuttle so we can just load it up and get the hell out of here. Now I'm thinking whatever we're looking for is inside the main part of the ship. We'll have to go in and get it."

Evie shook her head. "I don't think that's a good idea."

"It's not a good idea at all," Larkin agreed. "But I'm not seeing another option."

"Then maybe we should wait for the captain."

Larkin rolled her eyes. "She gets on my nerves. Self-important attitude, thinks she knows everything. I bet if we can't find what she's after, she'll blame us instead of their intel."

Ignoring Larkin's comments, Evie returned to the stack of data servers. Something about them felt off, and it was nagging at her. Why would the Coalition bother transferring old servers at all, instead of just furnishing new ones for the ships entering the fleet? Why not scrap these old servers? "I don't know, Larkin, I feel like something is up with this outdated equipment."

"Eves, it's nothing, I told you. They've even got the green 'declassified' labels on their sides, see?"

"Hmm."

"It's not worth wasting time on, I'm telling you," Larkin said, turning back to another stack of crates and dragging a dirty, damp lid from one box and dropping it to the floor.

Evie couldn't help thinking that there was something she was missing, some kind of clue or sign that the servers would be of use. She squatted down on the floor and squinted at the fine print etched into the base of each server. "Coalition property data server, penalty for improper use," she read aloud to herself. The bright green declassification label covered a serial number dozens of characters long, composed of numbers, letters, and symbols Evie had never seen before. They had to mean something, didn't they? She scooted to the back of the servers and examined the wiring, the ends cut and the copper fibers exposed. "Why would they cut the ends of these?" she called to Larkin. "Instead of just unplugging them from the data center?"

"Probably to splice them in with incompatible equipment?" Larkin answered. "Maybe wherever they're headed, the new systems can't take these older connections."

"That doesn't make any sense. The Coalition rolls out brand new ships and tech every week, they never reuse anything. Why these?"

"Who knows. Evie, just leave it, that can't be what we're looking for."

The tangled wires drooped towards the ground and coiled themselves into a mess of snakey tendrils at the base of the stack, the powerless cords woven in with each other and knotted in haphazard ways. Evie touched one wire that ran from one of the older, dustier servers to the ground. She tugged at the wire, but it wasn't loose like the others. There was tension on this cable coming from somewhere, and Evie knelt down to follow it. It dipped down beneath the nest of wires, which she pushed aside to find the cord in her hand leading down under the floor of the loading bay. With a quiet gasp, she ripped off the declassification label and found a blinking red light. "Larkin!" she shouted, pulling at the loose grate in the floor to follow the wire. "Larkin, one of them is on! It's transmitting some kind of signal!" She yanked hard on the cable running beneath the floor, and the crates Larkin was investigating started to wobble. The acrid scent of gunpowder began to leech into the air.

"Larkin!" Evie screamed. "It's a bomb!"

CHAPTER FOURTEEN

As soon as Evie screamed "bomb," Larkin leapt away from the stack of crates she'd been rummaging in, filled with loads of old crap that was no use to anyone. As the crates exploded, sending shrapnel screaming across the loading bay and into her arms, shielding her face, she thought, *of course it was a fucking setup.*

Chunks of metal flew unsettlingly close to her head, and she could swear one piece of flaming garbage singed the end of her dark braid as it went over her shoulder and landed on a stack of carrots. If there was one bomb, there might be others. She whipped her head around to Evie, who was busy yanking cords out of one of the servers in the center of the stack, copper wiring flying in every direction. "Evie, get away from that, it could be another—"

"Hey!" shouted a tall man whose thick muscles bulged through his thin Coalition uniform, as he punched through the ship's crew airlock. "What the hell do you think you're doing?" He advanced towards Evie, hands on his service revolver in the holster on his hip. "State your rank and ID number, right now!"

Larkin shrank behind the remains of the exploded crates and crouched down and out of sight. For now, he only knew there was one of them, and that was a distinct advantage. Her fingertips brushed the cold brushed metal of the gun in her makeshift holster. Captain Violet had said not to kill anyone, and had given them this piece of shit sedation gun instead. Still, it was better than nothing. Better than her bare hands against that absolute tank of a man; that's a fight she wouldn't win.

"Uh, I was sent here to transport these data servers," Evie said nervously. "I'm a... private, and my ID is..."

The man whipped his pistol from the holster and pointed it right at Evie's head. "No privates in the Coalition military, pirate." He took another step towards Evie and cocked the gun, a disgustingly smug grin oozing across his perfect meathead face. "I'm going to give you one more chance to tell me who you are, no bullshitting this time."

Larkin watched as all the color drained from Evie's face, the terror apparent. She felt a surge of anger towards the man and rolled out from behind the crates, pulling the gun from her holster as she silently righted herself. The man's finger twitched on the trigger and Larkin fired the gun, the sedative-laden rubber bullet smacking into the man's bare forearm. He whirled around, pulling the trigger on his own gun and sending an armor piercing round ricocheting off the wall of the loading bay. He stalked towards Larkin and she waited for the sedatives to take effect. They didn't.

"Oh, fuck," Evie said, and Larkin turned to run from the hulking man-beast that was now only a few steps away. The rest of the crew of the C.S. Blackwall would definitely have heard a gunshot in the loading bay, not to mention the fucking explosion, and it wouldn't be long before the whole goddamned barracks was in here with them. Where the hell was Alice with that transport? Larkin leapt over an overturned apple crate, looking over her shoulder to find that not only was this guy huge, he was fast, too, and closing the gap between them much quicker than she had anticipated.

"Radio!" Larkin shouted at Evie. "Use the radio!" The man behind her cocked his gun with a threatening click, so she turned around and punched him right in the face, sending him reeling. At least she still had the element of surprise, if nothing else. While he was stumbling backwards over a box of flaming scrap metal, Larkin punched him again and wrenched the gun from his hand, bending his wrist back and causing him to scream in pain.

"Bitch, get off!" he shouted, kicking at her with his massive boots. He caught her right in the kneecap, and she crumpled to the ground, tears stinging her eyes.

"Asshole!" she shouted back, cocking the gun she'd stolen from him. "Get back or I'll paint the walls of this loading bay with the inside of your skull!"

He raised his hands in surrender and backed away, crawling across the floor on one hand and both knees. She'd probably broken his wrist, and she smirked at him. Good, he deserved it, the Coalition stooge. "They're all going to come, you know," he said once he'd reached what he thought was a safe distance. "Even if you kill me, they're all on their way."

She pointed the weapon at his head. "Don't fucking move," she said in her most menacing voice, and when he reached for his radio, she shot him in the neck, sending uneven spurts of blood splashing across the crates.

"Larkin! Mask!" Evie shouted, and gestured towards the restraints on the wall. She was standing next to the emergency open level for the airlock, the warning lights flashing red. Why the hell was she opening the airlock? She tugged the mask up over her face and leapt over a box to strap into the wall. The pulleys engaged and the airlock started to open, the rapid change in pressure pulling at her organs, or so it felt. Unsecured boxes and flaming scrap were sliding out the widening door, which revealed the Cricket waiting outside.

"What the hell?" Larkin yelled over the noise, her hands in a death grip on the stolen gun.

The crew airlock screamed a warning that was barely audible over the din, and Larkin watched in horror as a dozen Coalition military members stalked through the doorway in magnetized steam armor, weapons drawn. "Oh, fuck." She raised the gun towards the soldiers in their steam armor, a weak and insignificant match against their huge cannons. The weapons on those suits were strong enough to take out ships much bigger than the Cricket. One good blast and sayonara, baby.

"Evie! Tell them to get away from the airlock!" she screamed, unsure if Evie could even hear her. When the woman didn't reach for the radio, she knew that this was it. This was how they all died, duped by a shitty amateurish setup and a bunch of assholes in steam armor. Goddamnit.

Evie was clutching at the restraints that held her on the ship while crates of produce skidded across the uneven metal flooring and dumped piles of flaming fruits and vegetables into space, where they immediately extinguished, their charred remains bumping against the side of the ship. The steam armored crew of the C.S. Blackwall advanced toward the open loading bay door, the heat guns on the arms of their suits powering up and growing red hot with inevitable death. Their steps were mechanical and heavy, one leg at a time as the mechanical locks disengaged and re-engaged to keep them secure on the rapidly depressurizing deck.

The soldier in steam armor at the front of their formation raised their weapons, and the rest followed suit, a small army of heat guns powerful enough to melt a hole in most ship's hulls, but especially an older model like the Cricket. The refurbished ship wouldn't stand a chance against them, and everyone aboard the ship would die. And then she would die, too. And Evie, though they'd probably send her back to Allemande at the high security prison first to torture more information out of her.

At the thought of Evie enduring more cruelty at the hands of the Coalition, Larkin raised the gun and shot at the soldier in front. She knew the bullet would have no effect against the steel plated, nearly impenetrable armor which had been increasingly over-engineered by Coalition paid armor manufacturers, but she could at least draw their fire until the crew of the Cricket got their act together.

To her shock, the soldier in front crumpled to the ground, holding their hands over a hole in the torso of their armor. Larkin held the gun in her hands, pushing out a round in the chamber. Hollow pointed and designed for maximum penetration, this specially designed ammunition was Coalition-made to fight pirates, brigands, and rebels. They worked just as well on their own kind.

By now the rest of the soldiers were slowly turning towards her, their speed limited by the heavy slowness of the magnetized boots. The heat guns were powered up and ready to fire on her and turn her into space dust, but to be honest, she wasn't ready to die yet. Not like this. She shot at the soldier who was first to face her just as they fired a blast from their heat gun. Her shot landed in the soldier's thigh just as the blast from the heat gun grazed Larkin's arm and burned through the left side of her restraint. She screamed in pain and fired at the soldier again wildly, this shot flying over their shoulder into the face of the one behind, who fell to the ground, their shattered helmet revealing the carnage within.

Another blast from a heat gun singed the hair of her braid and melted a bolt on the inside support beam that held her to the ship. She fired again just as the last of the loose crates sailed out of the loading bay into space, leaving only her, Evie, the soldiers, and the remains of the data centers, which she now realized were all bolted into the ground. Maybe not so amateur after all. This was an elaborate ruse, designed to snare as many pirates and rebels as it could. The Cricket had a mole.

Three soldiers now lay crumpled on the ground, with nine left in various stages of panic and duty. Two were tending to their fallen comrades, three were still advancing toward the loading bay door where they'd inevitably fire on the Cricket. Two were heading back to the crew airlock as fast as their slow, magnetized steps could take them, no doubt to report the attack to their superiors and call for backup. In this area of space, it wouldn't be long before they were facing half a dozen other Coalition ships, and they'd all have more weaponry and crew than the Blackwall did. One soldier was facing Larkin, raising their heat gun. They were so close that Larkin could count their eyelashes or punch them in the face, if a punch with her bare hand wouldn't break every one of her fingers in the process.

The final soldier was two steps away from Evie, heat gun raised and ready to fire. Larkin squeezed the trigger and watched the soldier near Evie fall to the floor. She pressed her mask against her face and looked across the loading bay to Larkin, her expression turning from hopeful to horrified.

The soldier in front of Larkin had the gun raised, and they fired their weapons in the same moment. Heat and pain slammed into Larkin's side, and it felt like she was melting from the inside out, the worst and most intense pain she'd ever felt. The soldier staggered backward, blood seeping from the gaping wound in their chest and hanging in the air around it like a macabre sculpture in a museum. Their eyes were empty and lifeless, their mouth stretched in a silent scream of pain and shock.

Examining her side, Larkin was horrified to discover that the heat from the gun had melted into her bloody, rapidly blistering skin. People didn't survive wounds like this. Not people like her, anyway - this level of care was only available at the heights of Coalition circles, with the best doctors and medications, experimental, life-saving treatments. She'd be lucky if she survived long enough to make it off the ship alive. Her body was going into shock, and she struggled to make sense of the scene. All she could think was that if nothing else, at least it wasn't Evie.

* * *

Time slowed down when Evie watched Larkin slump in her restraint, her body limp against the wide woven straps and clunky bronze buckles. She was watching the woman who just saved her life die, and there was nothing she could do to help her, not while the door was open, and not while the area was depressurized. There were still soldiers in steam armor between where she was and where Larkin hung on the other wall, soldiers with huge heat guns that were advancing on the Cricket, which was inexplicably floating in space like a sitting duck, as though they were waiting to be blown out of the sky. Communications had gone dark after Evie radioed after the explosion, so she had no idea what they were planning, or if they were waiting on her. There was nothing coming from the radio, not even static.

Three soldiers disappeared through the crew airlock, and were no doubt stripping out of their steam armor to alert all local Coalition vessels, if they hadn't been already. Someone planted that bomb, and meant for them to trigger it. If she hadn't found it, they'd both be dead right now. Obviously their intel had been wrong, and someone had fed the Coalition their plans. Evie was getting fed up with being set up, and felt anger blaze in her gut. No. Not again.

The soldier that lay dead at her feet was just within reach of Evie's short legs, and she stretched against the restraint to catch the lip of the helmet and pull it closer. She heaved and pulled with all her might as the three soldiers raised their heat guns to fire on the Cricket, but the magnets that held the steam armor to the ground were too strong for her to dislodge. She'd have to risk unbuckling herself from the wall to grasp the armor and pry it from the dead soldier's body to put on her own. If the other soldiers didn't notice her, and they might not now that they stood at the very edge of the loading bay ramp, she might be able to get to Larkin.

Reality spun back into itself with the threat of the soldiers firing on the Cricket, and Evie yanked open the buckle to free herself from the safety restraint. She felt the forces of de-pressurization pull and yank at her body, threatening to fling her into the void to die. Her fingernails bit into her palm as she clenched the strap and leaned towards the dead soldier on the ground. She hurled herself down to the floor and clung to the armor, held in place by the magnetized boots. She didn't need the full suit, just the boots, and struggled to unlatch them from the rest of the suit. She freed one boot, and then the other, leaving the dead soldier in just their bleached, pristine white Coalition issued socks. Their name was sloppily embroidered on the sole, probably by their mother. Evie retched.

Shoving her feet into the oversized boots, she pried their remote control from the gloved hand of the soldier. She wrenched the left sleeve from the suit, which held the armor's heat gun, and shrugged it on over her shoulder. With one eye on the soldiers at the edge of the loading bay, she began to cross the loading bay to get to Larkin, one painstakingly slow stomp at a time. The boots were slow to respond to the control, which meant they might be damaged or low on power. She just needed to get to the other side, and then she could figure out what was next.

The soldiers fired on the Cricket when Evie was halfway across the room, the heat guns glowing orange and red as they sent spirals of heated iron at the Cricket. If the heat didn't melt the hull, the coils would puncture it. She watched in horror, and the confusion, as the red hot metal bounced harmlessly off an invisible forcefield around the ship. One of the soldiers began to shout about magnetized shields, and the three Coalition soldiers lowered their weapons to recalibrate. Evie just needed them to stay focused in the other direction, and not turn around. She realized she was holding her breath when her lungs involuntarily gasped for air inside her face mask.

Breathe in, breathe out, she thought with the next few steps, her eyes on Larkin's unconscious form, sagging in the restraint, the side of her body a mess of blood, burned flesh, and scorched fabric. When she finally reached Larkin, Evie used the partially burned harness to secure the woman to her, threading the strap around her own waist and securing it with a sophisticated knot that wouldn't loosen. She shifted Larkin's body so that it was limp against her back, and she gently secured Larkin's arms around her own neck. Whatever was about to happen, she would need to have her arms free, and this was the only way to do that.

The soldiers at the edge of the loading bay were emptying the metal coils into space, where they drifted harmlessly into the dark void. They wore packs on the sides of their suit, and one by one they pulled long rods of shining gold and loaded them into their heat guns. Shit. If the Cricket's safety shield was magnetic, the gold rods would fly right through it and into the hull. It wasn't as strong as iron, nor as cheaply acquired, but it would be effective. She had to do something before everything went even more wrong than it already had. This was supposed to be a routine pillage and data extraction, and now people were dead, and Larkin would be too if Evie didn't get her the hell out of here - wounds didn't do well in zero gravity.

She engaged the heat gun she'd stolen from the dead soldier, breathing deep as it grew warm and glowed yellow with readiness. With a few more steps, she'd be right behind the three soldiers, but at the distinct disadvantage of there being three against one, and she didn't have a full suit of armor. Larkin's weight was heavy on her back, and Evie struggled to take each step with the heavy boots and keep Larkin's body from sliding in the harness. The last thing Larkin needed was more injuries after this.

The heat gun primed and ready, Evie swung it at one of the soldiers, and out of instinct they tried to leap out of the way. Hindered by their boots, they stumbled and fell back on their own weapon, shouting out in pain as the gun burned through the thick steel of the steam armor and melted into their skin. She dragged her boots across the deck, shoving the gun sailing into space, while another soldier tried to grab it from the air. She swiped at this soldier too, but they were prepared for her, and fired the heat gun over her shoulder.

"Surrender and you'll be shown mercy!" the soldier said.

Evie responded with a guttural scream and shoved one into the other, sending them both flailing for their weapons. She blasted both the heat guns with her own, melting the mouth of the barrels closed and rendering them useless. She stomped on one soldier's hand when they reached up for her own gun, and felt the bones in the soldier's hand crunch under her boot.

She turned out towards the Cricket and waved frantically. "I'm here! We're here!" she yelled. "Hurry, before reinforcements arrive!"

There was a strange hum as the Cricket disengaged its shield, and pulled closer to the C.S. Blackwall, their loading bay ramp extending as far as it could. Evie would have to jump from one ship to the other, and hope that the magnetic boots held. She took a deep breath, and jumped.

CHAPTER FIFTEEN

Evie landed hard on the deck of the Cricket loading bay, with one arm holding Larkin's body and the other to her side for balance. The three soldiers on the C.S. Blackwall that she'd disarmed were starting to regroup. It wouldn't be long until backup arrived. "Go!" she screamed into her radio, praying to the empty void someone would hear her. As if an answer to her prayer, she felt the Cricket lurch and shudder beneath her feet as the engines kicked into gear.

She bent her knees to brace for the force of forward motion that came as soon as the engines spun into high gear, but even with the heavy duty magnetic boots it was difficult to stay upright, as space tried to claim both of them for its own. Clutching the remote, she took five steps into the loading bay and yanked the airlock lever down, the pulleys for the enormous steel door groaning with the effort of doing so while at full speed. As soon as the room began to re-pressurize, with breathable air being pumped into the loading bay, she ripped off her face mask and Larkin's and started to shout into her radio while hot tears of panic welled in her eyes.

The speaker in the corner of the loading bay crackled. "All hands, all hands to stations. We need to get the hell out of here before half the goddamn fleet in on our asses," the captain's voice popped.

"Hyun, Violet! Anyone! Larkin's in bad shape!" she sobbed, laying Larkin down carefully on the unforgiving metal floor of the loading bay. She looked so small and vulnerable like this, nothing like how she was when not on death's door, and she was only there because of Evie. She'd sacrificed herself for Evie knowingly. A sob caught in Evie's throat and choked her back into the reality of the situation; she wiped the tears and snot from her face and bent to listen to Larkin's breath.

She was still breathing, at least for now, but she was looking ashen and unusually pale. "Hyun!" Evie shouted into the radio again, but there was no response. "Hyun!"

"I'm here," came a breathless voice from the crew airlock, still cracked and damaged from Evie's failed attempt at learning to be a sharpshooter. "What's her status?"

"She's breathing but took a bolt from a heat gun to the side. It grazed her, but she's got a really nasty burn."

"Jasper," Hyun said, pulling on gloves, "take her to the med bay, I'm right behind you. It looks like she has some serious damage to her ribs and maybe some internal bleeding."

"What can I do?" Evie called after them as Jasper hefted Larkin's body through the airlock.

"Stay out of the way," Hyun said in a tone much icier than Evie had ever heard from the medical tech before.

Anxiety lurched in her stomach, and she turned to vomit into an empty wooden crate. Evie retched loudly and brought up her breakfast easily, splashing into the crate with the putrid smell of bile and acid. She moaned and kicked off the magnetic boots, relieved to be freed from the heavy weight, and lay back on the floor of the loading bay, staring at the high ceilings with the yellow tinted bulbs hanging. Larkin was probably going to die, and for what? She never even wanted to be on this ship in the first place, and now the crew's ill-advised plan had failed spectacularly.

Worst case scenarios swam in her head, thoughts of Larkin's corpse being given the traditional dark space burial of being thrust into the void to linger as space dust for all eternity, or until some other ship smacked into the frozen body at full speed and shattered her into a billion tiny shards. No, she couldn't stay here and wait for news. She had to do something to help, even if Hyun wasn't interested.

When Evie burst into the medical bay, Hyun and Jasper were already hard at work irrigating the burn and evaluating Larkin for internal injuries. The grave look on the medical tech's face erased any hope that Evie had built up as she ran through the ship's long winding corridors, and her heart sank deeper into her chest. Hyun was inserting an IV into Larkin's arm while Jasper pulled fragments of cloth from the melted, burned skin with tiny tweezers.

"I told you to stay out of the way," Hyun said sternly, but softened slightly at Evie's horror-stricken face. "Elevate her legs, gently," she said, and Evie busied herself gathering a stack of folded sheets and blankets to put under Larkin's feet.

"She's breathing on her own, but there's definitely internal bleeding. I'm going to have to open her up to find the source."

"You can't do that here, it's not sterile! It's not safe!" Evie protested.

"If I don't, then she dies anyway. At least this way, she has a chance," Hyun said firmly, scrubbing her hands in the sink. "It's going to be a medical miracle if she pulls through this. Surgeries in space rarely go well, not in conditions like these, anyway." Hyun looked over her shoulder at Jasper's progress. "That's enough for now, cover the burn with bandages and get ready for me to scope for the bleed."

Jasper nodded and set to work laying gauzy bandages over Larkin's side, soaked in some kind of thick, shiny white paste. Evie watched as each strip was laid over Larkin's skin, and felt her heart grow heavier in her chest. A few weeks ago she didn't even know this woman, and now she couldn't imagine her life without Larkin in it. She'd saved Evie from the prison with a clever lie, and now she'd saved her from certain execution by heat gun on that Coalition ship.

Evie wanted nothing more than for Larkin to sit up in the medical bay bed, laugh, and say it had all been an elaborate prank, a ruse to determine how suited Evie was for piracy and adventure. As of that moment, she didn't think she was well suited for any of this at all. She was just an incredible liability to anyone around her, and it was her fault that Larkin was lying in that bed fighting for her life. They'd have paired her with a more experienced member of the crew if Larkin hadn't needed to lie to save her from prison.

Guilt bloomed in Evie's belly and sent tendrils of doubt snaking up her spine. How would she even pull this off without Larkin? The crew of the Cricket still thought she was some master markswoman who could keep them safe and help them steal the data from the armory, when she couldn't even keep herself safe from danger. Evie stepped back from the bed and watched Larkin's face for any sign of life. There wasn't one, not even a hint of the woman she knew. Evie fluffed the blankets under Larkin's feet, feeling completely useless and totally out of her depth.

"What in the hell happened over there?" Violet roared, slamming open the heavy door of the medical bay. "It was a routine job, and—" she swallowed hard when she caught sight of Larkin's unconscious form on the bed. "Gods."

"Not now, Captain," Hyun said, and Violet raised her hands in apology and backed out of the room.

"You can't be here for this," Hyun said to Evie gently. "Go with the captain. Tell her what happened on that ship."

Performing surgery without any training would probably be easier than talking to Captain Violet. She'd done well to avoid the captain so far, and now she'd have to keep all of her lies straight and tell her what happened on the C.S. Blackwall. "Okay," she whispered, with one last worried glance towards Larkin. "Can I wait outside after I talk to the captain?"

Hyun gave a heavy sigh, readying a bright silver tray of threatening looking medical instruments. "You can wait outside, yes. But don't come in unless I say so; most people don't do well seeing the inner workings of the human body."

Evie felt her stomach clench in preparation for another retch, but swallowed the bile back down and nodded before closing the door quietly behind her. To her surprise, Captain Violet was waiting right outside, fury burning in her eyes.

"The bridge. Now." The Captain turned on her impeccably polished boot heel and marched towards the ship's bridge, without so much as a backward glance at Evie, who shuffled along behind her, meek as a mouse.

The ship's officers were waiting on the bridge in various states of disarray.

Ned was nervously running his huge hands through his thinning ginger hair, his eyes fixed on a radar display flashing on his console. Kady was pacing near the far wall, wearing a hole in the thin carpet on the bridge, and Alice was leaning on the captain's chair looking stressed, her usually neat silver braids frizzy and loose. Violet whirled around and pointed in Evie's face when they reached the bridge. "What the hell were you two doing? It was supposed to be an easy job, and we barely all escaped with our lives." When Evie said nothing, Violet continued, "Explain yourself!"

Evie wanted nothing more than to run and hide, even if it meant throwing herself off the ship into space. How was she even going to begin explaining what had happened, and why Larkin was fighting for her life, and why Violet had risked the lives of her crew for two nobodies they'd already risked their ship for when breaking them out of a maximum security Coalition prison? "Captain," Evie said quietly after a moment. "There was an explosion."

"Well you don't have to tell me that," Captain Violet spat, her knuckles balled into fists. "Any ship within one hundred kilometers could tell you that, and we were a hell of a lot closer than one hundred kilometers."

"It was rigged into what looked like derelict data servers," Evie continued, struggling to keep her cool as the blood pounded in her ears. "At first, we thought it was nothing, just some old crappy equipment. But when I looked closer, I realized it was rigged into a whole lot of explosives, meant to detonate on a trigger in one of the crates we were searching. I'm afraid that when I discovered it, I caused it to go off early." She clenched and unclenched her fists in a desperate bid to calm her screaming nerves.

"And that's what happened to Larkin?"

Evie shook her head. "No, she escaped the main blast, as far as I know. Her current injuries are from a heat gun, fired by one of the soldiers."

"And what happened to the soldiers?"

"Three dead, I think, though I'm not positive what happened to the rest."

Violet swore under her breath. "This was a routine mission, Evie Anderson. How did you two manage to mess it up so badly?" The captain rubbed her temples angrily, her eyes squeezed shut in frustration. "This is why I told that goddamned assassin not to kill anyone. It always escalates faster, and then before you know it someone's jumping onto the ship and we're barely getting out unscathed." The captain turned to Ned. "How are we looking?"

"No sign of a tail or that we've been pursued. At our current distance, we're probably out of the woods, but we can't be too careful. These ships all have stealth shields now, so it's possible there's some Coalition around we just haven't seen."

"We can't go back to Bradach, not like this," Violet sighed. "If we do have a tail, we'd lead them straight to the settlement. We'll need to lie low for a while, make sure we weren't followed."

"But what about Larkin?" Evie interjected. "She needs real medical care, or she'll die!"

Captain Violet turned her steely gaze back to Evie, who then immediately regretted opening her mouth. "Larkin has some of the best medical attention she can get right here on the ship. It's unlikely she'd get better elsewhere, and we're at least a day from Bradach anyway. If she doesn't make it, it will not be the fault of Hyun."

Evie fell silent, guilt gnawing at her guts again.

"Why didn't you use the gun I gave you to sedate them, instead of letting Larkin take charge?" Violet asked, narrowing her eyes at Evie.

This was it, the moment they learned she was nothing more than a fraud, Evie thought, panic clawing up her chest and lodging itself in her throat. "Um," she started, but couldn't figure out how to admit the lie. Would they kill her here and now if she told the truth? Captain Violet, though not a fan of violence, didn't seem very merciful to those who lied to her or disobeyed direct orders. "Uh, well, actually, I..." she trailed off again.

"Well come on, out with it," Captain Violet said impatiently.

"You're not a sharpshooter at all, are you?" Kady said, pausing from her pace to consider Evie.

The bridge fell silent, and Evie shook her head. "No."

"For gods' sakes," Violet hissed. "Why did you lie?"

Evie stared at the captain, foreboding in her crisply tailored waistcoat and tight-fitting trousers that tucked into tall black leather boots. "I didn't plan to."

"You didn't plan to." Violet angrily smoothed back a stray hair from her bun and glared at Evie. "Do you know what you could have cost us? What we risked to free you from that prison? The complete trust we had in you?"

"I'm sorry, I—"

"We don't need your empty apologies," Violet said. "I want you off my ship at the next opportunity, I don't care if it's a Coalition-controlled trading beacon and they arrest you on sight to drag you back to that goddamned hellhole. I don't tolerate liars on my crew."

Evie opened and closed her mouth wordlessly. "I didn't ask to be part of your crew!" she protested finally.

"No, but you did ask us to save you, did you not? You lied and said you'd be an asset to our team, you begged me to open the cells before we left! Who knows what the consequences of that might end up being?"

"Violet," Alice said softly.

Captain Violet whirled on Alice. "No, you know I'm right, you all do! We almost all ended up as mincemeat back there because she lied to us. We never would have put her in that position had we known."

"No, but she did save us, in a sense," Alice continued. "Yes, she set off the explosive device early, but had she not, you, and I, and Jasper would probably be dead, too."

Evie really didn't like how Alice said "too," as though Larkin was already dead, but she swallowed the annoyance down and waited for her sentence.

"And, she kept those soldiers from boarding the Cricket, we'd never have gotten away in time if she hadn't."

Violet softened almost imperceptibly and turned back to Evie. "Alice is right, as usual," she said with a wry smirk. "If what she said is true."

"It is true," Evie nodded, though she wasn't sure how she felt about painting herself as the hero of the moment when it was her fault that Larkin was laying half dead in a medical bay with Hyun poking around in her rib cage. She closed her eyes in a desperate bid to focus on what she wanted to say. "Captain Violet, I'm no hero. It's true that I lied to all of you about my skills and put the mission at risk, and if I could do it all over, I would be honest from the moment you sprung me from my cell, no doubt. I understand why you want me off your ship and away from your crew, I just ask you let me stay until Larkin is well, or... or not."

Violet looked to Alice, who shrugged apologetically, and back to Evie. "You can stay, for now. But you keep out of our way and your mouth shut, do you understand? I'm still not convinced by your story about what went on over there, and Larkin has to answer for her own sins where that's concerned, but... but Alice thinks you should be allowed to stay with Larkin for now, at least, and I suppose I agree."

Evie nodded. "Thank you for that."

"Don't thank me," Captain Violet said, rolling her eyes. "Thank Alice. If it was up to me, you'd already be gone."

* * *

Every hour spent outside the medical bay while Hyun and Jasper worked inside felt like an entire day. Evie struggled to control her wildly flailing emotions, and spent her time sitting on the uncomfortable steel bench outside the med bay, alternating with crying jags and tiny slivers of hope that Larkin would be okay. Not many people survived injuries like that, and certainly not in space. She returned to her prison cell comfort activity, counting the holes in the grate floor, cracks in the ceiling, notches carved into the armrest of the bench. One thousand forty-two, thirty-seven, twelve.

Heavy footsteps approached from the boiler room, and Alice appeared with a strange contraption in her hands, with several sockets connected to a central plate with rigid wire. She nodded at Evie and knocked softly on the door. "Hyun? Will this work?"

"It will have to," Hyun said grimly, took the metal, and closed the door.

"What is that?" Evie asked, wondering what it could possibly be for.

"I don't know if I should tell you," Alice said hesitantly. "It might just make you worry more. I know I would."

"Please?"

Alice sat heavily on the bench and rested her palms on the worn knees of her green coveralls. "Hyun asked me to prototype a partial rib cage for

Larkin."

Evie's breath caught in her chest as she processed the information. "You *made* a rib cage? Why does she need that?"

"I'm not a doctor, or a med tech, I'm a mechanic who knows how to weld. I don't know the specifics, but it sounds like Larkin lost part of her rib cage from the burn. Heat like that doesn't just sear skin, it eats into the muscle and the bone, too."

"Gods."

"Yeah." Alice put an arm around Evie. "I know this must be hard for you, waiting to hear how she's doing. I know she means a lot to you, just how Violet means a lot to me."

Evie blinked at her. "Um, yeah," she mumbled, wondering what Alice had meant by that.

"Listen, I know Vi — er, Captain Violet - can come off harsh sometimes. I know you're scared about what's going to happen to Larkin. If you feel like you need a break from sitting here and waiting, you know where you can find me. If I'm not there, Ivy will be, and she's aces at making a cup of tea or foraging in the galley for some grub."

"Thanks, but I think I'll just wait here."

"I understand. If you change your mind— "

"I know where I can go, thank you, Alice."

The mechanic lumbered off back towards the boiler room, leaving Evie alone with her thoughts once again. The more she thought about the shiny rib cage, the more her own ribs felt strangely obvious and protruding. Humans could be so fragile, so vulnerable to injury that in most cases, our first instinct is for self-preservation, and yet Larkin's first instinct had been to protect Evie before protecting herself. Evie rubbed at her ribs, wondering how Hyun had the kind of skill and knowledge to perform such a complicated procedure, and outside a real hospital at that. Moments ticked by at an agonizingly slow pace, so drawn out and exaggerated that Evie began to wonder if time had actually stopped, and she was the only one left on the ship who hadn't been frozen in a second of toil or rest.

With the medical bay at the far end of the ship, away from any of the main corridors, there weren't any other crew members wandering by, which made the oppressive silence even more challenging to contend with. Evie briefly considered taking Alice up on her offer of conversation, but couldn't shake the feeling that if she didn't stay there on that bench, it would be her fault if Larkin didn't make it, if her body failed all attempts to be put back together again. So she stayed hunched on the metal bench and resumed counting the holes in the floor, the cracks in the wall, the notches on the bench. It gave her a way to occupy her mind, if nothing else.

She had to admit that it was difficult to adjust to the lack of day and night in space. Here, the only thing that kept you feeling like there was an actual waking and sleeping cycle of time was your own attention to a schedule, going to bed when your pocket watch said it was time, getting up and eating breakfast eight and a half hours later. On Bradach, and most other terraformed settlements, things still moved in a day and night cycle, even if it was in opposition to what the sky looked like. Settlements further away from the sun invested in more artificial sunlight, with timers that dictated when people got up and when they clocked off work to go home for the evening. On the Cricket, Evie struggled to get any good rest, except that one night when she'd accidentally fallen asleep in Larkin's room.

Evie rubbed her eyes and yawned, wondering how long it had been since Hyun had begun trying to save Larkin's life. It felt like three days had passed, even though it had probably only been a matter of hours. If Evie was this exhausted, how worn out must Hyun and Jasper be? Would they make mistakes in their sleep-deprived state that would cost Larkin her life, or simply give up trying because they had nothing left to give? If only there was a way Evie could help, but there wasn't, not really. Any knowledge of medical care was limited to standard first aid, nothing like advanced surgeries or even minor procedures.

Frustration began to build at the base of Evie's skull, an unsettled fury that made every second feel ten times longer. She bounced her legs on the balls of her feet, still fatigued from the weight of the heavy magnetic boots. The longer this went, the less likely Larkin would ever pull through. Her survival rate ticked down with every passing minute, and Evie couldn't bear the waiting, the not knowing what was happening or how she could even be able to cope if she never saw Larkin alive again, even a Larkin hooked up to tubes and machines to breathe for her while Hyun played a god, fitting Larkin's body with manufactured bits of skeleton.

Just when she thought she couldn't bear another second of waiting, the heavy medical bay door creaked open, and Evie nearly leapt ten feet into the air with anticipation. Hyun pulled a dust mask from her face with one hand, and rubbed her lower back with the other and sighed heavily. "She had a lot of extensive injuries," she began, and Evie resisted the urge to shake the information out of her. "Most people wouldn't have even survived to the ship, much less through that surgery. She's a fighter, that's for sure."

"Well, is she alright?" Evie asked impatiently.

Hyun looked at her with tired eyes. "No. I'm still not even sure she'll make it through the night."

Tears welled up and spilled over onto Evie's cheeks, dripping onto the wrinkled collar of her borrowed coveralls. "But—"

"Let me finish," Hyun said, putting a hand up to interrupt Evie. "I'm not sure if she'll make it, but the procedure went well. She's resting, but you can go in if you like."

Evie immediately turned towards the doorway, but Hyun caught her arm as she went past. "I did everything I could, but there's no guarantees."

"Thank you," Evie said earnestly, a hand on Hyun's shoulder. "You should rest."

"I intend to," Hyun replied, rubbing at her back again. "It's not every day you perform a twelve hour surgery, thank goodness." She straightened and massaged her neck, blinking profusely to counteract the pull of sleep. "Jasper is staying to monitor her condition, but he was in there as long as I was. If you want, you could keep an eye on things and just shout if something seems abnormal."

"Of course," Evie replied, nodding. "Anything."

With that, Hyun released her arm and shuffled off down the corridor, mumbling something about needing a shower and some dinner before bed. Evie just hoped there was someone in the mess hall to make her something, because she'd done enough for one day, that was for sure. Evie closed the door quietly behind her, and stifled a gasp. Larkin was lying in the bed with a mess of tubes and wires coming out of her, along with a large tube down her throat attached to a machine that was breathing for her. Hyun and Jasper had stripped her down to a loose fitting tunic with a hole cut into the side to allow for better monitoring of the huge wound on her side.

Evie carefully pulled back the crisp white sheet and felt tears spring to her eyes as she counted thirty-seven stark black stitches that lay just above the heavy bandages covered in the shiny white cream. She'd needed skin grafts, too. Evie pulled the sheet back up and turned to see Jasper behind her, making notes of some readings. "Sorry," she said automatically, but the man looked so exhausted she doubted he'd even heard her. She took the clipboard gently from his hands and pointed him at the spare bed, examining the chart for any evidence that Larkin would pull through.

When she finished, she sat in the squashy chair next to Larkin's bed, and took her hand gently in her own. Whatever happened next, she wouldn't be alone.

CHAPTER SIXTEEN

She'd been in and out of consciousness for what felt like a year, drifting to the surface of her mind and back down again, only aware of when the pain medication was syringed into her IV and the warm comfort of Evie's presence. She was always there whenever Larkin stirred, murmuring encouraging words and reassuring her that everything would be alright if she just rested. Her dreams were swirling, neon messes of incoherence, with guns that fired marshmallows and beautiful barkeeps with tousled bed hair serving her another double shot of rum with a broad, uncomplicated smile.

She'd have to fight her way to the forefront of her mind if she was going to make it out of this alive. Rest was essential, but so was keeping her wits about her. The crew of the Cricket had kept her alive, but for how long, and when would she be expected to repay their generosity? Gifts like these were never free in the Near Systems, not on Coalition planets or liberated settlements. And if there was one thing she hated, it was being in debt to strangers.

Blearily, she forced her eyes open and blinked cautiously. Hyun was still giving her sedatives and the best painkillers piracy could buy, so she was only vaguely aware of the dull pain in her side. She knew that Evie had saved her, had fought her way across that loading bay and strapped Larkin to her back. She'd been unconscious, but heard the others in muted whispers talk about what happened as they moved around her bed, checking dressings and making notes of readings on the machines that quietly whirred and beeped. Hyun had removed the tube in her throat at some point, which Larkin was grateful for, because having that tube rammed down her throat really, really sucked.

"Hey," Evie said, and grinned, reaching out gently for Larkin's hand. "How you doing, Princess Snores-A-Lot?"

Larkin laughed weakly. "I've been better."

"It's so good to see you awake. It's been a week, but Hyun says that's normal with injuries like yours."

"Feels like longer than a week."

"I know," Evie said soothingly, gently rubbing her thumb over the back of Larkin's hand. "I was so afraid I'd lost you."

Something in Larkin shifted, and she felt a rush of affection for the tender barkeep, but maybe it was just the excellent drugs she was being given. "You stayed," she said finally, her voice hoarse and thin. "The whole time, you stayed?"

"Of course I stayed. You saved my life."

"I know I was unconscious for a lot of what happened on that ship, but it would seem to me that you saved *my* life."

Evie gave a bemused smile and furrowed her brow. "That's what anyone would have done after someone saved their life."

"No, Eves," Larkin coughed, "most people wouldn't do that. Trust me." It wasn't lost on Larkin that the crew of the Cricket had also saved her life, but that felt a lot more transactional in nature. She wouldn't be surprised if Captain Violet burst into the room at any moment demanding payment for services rendered.

"Well, you look out for me, I'll look out for you then, deal?" Evie asked, and it was only then that Larkin noticed the deep circles under the woman's eyes. It was clear she'd barely slept since dragging Larkin back onto the Cricket.

"Yeah, deal," Larkin replied, even though Evie would be leaving as soon as they made it back to Bradach, back to the safety of her stable job at the Purple Pig and back to her reality, the one that didn't involve firefights and near misses with Coalition soldiers.

"Where's my necklace?" she asked, the reasonable part of her brain starting to wake up. "I didn't lose it, did I?" She reached out and scrabbled clumsily on the small table next to her bed. She'd never forgive herself if she lost it.

"Relax, it's just here," Evie said, pushing it off the table so that it cascaded down into her outstretched palm. The silver felt pleasantly cold in her hand.

"Thank you." Larkin cleared her throat, or tried to, only managing to irritate her already inflamed larynx. "So, how come we're not back in Bradach already, if it's been a week? We couldn't have been more than a day or so away when we boarded the Blackwall."

Evie cringed visibly, which Larkin knew meant trouble. "There was a little trouble getting back onto the Cricket, there were some soldiers about to board, and some more that raised an alarm with the entire Coalition fleet."

"Yeah, I remember something like that," Larkin said, her eyes squeezed shut with the effort of remembering what had happened that morning.

"Given the Coalition is always updating their stealth technology, it's difficult for Alice and Kady to stay on top of it. Captain Violet wanted to wait a while, to make sure we weren't being tailed."

"Right."

"But the good news is we should be on our way soon, and you'll be able to eat some real food if you're feeling up to it."

Larkin's stomach grumbled, and they both laughed. "Yeah, I think I'm up for that," she said with a grimace, regretting the laugh. "Only if I'm allowed out of this bed, though. I swear I'm getting bed sores."

"Hyun said you weren't to be moved, or it would risk the new rib cage dislocating the remaining bone structure."

"I'm sorry, the *what*?"

"I thought you'd have overheard!" Evie said, covering her mouth with her hands. "The blast from the heat gun burned through skin and part of your rib cage, so Alice made a new one from titanium in her workshop."

Larkin stared at her in disbelief. "Do you mean to tell me that I have a titanium skeleton under these bandages?"

"Well, only partially, but yes."

"That's fucking *cool*."

Evie burst out laughing and bent double in the well worn, overstuffed chair that sat next to Larkin's bed. "Only you would ever say that."

"I'm a bionic woman, Eves, who wouldn't find that cool?" Larkin smirked, gently prodding around the large incision peppered with perfectly neat stitches that held her skin together over the new piece of skeleton hidden underneath. "Very crisp stitches, impressive work," Larkin said, examining her side as best she could without moving too much. "Hyun does some excellent work."

"The stitches were me, actually," Jasper said, entering the room. "Thank you. Hyun made me practice on orange peels for months before she'd trust me with a member of the crew." He flashed a dazzling white smile and hung his jacket on a hook next to the door. "It's good to see you finally awake."

"Yeah, well, Eves here tells me that I'm what, 10 percent titanium now?"

"More like five percent, but yes, your existing skeletal structure in that area was irreparable." He looked up over the clipboard and raised a perfectly groomed eyebrow. "You know, you're incredibly lucky that you had Hyun treating you. Most wouldn't have survived injuries like that."

Larkin frowned, irritated that he would bring up her mortality to her when she was laying in what was almost her deathbed. "You don't have to tell me twice, I've got it," she grumbled. "Don't get me wrong, I'm glad that my corpse isn't quietly sliding through dark space right about now, but I am wondering what the payment is for something like this. I imagine the cost is fucking steep, if you catch my drift."

"You'll have to talk to the captain about that," Jasper said, looking back to the clipboard. "Hyun will be in a while later to discuss your recovery with you, but your numbers are looking positive. In any case, we'd say you've pulled through."

Evie heaved a sigh of relief, and brushed a tear from her cheek. "Thank you Jasper," Evie said, emotion making her voice thick, "I can't tell you how happy I am to hear that."

"You tell Captain Violet I want to talk to her," Larkin said, eager to turn the conversation away from her almost definite demise, "and I have a feeling that she'll be wanting to speak with me as well."

Jasper laughed and hung the clipboard back on the foot of the bed. "It's your funeral." He frowned and furrowed his brow and continued, "Well, you know what I mean." He gave a half wave to Evie, nodded at Larkin, and closed the door to the medical bay, leaving the two of them alone once again.

"What did you tell them?" Larkin said in a hushed voice, which was both practical because she didn't want any of the Cricket crew to overhear, and comfortable due to the swelling in her throat from the tube they'd removed only a couple of days prior.

"Don't worry about all that, just focus on getting well," Evie soothed. "There will be plenty of time for piracy and murdering when your ribs have all healed up."

"Evie, I'm serious. We don't know what the hell is going on here, or why there was a goddamned bomb on that freighter. That can't have been a coincidence, it being there and rigged up right before our job. Think about it."

"It wasn't meant for us," Evie whispered, having a furtive glance at the door. "Whatever the reason, it's for the crew of the Cricket to decide, not us."

"It means they have a mole," Larkin hissed. "Someone on the crew is leaking information to the Coalition about their plans, and setting them up. If you hadn't discovered that explosive device, well, then, we'd all be fucking dead."

Evie blanched with the realization, and stood to fill a cup of water at the small steel sink. "It's probably better if we don't get involved. Let's just get to Bradach, and we can..." she lowered her voice to a quiet whisper that even Larkin could barely hear. "...and we can just meld into the city, wait for them to leave. They can't force us to board the ship again, it's against the rules of the settlement."

"And what about when they go back to Bradach? It's not as if it's a place pirates don't visit *incredibly often*. What about when they see you at the tavern, or me wandering the streets trying to scare up some work?"

"Don't you want to just get a break from all this?"

"Well, yeah, but I also want to know who tried to blow us up so I can kill them."

"It's not our fight."

"They made it my fight when they almost got you killed," Larkin said, aware that her voice was increasing dangerously in volume. "It's complete bullshit what happened on the Blackwall, and I intend to make whoever's responsible suffer for what they put me through." She paused for a breath, and shivered with the sharp pain that shot through her chest. Obviously the strong pain medication Hyun had been giving her was starting to wear off. Perfect.

"Are you alright?" Evie asked, and offered the cup of water to her.

"I'm fine it just...it's weird to wake up in pain and know it's because part of you is missing, and replaced with a hunk of metal a mechanic smacked into shape in her makeshift workshop." She took a long drink from the cup and set it down on the table next to her. "Eves, I just have shit that needs dealing with. A contract I never got paid for, and now this. If I let these things slide, then I lose all my respect that I've spent years building up."

"You don't have to keep doing this, you know," Evie said quietly. "You could come back to Bradach with me and just, I don't know, maybe work at the Tavern with me, I could ask Tansy, and-"

"You think a renowned assassin can just give all of that up to work at a bar?" Larkin snorted. It was asinine to think she could just stay in one place and mop up ale, sleep in the same bed every night. Her past would never allow it. Evie's face fell, and Larkin instantly felt guilty for what she'd said. "Eves, come on, you know I didn't mean it like that."

"No, you did mean it like that. Don't worry, I'm used to it," Evie said with an icy tone, and left the room without another word.

"Evie, come on, wait—" Larkin shouted, but it was too late; the door slammed behind her leaving Larkin alone with her swollen vocal cords and partially titanium skeleton. "Perfect," she grumbled to herself.

* * *

Larkin trudged slowly to the bridge of the ship on orders from Captain Violet, and at the stern encouragement from Hyun to get back on her feet as soon as possible to speed her recovery. Everything hurt, from the follicles of her dark, shiny hair, down to the soles of her feet that hadn't touched the floor in over a week since the explosion on the Blackwall. Even though she had tried to shoo away Hyun's offer of forearm crutches to help her keep her balance, the medical tech had insisted with such authority that she'd had no choice but to relent; now that she was walking along the corridor of the ship unaided, she was grateful for them.

At Evie's suggestion, she'd avoided the captain for the past several days to the best of her abilities, which, being confined to the med bay, were frustratingly reduced under the current circumstances. This meeting wasn't going to be pretty, that was for sure, and part of her felt like she was making a long march to the gallows. Captain Violet was a brash leader who didn't trust anyone outside her own crew, and especially not infamous assassins. Why had the captain had even bothered to spring her from that Coalition prison, given her obvious disdain and suspicion of someone with a kill sheet longer than the length of the ship they were all trapped on together? She'd never liked spending more time than absolutely necessary in space, it felt claustrophobic despite the vast distance that surrounded them. Something about it felt unsettling in a way she didn't want to examine.

The crutches scraped quietly against the metal floor, the rubber tips at the ends dampening the sound, though it still echoed down the empty corridor, lined with old, yellowed maps of derelict trading beacons and rebel bases long since caved in. She could hear the low hum of overlapping voices on the bridge oozing into the hall, a mixture of friendly banter and brusque orders being given. This was a strange ship with an unexpectedly familiar vibe among its crew, and it made Larkin feel uneasy.

"Ah, good, you're finally here," Captain Violet announced to the room as Larkin shuffled through the doorway.

"It's not easy getting around on these, you know," Larkin said, gesturing at the crutches.

Captain Violet blinked at her blankly and turned back to the rest of the crew. "As you all know, the job on the C.S. Blackwall didn't go as planned.

In fact, it was a complete disaster, which ended in the deaths of several of their crew, and nearly those of our own people as well." The captain paused to allow the heavy emphasis of her words to sink in. "It has come to our attention that Evie's presence here on the ship was the result of a lie, and a lie that could have cost us everything."

Larkin scanned the bridge for Evie, but she was nowhere to be found. Only the officers had been invited to this announcement, except for Larkin. She felt panic pool at the base of her skull, sending waves of heat cascading down her neck, but kept her face even and calm. "Captain Violet," Larkin began, using every scarce ounce of reserve she had in her body, "I did lie in order to convince you to save Evie's life. But I'm sure you would have done the same for any one of your crew members."

"Nevertheless," Violet said, her hand held up to keep Larkin from continuing, "the lie resulted in several deaths. Though they were not our own, any loss of life is still a tragedy, especially ones that could have been easily avoided had we known Evie was in no way prepared for a job like that."

"Oh, please," Larkin said, rolling her eyes. She'd tried being civil, but the captain was still being unreasonably virtuous. "You know as well as I do that you can't hold all these lofty ideals about freedom and government, and keep knocking off Coalition ships and expect no blood to be spilled."

"Which is why we continually develop non-lethal weapons, which you declined to use in favor of armor piercing rounds." Violet's voice was laced with contempt that boiled just under her smooth, tailored appearance that exuded control.

"Your stupid gun didn't even work!" Larkin shouted, leaning forward on her crutches and feeling the metal gently bite into her forearms. "Bounced right off that soldier with zero effect."

"You're lying."

"I'm not lying, and that gun is a piece of shit."

"That's impossible," Kady interjected. "We tested it for weeks before we cleared it for use on a job."

Alice nodded. "We did. There's no way it wouldn't have worked. Did you fire at bare skin? Did you wait for the sedative to take effect?"

Larkin stared at them all, incredulous. "And how long was I to wait and see if this sedative took effect, before I let that soldier rip Evie to shreds? Before I let him waltz back onto his ship and call in that the explosives were tripped by some pirates?"

"It would only have been a few seconds," the captain challenged. "Given your apparently incredible skill at evasion, I think you could have managed that."

"Evie wouldn't have been able—"

"Ms. Anderson wouldn't even have been there, if it wasn't for you. If you'd have come clean, she'd have been safe here on the Cricket."

Guilt flooded into the space where her ribs should have been. She *had* put Evie into danger, and only to save her own skin. Still, the need to defend herself erupted up through her body and out of her mouth."You know, you assholes wouldn't even be here if Evie hadn't found that friggin' bomb. We'd all be space dust."

Captain Violet bristled, and Larkin knew she was about to explode. Against every neuron in her brain screaming at her to stop, she pushed the captain harder. "Did you even think to wonder how the hell that explosive was rigged to go off right when we were meant to be rummaging through their produce? Or did you just think it was some strange coincidence, an unfortunate happenstance that your crew, one of the most wanted crews in all the Near Systems, got a tip for an easy score on a Coalition ship that had enough explosives to blow us all to kingdom come set to detonate right when we pulled in? Did you think that was just a fluke, Captain?"

"Listen here, you mercenary," Captain Violet said, stepping so close to Larkin's face that she genuinely felt terrified, despite having faced down meaner, bigger assholes than Violet many times before. "We sprung you from that shit smeared cell to help us do a job, a job you've yet to help complete. When I trusted you with a simple run of the mill mission, people ended up dead. I'm wondering, are you a sociopath with a bad case of blood lust, or are you just that fucking obtuse?"

"Violet," Alice said in a gently warning tone from across the bridge.

"No, I'm not sure she quite understands her role on this ship. Here's a hint, Larkin: your job is to sit down, shut up, and do what you're told. This crew has managed hundreds of successful jobs where no one has needed to kill anyone, much less *three* Coalition soldiers."

Larkin raised her chin in defiance. "What do you care about Coalition parasites anyway?"

"Alice was Coalition once. So was Kady, so was I, so were many of us here on this ship. Life isn't back and white, and people aren't only good or bad. You don't know their personal life history, why they're serving in a corrupt military or within the ranks of an exploitative government."

"Who cares?" Larkin snorted, keenly aware that her attitude was only making Captain Violet's temper worse. "It's still their decision to go along with the bullshit. Everyone here left, you all made a choice to leave all that behind and fight against it. I'm hardly a rebel but it seems to me you've given everyone other than Evie and me the benefit of the doubt."

"I've seen what goes on behind closed Coalition doors," Violet said, leaning in closer to Larkin's face, her voice barely above a hostile whisper. "You're just a goddamned mercenary, a killer-for-hire I wish I could do without, you don't have any allegiances to anyone or any cause, you're only out for yourself," she spat.

"And why the fuck shouldn't I be, when I get treated like this?" Larkin said, hot tears rising to her eyes against her will. "I did the best I could on that ship with what I was given, and we barely made it out." She squeezed her eyes shut and felt the tears stream down her cheeks, which made her even angrier. "I lost part of myself, Captain, I'll probably never be the same, and for what? So that I can be dragged onto the bridge of your ship and be given a dressing down in front of all your officers? Are you serious?"

"Violet," Alice said again, this time quietly crossing the bridge to lay a hand on the captain's shoulder.

The captain shrugged off Alice's hand, but didn't even turn to look at her, choosing instead to keep a laser focus on Larkin. "How do you think I got to be captain of this ship? Do you think I just waltzed onto it one day, declared myself Queen of the New Systems, and expected people to follow me?"

"It sure seems like it," Larkin muttered.

"I worked hard to build trust with my officers and my crew. I have to make choices every single day that could either put them into danger, or keep them out of it. Assist the rebels, or sell our spoils and stay out of the politics, the way so many other pirate crews do. You, Larkin, are not part of my crew, and neither is Evie. You were given your freedom, and you chose to stay, and yet you act like you're more important than anyone else on this boat."

"It was barely a choice and you know that," Larkin hissed, and felt a throb of sharp pain like a spear through her chest. "If you dropped us anywhere except Bradach, we'd have been picked up and carted back to that goddamned prison. I'd be in a work camp somewhere bathing in radioactive bullshit, and Evie would be in some windowless room being tortured into confessing to every crime committed the Coalition couldn't pin on someone." Larkin set aside one of the crutches so she could gently press against the silvered bandages under her loose tunic. "And she was only there because her shitty girlfriend set her up to take the fall for scrapping a Coalition ship. It wouldn't have been fucking fair to leave her there."

"Damn," Ned whispered, and Larkin knew his tone held deep sadness for Evie's story. He should, it was a story that sucked.

"Regardless, you disobeyed orders, and you lied, and put us all in danger. What am I supposed to do, shrug my shoulders and chalk it up to a mistake?" Captain Violet shot back.

"A mistake? Captain, aren't you hearing me? That job was a setup!"

The captain stared at her intensely, her brows furrowed. "That can't be, our intel is ironclad. We have vetted all our sources over years of—"

"Captain, your intel is being tainted by a mole. Someone on this crew is betraying you."

CHAPTER SEVENTEEN

"That's impossible," the captain said as Evie crouched just outside the door to the ship's bridge, "We don't have a mole." Yes, it's true that Evie was eavesdropping, but she desperately wanted to know what was going on. Captain Violet didn't want to talk to them both together for some reason, though Evie suspected it was to corroborate their stories individually about what had happened on the Blackwall. It's why she had dragged Evie out of the medical bay before Larkin came out of the surgery anesthetic, to get her account of the events before she would have the opportunity to devise a plan with Larkin.

It was a smart way to approach a bad situation, and if she was in charge, she probably would have done the same thing. Evie had winced with every audible sigh and mocking laugh, wishing Larkin would just shut up and go along with what the captain wanted for once. The bridge was silent now, and Evie imagined them all looking around at their crew mates' trusted faces, wondering who had sold them out, or if the new interloper was the cause for the terribly botched job.

"Who could it be?" Hyun said quietly, after a long silence that felt like an hour.

"You must be mistaken," Ned said, presumably to Larkin."There's no way anyone on this ship has been leaking information. The officers in this room wouldn't, and no one else has enough information to be useful to the Coalition."

"You don't know that," Larkin responded coolly. "Unless your security protocols are the strongest I've ever seen, they're not impenetrable. Anyone with a background in coding or hacking data servers would be able to access flight paths."

"I wouldn't say anyone," Kady said. "It would take even the most gifted of hackers at least a few hours each time, and the bridge is never left unattended for that long. Plus without an officer badge, the door in here would stay locked tight."

"That still doesn't mean it's an impossibility," Larkin challenged. "Improbable, sure. But certainly not impossible."

"You seem to know a hell of a lot about this for someone who claims to be an innocent party."

"Really?" Larkin scoffed. "I'm an assassin, of course I know how to get around locks and security systems. That's something you pick up on day one of the career training summer camp, right before you all share an enormous ice cream sundae."

"Cut the crap," Violet interjected. "Unless you have more definitive information than that, I can't regard it as anything other than a desperate attempt to avoid punishment for disobeying a direct order. We may be an egalitarian ship, but the position of captain still supersedes the rest, especially during a job, and especially if something goes wrong. That's a safety measure, it's how I keep my crew safe."

"Captain, if you look at the timeline of everything that happened with that job, and your main takeaway from it is that I must be lying to save my own ass, well, then, I can't help you. Facts are facts, and in this case the facts are that there's far too many coincidences for it to all add up to be some big cosmic accident. You're a smart woman, you know this." There was silence a moment before Larkin continued, "Why do you think there was a whole squad of soldiers in friggin' steam armor on a ship taking produce and broken equipment to a trading beacon? That doesn't seem strange to you?"

"Larkin, you have to understand, this is a very serious accusation you've made. We've all worked together for a long time, and we have to trust each other, and here you show up with a fake sharpshooter telling us that someone in this room is selling us out to the Coalition? For what?"

"Money?"

The captain laughed, but the other officers didn't. "We have plenty of money and credits to go around, no one on this ship ever wants for anything."

"People always want more, it's how the Coalition remains in power. Why else do you think the bastards keep getting voted in?" Larkin asked with a snort. "People would rather believe that they might be a rich asshole too, someday, than overthrow a corrupt, fascist power and take back what was stolen from them."

"Rebels don't," Alice said. "They fight for freedom, they don't get caught up in all of that."

"That's what everyone fights for," Larkin pushed, "the possibility that one day they might be able to climb out of their shitty basements and become the oppressors. It's just human nature."

Before Alice could argue, Violet interrupted. "None of this is relevant. You've accused an officer of the highest infraction, treason, and expect us to just believe you."

"Of course I expect you to believe me," Larkin laughed, "how else would you explain any of this?"

"You lied about Evie," Kady said blandly. "Why should we believe you about this?"

Evie swallowed back a tickle at the back of her throat that threatened to expose her hiding place, and buried her face in the borrowed jumpsuit to stifle the sound of her breathing.

Larkin sighed heavily and shifted the crutches against the worn reddish carpet of the bridge. "I lied about Evie to save her life. I am not, however, lying about this."

"You could have just asked us to free her," Captain Violet said. "We would have."

"And how was I supposed to know that?" Larkin asked, audibly frustrated. "I'd never see a single one of you ever in my life before then. Besides, your resistance to free the rest of the prisoners, even though Evie asked before we boarded, was obvious. Don't lionize yourself to protect your image, it's fine. I wouldn't have freed an unresearched prisoner either, which is why, yes, I lied." Larkin sighed again, this time more exasperated, and continued: "What would be my reason for lying, anyway? To get out of spending a few weeks in your brig?"

"To prevent us from dropping you at the nearest Coalition base," Captain Violet threatened.

"Please, you wouldn't even think about doing that," Larkin said. "You'd be putting yourselves at risk just to punish me. What are the odds that someone wouldn't call in your position? The Coalition may have lost all data on this ship and its crew from that stunt you pulled last year, but that doesn't mean word won't travel about what Bad Captain Violet is up to these days."

Evie was always in awe of Larkin's confidence, of how she laid everything out like that, and how she always kept people off balance. It was a fascinating skill to witness, though it did make her wonder if Larkin had ever used that particular skill on her.

"This is going to go easier for you if you just calm down and cooperate," Ned said gently. "Now, let's back up. Tell us about the steam armor."

Larkin groaned loudly. "I told you, there were twelve soldiers with steam armor after the explosion. The initial guard had called for backup before he entered the airlock, but we didn't know that. I killed three, the first one that was powering weapons on the ship, one that was about to kill Evie, and the one that fucking shot me with a heat gun." She took a deep breath that still sounded slightly ragged from the pain the new ribs were likely causing her, and Evie flinched. "Three headed back towards the airlock, presumably to call in local reserves ships, three remained in the loading bay powering weapons towards the Cricket."

"That's only nine," Violet said coldly. "What about the other three?"

"I don't remember. Maybe I shot them too."

"You don't remember."

"No, I don't fucking remember!" Larkin shouted.

"Captain, she was under strong sedatives for nearly a week. Minor memory loss, especially after adrenaline spikes brought on by traumatic events and injury, is normal," Hyun offered. "I am personally impressed that she is standing before us at all. Her injuries were incredibly severe."

"Only standing here thanks to you, Doc," Larkin mumbled.

"In any case, I'm sure you can understand why these inconsistencies raise doubt about your version of events," Captain Violet continued. "We aren't just talking about a minor problem with the mission, it was a total disaster, the worst failure we've ever experienced. It went as badly as it possibly could have gone."

"It would have been worse if we'd all ended up dead, surely," Larkin said sarcastically. "You know, Captain, if Evie hadn't risked everything to rescue me and disable those heat guns, we'd all be fucking dead. You should be thanking your lucky goddamned stars that Evie Anderson was there that day, not dragging me through some pointless inquisition when one of you is the reason any of it went wrong in the first place."

Evie couldn't help but allow herself a private proud grin in her hiding place under the stairs, the metal of the support poles digging into her wide hips. Larkin was thoughtless and rude, but sometimes she made Evie feel more powerful and capable than she'd ever felt before in her entire life.

"Kady, can you access the ship's logs, and see if there has been any communication with Coalition data points in the last month?"

"Aye," Kady said, and her footsteps padded across the bridge to the main computer and remove the protective panel. "Just be a minute, but if anyone was contacting Coalition data points, it would have flagged on the ship's system. I made sure of it when Alice and I reprogrammed the security firewall after Ivy took out that data center last year. Better safe than sorry, you know."

One of the officers was shifting their weight back and forth, Evie could hear the quiet creak of the worn boards that lay beneath the carpet. Was someone nervous, or just impatient? Evie gasped for air and realized that even she had been holding her breath in anticipation. Whoever it was, they were the reason that six people died that day, and why Larkin was stumbling around with a partially reconstructed skeleton. They were why almost all of them had ended up dead.

"Captain," Kady said, her voice thin and tight with tension. "There were a number of communications sent to Coalition data points over the past two weeks. They were sent with Alice's override."

* * *

Larkin's breath caught in her throat when Kady said it was Alice who had been sending encrypted transmissions to someone in the Coalition. It felt like all the air had been sucked out of the room, and the stifled gasp she heard from the corridor was Evie's, probably hiding under the steps. Smart, no one would think to look there, and a good place for someone to listen in on a delicate conversation.

"Alice..." Ned whispered. "How could you?"

"No, it's not what it looks like," Alice protested, tears welling up in her eyes. "You all know me, you know I wouldn't betray you."

"After all we've been through, Alice?" Violet said, emotion tearing at the edges of her voice. "Why?"

"Violet," Alice said, crossing the room to take the captain's hands in her own. "Please listen to me."

Captain Violet yanked her hands away and hid her face behind her palms. "Take her to the brig until we figure out what the hell is going on."

"Violet!" Alice shouted, grabbing at the hem of the captain's jacket. "Just *listen*!"

"Whoever you were talking to, it doesn't matter, because there are no approved contacts, not anymore. You put us all at risk, and look what happened! People are dead, Alice. Larkin and Evie barely made it off that ship. We were almost fired on with Coalition heat guns that would have destroyed the Cricket and left all of us to die."

"Violet, I'm sorry, I was—"

"It doesn't matter. Ned, take her down to the brig."

As Ned reached for Alice's arm, she pulled it away. "I know where it is," she said, stomping off the bridge and down the steps towards the brig.

"Captain, should I-" Kady started.

"I don't care," Captain Violet said, and turned to face the window. "Just do your jobs."

"Boss..." Ned said quietly. "Maybe there's something else going on here? After all, Barnaby—"

"Barnaby was banned from this ship when we caught him selling parts and medications that were meant for rebel settlements, I'm sure you remember," the captain said sharply, her mood clearly off balance from what had just happened. "Not even you knew what he was up to, and he was sleeping in your bed. If she was relaying information to him, who knows what he was doing with it. It's the best answer we have right now as to why they'd been a step ahead of us for weeks. We haven't even been able to get back to Bradach because there's been a goddamn armored Coalition vessel right in the middle of every viable flightpath." The captain sighed heavily, and Larkin could almost feel the deep pain it was laced with.

Larkin didn't know whether to stay or go, but she did know that she needed to keep her big mouth shut. Nothing she said now would help the situation, and would only serve to inflame already dangerously overheated tempers. If she had the powers of teleportation, she would find herself back in her room, alone, away from all the chaos of human interaction. Though if she did have powers as such, she'd have teleported herself off the ship before they ever made it to the C.S. Blackwall to begin with.

"I'll be in my quarters," the captain announced, her voice gravelly and thick with emotion, before turning and marching off the bridge. Hyun followed a moment later, shaking her head and waving to the others over her shoulder.

Kady sighed and snapped the console's case back together. "Ned, I'm leaving this accessible while I go grab some coffee. It's going to take a few hours to find out who was receiving that data."

"Yeah, yeah, don't worry," Ned mumbled, waving her off.

When she was gone, Larkin cleared her throat as though to remind him she was still there. "So, who was Barnaby?"

Ned looked up from his screen and blinked at her. "It's a long story."

"What happened? Betrayal? Sabotage?"

"Of sorts," he grunted.

"And you and he were...?"

"Don't you have somewhere else to be?" he snapped. "You know what, never mind. I have some charts I need to look over, try to find some other way back to Bradach." He squinted over his thick black rimmed glasses. "You'll do well to mind your business, Larkin." He shuffled off his chair and leaned on his cane, looking more pained than usual with his heavy, lumbering gait.

Just like that, Larkin was left alone on the bridge of the ship with an accessible console ripe for the taking. If she wanted to tap into the communications, she could contact the nearest Coalition base and inform them of the Cricket's position, possibly in exchange for clemency for her and maybe Evie, too. She crossed the bridge and rested her palms on the console, feeling the slight heat radiate into her skin. Her index finger hovered over the button that would allow her to direct a text based message to whoever was within receiving range, and prepared what she would say.

"Dear Coalition," she rehearsed in a barely audible whisper, "I have valuable intel on the location of the Cricket and its crew in exchange for two expunged records." This would work, this crew had been so desperately sought after the situation with the crew of a trading vessel as well as dozens of soldiers being stranded on a derelict rebel base for a week, that the Coalition would jump at the chance. The bridge was empty, not a single soul around. She depressed the button, which started the recording, but hesitated. *Why was she hesitating?*

"Larkin, what are you *doing*?" Evie demanded, after appearing in the doorway like a goddamned ghost. "Cancel message," Evie said loudly, and the recording vanished.

"Eves, are you kidding me? This could be our ticket out of here!"

"Are you a total *fucking* grapefruit? That's a terrible idea."

Larkin stifled a laugh at Evie's outburst. "It could work."

"And what about everyone on this ship? You just want to condemn them to the same torture from freaks like Allemande that I had to endure?"

Larkin shrugged, but felt the tiniest seed of guilt plant itself deep in her chest. Well, it was either guilt, or internal bleeding, and she knew which one she preferred; death was infinitely more easily accepted than blame. "I thought you wanted to get off this boat," she said nonchalantly.

"Not at that cost," Evie said, reaching out and moving Larkin's hand away from the console. "I think this crew has had enough misery and upheaval for one day, don't you think?"

"What about us, Eves? When will we get what they promised us?"

"I heard Ned say he was working on charting an alternate course back to Bradach, did he not?"

"That's no guarantee, and besides, this crew obviously has major problems of their own. Moles, leaked information? It's a mess. There's no telling when they'll make it back to Bradach if we wait for them to get it together."

Evie dropped her arms to the side and shook her head sadly. "Yeah, Alice, who'd have thought? I mean, I know she's ex-Coalition, but..."

"Just goes to show you, you can never trust those assholes, even if you think they're reformed. Too much crap embedded into their skulls to think clearly on a long term basis." Larkin moved away from the console, worried the noise of their casual conversation would draw Kady and Ned back to the bridge, where they'd see her fiddling with the console. That open line might be their only opportunity to get the hell off this ship before the Coalition found them, or they all imploded from their messy interpersonal bullshit. Other people were why Larkin had always preferred to work alone.

"Come on, Hyun said you need to eat to keep your strength up, and I heard that Ned left some couscous in the kitchen." Evie tugged gently on Larkin's jacket and wiggled her blond eyebrows. "Let's go, I'm hungry."

It was too late, now. Kady would be back any minute, and if they found her sending a message to the Coalition, they were more likely to throw her out an airlock than to grant her the mercy of the brig. "Yeah, yeah, alright."

* * *

Evie piled couscous high on their plates, and added some roasted peppers on the side while Larkin watched, leaning heavily on her crutches. She'd only been out of bed a few times, and was probably exhausted already, no doubt, especially since she was still confined to the medical bay where Hyun and

Jasper could keep an eye on her recovery. Replacing part of a rib cage was no easy feat, and Evie had heard them whispering their amazement that Larkin had survived at all.

"How's this, good?" Evie asked, gesturing at one of the plates.

Larkin nodded in approval and cocked her head towards the empty table in the corner. "Let's sit there."

She followed as Larkin ambled slowly across the room, her breathing still a bit ragged. "Just take it easy," Evie said gently, watching Larkin struggle.

"I'm fine."

"I know you're fine, I just don't want you to overdo it. Who knows what's in store for us, and I need you fighting fit. Who else is going to save me if you don't?"

Larkin snorted. "You're hardly a damsel in distress, Eves. If I recall correctly, it was my half dead corpse you dragged back onto this godsforsaken ship."

"Yeah, well, who knows if I could do that again," Evie said, sliding into one of the many hodge podge chairs around the small circular table. "It was like I was someone else, watching me do all those things."

"Adrenaline." Larkin eased herself down onto a padded chair and leaned her crutches against the wall. "Adrenaline can make you do things you never thought you could. Afterward, you're not even sure it was you who did all of that."

"I guess," Evie conceded, shoving a fork of food into her mouth, where the intense spicy flavors warmed her from the inside out. "This is good, have some."

"Alright, alright," Larkin said teasingly, poking at her food. "I know I should be hungry, but I just have no appetite since I got turned into a cyborg."

"Hyun said that was normal, and that you should still try to—"

"I know what Hyun said," Larkin interrupted with a slight edge to her tone. "Just let me do things at my own pace."

Evie closed her mouth and looked down at her food, unsure what to talk about if Larkin's recovery was off the table as dinner conversation. It's all she'd thought about since the explosion, pouring all her mental energy into doing whatever she could to aid in Larkin's recovery, from reading to her as she dozed in her medicated coma to taking readings from the various machines she'd been hooked into. It's not as though she had anything else to be doing on the ship anyway, no real way to contribute or help with the issues in getting back to Bradach. At least when Larkin was sick, she needed Evie. Now that she was recovering, Evie felt her pulling away to retreat back into her cave of solitude, where no one else was allowed in.

"So, what do you do for fun?" Evie asked finally. She was realizing that she didn't actually know much about Larkin at all, other than what they'd gone through together. For all she knew, Larkin was nothing more than the cold-blooded killer she'd made herself out to be.

Before Larkin could answer, a young woman with a bright braid of green hair staggered into the mess hall, a half empty bottle of what looked like whiskey in her hand. She was sobbing loudly and muttering something unintelligible, and clearly didn't see the two of them sitting at their table in the corner.

"Who the hell is that?" Larkin asked, looking mildly horrified at the girl's overt display of emotion.

"It must be Ivy, she's Alice's apprentice," Evie whispered.

"Oh, shit."

It was obvious the lanky girl, wearing bleached denim dungarees, was incredibly drunk, and perhaps for the first time by the looks of it. If someone didn't step in, she'd end up out cold on a bathroom floor. "Hey," Evie said gently, her years of comforting heartbroken drunks at the Purple Pig rising to the surface, "you okay?" It was obvious she wasn't okay, but it was as good an opener as anything else.

"No!" the girl shouted, and collapsed into a squashy chair near the doorway, her head in her hands and the whiskey dangerously close to spilling out all over the floor.

"Here let me help," Evie said, exchanging a glance with Larkin before moving in to rescue the perilous bottle. "Can I get you some water? Some food?"

"Water?" the girl sniffled, peeking out at Evie from behind her grease stained fingers.

"Absolutely," Evie said with a reassuring smile, setting the bottle of whiskey on a nearby table. She filled a mug with water from the tap and handed it to the girl, and crouched down in front of the chair. "Do you want to talk about it? You're Ivy, right?"

"I'm Ivy," the girl said, her voice thick with emotion and snot. She drained the mug of water, and Evie took it from her to refill it. She'd need a lot of water after that much swill, or she'd end up in the med bay hooked up to an IV, and would probably have to endure a stern lecture from Hyun.

"Alice," Ivy sobbed, her green eyes filling up with tears again. "They put Alice in the brig, they said she was sending information to the Coalition, but that doesn't make any sense, she'd never do that, she'd never betray us, not ever, and she'd never keep something like this from me, and especially not Violet, and-"

"Slow down a minute," Evie soothed, gesturing for Ivy to drink more water from the mug. "Just breathe, okay? It's going to be alright."

Ivy buried her face again, her fingers pulling at the wavy tendrils of green hair that escaped from under a grey tweed cap. "I'm just an apprentice," she said in a shaky voice. "I've learned loads from Alice since she took me on as an apprentice, but I can't do this by myself. There's tons I don't know! What if something happens and I can't fix it, and everyone is depending on me, and I let them down? What if Captain Violet hires a new lead mechanic and they don't like me, and won't train me, and then she has to get rid of me or give me some other job I'm not good at?"

"Well, first things first," Evie said, brushing the girl's hair back from her forehead, "the ship is in good condition, and from what I hear you're a very quick study with mechanical engineering. I for one feel very safe with you in the boiler room."

"You do?" the girl sniffled, looking up at Evie.

"I do. And second, Captain Violet seems like a... very fair person, and I don't think she'd hire a new lead mechanic that wasn't willing to let you continue your apprenticeship."

"But what about Alice?"

"That I can't answer, I'm afraid. You must be so upset, poor thing. Who told you?"

"Kady did. She's nice and all but I already miss Alice."

"I bet you do," Evie said softly. "Listen, how about I slap a plate together for you, how does that sound?"

Ivy nodded and took another sip of water. "Yes, please."

"Toast okay? With some..." Evie rifled in the kitchen, opening cupboards and poking through piles of produce. "With some tomatoes and eggs, maybe?"

Ivy nodded again. "You're Evie, aren't you?"

"Yes."

"I heard you saved Larkin. I heard you took down a dozen soldiers on your own."

Evie caught Larkin's bemused expression from across the room, and stifled a laugh. "That sounds a little embellished, if I'm honest with you. I just did my best, which is all any of us can do. Who did you hear that from?"

"Alice told me."

Of course, it was just Evie's luck that one of her only advocates on the ship had turned out to be a damn spy for the Coalition. She sighed heavily and tossed some chopped tomatoes and a few eggs into a hot pan, the flames licking at the sides. All she could think to say was, "I see."

"She said that you could help us get into the armory, both of you," Ivy said, nodding at Larkin, still silent in the corner. "She said that once we got back to Bradach, we'd have some shore leave, too." She began to cry again, her red rimmed eyes puffy now.

"I like Bradach," Evie said cautiously, "don't you?"

"Not anymore!" she sobbed and angrily wiped away her tears. "I loved her, and now she's gone!"

Evie glanced at Larkin, who looked as confused as she felt. "... Alice?"

Ivy scrunched up her face. "No, not Alice! My girlfriend! Or I guess I should say, ex-girlfriend."

"Ah," Evie said, scraping the egg and tomato mess onto some toast. "Well, we've all been there." She handed the plate and a fork to Ivy, who eagerly took a bite.

"We have?"

"Well yeah, of course. It sucks to have your heart broken."

"She said 'It's not you, Ivy, it's me.' And that was it."

"Ouch," Larkin said from across the room.

"Yeah, ouch. She wouldn't even talk to me, wouldn't tell me what changed."

"Sometimes people change. They can grow apart, and it's no one's fault. Especially when you're young."

"If you think that's bad, you should ask Evie what her ex did," Larkin said, and Evie shot her a warning look.

"What did she do?" Ivy asked between mouthfuls of food.

"It's a long story, but she set me up to take the fall for something she did. It's why I ended up in that Coalition prison."

"Oh, gods," Ivy whispered after she swallowed the last mouthful. "That's *terrible*."

"It didn't feel good. It still doesn't." It had only been a few weeks since she was arrested on that ship, with Holly selling her out, but it felt like a lifetime ago, even though the pain was still sharp and present. She plastered a smile across her face and said, "All done?"

"Yes, thank you so much, Evie. I'm sorry I'm such a mess."

It was obvious that the food and water had sobered her up a little, but she'd likely still have a horrific hangover in the morning. "It's alright, it happens," Evie said. "Why don't you go and get a good night's sleep, and we can talk more in the morning?"

Ivy yawned and stood, stretching her arms high over her head. "That's a good idea." As she left the room, she greeted the captain, who sidled into the room looking rough, as though she'd been crying for a good long while.

"Evening, Captain," Evie said cautiously. "How long have you been standing out there?"

"Long enough." Captain Violet sat into Ivy's vacated chair heavily, and reached for the abandoned bottle of whiskey. "Thank you for that, I'm not sure I could have given her what she needed tonight." She took a long drink straight from the bottle, and wiped her mouth with the back of her hand. "Too many problems of my own."

"Yeah," Evie said, because she couldn't think of anything else to say.

"You know, you never needed to lie."

"What?"

"About being a sharpshooter. You have other skills, clearly. People skills. Research. Not everyone can be a warrior, you know."

"Okay," Evie said, not wanting to explain she'd have had no way of knowing that earlier on, and that she'd been convinced the crew would have shoved her out an airlock if they caught her in the lie. Most pirate crews wouldn't abide it.

"Don't worry, I won't stay long. Just wanted a swig of this. It's usually locked away, but Alice must have had a bottle hidden in the boiler room." She took another long drink, longer than Evie had ever seen someone drink straight whiskey. "I guess that's not the only thing she hid." The captain saved Evie from having to reply by standing up from the chair, casting a frosty glance at Larkin, and leaving the mess hall with the half empty bottle of whiskey. Her footsteps faded down the corridor, and Evie went back to her plate of couscous, now cold.

"Let me heat that up for you," Larkin said, taking the plate. "Hell knows I couldn't have done that. You're a good one, Eves."

CHAPTER EIGHTEEN

"Here, you'll need this," Captain Violet said, laying a heavy revolver with a long barrel in Larkin's outstretched hand. "And please, be careful this time, I can only imagine how the airlock ended up cracked a couple of weeks ago," she said with an unwavering, steely glare, gesturing at the spider-webbed cracks in the glass. "Given my old standard issue pistol was missing from its hiding spot, I assume you pilfered it for yourself before returning it a few days later." With an eyebrow arched, she continued, "Yes, Larkin, I noticed." The captain was hard as nails, especially considering the woman she'd shared a bed with for over a year was sitting in the brig and refusing basic rations. "Ned left an appropriate backstop in the loading bay for your use. Obviously we know now that Evie is no sharpshooter, but she should at least know how to handle herself if we get into trouble which seems unfortunately unavoidable at this point."

"Shouldn't we get two guns then? One each?"

"I would assume you have your own ways of handling yourself which don't involve firearms," Violet said icily.

"Sure."

Captain Violet raised an eyebrow. "You've proved useful to the crew so far, but you'll need to keep it together if we're going to keep you around."

Evie nodded, her hands clasped behind her back. "Yes Captain."

"Larkin, I am leaving this in your, I'm assuming, capable hands. If I had any other options I would eagerly take them, but I don't. We can't have helpless crew members wandering around on the ship, vulnerable to attack or manipulation."

"You can't be serious. I seriously doubt everyone on this ship has been combat trained," Larkin protested. "I mean, don't get me wrong I'm happy to train her, but-"

"Larkin," the captain said, her eyes squeezed shut with frustration. "Can you not just do what's asked of you, even once, without argument, or making a goddamned mess of the whole thing? Is that even within the realm of possibility for someone like you?"

"Sure," Larkin said grumpily, but closed her mouth nonetheless. The captain was probably closer to the edge of a breakdown than any of them realized, and Larkin really didn't want to be the person who pushed her over that edge. Hell only knew what kind of havoc a woman like that would wreak, given the opportunity and motive. She turned on the heel of her impeccably polished boots, and left Larkin and Evie alone outside the loading bay.

"Well, shall we?" Larkin asked with a grin, making a broad sweeping gesture towards the airlock. Evie laughed and they both squeezed through the narrow passage into the large open space of the loading bay. They took their places a few feet away from the makeshift backstop Ned had dragged out of storage for them, cobbled together out of planks of pockmarked hardwood backed with a thick layer of steel.

"Okay, so just run me through this again," Evie said eagerly, her eyes bright and sparkling with curiosity. Larkin had never in her life met someone as voracious for knowledge and information as Evie, and it was incredibly endearing.

"Okay, so this here's the barrel, and-"

"No, no, I know all that," Evie said impatiently. "I read about it in some books Alice lent me while you were recovering. Before... well, you know."

"Yeah. Okay. So anyway, the length of the barrel-"

"The length of the barrel dictates accuracy, yes, I *know* all that. Show me things I can't learn in a book."

Larkin had the sudden urge to grab Evie and kiss her right there, and shook her head violently. *Where the hell did that come from*, she thought.

"Are you alright?" Evie asked with a smirk.

"Thought I was going to sneeze," Larkin lied, and cleared her throat loudly. "Alright, so first things first, you have to get comfortable with the weight of the thing." She emptied the cylinder into her palm and pocketed the ammunition, dropping them one by one into the inside of her jacket and then thrusting the revolver into Evie's hands.

"It's heavier than it looks."

"Yeah, that's good though."

Evie nodded and turned it over in her hands. After a long moment, she asked, "What does it feel like to kill someone?"

"What?"

"You know, how does it feel to snuff out a life, to watch the light fade from their eyes?"

The truth of it was, Larkin was rarely around to see that part of it. She was always long gone by then, downing shots of rum in some dingy tavern or hitching a ride to her next job. In fact, the soldiers on the C.S. Blackwall were the first she'd been face to face with in a long time, but their darkly tinted visors meant she didn't even know what any of them had looked like. She didn't feel like it was the right moment to be divulging all of this, though, and so she shrugged and said "I dunno."

"Really? You don't get some kind of weird rush from it?"

"Don't be dark, Evie. It's a job, I get in, I do my work, I get out. I don't get all analytical about it."

"So you don't enjoy it?"

What Larkin really *didn't* enjoy was where this line of questioning was headed, and huffed out of annoyance. "Well, I don't know, Eves, how did it feel when you nearly melted the faces of those soldiers on the Blackwall?"

Evie stared at her, the gun balanced on her flat palm. "That was for survival. It's different. And I didn't kill any of them."

"That you know of," Larkin shrugged. "Anyway, my job is also for survival in a lot of ways, it's just more... meta." She cleared her throat again and hoped that Evie would leave the conversation there; instead of giving her an opening to question her again, she squared her shoulders and said, "Here, reload it," and dropped the bullets into Evie's outstretched palm.

"Did you know that gunpowder has its own oxidization? It's why guns can still fire in space."

"As long as it fires, I'm not that interested in the particulars."

Evie loaded the rounds into the cylinder easily, and snapped it shut. "Sometimes, it's the particulars that keep a person alive. Knowing the specifics, why something works the way it does."

"I'll leave the particulars to the big brains like you, Eves." Larkin smiled and held her arms out wide. "Let's see your stance, then."

"Don't laugh."

"I'm not going to laugh."

Evie grasped the revolver with both hands and straightened her arms out in front of her, her shoulders tense and high. "How's this?"

"You need to relax your shoulders," Larkin said, watching appreciatively. "But for a start, that's not bad at all."

"I am relaxed," Evie argued, her elbows locked into position.

"If that's relaxed, then I'll bet you shit diamonds," Larkin laughed.

"I told you not to laugh!"

"Right right, sorry," Larkin said, moving closer to Evie. "Just ease those shoulders down, yeah? And loosen up a little, being that rigid is only going to hurt your aim." She smirked and raised an eyebrow at Evie. "Though I'd have thought a master markswoman would have known that."

"Yeah, well, that wasn't exactly the first cover story I'd have gone for," Evie grumbled, rolling her shoulders backwards and forwards. "Why couldn't you have made me something cool, like..."

"Like an assassin?" Larkin finished for her. "I can tell you from experience, it's not all it's cracked up to be. Pretty boring, actually."

"Somehow I don't think that *boring* is why the crew infiltrated a high security prison to break you out and pressure you to join them," Evie snorted. "I think it probably has more to do with the whole 'being excellent at murdering' thing." She took a step back from the backstop and aimed with the revolver, closing one eye to look through the iron sights on the gun. "Your reputation precedes you with the whole Lionel Cabot thing, you know."

"Mm." Larkin wasn't interested in this line of questioning, not even from Evie. Lionel Cabot's death may have launched her career as a mercenary, but she'd rather he stayed buried in the past. There was no sense dredging all that up again, not even to explain herself or her motivations. "Eves, you're still looking pretty tense, there. If you don't relax those muscles, the recoil is going to knock you off balance."

"I'm trying!" Evie protested, but the more she tried to relax, the more tense she got, with her shoulders hiked up somewhere around her ears. "This is as relaxed as I'm going to get, I'm hardly going to be nonchalant when handling a weapon like this."

"Here," Larkin said, stepping up behind Evie and placing her hands on the woman's shoulders. "Feel the weight of my palms?"

"Yes."

"Just let your muscles relax into the pressure." She pressed down gently on Evie's shoulders and instantly felt her relax a little bit more. "Good, almost there." She drew her thumbs firmly down the base of Evie's neck and into the knots of tension between her shoulder blades. "So this is where you hide all that anxiety," she said quietly.

Evie didn't respond, except to lower the revolver to her side and lean back into Larkin, whose breath caught in her throat. Her heart began to pound, and she felt like she was going to be sick for just a second, before her stomach settled back where it belonged. Larkin coughed nervously and moved her thumbs in tight circles over Evie's shoulders. "How about you try the stance again, Evie."

The polished revolver sparkled in the dim light as Evie raised it again, grasping it with both hands. This time her stance looked textbook perfect, with one arm locked and the other slightly bent, her feet solid on the floor of the loading bay. Larkin released her shoulders and stepped back, willing her lungs to remember how to breathe, wondering if she was having some kind of strange side effect from the surgery. She'd have to see Hyun later, just in case. The assassin swallowed hard and nodded approvingly, even though Evie couldn't see her. "Much better."

"Yeah, that, uh, feels better," Evie mumbled. "Maybe I should try shooting now?"

"Huh? Oh. Right," Larkin said.

"I think I've got it now," Evie said, pulling the hammer back and raising her arms back to the stance she'd just perfected. "You can learn *some* things from a book, you know."

"Eyes open, Eves," Larkin said, leaning against a crate full of shiny red apples that smelled of sweet dirt and terraformed orchards thick with chemically manufactured fertilizer. "You don't want to miss your target, do you?"

Evie squeezed the trigger and the shot rang out across the loading bay, echoing noisily against the steel walls of the ship. Larkin was proud she hadn't shifted her stance or jumped back in surprise like so many beginners did. She'd seen enough baby faced armed guards to know what inexperience looked like, and it was often a gangly teenage boy firing wildly before cowering under a desk. Still, the cowering had kept them alive, at least when it was Larkin they were up against. She couldn't say the same for other assassins. "Nice job," Larkin said casually. "Where did the shot hit?"

"Top right quadrant," Evie said, the disappointment obvious in her voice.

"Alright, well, that's a good start. You hit the backstop at least, so a definite improvement on last time."

Evie turned and scowled. "That old gun was so warped I'm shocked we didn't end up shooting each other on accident."

"In any case," Larkin said with a wide smile, pushing herself back into standing upright, leaning on her crutches, "your left shoulder is still too high, it's rotating your wrist just enough to cause problems." She stepped back into position behind Evie, ignoring the persistent throb of pain pulsing from her brand new rib cage. She wrapped her hand around Evie's left shoulder and moved it into place, with her other hand on the woman's right hip so she wouldn't lose her balance and send them both tumbling to the ground; she still needed the crutches to steady herself. "Try this now," she said into Evie's ear.

Without a word of response, Evie pulled back the hammer, took a deep breath, and fired, sending the shot straight to the dead center of the target.

"Well, Ms. Anderson," Larkin said, keeping her hands in place, "you might make an excellent sharpshooter yet."

Turning in her grip, Evie turned and gave her a broad grin of achievement. "You know, if the assassin thing doesn't work out, you could always get a job in Bradach as an arms instructor. I'll even be your first verified review, you can take a photo of me next to a target riddled with holes in the middle."

Larkin considered making a snarky comment about how she'd sooner jump out of the airlock than teach fools how to handle firearms, but the words got stuck in her throat. She'd never felt like this, and couldn't put her finger on what exactly it was; she just knew that she could barely breathe, her hands were tingling where they rested on the tattered material of Evie's coveralls, and the thought of kissing her was playing in her mind like a projector she couldn't get rid of. "Eves..." she managed to say, but no words after came out. The woman was staring at her with those huge eyes that looked like a whole world was trapped there, and didn't say a word.

"I..." Larkin tried again, but words still failed her. She leaned forward and kissed Evie softly, pulling the woman's hips toward her own. The room spun around them and Larkin's mind lit up with fireworks when Evie kissed back.

Then Evie pulled away, shaking her head. "No, Larkin," she said with quiet but firm determination, "I can't do this." She turned, set the now empty revolver atop the apple crate, and hurried back through the crew airlock, leaving Larkin alone with the weapon, the same place she'd always been.

* * *

Larkin stopped to angrily brush a tear from her cheek as she wandered the halls of the Cricket, unsure what the hell had just happened. She didn't even really understand why she had kissed Evie, but watching her leave the loading bay felt like her shiny, brand new titanium ribs were collapsing in on themselves and crushing her lungs into a fine powder. The soft click of her crutches against the floor made for a punishing rhythm that pushed her further and further down dark, empty corridors with cobwebs stretched across the corners. *Even the spiders didn't want to stick around here*, she thought to herself, examining a long-abandoned web littered with clumps of sawdust and bits of shredded paper.

Her appetite had vanished as soon as Evie left the loading bay, quite a feat for someone who enjoyed her food as much as Larkin did. The scent of hot, spicy food wafting from the kitchens was a clear sign that Ned was cooking again tonight, but couldn't bring herself to loop back to the mess hall to eat. Evie might be in there, and until she knew what to say, seeing her was best avoided. Would 'I'm sorry' suffice, or would she have to give a more thorough explanation? Still, Evie had kissed her back before pulling away, and that's what was most confusing of all. Larkin felt like she was on a perpetual spiral staircase, marching forward step by step, without actually progressing to a destination.

The pendant she wore around her neck was a comforting weight in her hand as she balanced it on the tip of one finger, and then the next, feeling the soft shift of the chain through the ring that held them together. Walking was the best way to clear her head, and cursed the Cricket under her breath for being much smaller than more modern ships. It had long, winding corridors, of course, but she had already memorized those, and itched for some new surroundings.

Growing up, she took great liberties in disappearing into the woods behind their house for hours when she felt upset, and no locale had ever come close to rivaling it. Huge trees that climbed high into the sky, leafy vines that wound their way around old, broken down fences, a plethora of flora that deserved investigation, but she was young then. She was grown now, with responsibilities, and a history, and an infamous tale to go along with her name that was only half true. Maybe when they got to Bradach, she could lose herself in several pints of ale, forget the indiscretions and the bullshit with Evie.

This part of the ship was devoid of crew, and served as storage for pillaged loot that wouldn't spoil. Small utility closets stacked with boxes of broken droids and ship parts they'd probably sell for scrap at some point. One was piled high with bags of raw wool, probably stolen from one of the Coalition merchant vessels that transported goods from the established terraformed settlements to the struggling ones without resources, where people worked twelve and sixteen hour shifts just to survive, and got paid nothing in return. Muffled voices from the next corridor, where the brig was located, crept down the hall and stopped Larkin in her tracks. She stopped, keen to silence the soft clicks of her crutches. She leaned them gently against a wall and crept towards the corner.

"Ned tells me you're still refusing rations," Captain Violet said coolly.

"I wanted to see you," Alice said, and the exhaustion was apparent in her voice. "If you would just listen to me, I— "

"What exactly is there to listen to? You were caught sending encrypted information off ship to Coalition contacts, Alice. You forced my hand. We agreed that when it comes to these matters you'd be treated the same as any other officer on the ship." Captain Violet rubbed her temple, her other hand on her hip. "You're lucky this is my ship, on anyone else's the punishment would be getting shoved out a goddamned airlock."

"Well this isn't anyone else's ship, it's yours. And as captain, you can make whatever decision you see fit regarding these matters."

"Alice. Every officer on the ship was standing there when Kady said that, as well as our resident assassin who does everything in her power to irritate me into madness. You know I couldn't have let it slide, especially when we were leaving the console open to see if she'd sell us out."

"You could have warned me," Alice hissed.

"Had I known you were contacting Barnaby every day, I would have!"

"It wasn't just Barnaby." Alice sighed and scraped her boot against the dusty, unused cell floor. "I was getting information from Jhanvi about how to circumvent the data protections when we hit the armory."

"Jhanvi?" Violet asked. "I thought we agreed we couldn't trust her as a source!"

"Yeah, well, the data protections are stronger than they were a year ago. They've beefed everything up since Ivy erased all that information from their systems. They don't want to end up embarrassed again, and certainly not by us."

"What about the Blackwall?"

"I didn't tell either of them about the Blackwall, Violet. I wouldn't. You should know that. I'd never gamble with the crew's lives like that." Alice paused and shuffled in her cell. "And you should know that I'd never put *you* in danger like that, either."

Captain Violet sighed, and Larkin peeked around the corner to see the captain reaching her fingers through the wide bars of the cell. "You don't have to stay in there, you know."

"Oh, no, we agreed, I get the same treatment as anyone else, remember? I guess I'll just have to stay in here until you decide I'm innocent."

"Well, you're not that innocent," the captain said with a husky laugh. "You did communicate with two people with ties to the Coalition without telling me, or any of the other officers for that matter. And for that, I am still very much angry."

"Yes, well, had I known you were going to spring a trap for her, I might have made sure to at least inform Kady what I was up to, so she could keep quiet about it. Damn, Vi, you need to keep me in the loop about these things."

"I didn't think you'd agree with me on my methods, and besides, you didn't exactly keep me apprised of what you were sneaking around with, either."

"For the record, no, I don't approve of your methods. Larkin has had multiple opportunities to sell us out, and she never has. Hell, she could have landed on the C.S. Blackwall and pleaded to the Coalition for mercy, giving up our position as leverage."

Larkin's jaw dropped open, and she felt anger and righteous indignation rising in her throat. They'd left the console open to lure her into using it, to prove she was just as shitty as Violet and Kady thought she was, and they were right. The only reason she hadn't was because Evie had stopped her. She was also feeling irritated with herself for not thinking of the Blackwall idea earlier and saving herself the trouble of a rib reconstruction and a lifetime of consciously avoiding metal detectors. It was going to impede her career as an assassin, that was for sure.

"No, she didn't take the bait on the bridge the other day." Violet admitted, holding Alice's hands through the bars. "I guess you and Ned were right.

She can be trusted. It doesn't change the fact that her story doesn't add up, though. If you didn't tell Barnaby or Jhanvi about the Blackwall job, how the hell did the Coalition know we were coming? It's impossible."

The seed of guilt in Larkin's chest germinated into a sprout of regret that grew roots right into her stomach. Alice and Ned had vouched for her against the captain's gut feeling. She desperately wanted to say something, to defend her character to these strangers, but she felt paralyzed by her own silence.

"Something is getting out somewhere, that's for sure, but it's no one on this crew," Alice said.

"Come on, get out of there," Violet laughed, and tugged on the noisy sliding door, wrenching it open. "You're going to have to explain yourself to the rest of the crew." When Alice opened her mouth to protest, Violet pressed a finger to her lips.

"I'm sorry I didn't tell you about the trap. And that I sent you to the brig. But you know I have to keep a strong character in front of everyone. It wouldn't be right for them to see their captain be weak, even for her wife." She stood on the toes of her polished boots and kissed Alice slowly, biting at her bottom lip.

"You're going to have to tell the rest of the crew about that some day, you know," Alice said, stepping out of the cell and pulling Captain Violet into a tight embrace. "How else are we going to get well-wishes and gifts for our elopement?"

"Hush," Violet mumbled into Alice's chest, "We will, in time."

Alice raised the captain's face to her own and kissed her again, deeply and with hunger that Larkin could sense all the way at the other end of the corridor, and it made her stomach turn with envy and regret that her kiss with Evie hadn't ended the same way theirs was going to. Using the couple's amorous distraction, she skulked back down the hall, and carried her crutches all the way to her room, holding her ribs and wincing with every step.

CHAPTER NINETEEN

Evie stepped off the Cricket and into the terraformed sunlight, beamed down into the city from giant mirrors above the buildings. Fake or not, the warmth was welcome on her face, though her arms remained bandaged. The scabs were flaking off every night now, and the iodine burns nearly healed. Hyun said the scars would remain with her forever, but she was growing to like them. Proof she was a survivor.

She'd barely slept in the several nights after Larkin had kissed her, and instead spent the entire night at her desk in the small quarters on the ship, reading up on the technology Kady and Alice used to stealth the ship. Most of the jargon was far over her head, but it was a welcome distraction from replaying the scene in the loading bay over and over in her mind.

Evie didn't even really know how she felt about the whole thing. Gods, she hadn't even noticed that Larkin even felt that way about her. She liked Larkin, but that kiss felt dangerously distracting, the kind of thing that could unravel the entire friendship. Though if she was staying in Bradach, it wouldn't matter, anyway.

It felt odd to be back home, even though she'd spent weeks pining for it. On the Cricket her days had a satisfying rhythm with Larkin healing much quicker than Hyun and Jasper had anticipated, and Evie was enjoying helping around the ship with small jobs, and reading anything she could get her hands on that might help the crew at some point. It had been her late night research into old, abandoned flight paths that gave her the idea to suggest a different route back to Bradach, and now here they were, being given shore leave.

Captain Violet hadn't told Evie to come back, not specifically. When she gave everyone else's assignments, she looked right at her, said nothing, and continued onto the next crew member. Did that mean she was free to go, now that they knew she wasn't a sharpshooter? It seemed strange to ask, so she didn't. Bradach was home, and she supposed she would just go back to the way things had always been. There was nothing wrong with her life before, she realized that now. Home was certainly safer than anywhere else she'd been in the past several weeks, that was for sure.

Her key slid into the lock of her rented room, and she was almost surprised that it looked exactly the way it had the morning she'd left to meet Holly at the docks. Something about the haphazardly folded shirts on the rickety desk made her stomach turn, like something jumping out of time. She hadn't known when she left that it would be weeks before she returned, that when she did, she'd be covered in burn scars and have saved the life of a woman she barely knew, after spending a week in a Coalition prison being tortured by the sadistic Inspector Allemande.

She shook her head to clear her thoughts, and stripped off the over-sized jumpsuit she'd borrowed from Alice. It was so worn and tattered, she couldn't imagine she'd want it returned, but Evie placed it into the nightly wash basket anyway. If she was lucky, it would be clean and pressed before the crew left Bradach in a few days.

The buttons on her crisp white shirt felt oddly clumsy after weeks wearing jumpsuits with wide toggles, but she tucked it into a pair of well worn linen trousers anyway, and pulled a black waistcoat from the tiny wardrobe. Moths had eaten a hole under one of the arms, but Evie hoped no one would notice once she had it on. If she was going to beg Tansy for her job back, she had to look like she cared.

Walking back to the Purple Pig felt strange, like they weren't roads that belonged to her anymore, but once she pushed open the heavy swinging door into the opulently decorated tavern, she felt at home for the first time since she'd left the settlement. Gabe was behind the bar, looking flustered and run ragged trying to keep up with the constant stream of patrons; Evie knew it would only get busier as night approached and people wandered in looking for a nightcap or someone to spend the evening with.

"Holy shit. Evie." Gabe nearly dropped the brown bottle of rum in his hand as he vaulted over the bar to wrap her in a hug. "We never thought we'd see you again! The broadcasts called you all kinds of things. Tansy was ready to skin you alive when you didn't show up for work, before we knew." He looked at the bandages on her arms and grimaced. "Though it looks like someone else got to you first."

"It's a long story," Evie said, sliding onto a barstool and running her fingers through her short, unruly hair. "Is Tansy here?"

Gabe shook his head. "No, and I don't know when she'll be back, either. She's barely been here the past few weeks since you left, I've been trying to keep everything together and train the new barkeep, and I've gotta be honest with you Evie, this is hard work."

Evie snorted. "Yeah, I'll bet it's the first bit of hard work you've ever been subjected to without me here to clean up your messes."

"After the past few weeks, I'd say we're even on that," Gabe sniped. He cracked a smile and set a pint of dark red ale in front of Evie, where it teetered perilously on top of an uneven coaster. "After the first couple days you were gone, Tansy got real worried. She called up to your landlady, who hadn't seen you either, and then she was contacting every captain she knows, asking if anyone had heard of you. No one had."

"Yeah," Evie nodded. "Like I said, it's a long story."

"So what are you doing back? Are you back for good then?"

Evie shrugged. "I don't know, actually. I was going to ask Tansy for my job back, but it sounds like it's already been given away. I don't really know what to do now, everything seems so different, yet somehow the same."

"She might be back late tonight, or tomorrow maybe," Gabe shrugged. "She's barely in her office anymore, and when she is she's always making calls and responding to letters that come in with the post. Who knows what she's up to."

"I guess I'll just hang around here tonight, then, if that's alright?"

"Of course it's alright," he said, ruffling her hair with a grin. "Could you just watch the bar for ten minutes? I still need to show the new guy how to log trades, and if I don't get some food soon, I might start gnawing on some patrons."

"Of course," Evie said, laughing and rolling her eyes. "I'm not back more than five minutes and you're already running for the hills."

With an apologetic wave, he backed into the kitchen area, untying his apron as he went. He called to the new hire, and Evie took a deep drink of her ale. It was smooth and rich, just how she liked them, and slightly chilled. Gabe may be a pain in the ass, but he always remembered what people liked to drink, and Evie admired that about him. She was surprised that he'd stuck around to do the majority of the work after she left, given his usual proclivity for hangovers and calling off work, but some people work better under pressure, and maybe Gabe was one of them. In any case, she was happy to see at least one familiar face.

"Oh my gods, EVIE?"

Evie swung the barstool around, and her jaw dropped. Make that two familiar faces, though this one was significantly less welcome. There was Holly, dressed to the nines in a stunning black dress, cinched at the waist with a silver silk corset that accentuated every perfect curve. Evie nearly choked on her ale, but just barely managed to keep her cool with an arched eyebrow, one forearm resting casually on the bar.

"Oh gods, Babes. I missed you so much!" Holly threw her arms around Evie's neck and pressed her breasts against her. "How did you get out?"

Evie stared at her, not sure what to make of this oddly familiar outburst from a woman who sold her out to save her own hide. "*How did I get out?*" she repeated. "Do you have any idea what's happened to me over the past few weeks, or even care?"

"Of course I care! I tried finding you, I tried everything, but no one could find you!" Holly began to cry, and Evie resented how much it made her soften towards her. "I'm so sorry for what I did, I know you'll never forgive me, I had no idea they'd send you to that prison and try to pin all those other horrible things on you."

"How did you know about that?"

"Babes, your face was all over the public transmissions. They called you a terrorist, an enemy of the Coalition." Holly pulled her into another embrace, this one tighter and more fervent, sobbing, "I couldn't believe what I'd done to you, I thought I'd sentenced you to death!"

"You did," Evie said, pulling away. "You let me take the fall for all those things you did."

"All those— Babes, you don't think I did *everything* they tried to blame you for, do you?"

"How should I know? It's not as though you'd be honest with me about anything from the moment we met. I was what, just some stupid, silly lovelorn girl to take the fall for you?"

"No, of course not, I—"

"Then what?" Evie demanded. "You left me on that... on that *fucking ship*, and made me take the blame for you! You let me rot in a goddamn Coalition prison while some sadistic asshole took slices out of me until I confessed to things I could never have done."

Holly traced her fingers lightly over the bandages on Evie's arm, and she shivered involuntarily. "Oh, Evie. I could never make it up to you, I could never do anything that would undo the hurt I've caused you." She leaned in, and Evie could smell the expensive perfume she had dabbed on her neck. "I am deeply, incredibly sorry for what I did." A single, glistening tear trailed down her perfect cheekbones, and Evie found herself resenting that Holly was flawlessly beautiful even when crying. She got down on her knees and buried her face in Evie's lap. "Tell me anything I can do to make you forgive me, and I'll do it. I'll throw myself under a tram, or give you every last credit I have, or vow to be your servant forever."

Evie raised an eyebrow at that last suggestion, but said nothing.

"Is that what you want? For me to be your servant?" Holly said, rising to her feet and wrapping her arms around Evie again. "You know I'd do anything for you, anything to undo this pain." She leaned in, her pout lips soft and inviting. "I'd even take you on another pleasure cruise, with a stealth vessel this time," she said, her voice low and husky. Holly kissed Evie and leaned into her with a delicate sigh.

Evie rested her palms on Holly's waist, and felt the steel boning of the corset push back. She let Holly kiss her again, deep enough to feel her tongue against her own, and lost herself for just a moment. When Holly released the kiss, Evie whispered, "Can I ask you a question?"

"Mm?"

"Do you think I'm a fucking idiot?"

* * *

Larkin almost couldn't believe what she was seeing, but it was right there in front of her, gripping her stomach in a clenched iron fist. Evie with her hands on Holly's waist, deep in a kiss. She felt like she was going to be sick, and wrapped her arms tightly around her middle. So this is why Evie left the airlock, she had plans to meet up with her scheming ex-girlfriend and take her back, probably just so the asshole could set her up again. Part of her wanted to burst through the door of the tavern and demand an explanation, but the other part of her wanted to curl up into a ball and wait for this all to pass, and leave her the same disconnected assassin she'd always been.

Women, Larkin thought darkly, turning away from the window of the Purple Pig. This was why she never got attached, why she always kept her distance from the women she'd been with before, in dark dingy taverns across the Near Systems, or a quick fuck in the middle of a cold, black night on a settlement far away from here. None of those times had left a lasting impression. Yet here she was, brought nearly to her knees by a quirky barkeep with an insatiable hunger for learning, and there was nothing she could do about it.

She'd seen Holly before, the first time she'd ever met Evie right there in that tavern, sitting on that exact barstool. She was the kind of woman that men started wars for, the kind of woman you'd cut your own kidney out for, before you served it to her on a silver platter, garnished with fresh herbs. Holly was the picture of perfection, curves that hypnotized anyone who looked at her, and it wasn't hard to understand why Evie would take her back, even after everything she'd done. Women like Holly always got what they wanted, and never paid the price for their sins, skating through life on impeccably good looks and dangerous charm.

The mirrors were shifting the light away from the city, a manufactured darkness that made Bradach feel like she was back home. It was common in terraformed settlements, of course, but the makeshift cobblestone roads and lack of steamcars made the city feel like it was trapped in time, a moment long ago when street lamps like these were common in cities on Gamma-3. Larkin stared up at one of the lights and watched as it grew brighter in the absence of sun, quickly becoming the brightest source of light on the street, along with the other identical lamps. She had to get away from the tavern, back to something that felt predictable and familiar.

Each step along the uneven road was painful and uncomfortable with her crutches, but she made her way back to the Bronze Bell pub in search of a stiff drink and some unrepentant scumbags she could find some work with. Larkin had no doubt that no captains in Bradach would take her on knowing she had a debt to repay to the crew of the Cricket, but what they didn't know wouldn't hurt them, and she wasn't interested in being Captain Violet's errand girl. Sure, they'd busted her out of prison, but she hadn't asked them to, and she had no intention of participating in their harebrained scheme to steal tech from the Armory. Even she had limits, and one of her limits was not accepting work that would lead to her inevitable demise. Hell, she'd already almost died on the C.S. Blackwall, and that had been enough excitement to last a lifetime. There was a reason she preferred poison: she was rarely around when the shit hit the fan.

She hid her crutches behind a dumpster behind the pub, knowing no one would hire an assassin who was barely healed from experimental rib replacement surgery. Walking without them was painful, but she'd had a lifetime of practice at hiding that. With a purposeful scowl on her face, she heaved open the door and ducked inside the dimly lit room, crawling with scumbags. *Excellent*, she thought to herself, motioning for the barkeep to set her up with a flight of rum. If luck was on her side, she'd have a new mark by the time the alcohol hit her bloodstream, which wouldn't be long on her empty stomach. The amber liquid sparkled as the bartender poured it into the small glasses.

"YOU!"

Larkin turned just in time to receive a perfectly placed right hook right to the jaw so powerful it knocked her off her barstool. Her head swam and she blinked furiously, willing her vision to clear. It was Gold Earrings, one of the pirates who had hired her to take out that security manager, Robert. "What the hell?" Larkin demanded, trying to ignore the searing pain in her ribs as she stood up.

"You never followed through on our deal!" Gold Earrings shouted, and drew her arm back to deliver another punch.

"I fucking did!" Larkin said, ducking under the punch and tossing back another shot of rum. Whatever happened next, she was going to need it. "He's dead as a sewer rat in a flood!"

"You never liaised with us, how were we supposed to know? Now that site is fucking swarmed with goddamned security droids and we'll never get in there to strip it out! Do you have any idea how much you've cost us?"

"Listen, asshole," Larkin said quietly, willing the bartender to intervene before she got the shit beat out of her, "I held up my end of the bargain. It's not my problem that you were too chickenshit to strip that site before the Coalition swooped in."

"We want our money back," said the other one with the Crystal Beard.

"I don't owe you shit," Larkin spat, irritatingly aware of her empty credit account. She couldn't pay them back even if she wanted to. "I suggest you back the hell up before you really make me angry." She tasted blood in her mouth and knew the punch had split her lip.

"Give us," Crystal Beard said, pulling a switchblade from his pocket, "our money back, or we take it out of your flesh."

Larkin rolled her eyes. "Really, a knife? That's all you've got? Buddy, let me tell you, two assholes with a knife have never managed to stop me." She was bluffing now, hoping she could scare them off before they realized she was definitely not in good shape for a tavern brawl. "In fact," she added, raising her voice above the din of the room, "I bet anyone in here a thousand credits that I kick your ass before you land even one hit on me." She smirked and raised an eyebrow. "You've got a mean right hook, Earrings, but you caught me off guard."

Despite her announcement, no one in the Bronze Bell looked particularly keen to place a bet on a fight. A few watched with passing curiosity, while the rest ignored her outright. "After all," she said loudly, "I'm the one who killed Lionel Cabot." She really didn't like pulling that card, but sometimes, like when you're recovering from a partial rib replacement, it was necessary. A hush fell over the pub and all eyes were on her, a feeling she despised. One usual benefit to being an assassin was the relative lack of attention.

"You couldn't have been the one killed 'im," said a burly bald-headed man in the corner. "You'd have been just a kid."

Larkin stared the man straight in the eye and winked. "Yup." She turned back to Earrings and Beard and shrugged her shoulders. "I don't know, friends, are we doing this or not? Because I've got plans tonight and they don't involve putting you into a med bay." She cracked her knuckles convincingly and raised an eyebrow. "Whaddaya say?"

"I've got a sack of raw diamonds says she'll get her ass beat," said Baldy, his pallid skin weirdly translucent in the dim lighting.

Shit, thought Larkin, *this wasn't how that bluff was supposed to go.*

"I'll bet a round she's out in two hits," said a dark skinned woman in the corner, her waist length braids swinging as she turned her head towards the bald man. "I mean, look at her, one punch to the jaw and she's wobbly."

The woman wasn't wrong, Larkin was unsteady on her feet - but it was the sharp throbs of pain pulsing from her ribs that was distracting her, not the split lip or the sore jaw. Truth be told, she was lucky that right hook hadn't knocked out any teeth. The patrons of the Bronze Bell were beginning to murmur hungrily, and Larkin knew she was screwed. She probably would be out in two hits, and she sure as hell wouldn't be able to take on the both of them. "Why did I have to come to this fucking pub," she grumbled under her breath, clenching her hands into fists at her side. If she didn't end up back in the med bay, or worse, dead, it would be a goddamned miracle.

Earrings smirked and wound her elbow back to throw another punch, and Larkin braced for the inevitable impact.

"What in the hell is going on in here?" bellowed an irritatingly familiar voice, and Larkin opened an eye to see Captain Violet, Alice, and Ned in the doorway. Maybe not an improvement, so much as a further detriment to her evening.

"I'm sorry, have the rules on Bradach changed since I was last here?" Violet demanded, staring so fiercely at the bartender that he wilted under her glare. "Because as far as I know, brawls are forbidden in all public spaces on pain of being indeterminately ejected, no? Furthermore, establishments are bound to eject those who brandish weapons?"

With a reluctant nod, the barkeep gestured for Earrings to exit the tavern. "Out the way you came, friend." Earrings and Crystal Beard huffed and spluttered with indignation, but by now, no one was interested. The other patrons grumbled and turned their attentions back to their tables, happy to abandon the allure of an illicit fight between two stupid brawlers and a frail looking mercenary. There had been better match ups in the old days, anyway. The door slammed with the exit of her harassers, and Larkin heaved a sigh of relief. Saved by the Cricket crew, again, much to her chagrin

Captain Violet turned her steely glare back to Larkin, and narrowed her eyes. "And what in all the gods' names are you doing here?"

"Just having a drink," Larkin replied feebly, feeling blood from her lip drip down her chin.

"Is it possible for you to ever stay out of trouble?"

"Apparently not."

Captain Violet sighed heavily and sat down at the bar. "And what do you think would have happened, if we hadn't happened to wander through the door at that precise moment, do you think?"

Larkin shrugged petulantly and resented how every time the captain spoke to her, it felt like she was being scolded by a school teacher. "I'd have gotten my ass beat. Wouldn't be the first time I've had to fight for myself, and it won't be the last."

Alice exchanged a look with the captain and sat down on the other side of Larkin, and she was surprised to see the usually grubby, grease covered mechanic in sleek, tailored clothes with her long silver hair hanging loose to her waist. "So, what, you were trying to find yourself a job here? Because that's the only reason I can think of that you'd be in a place like this your first night on shore leave."

"You're here the first night of shore leave," Larkin shot back, and downed another gulp of the cheap, grainy rum.

"We have business with a former colleague to attend to," Captain Violet said sharply. "And unfortunately, this is his chosen venue. I'd rather be at the Pig, personally, but given his reputation, he's no longer able to frequent more civilized establishments."

A well dressed man in an expensive looking top hat and brocade waistcoat swung through the doors of the pub, his boots shiny, as if he'd never done a day's hard work in his life. "Ned, my darling," he said, holding his arms out to wrap the huge man in an embrace, "you look fantastic, as always."

Ned held his arms stiffly at his sides, and pulled away from the man after a short moment. "Barnaby," he mumbled.

So this was the infamous Barnaby that she had overheard them talking about, the one who was no longer allowed on the Cricket after he tried to sell some supplies out from under them. It took some guts to do that to someone like Captain Violet, and Larkin was almost surprised that he was still able to walk around, and that his frozen corpse wasn't floating through dark space somewhere.

"Al," he said, smiling at Alice, "how have you been?"

"Oh you know," she replied in a non-committal tone. "Same old."

"Alright, can we cut the crap, Barnaby? Tell us what you know," Captain Violet said sharply. "And make it quick, I don't have all night."

"There's no need for hostility, Violet," Barnaby said dismissively, and the captain bristled. "It's not like *I've* been the one feeding the Coalition information." He turned and raised an eyebrow at Larkin. "I suppose this is your new toy, the assassin, is she?"

"Barnaby," Alice said, warning him, "just tell us why we're here."

"Well, I heard through the grapevine that you've been very busy bees indeed. Something about a high security prison break?"

"Something like that," Captain Violet confirmed.

"Your little stunt caused a lot of problems for the Coalition, so I'm told. Releasing all those prisoners and unlocking the weapons closet was a masterful bit of subterfuge, Captain, and it's why they still haven't regained control of that base. From what I understand, those poor Coalition grunts barely made it out before all hell broke loose."

Captain Violet sat up straighter, clearly interested. "Really? We've not heard anything on the public broadcasts."

"Don't be naive, my dove, they certainly wouldn't announce they've lost control of one of the most locked down prisons in the Near Systems. Although, my sources seem to be hinting that they didn't expect an attack quite so vigorous."

"What does that mean? Were they expecting us in any capacity?" Alice pressed.

Barnaby shrugged. "Who can say? I only report what I hear, and what I've heard is that they weren't prepared for an attack quite like that. In fact, others who have attempted to break out their fellow crew members and rebels are fascinated with how you achieved it in the first place. Though I should warn you, Violet, I've seen your old friend *Captain* Josie strolling around down by the docks. Seems she's one of the lucky few who managed to escape."

"Fantastic," Captain Violet muttered, rubbing her temples. "What else?"

"I'm not the only one who heard about that, so I'd keep my wits about me in places like these, if you know what I'm saying." He turned back to Larkin and motioned for the barkeep to refill her rum. "And you, so I've heard, are a very interesting addition to the crew."

The captain shot Alice a look, who withered slightly under her glare. "I don't suppose your source on that was our very own lead mechanic?" Violet said through gritted teeth.

"Now now, Captain, Al and I go way back. Of course she's going to share minor information about crew assignments with her oldest friend."

Alice cleared her throat. "Barns, is there anything else?"

"Yes, actually," he said, leaning on the bar in a nonchalant manner. "It seems as though the Coalition is planning something." He handed over a scrap of paper with some numbers and symbols all jumbled up. "It's coded, though. Can't say for sure what it is."

"Where did you get this?" Alice asked.

"I have my sources, Al, you know that. According to them, whatever it is, it doesn't bode well for your friends in the settlements."

Captain Violet's eyes widened with horror, and she reached for Alice's hand. "Shit," she said quietly. "We have to warn the rebel bases. It could be a full-scale attack."

CHAPTER TWENTY

The streets were dark now, and a ring of yellow light surrounded each lamp. Holly leaned against Evie and hiccuped, a side effect of all the bootleg whiskey she'd had in the Purple Pig. She stumbled over her own feet, clad in knee length crushed velvet boots that matched the bodice of her dress, but Evie caught her before she fell. Despite everything, she felt like she should at least make sure Holly got home safely.

"I can't believe you thought I never loved you," Holly mumbled, picking at a snag in the fabric of her skirts. "I can't believe you believed that bitch Inspector Allemande when she said I set you up." She gazed into Evie's eyes and caressed her cheek tenderly. "I told you, it was a total coincidence, and I can never repay you for what you've done for me."

"Mm," Evie mumbled, still unconvinced of Holly's innocence, though softened enough that she'd agreed to walk her home when the tavern closed up. Gabe had rolled his eyes when he saw them leave together, but he didn't say anything other than for them to have a pleasant evening. Larkin would probably have some choice words to say if she saw them together, but Evie quickly pushed the thought out of her mind. Things were complicated enough without adding her into the equation, that was for sure. A prick of guilt began to pierce her half-drunk haze, and it made her feel uncomfortable.

"Babes, why won't you say you forgive me?" Holly pouted, pushing out her perfectly plump bottom lip. "I said I was sorry, I even got down on my knees and begged for your forgiveness, but you've hardly said anything to me at all."

"It's a lot to process," Evie said simply. "You have to understand, I'm not the same person as I was before. Things have changed."

Holly pulled her down a tight side street lined with red buildings and verdant ivy that climbed from window to window, casting odd shadows against the brick. "I think it's amazing you escaped that prison, I was wracked with torment the whole time you were away, I could barely even get out of bed I was so distraught."

Evie decided not to question what she was doing in the Purple Pig earlier that evening then, dressed to kill and looking for the swankiest party she could talk her way into. Her stories of distress and guilt was, she suspected, almost entirely fabricated. "I told you, I wouldn't have been able to escape on my own. I got lucky, that's all."

"Oh, lucky, please," Holly scoffed, entwining her fingers with Evie's. "You're an absolute star, a complete and total wonder. I never knew I was dating someone so interesting and full of intrigue." She giggled playfully and tugged on Evie's waistcoat. "I guess you should be grateful that you got sent to prison, otherwise you'd still be the same old Evie."

Evie prickled at this. "Mm," she mumbled again, unsure of how to respond to something so ridiculous.

"This is nice, isn't it?" Holly prodded. "Walking together in the lamplight, reunited after such a painful and traumatic separation. Some poets would kill for that kind of inspiration, you know."

Evie smirked. "Well, I'll be sure to tell a poet my story if I ever meet one, but assuming things are still pretty much the same around here, poets aren't all that common in Bradach."

"Well, you might meet one on your travels, then!"

"I don't know if I'm leaving with the ship," Evie admitted, and even the sound of the admission sat heavy in her gut. "I might decide to stay here, get my old job back if Tansy will have me, focus on some research maybe, I don't know."

Holly wrinkled her nose. "You're going back to your old job at the tavern?"

"I don't know. I might."

"Don't you want to have more adventures, Babes? Have interesting stories to tell, make some better credit?"

"It's possible I've had enough adventures for a couple of lifetimes," Evie laughed, but the joke didn't seem to land with the woman next to her, who frowned.

"You should really think about getting back on that ship. Think of everything you could do!"

"Like get arrested for my girlfriend's crime and be sent back to a maximum security Coalition prison?" Evie snorted.

Holly yanked her hand away and turned to face her. "You can't keep throwing that in my face, Evie, I already said I was sorry."

"Yeah, well, I'm sure it will be a hilarious joke for us to tell at parties someday," she said, and Holly's expression softened before she turned back down the alleyway.

"Parties, I like the sound of that. Ooh, Babes, imagine all the places you could get us into, knowing Captain Violet!"

"She doesn't strike me as one for parties."

"Shame," Holly said, and tugged gently on Evie's sleeve. "Come on, my place isn't far."

It struck Evie as strange how she'd never been to Holly's suite in all the months they'd been together, she was always too busy, or setting off on another salvage job, or hobnobbing with important people at parties Evie would never be allowed into, with even her nicest clothes being moth eaten and ragged to the trained eye. "So," she said casually, "I finally get to see where you live."

"Don't be silly," Holly said, sliding a bronze key into the lock of a heavy gate that swung into a lush, private garden. "I don't always live here, you know that. Most of the time I'm away on salvage missions." A crisp white trellis lined the boundaries of the garden, covered in blue roses that wept petals gently to the soft grass below.

"Wow," Evie whispered. "It's beautiful."

Holly shrugged. "It's fine, for now. Someday I want a much nicer place than this, and definitely not in Bradach."

"What's wrong with Bradach?" Evie asked, stepping over the threshold into a wide hallway with marble floors and dimly lit lamps lining the walls.

"Oh please, Evie, Bradach is such a backwater. It's practically a developing settlement."

Evie didn't say it, but nothing about this building said *developing settlement* to her. It made the impeccably decorated Purple Pig tavern look cheap and tacky, which it definitely wasn't. Holly led her through a frosted glass door into a parlor with daybeds draped with silk scarves and fresh flowers in all of the many vases lined up on the narrow tables which stood beneath huge paintings of Holly in various states of undress.

"So, my little adventurer," Holly said, motioning for Evie to join her on one of the daybeds, "when do we get to pick up where we left off?"

"Um..."

"This seems as good a time as any, doesn't it?" Holly whispered, leaning forward to kiss Evie on the neck. "After all, I seem to remember that before we were so rudely interrupted on the cruise I so lovingly planned for us, that we were very close to taking things to the next level, shall we say."

Evie swallowed hard and felt a hot flush begin to crawl up her neck. "Holly, I—"

"If you're going to deny me forgiveness, you can't deny me this too." She began to unbutton Evie's waistcoat slowly but deliberately, with one perfectly shaped eyebrow arched. "Won't you let me make it all up to you, Babes?"

The pinprick of guilt widened and seeped inky restlessness into her mind. "Holly, I think we should wait, don't you?" It didn't feel the way it used to; that hunger was gone, smothered by the experience of the prison. "I've only just got back, and—"

"And you'll be leaving again soon, so we should make the most of this time together, don't you think?"

"Well, I might be leaving soon, but I might be staying, and I—"

"Oh, Evie, stop this foolishness," Holly said, perturbed. She sat up straight on the day bed and smoothed her skirts purposefully. "We both know that you're going to get back on that ship to build a better life for yourself. Don't be an idiot, staying here is practically a death sentence."

"A death sentence?" Evie barked a laugh and ruffled her hair casually. "Holly, you realize you're talking to someone who literally did have a death sentence, right?"

"Oh, please," Holly rolled her eyes, "you made it out just fine. Honestly Babes, you're so melodramatic sometimes."

"It didn't feel melodramatic when that Coalition inspector was carving chunks out of my arm with a fucking pen," Evie said angrily, gesturing at the bandages on her arms. "It's just a story to you, something impressive to tell people at fancy parties, but it actually happened to me. I had to live through that. Hell, I'm still living through it now!"

"Alright, just calm down," Holly said sweetly. "You know I didn't mean to offend, let's not waste this time together." She flipped open the top two silver toggles at the front of her corset and stopped, letting Evie take in the view of her cleavage. "You wouldn't want to leave this behind without a taste, would you?"

Evie hesitated, weighing the options in her mind. She reached out a hand, and then pulled it back. "I don't know," she said, before Holly pulled her into a kiss. She wanted to allow her resolve to melt away, but in that moment, all she thought of was Larkin and their kiss in the loading bay.

The frosted glass door swung open with such force that it smashed against the parlor wall. Holly sprang back from the kiss and stood up from the daybed, quickly closing the delicate silver toggles. Evie turned, and a lanky, impeccably dressed woman in a crisp tailored charcoal suit and a jet black top hat stepped over the glass.

"Who the hell is this?" she bellowed at Holly.

"She's just a friend!" Holly shouted back "And you're not supposed to be back for two more weeks!"

Evie looked from Holly, to the woman, and back again. "Who the hell is she?" she demanded.

"Who am I? I'm the sucker she roped into paying the rent on this place. I'm her wife, not that she bloody well acts like much of a wife herself."

"Well, my good lady, I think we've both been had, haven't we?" Evie said, rising from the daybed, glaring at Holly and feeling her heart harden into stone in her chest. "Here I was, ready to forgive her after all the bullshit she put me through, taking the fall for a shuttle she scrapped with *her* own two hands—"

The woman interrupted her with a loud guffaw. "Her? A scrapper? Hardly. More like she hired some cronies to do her dirty work, because that's what you do, darling, isn't it?"

Holly was silent like a petulant child, her jaw pointed in disagreement.

"I don't know who you are," she said, waving her hands around, "but she's no scrapper. She's the mastermind there, hiring a crew to scrap a ship so she can organize the trade, scrap for credits, and then she never pays the fucking crew. Oh, sure, she wears the coveralls, to make them feel like she's one of the team, but once they start looking for her, she runs back here to Bradach, to hide in the safety of this fucking house."

Evie stared dead ahead, not wanting to make eye contact with either of them. This entire thing was a complete and total disaster, and she wanted nothing more than to go back to the Cricket and forget any of it ever happened. Awkward didn't even begin to cover the situation.

"Why do you think I'm back so early then, eh?" she asked Holly, who remained silent. "Some of that crew you stiffed figured out you're my wife, and attacked my ship. We lost everything Holly, and I come home to this?"

"You lost *everything*?" Holly screeched. "How could you let that happen?"

Evie burst out laughing at how clear it all was now. "I'm out of here," she said, throwing up her hands in disgust. "Best of luck with her, friend, because she's a goddamn nightmare." She turned on her heel and stepped over the shards of glass from the door, leaving her waistcoat partially unbuttoned, into the garden and back out to the alley, leaving the gate swinging wide open. Running her hands through her hair, she was trying to make sense of it all when she saw Larkin crossing in the square.

"Larkin, hey!" she called. It was like the fog was lifting in her mind, everything so obvious and apparent now. Holly was a closed chapter, and the finality was settling in like the finishing touches on a canvas. All Evie wanted was to tell Larkin everything, stay up all night in the kitchen laughing and joking.

The assassin turned, her black jacket swinging easily with the motion, and looked at Evie head to toe, before scowling and disappearing into the shadows.

* * *

Fucking bullshit, Larkin thought, kicking a loose cobblestone down the road, where it skidded into the bushes. It was obvious now that Evie hadn't just kissed Holly, she'd slept with her, too. Seeing her all unbuttoned in the alleyway was proof enough of that, and it burned in Larkin's guts like a hot coal fresh from the furnace.

The city was quieter than usual, most businesses long dark inside, and even the taverns had dumped patrons out onto the streets.

The captain and the others were headed straight back to the ship, at least that's where she assumed they'd all sprinted off to when Barnaby revealed the news. Larkin had never been very political, she just did the jobs she got paid for, though she did always have a morsel of sympathy for the rebel cause.

The Coalition was corrupt from the top down and the inside out, at every level of management. The only employees that weren't at least partially full of shit were the laborers at the bottom, the cleaners, the mechanics, the ones who inadvertently sold themselves into indentured servitude chasing opportunities that had never really existed except in propaganda filled public broadcasts. If the Coalition was planning a massive take down of rebel bases, there wasn't much a small ship with a limited crew could do to stop it. Captain Violet was an idealist, something rare in battle-hardened pirates, and a part of Larkin admired that the captain had never abandoned her principles, even in the face of certain defeat.

No one had said anything to her when they left the tavern, not whether they were leaving immediately, nor whether they were going to proceed with their ham-fisted plan to infiltrate the armory and steal weapons tech. If that plan was abandoned, they wouldn't have much use for Larkin. She was a leaf, blowing in the wind. No obligations, but no opportunities, either, the assholes at the Bronze Bell had seen to that.

Oddly, the market in the center of the city was still bustling with people, and in fact, it was busier than it had been than when she'd seen it during the day. This was where people went late at night in Bradach, with groups of friends shrieking with drunken laughter, stuffing their faces with noodles, tofu kebabs, and fried potatoes artfully drizzled with some kind of garlic sauce so potent that she could smell it from across the square. Her stomach grumbled angrily, and she was reminded she hadn't eaten in a while.

Larkin sighed heavily and scanned the marketplace, half hoping and half dreading that she would see José cooking paella at his market stand. She'd done an excellent job of disconnecting from her past, having no communication with anyone that knew her before the Lionel Cabot incident. It wasn't too hard, considering she had no family left, and truth be told she hadn't thought about José in years, not until she saw him in this very market only a few weeks ago. Catching up with your past was a dangerous business. The night was chilly, and she pulled the light jacket tight around herself.

There was a pack of young friends that couldn't have been older than eighteen or nineteen cackling over a tray of tapas balanced precariously on top of an old tree stump. One of them was Ivy, her bright green hair tousled and carefree, her arm around a pretty girl with long blond braids. Larkin couldn't help wondering if that was the same girl Ivy had been crying about in the kitchens not long ago, but decided it wasn't any of her business anyway. She sidled past the group quietly, pulling her collar up to hide her face and stepping around one of the group members splayed out on the yellowed grass, laughing so hard they snorted.

"Larkin." The voice was soft but insistent, and she turned to see José with his arms open wide. "I was hoping you'd return." He wrapped her in an embrace she couldn't quite bring herself to return, keeping her arms stiff at her sides. "When I didn't see you for a few weeks, I was starting to think maybe you'd moved on again, and I'd go another decade without seeing your face."

"Heh," Larkin muttered, regretting the half of her that hoped this would happen.

"Where did you go?"

"I had a job, I told you."

"And? How did it go?"

"It went off without a hitch," she lied. "As usual."

He lazily diced a handful of bright red chillies and tossed them into a pan sizzling with oil. "You can't run from it forever, you know."

"Sure I can."

"When are you going to settle down, eh? Find yourself a nice girl and put down some roots."

An image of Evie, half unbuttoned, leaving Holly's suite tugged at Larkin's mind, and she shoved it away angrily. "No such thing as a nice girl. They'll all break your heart. Anyway, roots are for suckers." She forced a smirk and picked off a lightly charred pepper from the enormous pan of paella. "What would I do anyway, make paella?"

"You could," he shrugged. "You could do anything you wanted to, you're smart enough."

"Smart is one thing, wise is another."

"True, true." He pulled an onion from a tall paper bag and began to peel away its yellow skin, letting the crisp, paper thin chunks float gently to the ground. "So, who's the girl?"

Larkin's head snapped up. "What?"

"The girl, whoever you're thinking about."

"I'm not thinking about anyone."

He jabbed a fork playfully in her direction, shaking his head. "Don't lie to me, I'm too old to be fooled."

"You're not so old."

"Old enough to know better." He set the peeled onion aside, and pulled another from the sack. "You don't have to tell me, I understand. I've not seen you for long enough that I don't even really know you anymore, I suppose."

"José..." Larkin started, and felt guilty that she'd lied to him. Here was a man who'd risked everything for her, and she was resenting being reminded of his existence. Maybe she'd spent too long by herself, creeping through the shadows. Maybe she was forgetting how to even have a connection with someone else. "It's complicated," she sighed.

"It always is."

"She's with someone else."

"Ah." He nudged the sack under his stand and set the peeled onions atop a worn, notched cutting board, and sliced into one of them. "Yes, I would agree that complicates things. Is she happy with this other person?"

"She is, but she deserves better," Larkin said, picking another pepper off the paella and closing her eyes to enjoy the smoky burst of flavor in her mouth. "This girl she's with, she doesn't treat her right. In fact, she's a complete asshole."

José laughed, pausing from his chopping to pile a bowl high with rice and vegetables before he handed it to Larkin. "Here, stop picking at the merchandise."

Larkin took it, but couldn't bring herself to dig in, despite her hunger. Thinking about Evie planted a strange melancholy in her chest that she'd not felt for a long time. "I don't know, nothing makes sense anymore. I've barely known her a month but it feels like we've been through years together."

"Love rarely makes sense."

The word rolled around in her mind, and dropped a rock into her stomach. Was this love? If so, it sucked. "I didn't say love."

"You didn't have to, mija. It's written all over your face."

Tears sprang to Larkin's eyes, and she turned away in shame. "Fucking onions," she grumbled angrily. "Making me tear up."

"Yes, yes, the onions," he agreed, but it was clear from the concern on his face that he didn't quite believe her excuse.

"Anyway it doesn't matter, it's never going to happen. If it was meant to be, she wouldn't have jumped back into that woman's arms the second we landed in the port." She wiped the tears away with the back of her sleeve and flipped the tail of her long dark braid over her shoulder.

"Eh, never say never," he mused, scraping the pile of neatly diced onions into the large pan, where they joined the smoky chillies. "You know, Magdalena and I were friends for years before anything happened." A sadness descended over his face, and guilt pulsed through Larkin's veins. "She was in love with someone else in the beginning, too, but I stuck it out. We got to have ten years together before..." he trailed off.

"Yeah. I'm... sorry." An apology was never going to be enough, not after what happened. Not when the whole thing had been her fault.

José waved her away. "Enough sadness. That was a long time ago, and I'm grateful for the time we had together. Love is what makes a life, you know."

"Mm," Larkin murmured in a non-committal way.

"How long are you staying for?"

Larkin shrugged. "I don't know. I was sort of contracted for a job, but it might all be falling apart. Crew has changing priorities. Might scare up some other work here, might catch a lift to another settlement to see what jobs I can pick up. Lots of people need killing these days."

"You're always welcome here, you know that right? You don't have to keep chasing all over the place. What has it gotten you in life so far, anyhow? Money? Friends? Influence? Or are you talking to a lonely old man in the middle of the night, wearing secondhand clothes?"

It unnerved Larkin that he could see straight through her, even to recognize that her clothes weren't her own, they were borrowed from Kady, and her account was empty due to that contract welching on their payment after the job was done. "It's a life."

"It's half a life."

"Well, either way, it's not something you can just stop doing. I have a reputation to uphold," she said with a forced wink. "I bet the next time you see me, I'll be draped in the latest fashions, drunk on the finest wine in the Near Systems, with ten girls on each arm." The only girl she wanted on her arm was Evie, but that was obviously never going to happen.

José laughed and tipped a jug of seasoned vegetable stock into the pan. "So there's a next time? You promise it won't be another ten years before I see that face?"

Larkin drew an X over her chest and said, "Cross my heart."

"I'll believe it when I see it," he scolded gently, shaking a spatula at her. "Don't let life pass you by, eh? Tell that girl you love her."

"No chance," she replied, rolling her eyes. "You've got customers, old man, better get back to work."

CHAPTER TWENTY-ONE

Larkin found herself silently slipping through the open loading bay of the Cricket, full of regrets and emotions she thought she'd buried long ago. Coming back to the ship felt strange, and she still wasn't sure if it was the right thing to do, but she was broke and had nowhere else to sleep except José's, and she sure as shit couldn't stay there, not after everything, so it would have to do. Besides, it was possible that Captain Violet and the other officers would be occupied dealing with whatever information Barnaby had unearthed for them, and they might not even notice she was back. Even better.

The ship was eerily quiet without the persistent hum of the engines and the quiet chatter of the crew, who were all off on shore leave, probably getting drunk in back-alley speakeasies that required your name on an exclusive list to get in. She hadn't felt much like drinking anyway, not alone, and not after seeing Evie leaving that suite earlier in the evening. It just wouldn't have sat right with her, no matter how hard she tried to bury it, or ignore it, or forget she'd ever seen it, and it was because that Holly woman was bad news. She had thrown Evie to the wolves once before without a second thought, who was to say she wouldn't do it again?

She paced the silent halls, the only sound the quiet shuffle of her crutches against the grate. She was almost surprised no one had stolen them from behind the Bronze Bell to fence for a shot of booze. No one would be looking for her, and she was free to be alone with her thoughts for the first time in weeks, and yet it's the last thing she wanted. Shit, what she wouldn't give for a messy game of cards, or inane chatter about shore leave, or anything other than the crushing solitude she had to endure. She was starting to regret not digging up a bottle of rum from somewhere to drink herself into a dark and dreamless sleep. Sure, she'd have a hangover in the morning, but there's no way it would be worse than how she was feeling at that moment.

"Hey." Ned appeared at the end of the corridor like a ghost, and Larkin remembered that was the location of the secret hold in the ship. "Boss was looking for you, she's up on the bridge with the others."

"Looking for me? Why?"

"We might have a hell of a fight on our hands soon," he said, running his hands nervously through his long ginger hair. "Boss thinks maybe you might be able to help us out where that's concerned, if you're willing."

Larkin shrugged. "No harm in hearing her out, I guess." Truth be told, she was grateful for the distraction from her own mental staircase, turning around and around and never getting anywhere. She cracked her neck and followed Ned, more solemn than she'd ever seen him, up to the bridge where Captain Violet was pacing the width of the window.

"Captain," Larkin said evenly. "I heard you were looking for me."

"What did Zane say?" the captain asked Kady, who was leaned against the wall, stiff as a panel of steel.

"He said they haven't recorded any Coalition troop movement, nothing that would suggest the scale of attack Barnaby implied."

"Well, how else would they be planning something without staffing battleships with crews? It's not as though they can magic up man-eating dragons or anything, where the hell would they be coming from?"

"We identified a vulnerability with some of the older terraforming equipment. It's possible they could be manipulated to spread some kind of toxin," Alice offered. "Zane said he's got his people on it, so if that's what the Coalition is planning, they'll be stopped before they can even initiate an attack. So far, none of the vulnerabilities seem to have been tampered with in any of the bases."

"Er, Captain?" Larkin tried again. "Did you need something from me?"

"We may require your services sooner than we had anticipated," Captain

Violet responded. "If the Coalition is planning this kind of wide scale attack, the sooner we get our hands on whatever tech they're developing, the better. If the rebel colonies are left without intel or support, they'll get flattened."

"Not to question your judgment or anything, but why bother with the rebels at all? It's not as though they've done much to stop the Coalition's march across the Near Systems. In fact, your crew did more to advance the cause with your little stunt last year than anything else."

"I won't leave people to die," the captain said firmly, turning her unnerving stare towards Larkin. "Those rebel camps are full of people just like us. Families. Friends." She stole a glance at Alice. "Spouses. And without our help, and the help of others like us, they'll all be wiped out just like that."

"So what do you want from me, then?"

Captain Violet sighed. "To be honest, we're not sure yet. We don't know what they're planning. It could be anything, or it could be a ruse to draw some of the rebel groups out of hiding, there's no way to know for sure unless we can get our hands on that intel. Plans will have to be fluid."

"Alright," Larkin said carefully, "then when do we leave?" There was no point in pretending she had any other options anyway; without credit, she wouldn't be able to book passage to anywhere else, and thanks to those two assholes in the Bronze Bell, it would be challenging to pick up work in Bradach, at least until they calmed down. Flying with the Cricket was as good of work as anything, really, and at least the food here was better than most ships. At least she didn't have to spend almost the entirety of this job crushed into a utility closet.

"Glad to have you on board," the captain said, and Larkin detected a hint of relief in her voice. "We leave as soon as the crew is all back on board."

* * *

Evie peered in through the tinted windows of the Purple Pig, hoping that Gabe was still inside cleaning up. She could easily go home to her small rented room, but it felt foreign to her now, after everything that had happened. It felt suffocating, as though all the air had been sucked out in the time she was away. Now it felt more like a stranger lived there. The Cricket wasn't really her home, either, and besides, Larkin wasn't speaking to her. She banged her head softly against the thick glass and growled softly under her breath. Nothing was going right: Holly was married, not to mention she really *had* done everything the Coalition tried to pin on her in that prison. Evie's only real friend wouldn't speak to her, apparently, and everything was a big confusing mess.

The chandeliers that hung from the rafters of the tavern glowed softly through the darkened pane, and Evie mulled over the fact that the Purple Pig was the only place that had ever really felt like home. Sure, it was just a job, and one most people took for granted, but she was good at it, and in the weeks she'd been away, realized how much she missed pulling pints of ale and pouring shots of bootleg whiskey into glasses for jubilant pirates fresh from a successful job.

The heavy door swung open, and Tansy appeared in the gap, a mug of steaming liquid in her hand. "Fancy meeting you here," she said, the familiar kind smile spreading over her high cheekbones. She pulled Evie through the narrow opening into a tight hug. "I'm so glad you're alright."

"I'll be honest, there was more than one moment I wasn't sure I'd make it."

"You look like you need an ear. Come on, I'll fix you a tea."

"Thanks."

"Care to fill me in on what's going on?"

"It's a long story, I went on a trip with— "

"No, no," Tansy said, waving her hands. "I know all that, you were all over the public broadcasts after the prison break. I mean, why are you standing outside like a sad puppy after closing time, like you have nowhere to go?"

"I don't know," Evie mumbled, fidgeting with her hands. "Everything else feels different, now."

Tansy nodded. "Yeah, having adventures will do that to you, I'm no stranger to that." She knocked on her titanium leg, a sparkling diamond ring making hollow taps on the metal that echoed prettily around the empty tavern. "You know, when I came home with this new leg, I couldn't wait to get back up in the sky. It took me months to recover, to get used to how my body moves now, and the whole time I felt like I was trapped here in Bradach, like I had no purpose or meaning."

"Yeah," Evie agreed, letting herself behind the bar to make a hot tea to mirror Tansy's.

"I was miserable until I found this old place," Tansy said, craning her neck to look up at the rafters. "It was a pile of shit and bricks back then, nothing to look at, and nobody did. I bought the plot with every last piece of crap I had to trade, and I came in here every damn day, working to fix it up. First were the structural problems, then lighting, picking out furniture, hiring an artist to put gold leaf on the walls, stocking the bar. With every victory in putting this place back together, I felt a little more like myself." She took a thoughtful sip of her tea and set the mug on a mismatched coaster. "Sometimes you need a project, or a distraction, something to call your own."

"I don't really have anything that fits the bill," Evie admitted, sliding onto the bar stool next to her boss. "I don't even know if I should stay or go."

"Sounds to me like you had a hell of an adventure."

"Sure, maybe a few too many close calls, though. The Cricket leaves in a few days, and I don't know if I should get back on that ship or not. It doesn't feel like I have much of a purpose, to tell you the truth." She watched the tea leaves swirl and dance in the hot water. "No barkeeps needed on a ship like that."

"Whatever you choose, you can always make a different decision next time. Getting back on that ship doesn't mean you'll be on it forever, and it's possible you need a little more time to figure out who you are, and what you really want out of life." Tansy sighed heavily and pulled herself up to sit on the bar. "If I were you, I'd be back on that ship in a heartbeat."

"Really?"

"Absolutely. I love this tavern with my whole heart. It brought me back to life and it has thrived, but my own sense of self is having a bit of a crisis. I feel itchy and impatient, like something else is out there waiting for me." She looked out through the window of the tavern, a view that crossed the city and sparkled with a clear view of the docks and the ships lodged there.

"I don't know what it could be, though."

"I know what you mean. I have this strange feeling that something big is right around the corner, but I can't quite figure out what it is yet."

"Exactly," Tansy nodded, and then shook her head with a quiet laugh. "Isn't that just life, though? We all just bumble through and hope for the best. Hope for a good job that doesn't make us want to scream, hope for a love that's kind and true, hope for something to make you feel like you've made a difference."

"You've made a difference though, I mean just look at this place! It's where everyone in Bradach wants to go, it's beautiful, it means so much to so many people."

"Yeah, yeah, but I still feel like there's something else waiting for me." Tansy took another sip of her tea. "And what about you? You could be in your own place, or back on a ship destined for adventures and meaning, and yet you're here with an old lady, drinking tea before sunrise."

"Sometimes you have to do what feels right, I guess. Tonight it felt like everything started to fall apart, even more than before, and this is where I ended up."

"Can I just say something?"

"Uh, sure?" Evie replied, apprehensive.

"I really hope you don't end up back with that bitch who sold you out. Gabe said that you left with her, and—"

"That seems very unlikely at this point, given she's got a wife and about a dozen different crews after her."

Tansy gave a low whistle. "Well, that's something, isn't it."

"It sure is."

"You know, Evie," Tansy said, hopping down from bar, "Captain Violet is a good woman. An excellent captain, and if you're looking for the kind of experience that makes you realize what you're really after in life, then flying with her is as good as anyone could ever get."

Evie raised an eyebrow. "And you know this from...experience?"

"It was a lifetime ago, long before the tavern, or my shiny leg here. I wasn't on her ship for very long, it turns out that while Captain Violet and I share ideals, we do not share the same methods of approach. We were oil and water." She paused, and laughed quietly. "Maybe more like a blowtorch and a very short fuse."

"Do you still talk?"

"She tends to drop into the tavern now and then, when her ship is docked. Though I've not seen her this time around, but then, I'm rarely here these days."

"What, some exciting new project? A new tavern, maybe?" Evie asked.

"Nah, nothing like that."

Her boss didn't seem to want to offer up any more information on that front, so Evie closed her eyes and enjoyed the heady smell of the herbal tea, the scent of which always made her feel calm and at peace. Tonight though, it was barely even touching the firestorm of wasps in her mind, all fighting for dominance as they devoured each other alive. The kiss with Larkin, her tenuous obligation to the Cricket and Captain Violet, the total disaster with Holly, and how she'd almost been stupid enough to fall back into that stupidly sexy web of lies. Evie blew gently on the hot liquid, watching the tendrils of steam spiral in a lazy dance to the ceiling.

"I've not seen someone with this much on their mind in ages," Tansy said, interrupting Evie's thoughts, "and for someone who owns a tavern in a pirate settlement, that's one hell of a feat. What else is going on?" She reached for a large bottle of whiskey and poured a generous helping into a mug with some hot water, lemon, and added a cinnamon stick for good measure. "I feel like whatever it is, it needs this." She pushed the mug across the bar at Evie, who wrapped her hands around the smooth fired clay of the cup.

"I don't know. It's complicated."

"When isn't life complicated?"

Evie laughed with a slight edge of bitterness. "Yeah, and isn't that the truth." She lifted the mug to her lips and took a long sip of the hot cocktail. "It's not just whether I should go back to the Cricket, and things are definitely over with Holly now."

"Okay," Tansy said encouragingly, and nodded her head, "go on." When

Evie wouldn't look up from her mug, she continued, "is it about a lover?"

"What? No!" Evie responded, a deep crimson blush creeping up her cheeks. "No, it's nothing like that."

Tansy shrugged. "Okay, just thought I'd ask. I've been hung up on all kinds of folks in my life."

"I can't imagine you hung up on anyone."

"You'd be surprised. Matters of the heart are rarely things that we feel in a mediocre way. People can crash into your life and cause all kinds of mess and havoc if you let them, or if they're special enough that even their presence seems to throw you off balance." Tansy took a sip of her tea and raised an eyebrow casually. "But that's none of my business."

"We're just friends," Evie blurted out. "But it's all wrong now, and she won't talk to me, and I don't know if I can even do the kinds of things I'll need to do on that ship if she's not with me."

"From what I hear from Vi, you're perfectly capable on that ship. Saving lives, helping one of the most gifted navigators I've ever met chart a course? You don't need anyone else to be you, Evie." She set her mug down on the bar, and pushed a cork back into the bottle of whiskey. "That said, it sounds like you have some things to work out with this woman." She squinted out the window, which was glimmering with the early promise of a dawn brought by the huge mirrors over the city. "And if you want to work it out, you'd better go now. Looks like the Cricket is getting ready to leave port a few days early."

"Oh, gods. Fuck." Evie downed the rest of her drink and tossed the mug to Tansy, who caught it with one arm behind her back. "I have to go. Thank you!" she shouted, bursting through the door and running full pelt back to the docks, where the loading doors of the Cricket were already closing, the metal chains grinding against the pulleys.

CHAPTER TWENTY-TWO

Evie ducked under the slow airlock door and bent double to catch her breath. Hefting huge boxes full of swill was all fine and good, but wouldn't prepare anyone for sprinting across Bradach on a mostly empty stomach, except for the hot whiskey and lemon that sloshed angrily in her belly. "Fuck me," she wheezed, unlatching the handle for the crew airlock. "That was close." She tumbled through into the ship and nearly crashed into Larkin, who was standing at the other side, waiting to call the all-clear for liftoff, radio in hand.

"It's Evie," she said into the radio, staring deadpan. "We're all good to go here, as soon as the doors seal in three... two... one... we're locked, Ned." The radio transmission clicked off, and Evie felt the gentle rumble of the ship as the engines kicked into gear and the air filtration system began their deep hum.

"Almost didn't make it," Evie said, still breathless from the run.

"Yeah, well, I guess you've been busy," Larkin said flatly.

"I thought we had shore leave for two more days?"

"Circumstances have changed."

"Okay, what circumstances?" Evie felt annoyed that Larkin was being so evasive, like she was intentionally withholding information to irritate her. "You gonna clue me in here, or what?"

Larkin clipped the radio to her belt and tilted her head slightly. "We assumed you'd be too *busy* to come back and join us."

"Yeah, because I have so many other more important things to do," Evie laughed, allowing a slight iciness to settle at the edges of her tone. If Larkin could play this game, so could she. "I'm just saying a little advance notice would have been appreciated."

"All appropriate crew members were notified, so I'm told."

"What, so I'm just extra baggage? A spare wheel, or what?"

Larkin shrugged coolly, and Evie felt the heat of confrontation prickle at the back of her neck. "I told the captain that you were... otherwise engaged."

"What the hell are you talking about?"

"I think you know damn well what I'm talking about."

"I can assure you, I have no idea why you're being so openly hostile right now."

"Really? You have no idea?" Larkin's smirk twisted into a sneer, and Evie could all but see actual flames in her eyes. "Maybe I should just leave you alone to consider your options, shall I? Perhaps it's for the best."

"Could you give me a hint here? I know we left things a little weird, but—"

"Why did you even bother to come back?" Larkin snapped. "You have everything you need here in Bradach, and yet here you are again, like a shadow too stupid for its own good."

Evie's jaw dropped open and tears sprang to her eyes from the biting words. Before she could form any kind of cohesive response, Larkin abruptly turned and stalked off down the corridor. "I came back for you, you asshole," Evie said to herself, and wiped her tears away with the back of her crisp white shirt.

* * *

"Ah, Evie, we're glad to have you back on board," Alice said warmly, wrapping an arm around her shoulders. "We weren't sure you'd be back, not after everything that's happened, and it's not like you signed a contract with us," she laughed.

Evie just nodded, not willing to allow herself to talk about the upsetting interaction she'd had with Larkin only twenty minutes prior.

"Since you missed the memo, so to speak, Ivy and I thought we could fill you in down here in the boiler room," Alice said, and gestured around the room proudly. "In any case, our informant has uncovered some information that suggests the Coalition is making plans for a huge attack on some of the rebel settlements we've assisted in the past. Now, we have no idea what kind of attack this could be, so Captain Violet thinks it best if we accelerate our plans to infiltrate the Armory, to hijack any information or tech that can give us some kind of idea as to what they're planning."

"It could be a wide scale attack on communications infrastructure, or even something like toxic additives into their water supply, or their terraformers," Ivy added. "We've already been in touch with some of the settlements to tell them to be on their guard, but none of them have reported any signs of tampering so far."

"Oh, shit," Evie breathed.

"Yeah, 'oh shit' is right," Alice grumbled, releasing her and reaching for a rolled up blueprint that sat jumbled amid piles of paperwork, schematics, and maps. "Honestly, getting into that armory is our best bet for getting the drop on them. If we don't, lots of innocent people could wind up dead."

"So what can I do?" Evie asked. "Obviously I'm not a real sharpshooter, but— "

"They don't know that," Alice said mischievously, a grin spreading across her face. "You're Bradach born and raised, and the Coalition already has you on record as a criminal mastermind who managed to hijack and scrap nearly a dozen of their most impressive ships single handedly. We think we could use that to our advantage."

"I'm not so sure that's a good idea," Evie stammered, her palms suddenly feeling clammy. "I'm not a very good liar."

"You don't have to talk to anyone, we just have to let you be seen once we land. Maybe if they're busy chasing after what they think is supposed to be a scrap mission, they'll miss Kady slipping into their data server rooms and extracting mountains of information."

"Is that really our best plan?"

"Well, there's plenty of moving parts involved, but that's the general idea, yes."

"What if I hadn't come back?"

Alice shrugged and grinned. "We always have a plan B on this ship."

"Yeah, last time I was the plan B," Ivy said, laughing, "but that all turned out for the best, didn't it?"

"You're damn right it did," Alice said, and it was clear how proud she was of her apprentice. "So we're aiming to reach the Armory in a day or two, depending on whatever flight path Ned thinks is best to keep us out of trouble until we get there. I think Captain Violet is planning to have a big briefing later tonight, in the mess hall, and then we'll all break into small teams to make sure everyone is clear on what the plan is."

"Wow, so it's all going to happen pretty fast."

"Yep, that's the plan. The longer we wait, the more likely they'll start to cover their tracks on what they're planning, and then it will be too late. If we get in and out now, we might be able to get enough intel to give us some kind of clue, and then maybe we can work on a way to fight it before it even happens." Alice spread the blueprints on the workbench, securing the curled ends with various tools she pulled from the tool belt hanging at her hips. "The best way to win a war is to know what the assholes are up to. The ones who win the wars are the ones with the most information, every single time."

"I can imagine that's probably the case," Evie mumbled, fiddling with an adjustable wrench that was holding down a corner of the paper. She felt anxiety rubbing at the edges of her mind like sandpaper, wearing away her thin facade of calm. "You know, Alice, I don't know how comfortable I am with all of this. It seems like an incredibly risky move, and you're depending on me to provide, what, some kind of diversion? And what if that doesn't work? What if your source tells them we're coming?"

Alice furrowed her brow and used a straightedge to draw a line from one side of the page to another. "My source hasn't been informed of our plans, so I wouldn't worry about that."

"Why not?"

"Because he's kind of an asshole," Alice sighed, setting down the tiny worn stub of a pencil. "He used to be here on the ship with the rest of us, until Violet— er, Captain Violet, that is, caught him selling things out from under her for a profit. She kicked him off at the next trading beacon, and rightfully so. The fool's lucky she didn't push him out an airlock."

"So why does he do this for you, feeding information?"

"Penance."

"And someday he'll be allowed back on the ship?"

"It's unlikely."

"So why bother?"

"Feeding Captain Violet information guarantees she won't turn him in to the Coalition or to any of the probably dozens of people looking for him," Ivy offered, mirroring the line Alice had drawn with another, this one thicker, leaving a trail of graphite along the paper. "And he used to be friends with Alice." She tucked the pencil back into her hair, scrunched up into an unkempt bun with short bits sticking out of the sides. "And he dated Ned."

"Then why would he betray the crew in the first place?"

"Because Barnaby is, above all else, a greedy, pigeon-livered ratbag," Alice interjected, scribbling a note into the margin of the paper. "He thinks only of himself, and only does things that will benefit him. Yes, there was a time he was my oldest and best friend, but until he learns a little humility, or at least how to behave like a decent human being, I keep my distance. Fuck knows I don't need him selling me off to another pirate ship."

"He - what?" Evie asked. "What ship?"

"This ship." Alice marked three large Xs in the building outlines on the map with a fountain pen dripping red ink, and Evie had the unnerving thought that it looked a little too much like blood for her comfort. "It's a long story, anyway. I'm sure if you stick around, you, too will get bamboozled by the little liar."

"What about Ned?"

"He didn't take it well," Ivy said, pulling the cap from a marker she pulled from the large front pocket of her blue denim dungarees. "Alice reckons he's been heartbroken ever since."

Evie nudged the wrench out of the way as Alice drew another line across the page. "Well, I've had my fair share of betrayal, so I can't say that I blame him." The memory of Holly's appearance in the Purple Pig the night before was still fresh in her mind, along with the revelation that she really had just been using Evie to take the fall for her, maybe even to set her up again. "Fool me twice..." she mumbled.

"Exactly," Alice agreed, and pushed her green goggles back onto her forehead. "We're all better off for having told him to take a hike until he gets it together. We have a lot of people depending on us, you know, we couldn't risk it to keep Barnaby on board. Who knows what he'd have planned if Violet hadn't caught him with his hands in the cookie jar. Sold us all back to the Coalition in exchange for a clean record, probably."

"Do you really think so?" Ivy asked.

Alice shrugged. "Probably." The mechanic stood back from the workbench, analyzing the blueprints, and nodded thoughtfully. "Yeah, that will about do it, I think. What do you reckon, Ivy?"

"Looks good to me," Ivy agreed.

"What exactly are you doing?" Evie asked, eyeing the marks on the crisp white paper.

"Making notes of the potential breakout points," Alice answered, pointing at the large red X nearest to her. "They indicate where data servers are stored. They're all interconnected with a local communications network, so really we only need to get into one of these rooms to pull this off, but they're all pretty heavily guarded."

"Won't they know once we tap into the system?"

"Hell yeah, and that's why this is more of a smash and grab than a graceful cat burglar situation. As soon as we touch one tiny byte of that data, it's going to be red alert all across that base, and we're going to have every Coalition soldier in a twenty mile radius on our asses. We need to get in, get the information, and get the hell out before they nab any of us. It's definitely risky, but if we want a heads up on whatever they're planning, it's our only option."

Evie nodded, but couldn't bring herself to say anything. The whole idea sounded ridiculously dangerous, and she couldn't imagine it ever succeeding. Sure, the crew had managed to infiltrate a high security prison, but the Armory was another level entirely. Stuffed to the gills with military personnel and more guns than you could ever need, even beyond the Near Systems. No one knew for sure what kind of weapons the Coalition was developing there, but whatever it was couldn't be good news.

"Why don't you go grab Larkin before the meeting? Captain Violet will probably have you two working together at the Armory, since you've already proved you function well as a team."

"Sure," Evie said, but her heart was heavy with guilt and dread. It was obvious Larkin didn't want to speak to her, but she should at least try, for the sake of the mission if nothing else. "See you there," Evie mumbled to the mechanic and her apprentice, and trudged up the steps into the corridor.

CHAPTER TWENTY-THREE

Larkin sat perched at the edge of her bed, staring at the blank wall in front of her. Her mind was a jumbled mess of rage, frustration, and sadness, more tangled than a pit full of drunk snakes. The ship was gliding full steam ahead towards the Armory, and soon she'd have to help the crew of the Cricket extract top secret information in the hopes they'd be able to stop whatever attack was being planned. It was a bold move, to be sure, but also possibly a very stupid one that would get them all killed. She sighed angrily and flopped back on the bed, enjoying the cool smoothness of the crisp cotton sheets against her face.

There was a soft knock at the door, and Larkin turned her head to face it. She knew that it was Evie. She also knew that she didn't want to talk to Evie right now, and in fact was angry she made it back to the ship before they left. When she'd lied to Captain Violet and said that Evie decided to stay, she wanted that to be the end of it. No more Evie, no more distractions, no more confusing feelings racing around in her mind. If nothing else, she just wanted things to go back to normal: do a job, get paid, move on, end of story. Emotional entanglements were dangerous and quite frankly, annoying as hell. She ignored the knocks, and soon, steps retreated back down the hallway.

It wasn't long before the big meeting in the mess hall, anyway, and she'd have to deal with seeing Evie there. No need to make things more difficult by rushing it, that was for sure. Larkin craned her neck back and examined her face staring back at her through the open bathroom door, her thick, dark braid coiled next to her on the bed, and her deep brown eyes reflected in the mirror. She really hoped that this job went off without a hitch, and she could get paid and start looking for her next contract wherever they dumped her. She'd need another new Coalition ID, again, but at least she wasn't still rotting in that prison. At least she'd been able to see José again, one last time.

The guilt she felt when he spoke about his dear departed wife Magdalena was too much for her to bear, and there was no way she could deal with dredging up the past like that. Everyone had their limits, and that was hers. Larkin huffed angrily and rolled off the bed, rising to a standing position, still facing the mirror. There would be time enough for self-indulgent ruminating later, right now she had a meeting to get to, and a job to plan. Carefully tucking a loose lock of hair back into her braid, she tugged her jacket back into place and tightened her belt; the knives she'd stolen from the kitchens and sewn into her trousers were heavier than the last ones.

With a loud click, the door latched close, and Larkin moved silently to the bridge, which was unattended. No doubt they'd put the console on lock again, only accessible to the crew, but she itched to know for sure. If she could just send a message, maybe she could get paid and not have to go through with whatever harebrained, reckless plan the captain had in mind. She hesitated at the doorway, her fingers wrapped around the metal of the jamb. It would only take a minute, and she could just lie and say she fell asleep, and that's why she was late to the meeting. Maybe they hadn't put the lock back on. Larkin scanned the room, wondering what the odds were that this was another trap, maybe fifty-fifty if she had to guess, because it was clear that Captain Violet didn't yet trust her, not entirely.

The room was empty, the displays above Ned's station blank. Just as she stepped over the threshold, the sound of footsteps sent her swiveling on the heel of her boot.

"What are you doing?" Evie asked flatly.

"Nothing."

"You're going to be late."

Larkin shifted her weight from one foot to the other, wondering how she could get rid of her and have the bridge to herself for just a few moments. "So will you," she replied. "I just want to check something, that's all."

"You want to send a message to the Coalition, sell us all out."

"No, that's not it. There's someone who owes me credit for a contract I completed, and—"

"Why don't you just ask them to send it for you?" Evie interrupted.

"Because they don't trust me."

"And you think that sneaking around behind their backs is going to change that?"

Larkin didn't want to admit that the only reason she hadn't been caught in the crew's web last time was due to Evie's intervention. If she hadn't kept her from sending that message, she'd probably be rotting in their brig, or worse, an icy corpse floating in the desolate backwaters of space. "You wouldn't understand," she said instead, "it's complicated, and my clients like to retain their anonymity."

"You're going to get yourself killed, you know," Evie said angrily. "You think you're such hot shit, that you're invincible, untouchable. But you nearly kicked the bucket back on the Blackwall, and it's only because of me that you're standing there with that titanium rib cage and not in some Coalition morgue. Yet here you are, causing more bullshit for yourself because you can't even imagine possibly letting someone in." She threw up her hands in disgust and shook her head. "Whatever, do what you like. But when this all comes back to bite you in the ass, don't expect me to bail you out." Evie turned to walk back down the corridor when Larkin felt words bubbling up inside her, with nowhere to go but out.

"Yeah, well, you're one to talk!" she shouted. "You'd still be in that prison with Allemande, or dead, if I hadn't vouched for you. But the only people you let get close are assholes and hustlers who screw you over and don't care about you at all! You can't even see what's right in front of you!"

Evie stopped, paused, and then turned back to face Larkin. "What the hell are you talking about?"

"I know you went home with her last night."

"*Excuse me?*" Evie's eyes flashed with fire, and Larkin took a step backward.

"You have no idea what you're talking about."

"Oh really? Then how come I saw you slinking around in that alley, looking like you'd just had the time of your life, huh?"

"I didn't sleep with her!" Evie snapped. "But even if I had— "

"Well you damned well kissed her, I *saw* you!"

Evie's jaw dropped open. "You were spying on me?"

"No, it was accident, I didn't mean to— "

"You didn't mean to follow me to the Purple Pig and creep around looking through the windows to see what I was up to? Well damn, Larkin, next time you should just pull up a fucking chair because you missed that I told her to take a hike."

"Bullshit, then what were you doing later?"

"That's— ugh! It's more complicated than that!"

"So you did sleep with her."

"No." Evie ran her hands through her hair, tousling it and creating a cowlick at the back. "She's married, anyway. And has about two dozen pirates trying to pin her down for payment. Yes, I walked her home, and yes, she wanted to get back together. The next thing you know, her wife is bursting in through the door, screaming and demanding to know what the hell was going on."

Larkin's stomach churned with the image of Evie in Holly's arms. "And if her wife hadn't come home?"

"Larkin... don't."

"No, I want to know. Would you have slept with her? Would you have stayed?"

"Uh, ladies, we're all incredibly late," Ned said quietly from around a hidden corner. "I hate to interrupt, but it's not really an appropriate time to be late, if you catch my drift. Big plans in motion, you know. Important meeting." He coughed and shrugged his shoulders apologetically.

"Goddamnit," Larkin muttered as she pushed past Ned, stomping painfully towards the mess hall. She was regretting leaving her crutches in her room, but she wasn't about to double back now and make an even bigger fool of herself. Instead, she accepted each throb from every heavy footstep as atonement for everything she should have said, but didn't. She couldn't wait to get off this fucking ship.

* * *

When the captain stepped over the threshold of the bridge, the ship shuddered and the lights flickered. "What the hell was that?" Larkin asked, bracing herself against the door frame.

"Yes, Ned, what was that?" the captain echoed.

"Stealthed vessel, coming in hot from port side," he said, sliding into his chair as fast as he could.

"Why didn't we detect them?"

"We did, it's a friendly signature."

"Then why the hell are they shooting at us?

Ned swiped through several displays. "That, Boss, I can't tell you."

"Wow, you guys really do make a lot of friends out here, don't you?" Larkin snarked.

"Be helpful or get off my bridge," the captain snarled. "Your sarcasm isn't adding anything to the situation other than raising my blood pressure."

"Alright, geeze," Larkin muttered. The captain's console display was flashing from one view of the ship to another, between a wide angle blueprint and the location of the hit.

"They're going to try to board us," the captain said, rubbing the bridge of her nose. "Ned, do we have comms yet?"

"They're blocking our comms."

"Gods be damned." She sighed heavily. "They're waiting for us to bank to get away from them, and they're going to ram us where the loading bay is."

"Yup," said Ned. "My vote is that we don't bank."

"You're just going to let them board you?" Larkin asked, incredulous. "Why?"

"We're on a schedule, we can't be risking taking weeks to have the ship repaired properly in Bradach, and nor do I want to be heading into the Armory with a weakly patched vessel."

The captain had a point. The rig was decades old and sourcing parts was probably a nightmare.

"Attention all crew, stay where you are and do not go near the loading bay. We're about to be boarded by another ship that has fired on us. I and the other officers will meet them and hear their demands." The captain's voice boomed from every speaker on the ship, the echoes through the corridors overlapping against each other like the tides on a beach.

The radio at the captain's hip crackled. "Hey, Violet, remember me?"

"You've got to be joking," she groaned. "This asshole again? Really?"

"Don't bother trying to radio back, we're blocking your frequency. Meet us in your bay and we'll tell you our demands, one of which is you coming with us for an extended lesson in why you never should have crossed us in the first place. Say no, and we keep firing."

"Right, people, let's get a move on," Captain Violet said to the other officers with a beleaguered sigh. "If we're lucky, they won't shoot through our loading bay with heat guns."

She hadn't been invited, but Larkin followed them through the corridors anyway. They might need some help with whatever assholes were on board. She noticed Evie hang back, and then turn down a forked hall towards the mess hall. Great. An idea sparked in her mind. The crew couldn't be without a captain, but maybe they could do without an assassin. She jabbed Ned in the ribs. "Hey," she whispered. "I need you to back me up. I have an idea."

"It better be good," he hissed.

"It's good. It's me instead of the captain. Please, Ned. Just trust me. I know the captain doesn't, and Kady doesn't, but..."

"Alright! Fine. But this better work or she'll have your head on a gilded platter."

"It will work."

Ned nodded, and then cleared his throat. "Uh, Boss? What if we... let our hired assassin have a word?"

"We don't have time," she snapped, continuing her march down the hall. "They're going to be in our bay any minute."

Larkin caught her by the arm."Captain, please—"

"Unless you have a way to keep me on the ship and keep the ship intact, we better just get this thing moving. Already going to cost us days in transit time, huge setbacks..." The captain trailed off, and then stopped and spun on the heel of her boot. "Larkin, are you thinking what I'm thinking? Because if you are, then I can't condone that kind of risk, not when—"

"I know I haven't given you many reasons to trust me, Captain, but if you and the other officers take cover in the old hideaway, I might be able to convince them to take me instead."

"I don't want them killed. We have enough blood on our hands as it is."

"I won't."

"And if they don't take you instead of tearing the ship apart, piece by piece?"

"I have a feeling that they're in a hurry. Besides, from what Ned told me, they hardly seem the type to properly execute a siege."

The Captain stopped and chewed at her lip. "This could work. Larkin, don't do anything stupid."

"I'll try."

"Don't get killed, either."

"No promises," Larkin said with a reassuring grin, patting her side where the titanium ribs hid beneath her scarred flesh. "But I figure I've got about seven of nine lives left."

The others looped around to the left, leaving Larkin on her own. Her hands ran over the small silver knives strapped to her thigh, insurance against getting her ass beat again. It wouldn't do much against a gun, though, and she swallowed hard. She was about to bring a knife to a gun fight, and she'd have to hope to shit she didn't fuck it up. If the invaders didn't kill her, the captain might.

"Hey! You!"

She came face to face with some woman she didn't know, and her old friends Beard and Earrings. "Oh, it's you blockheads again," she said with a laugh. "Come back for round two?"

"We didn't even get round one, you lily-livered chicken shit," Earrings said. "That captain made sure of that."

"What captain?"

"The captain of this ship, you numbskull," Beard growled. "We're here to take this ship from her."

Larkin shrugged. "No captain here. Just me."

"Cut the crap, I've been on this hunk of space junk before and I know this is Violet's ship," the woman said. A memory clicked into place, and Larkin nodded with understanding.

"You're Josie."

"You're damned right I am. Violet's the reason why my beloved Leo is dead, and why I spent a year locked up in that disgusting prison!"

"Well, she's not here. Can I take a message?"

"Tell us where she is, or I'll tear this ship apart piece by piece!" Josie screamed, color rising in her pale, gently freckled face.

"What are your aims, here?" Larkin asked, resisting the urge to rub her thumbs over the knives. She didn't want to escalate, not yet. Not until she had the upper hand. Timing, as always, was key.

"We want the captain."

"For what? Charades?"

"No, you piss ant, we want to capture her and make her pay for what she's done."

Larkin raised an eyebrow. "And you two," she said, gesturing at Beard and Earrings, "other than keeping you from kicking my ass seven ways from Sunday, what has she done to you?"

"She needs to be taught not to intervene with someone's private business!" Earrings spluttered.

"Ah. So you found yourselves a captain, your friend Josie here, to come enact revenge? Yet, you aren't interested in me?"

"We'll deal with you once we have the captain," Beard snarled.

"Was that your idea, or Josie's?"

Beard and Earrings exchanged a look. "That doesn't matter!" Beard retorted. "We're the ones in control, here!" He brandished a silver revolver with a thick, long barrel. "*We're* boarding *you*!"

"Alright, alright," Larkin said, holding her hands up. "Search the ship if you must, but I told you, she's not here."

"You're damn right we're gonna search the ship," Josie said, pushing past her, "and if any of the crew shoot first then we're turning this into a bloodbath."

Larkin gave her a fake smile and a shrug, hoping she'd stalled long enough for Ned to get the captain into the hidden hold. These bright sparks sure as hell wouldn't know it was there.

"You wait here," Josie barked at Earrings. "Stay here with her, make sure she doesn't do anything to our shuttle. And keep your gun trained on her, she looks like she's up to something."

"I wouldn't dream of it!" Larkin said, beaming.

"And keep your finger on the trigger," Josie added.

Larkin perched atop an overturned empty crate which still had the vague scent of cabbage. She swallowed back a retch. Cabbage was disgusting.

"Don't move," Earrings said, pulling back the hammer of the gun. "Or I'll blow you away."

"Calm down, no one is moving anywhere. I told you, the captain isn't here."

"If she's not on her ship, where the hell is she?"

"Somewhere captains go? How the hell should I know, I'm not privileged to classified information on this vessel. I just got here."

"You really fucked us over in Skelm, you know. We could have had that whole station stripped, but you just decided to ignore our repeated messages."

"I got arrested for jaywalking, Shit-For-Brains. I couldn't have responded even if I wanted to."

"What kind of shitty contractor gets arrested for *jaywalking*?"

Larkin sighed angrily. "Listen, how about we agree to just sit here in silence until your benevolent dictator gets back?"

"She's not our dictator, we're a team."

"Sure, in the same way that wolves and sheep are on the same level."

"Shut up!"

"Alright, where is she?" Josie asked, stomping back into the loading bay.

"I know you're hiding her here somewhere."

"I told you, she's not here. She hasn't been here since we left Bradach."

"I find that hard to believe."

"You searched the ship yourself! If she was here, you'd have found her. She's not here. I don't know where she is."

"Well that's too bad for you, then."

Larkin tilted her head. "And why is that?"

"Because we'll be taking you, instead. Congratulations, you're now our hostage. If Violet wants you back, she'll have to pay a handsome ransom and give herself up in your stead." Josie smirked. "She's such a penitent do-gooder, I bet we won't have to wait very long."

"No, please," Larkin pleaded, forcing a tear from her eyes. "Please, I just want to stay here, I'm broke and I need to get paid, and—"

Josie pointed her gun. Two guns pointed right at Larkin's chest, now. "Too bad, scum. Let's go. Get on the shuttle."

Timing. The timing was everything. "What will you do to me if she doesn't come?"

"Oh, she'll come. But on the very small chance that she doesn't, we'll kick you ass-first out of the airlock."

Time to make it convincing. "No, I won't go! You can't make me, I'll fight!"

"I'll blow a hole in your skull so big there won't be anything left of your ugly face," Beard said, pulling his gun, too. "Let's go."

With a sob, Larkin jumped down from her perch and boarded their shuttle, three guns at her back. Not long, now. It was all going to plan. People like these were so predictable. Buckling herself into the seat, she felt the shuttle lurch as it pulled out of the Cricket's loading bay and ease into dark space. Josie was at the helm, pushing the shuttle to maximum speed. Their ship couldn't be far, these things didn't have much range. Larkin settled back into her seat and started to drift off when the shuttle landed in their ship's bay with an unsettling crunch.

"Not much good on the landings then, are you?" she muttered.

"Keep your mouth shut or I'll expedite your trip back to the Cricket by way of the cannons," Josie shot back. "Get out."

Larkin eased out of the shuttle, eyeing the underside for damage. Luckily, it looked like the damage was only cosmetic. Excellent. "So what now?"

"Now we send a message to the Cricket and tell them they have forty-eight hours to get us ransom money and *Captain* Violet or you die."

"Just out of curiosity, what makes you think she's going to care that you have me? For all you know, we didn't have an amiable relationship. Maybe I think she's a bastard, too."

"She will."

"If you say so."

Josie grabbed her by the collar of her borrowed jacket. "You're damned right I say so. Now get into the airlock. You'll be spending the next two days in the brig."

"You know, I'm not so sure that plan works with my schedule," Larkin said, snatching Josie's gun right out of her hands. She was the biggest threat.

"Hey!" Beard and Earrings yelled in unison, pointing their guns at her.

One hand on the stolen gun, she pulled one of the concealed knives from her thigh holster and flung it. She was aiming for their hands, but if she missed, the world wouldn't be much worse off. The knife lodged in Earrings' wrist. She screamed, the gun dropping to the ground. As Larkin knew he would, Beard bent to pick it up off the floor, and when he did, Larkin jumped forward with the other knife, punching Beard's gun hand with her stolen revolver and slashing at the one grasping for the fallen one. Beard stumbled backward, and Larkin swept the guns from the floor.

"See, now I have three guns, and you all have none," she chirped. Nothing put her into a better mood than a plan well executed. "What should we do about that?"

Josie scrabbled along the floor and grabbed for Larkin's knees. "No, no, I don't think we'll be doing that, thank you," Larkin said, smiling, a gun trained on Josie and one trained on the other pair, the third gun wedged into her pocket. "Drop the keypass for the shuttle and get into the airlock."

"We'll be back, you know," Josie spat. "We'll keep coming back until we get what we came for."

"I don't think that's true, actually. In fact, I don't want to see any of your faces ever again, do you understand me? I killed Lionel Cabot, you know-nothing scrubs, I could have killed you all in a heartbeat but I'm leaving you alive out of respect for Captain Violet."

"You didn't kill Lionel Cabot," Josie sneered, with an arched eyebrow that made Larkin very uncomfortable.

"I did. And if you come at me, or any member of the Cricket crew again, I'll be wearing your teeth as a shiny new necklace." She smirked. "Assuming you have any left in your skulls by then, given the way you seem to pick fights you can't win."

"Fuck you, you hack-ass conwoman," Beard spat, his hands up in the air. "I bet you didn't kill him. You run around telling that story to anyone who will listen to get yourself out of trouble."

Larkin stared. "It really was a pleasure doing business with you. However, I have places to be and people to see, so I'm going to take my leave. Oh, and I'm stealing your shuttle. It's my fee for threatening my friends." The word felt strange in her mouth - *friends*. Is that really what the crew of the Cricket was to her now? "Alright, into the airlock," she said, gesturing with the gun. "Don't want you getting sucked into space, that would completely defeat the purpose of not killing you on sight the moment I set eyes on your ugly faces."

The trio backed into the crew airlock and the door slid closed, Josie's glare all but boring a hole through the thick glass. Time to go, before they regrouped and came back with heat guns or some shit. Larkin climbed into the shuttle, waved the keypass over the console, and fired up the boiler. She was a shit pilot but it would have to do, unless she wanted to stay with this merry band of miscreants and end up getting killed because their plans royally sucked.

The trip back to the Cricket was quiet and smooth, coasting through dark space. She could have saved herself the trouble if she had just killed them on sight, but Captain Violet's ship, Captain Violet's rules. Larkin hated the quiet. Too much time for her mind to wander to dark places, to dwell on things that ached at the center of her being. Silence told too many truths.

At least on a job, she had someone's habits and schedule to observe, blueprints to memorize, strategies to consider. This short trip was reminding her why she hated flying.

When she landed the shuttle in the loading bay, it scraped against their existing shuttle, scratching the faded paint job. The captain's glare was visible from twenty paces through the cracked airlock glass, and Larkin's stomach lurched. Better face the consequences.

The loading bay door latched and the room pressurized before Larkin climbed out of the small transport.

"What the hell are we supposed to do with two shuttles?" the captain asked over the quiet hiss of the crew's airlock door. "We won't be able to fit a single crate of freight in here, now."

"Er—" Larkin started.

"Thank you."

Larkin blinked. "What?"

"Thank you. For what you did. I know that you didn't kill them, even though you could have. I know you did that for me."

"How do you know that?"

"They radioed over as soon as you took their shuttle. We didn't grasp much other than a string of very offensive expletives, but they're alive, even though they probably don't deserve it." Captain Violet turned and shook her finger at her navigator. "And if you ever, *ever* lock me in that storage room ever again, Nedrick, you'll be looking for a new job."

"Aye, Boss," Ned said with a laugh. "Sure."

"What did they want, anyway?" the captain asked, flicking her stare back to Larkin. "Money? Scrap?"

Larkin nodded. "And you."

"Of course. Fools."

"I don't think it's the last time you'll see that Josie woman. I might have scared the other two off."

The captain sighed. "No, I suspect she'll continue to be a thorn in our side. She's getting braver, smarter. Where the hell did she even get that ship from, anyway? It's not her old one, the Coalition would have scrapped it."

"I don't know."

"That might have taken days to sort out if they'd taken me on board," Captain Violet admitted. "At least now we've only lost a couple of hours."

"What about the shuttle?" Alice asked, eyeing it. "Might be worth checking it out."

"You can't keep it. We don't have room, you gearhead."

"Might be better than our old model. I'll send Ivy to do my rounds and check it out. Could be a good thing, Vi."

Evie's absence in the loading bay hit Larkin like another heat gun bolt to the ribs. Evie didn't even care that she'd made it back okay.

* * *

"Alright, people, now that some of us have *finally* decided to show up," Captain Violet boomed from atop a table with a smirk, "let's go over the general plan." She unfurled a large blueprint of the armory, marked with solid and dotted lines, and the large Xs that Larkin knew would be the end goals for this job, the rooms with the data servers. "This is a smash-and-grab. Our previous plan is scrapped, we don't have time for that now, not when the Coalition is planning something big." She exhaled loudly and rested her hands on her hips. "We'll all be assigned to pairs or teams, but most of you will be remaining on the ship. The fewer of us risking our asses down on that base, the better."

"Alice and the rest of the usual maintenance crew will stay here on the ship to keep things running smoothly, and to make sure the cloaking shields stay up," Kady announced, climbing up onto a chair so she could be seen by everyone. "Ivy will pilot the new shuttle down initially, and use an artificially generated security code to grant her access to one of the larger transport vehicles, and return to pick the away team up so we can all travel together. As all of the transport bays in the Armory are automated, she should be able to get in and out without having to actually speak to anyone."

"We're stealing a transport?" Larkin asked. It was an incredibly risky move, and an unnecessary one. "Why not just send me down to get the data?"

Captain Violet considered this for a moment, and then shook her head. "No. If you get caught, then that's our one shot. We run a higher risk of being targeted, yes, but also a higher possibility that we will be able to uncover what we're looking for. Which is why we'll be hitting all three data centers, the worst that will happen is we end up with duplicate information. It's unlikely that all three teams will succeed, but hopefully at least one will."

"Why not take both shuttles, then?"

"Also too risky, especially because that one you commandeered from our friend Captain Josie has a pirate signature. The Armory would shoot it down before we even hit atmosphere, and we don't have the time for Kady to reprogram it."

Larkin huffed quietly. "Okay."

"As I was saying," Kady continued, "we will all go down together, and disembarking from the transport is where we're most vulnerable. We'll all have orange jumpsuits to disguise ourselves as janitorial staff, but we can't attract any more attention than is absolutely necessary." She pointed at the blueprints, one arm behind her back and an impeccably straight posture. "Each of the data centers will have an armed guard posted outside the door, but they rotate every twenty minutes. If we get in, get the data, and get out before their replacement arrives, it will be a miracle." Kady pulled a small, circular disk from her pocket. "Which is why Alice and I have developed this. In the event we cannot access the rooms, you will be able to use these small explosive devices to get inside."

"So much for not attracting attention," Larkin scoffed, which earned her a withering glare from Kady. "And I sure hope these are better than the last invention you two cooked up, because that sedation gun sucked."

"Why don't you come over here and test it on yourself?" Kady asked sweetly. "If we're lucky you might earn yourself the other side of a titanium rib cage."

"Alright," Alice interjected, "let's stay focused, shall we? Kady and Jasper are one pair, heading for the northernmost data center. Captain Violet and Ivy are the second, going for the eastern block, and Larkin and Evie, you're the final pair, aiming for the southern location. This is a smash and grab, but don't attract any more attention than necessary, and definitely don't hang around. Get back to the transport as soon as you have the data, or if you hear the alarm. The alarm means the Coalition know we're there, and we need to get the hell out."

"Obviously," Larkin said under her breath, and Alice gave her a warning glance. "Sounds good," she said louder, with plenty of faux enthusiasm. She just got back, and here they were sending her out again. Evie was standing as far away as she could on the small bridge, and refused to make eye contact. Larkin tried for a smile. "Buck up, Inmate, looks like we're in this together, like it or not."

"Yup," Evie said shortly, and Larkin resisted the urge to make another barbed comment about Evie's poor decision making skills. Now wasn't the time, but if they both survived this self-destructive mission, she planned to get an answer to her question. Evie pulled away from the kiss because she was still in love with Holly, but Larkin wanted her to admit it out loud; maybe the sharpness of the words would nip her distracting feelings in the bud and let her get back to work, somewhere far away from here.

* * *

"This place smells like ass," Larkin said, climbing off the transport. "Worse than the public washrooms in any tavern I've ever been in."

"It's the sulfur, from the explosives they build here," Evie said flatly. "I'd have thought an experienced killer-for-hire like you would know that."

Larkin narrowed her eyes, and then sighed. "Whatever. Still smells like ass."

"Can we please keep it together?" Captain Violet hissed, following them off the ship. "Stay focused." She looked back to Ivy, who was unclipping the safety belt as the engines whirred softly. "You ready?"

"Aye," Ivy said, and Larkin echoed her.

"Right. Get in, get what we need, back on the ship. Whoever gets in first may trigger the alarm, so don't hang around once you hear it. We've got twenty minutes before our generated security code gets purged from their system."

The three pairs exchanged radios, which they clipped to their garish orange janitorial jumpsuits, emblazoned with the Coalition crest across the breast pocket. They were all covered in faded stains that Larkin definitely didn't want to know the origin of. She motioned for Evie to follow her. "Keep your fucking head down, just in case one of them remembers your face from the public broadcast."

"Alice said I might make a useful distraction."

"Yeah, well, you're not going to be used as fucking bait as long as I'm around. This whole thing is stupid, let's just get what we need and get the hell out of here."

"What, never infiltrated a Coalition base before?" Evie asked, teasing.

"Of course, but I've never attempted to steal data from the goddamned Armory, the most densely weaponized place in the Near Systems. You ask me, this plan is asinine. I'll be shocked if any of us make it back with this magic information they're looking for."

"Ah come on, Larks," Evie said, playfully jabbing her in the only original ribs she had left. "It might be fun. No better way to settle an argument than a bit of friendly competition, right? After all, you did just save everyone's asses with those other pirates."

The abrupt swerve in tone caught her off guard, but she wasn't about to let a petty argument get them caught. She'd seen enough of the inside of a Coalition prison cell to last her a lifetime. She smirked and jabbed Evie back. "I bet we can beat the other teams to the data center."

"You're on," Evie replied, picking up her pace to somewhere between a purposeful walk and a shuffling jog. They couldn't run, not if they wanted to make it to the southern center without getting caught. She grabbed a wheelie bin from the side of a small communications tower and pushed it in front of her. "See, now I look legit."

Larkin stifled a snort and walked alongside her, as though they were on the way to clean up a conference room, or a toxic spill. Their radios remained silent, which was a good sign. It meant the other two teams were still en route to their data server rooms, and no one had gotten busted yet. She'd imagined the Armory would have more of a bustle, given the number of soldiers stationed here, and the immense number of weapons stored in basement bunkers far beneath the surface. In fact, it was nearly a ghost town. She pushed the uneasy feeling down as they approached the small grey building. It was probably nothing.

"Here we are," Evie whispered, eyeing the guard from behind a nearby shed filled with cleaning products and waste bins. "If my watch is right, they should be rotating posts any second now." As if on cue, the guard checked his shiny silver pocket watch, which glinted in the reflected sun from mirrors similar to those on Bradach. He sighed, turned, and marched off towards the western data center, which was on the other side of the Armory.

"Now or never," Larkin said when the guard was out of sight. She strolled up to the door like it was the most natural thing in the world, the small explosive ready in her pocket. "Huh," she said over her shoulder to Evie. "They don't use digital locks. That seems odd."

"Maybe they haven't upgraded yet?"

The nagging feeling in Larkin's spine grew heavier. "Yeah, maybe." She pulled a lock pick from inside her bra. "I can get us inside without the explosive. The quieter, the better, that's what the captain said, right?"

"I'll keep a lookout," Evie said, positioning herself and the trash bin in front of Larkin to hide her from view.

"No need, I'm already in," Larkin smirked as the lock popped open.

"That's irritatingly impressive."

Evie's approval made Larkin's stomach flip flop, which was an interesting, yet distracting addition to the unsettling feeling that they were being watched. She reached for the chain of her pendant, a familiar comfort even in the most uncomfortable spaces. "Come on, inside," she said, and ushered Evie inside before closing and locking the door behind them. "We've got maybe a few minutes before the next guard shows up and traps us in here, so let's get a move on."

"Already on it," Evie smiled, inserting a small square disk into the main console. "Kady said the display should show whatever it's writing to— what the hell?"

Larkin turned and furrowed her brow at the display. "What does it mean, no data available? Try it again." Evie pulled the disk out and reinserted it, but the same message flashed on the screen. "Fuck. Can you do it manually?"

"Yeah, it will take longer though."

"Do it."

Evie fiddled with the knobs below the display, and swore under her breath. "Larkin, there's nothing here. This data server is empty."

"What do you mean, empty?"

"There's nothing on it! No data!"

The weight of what Evie said sank horribly into Larkin's guts, and lodged itself there when she realized what it all meant.

"Fuck. They knew we were coming. Again."

CHAPTER TWENTY-FOUR

The alarm began to sound, a loud, aggressive whine pumped through speakers in every building across the base. Red lights flashed from the console with ERROR scrolling across. She turned to Larkin, who was stone faced, with a large throwing knife in each hand. Somehow, she hadn't noticed the bulky sash made of similar knives that she'd hidden beneath the garish orange jumpsuit. "What now?" she shouted over the din of the alarms.

"We get back to the transport, and hope to fuck no one else gets nabbed." Larkin adjusted the knife belt that was slung over her shoulder and leaned against the door. "You ready? We're gonna have to be quick."

With a nod, Evie shoved the disk back in her pocket, not that it mattered, being empty and useless. They were the furthest from the transport and the most likely to be caught, especially if their tampering is what triggered the alarm. "Let's go."

Larkin eased open the door, knife in hand. "Coast is clear." She motioned for Evie to follow her, and darted behind the shed next to the building. If they could stay out of sight, their odds of not getting killed would significantly increase. The blaring siren dulled any sound of voices or footsteps, which was good for remaining undetected, but terrible for hearing if anyone had spotted them. She pushed a tuft of blue hair out of her face and peeked around the corner to see a group of soldiers running full pelt towards the building, every single one of them armed to the teeth with revolvers and heat guns. If Larkin had to use one of her knives, then her aim better be damn good. The soldiers were inaudible over the noise, but definitely shouting directions to each other. The group split into pairs that headed off in every direction, including towards the shed.

Evie tugged at Larkin's sleeve, pointing at the pair headed their way. There wasn't much between the shed and the transport, nothing more than a long way to run in the wide open, a perfect place to get shot. If they made a break for it now, they'd be dead in three steps. The pair of soldiers approached, weapons drawn, but they hadn't spotted them yet. Larkin ran her thumb over the hilt of the silver knife, poised like a cat ready to strike. As the soldiers neared, their voices emerged from the chaos of the alarm.

"They've gotta be here somewhere," one of them said. "The lieutenant said they were on their way."

"They wouldn't be stupid enough to hide behind a shed—" the other said, nearly stepping on Evie as she rounded the corner. "Oh, hey, would you look at that, they *are* that stupid," the soldier smirked, pulling back the hammer on the pistol. "Alright, scum, hands where I can see them or I blow your brains into next week."

The sun glinted on the knife as it streaked past Evie's face and buried itself deep into the soldier's thigh, which bloomed red blood flowers across her immaculately tailored uniform. "Oh, fuck—" the soldier screamed, ripping the knife out of her flesh.

"Shouldn't have done that," Larkin said easily, flinging a second knife into the other soldier's shoulder. "Makes the bleed worse." Before she had even finished her sentence, the soldier's leg began to pump her lifeblood into the ironed, bleached white woven fabric of the Coalition uniform. She'd be unconscious soon. The second soldier left the knife in her shoulder, heat gun raised and ready to fire.

"You bitch!" the second one screamed, and as she hefted the heat gun from one arm to the other, a flicker of recognition flashed over her face. "Hey, I know you! You're the one who escaped from the prison!" The soldier fumbled with the heat gun, reaching for her radio, but Larkin knocked the gun to the ground and tossed it to Evie, pausing to twist the knife in the soldier's shoulder, sending her screaming to the ground.

"Here, arm yourself. It's time we put these two down." Larkin turned back to the bleeding soldiers, two more knives in her hands.

"We don't have time for that, come on," Evie urged, clambering to her feet. "They don't have anything on me worse than what I've already got. One or two extra charges on my rap sheet won't make the difference with what they do to me if they catch me."

Larkin nodded, and then hesitated for a brief moment. She snatched the radios from the bleeding soldiers, crushing them under her boot with a satisfying series of electrical pops. "We're going to need to run for it, now," she said grimly. "I don't think we'll make it in an all out firefight. We need to get back to that transport."

The soldiers were shouting to their crew, but they were unheard over the cacophony of the siren. It was now or never, but both of those options were likely to end in imprisonment, torture, and death. Evie steeled herself, willing herself to become one with the weight of the heat gun, and realized she'd rather go out swinging than deal with the likes of Allemande again. The choice between a quick death and a slow, painful one was easy to make, at least for her. She nodded and kicked the crushed remains of the radios out of the reach of the soldiers, just in case. "Race you there," she said, and tried to force a smile past the terror she knew was evident on her face. "Whoever wins, buys the drinks at the next tavern."

"See you at the transport, slow poke," Larkin replied, and underneath her humor, Evie could hear the sharp edge of training and adrenaline that lay just beneath the surface.

"Yeah, I'll see you there," Evie said, and reached out to squeeze Larkin's hand. "Don't be late."

"I would never."

Evie launched herself into a run, willing the din of the siren to dull the sound of her heavy steps as her boots crunched gravel under the soles. A trio of guards burst into the small grey building, and the telltale sparks of revolvers firing lit up the room. The transport was ahead, and Ivy was already powering up the engines. They must not have been far from the vehicle when the alarm was triggered, but if they didn't get the hell off this base soon, they'd all spend the evening getting autopsied in the morgue.

"Hurry up!" Larkin shouted, and prodded her in the back. "Don't look back, okay?"

Of course, Evie did look back, and when she did, there was a second group of soldiers emerging from their barracks. They didn't have long before they were spotted, running across this empty storage yard. She urged her legs to move faster, but the extra weight of the heat gun was weighing her down. If she dropped it, she'd draw attention and also not have something to defend herself with.

One of the soldiers turned over their shoulder and spotted her, stumbling over her own feet. She couldn't hear what they said, but every other soldier turned towards them, weapons drawn. "Oh, fuck," Evie said. The transport was half empty. Kady and Jasper hadn't made it back yet. If Evie alerted the soldiers to the transport, none of them would make it out alive. She steeled herself, and planted her feet where she was stood, heat gun raised and ready to fire red hot bolts of steel at the growing platoon of Coalition troops.

"Evie, no!" Larkin shouted.

"Go! Keep the others safe!"

"Are you out of your goddamned mind?"

"I'm not going back to that hellhole, Larkin!"

Larkin planted herself next to Evie, twirling a sparkling knife between her knuckles. "And neither am I." Her fingers brushed against the delicate silver chain around her neck. "Come on, barkeep, let's waste these fools."

"Or die trying."

"Or die trying," Larkin agreed, nudging her shoulder next to Evie's.

The platoon approached, while a few in the back peeled off to attend to their fallen comrades, who were still screaming and swearing despite their significant blood loss. Evie was glad she couldn't hear them over the alarm, which continued to bellow and ring in her ears. The soldiers in front were four across, all holding revolvers with long, intimidating barrels. They pulled the hammers back in unison, but before Evie could react Larkin flung two knives, and then two more, dropping the soldiers where they stood. "Fucking hell, you really are an assassin, aren't you?"

"Born and raised," Larkin said, swiftly pulling two more from the rapidly emptying belt. "Take the left two."

Evie aimed the heat gun and fired, the recoil nearly knocking her on her ass. The smoking steel zinged between the two she'd been aiming for, singeing their uniforms, and knocking into the soldier behind them.

"Go again," Larkin said coolly, taking out the two on the right. "One less to deal with behind them, now."

Bullets whizzed by Evie's head, and she danced from foot to foot to be as difficult a target as she could be. Shots rang across the yard, barely audible over the siren, and when they stopped to reload their guns, she took the opportunity to fire the heat gun again, this time sending a red hot bolt ricocheting off the ground and into the stomach of a soldier who keeled over from the force and screamed as the bolt burned through his uniform. "I can't aim with this thing!" Evie shouted, as Larkin pulled the last three slender knives from her belt.

"You have to," Larkin replied.

Evie's eye's swept over the empty yard, and her gaze fell on a curious fluorescent yellow barrel to the left of the advancing platoon. She ducked to avoid the trajectory of an oncoming bolt from a heat gun. It was time to gamble with their lives, and it would either save them or kill them, but she didn't have the luxury of time for debate. Evie aimed at the barrel and fired, the steel bolt glowing with heat as it penetrated the barrel.

The explosion was instantaneous, the blast toppling the rest of the platoon. Some were probably dead, but others just blown across the gravel yard, their moans inaudible beneath the alarm. She turned to Larkin, who was motioning for her to follow back to the transport. Evie dropped the heat gun and ran for her life, towards the beckoning hands of Kady and Jasper, the latter of whom was whiter than a sheet of paper and looked like he might be sick. Ivy was hovering the ship off the ground, her mouth open in a desperate scream inaudible over the alarm. Evie jumped onto the transport as it began to rise up and away from the base, and held her arms out to catch Larkin's wrists and pull her aboard before slamming the door shut.

The noise of the siren began to fade, but rang in Evie's ears so loudly that she could barely hear what the captain was asking her. "What?" she asked again, for the third time.

"Did anyone get the data?" Captain Violet asked again.

Kady shook her head. "There was nothing."

"They knew we were coming," Larkin said, out of breath from their sprint to safety. "They knew we were coming and they wiped the servers."

Captain Violet clenched the loose fabric of her jumpsuit. "How the fuck did they know we were coming?"

"I don't know, but we better get back to the Cricket before those assholes catch up to us," Kady said urgently. "Ivy, what's our status?"

"We should be back in about ninety seconds, I'm pushing this thing as fast as it can go."

The shuttle hurtled through dark space, much faster than the old two person transport could go. The only sound in the vehicle was the strained, whining engines, and the heavy gasps from Evie and Larkin as they struggled to catch their breath. They were flying blind without radar. Transports this size weren't fitted with navigation systems, only meant to bring soldiers from base to their assigned ships, not escape from one of the most heavily armed areas in the Near Systems. For all they knew, there were a dozen ships lifting off to chase them.

Ivy pulled into the loading bay smooth and soft, and they waited for the heavy, slow door to latch closed, the steam hydraulics that powered the door hissing in protest. "Fuck," Captain Violet said, opening the door of the shuttle.

The large speaker bolted above the crew airlock crackled. "Crew to your stations, we've got company!" came Ned's voice, laced with panic. "Boss you'd better get up here, it's like they're tracking us somehow."

"All of you, strip down and burn your clothes, just in case there's a tracker on one of you." Evie started to slowly unzip her jumpsuit. "Now!" the captain shouted, stripping off her own jumpsuit. "Better thought, leave them on the floor. Ivy, don't secure the shuttle. When we're all through the airlock, open the loading bay and let everything go. If there's a tracker let them follow it there and we'll be long gone."

They all shimmied out of the ugly orange jumpsuits and dropped them to the metal grate, shivering as they packed into the crew airlock and watched the jumpsuits sail into space. "Go get dressed, all of you." Captain Violet stood in her black lacy underthings, and somehow was even more terrifying without her clothes than with them, given her steely glare and total lack of embarrassment. "Hurry up!"

They all scattered to their quarters, footsteps pounding against the metal grates. Evie dove into her quarters and threw on her shirt and trousers, regretting that she'd left the oversized jumpsuit in her old rented room. It wasn't flattering, but it was sure as hell practical. She skidded back into the corridor, tugging on her boots and buttoning her shirt, only to realize she didn't know where she should actually be in a situation like this. The speaker on the wall crackled. "Boss, we're still being followed, and we're losing ground fast. These newer Coalition vessels are fast as fuck!" The speaker continued to crackle as Ned kept the transmission going. "Kady, I think you should use the EMP gun on the newbies, just to be safe. Just in case."

Evie jumped when she heard Kady behind her speaking into her radio: "Roger that, Ned, EMP is on hand." Kady pulled a small, silver, snub nosed gun from the inside breast pocket of her jacket. "Don't worry, it doesn't hurt."

Larkin tumbled out of her quarters, buttoning up her shirt with clumsy fingers.

"Hey, you too," Kady barked, and gestured to the small gun. "I need to disable any Coalition chips you might have, just in case they're being used as trackers." Larkin held out her arm and tossed her long, shiny braid.

"There's no way that's possible, my chip is from a grey market dealer. It's the third one I've had, along with identities."

"Yeah well, we have to be sure, with these assholes picking up speed. If they catch up to us, there's no way this ship would survive a firefight." The gun chirped and flashed green. "You're not being tracked," Kady said, a hint of disappointment in her voice. She turned to Evie. "Now you."

Evie obediently held out her arm, hidden beneath the sleeves of her shirt.

Kady pushed the sleeves up and pressed the gun to her skin, the light flashing yellow.

"You don't have a chip?" Kady asked.

"No, I never have. Bradach born and raised."

"Of course, right. I remember scanning you when you first joined us from the prison." She narrowed her eyes and let her gaze fall on Evie's arms. "Hm." Kady peeled back the bandages and stared down at the angry scars that bubbled up from Evie's skin, the remnants of the torture Inspector Allemande had inflicted. Her eyes grew huge, and she gasped. "Evie, I think they may have hidden a tracker in your wounds."

"No. No, that's impossible," Evie said, fear taking root in her stomach and sending bile to blossom angrily in her throat.

"It's not impossible, and it's the best lead we've got," Kady said, pulling her along the corridor. "We'll have to cut open the scars and see if there's a tracker embedded in your skin, something new that doesn't respond to the EMP gun."

"Just try the gun again," Evie pleaded, trying to wrench her arm away from Kady. The petite woman was stronger than she looked, and pulled Evie behind her. "Maybe the gun will work, please—"

"I've heard of trackers like these," Kady said, ignoring Evie's desperation. "They utilize tiny Faraday cages to protect the trackers from being disabled remotely, like with my EMP gun. The only way to stop them transmitting is to rip them out and crush them."

"Please, stop—"

"Everyone on this ship will die if we don't find out what's allowing them to follow us. No amount of cloaking shields will give us a chance in hell of surviving, do you understand that? I'm so sorry Evie, but we have to."

"Please don't cut me open," Evie begged, hot tears flowing freely down her face now. "Please!"

* * *

Larkin felt a feral anger build in her chest. Who the hell did Kady think she was, dragging Evie off to subject her to the same torture she'd undergone in the prison. *Hell no*, Larkin thought, *not on my watch.* The rest of the crew be damned, she wasn't about to let Evie get carved up in some desperate search for a tracking device. She shoved Kady into the wall of the narrow stairwell and pried Evie's arm free.

"Don't fucking touch her," she snarled. "Don't you have any idea what she's been through? You want to slice her open just like that monster Allemande did, on a goddamn hunch? Have you completely lost your goddamned mind?"

"We don't have time for this," Kady hissed, leaning into Larkin's face. "If we don't find how they're tracking us, we're all dead."

"Yeah, well, maybe don't have cutting open someone who spent a week slowly being chopped to pieces be the first thing on the table." Larkin stepped between Evie and Kady and scowled at the scientist whose jacket she was wearing. "Try. Something. Else."

Kady looked panicked, as though the idea that Evie was carrying the tracker was the only possible solution she'd considered. "But it has to be her!" Kady spluttered. "Who else could possibly be carrying a tracker that has to be embedded that deep? I'm damn sure we'd remember that procedure."

"You're telling me there's nothing else, anywhere on this ship that might be carrying a tracker? It's impossible that someone brought one in accidentally on the sole of their boot, or had one hidden in a stolen shipment of produce?"

"No." Kady shook her head. "These kinds of trackers draw energy from heat, and the electrical charge of human physiology. They wouldn't work on a boot or in a pile of lettuce."

"You don't know for sure that's even how they're tracking us!" Larkin shouted, and felt Evie flinch behind her. "It could be more sophisticated radar, or a lucky guess!"

"That's not how any of this works," Kady scoffed, and reached around Larkin to grab Evie's arm again. "I'm telling you, it must be in her arms somewhere."

Larkin blocked Kady's grab, leaning forward on the stairs to pin her to the wall. Her necklace slipped out from under her half unbuttoned shirt, and caught the dim yellow light before she could stuff it back behind the borrowed white fabric. "I said, try something else."

"What was that?" Kady asked pointedly. "Why have you got it hidden?"

"None of your business," Larkin snapped.

Kady's arm darted out and snatched at the necklace, snapping the silver chain links that held it around Larkin's neck. "This looks like it's big enough to hold a tracker," she said, before sprinting down the stairs into the boiler room. Larkin followed, leaping down the steps two at a time despite the sharp throb under her shiny new rib cage.

"Wait!" she shouted after Kady, who was already out of sight. "Stop! That's mine!" Larkin was vaguely aware that Evie was following her, sniffling softly. Larkin turned and squeezed Evie's hand, trying to quell the trembling in her palms. "Don't worry," she reassured her, before jumping down the rest of the stairs into Alice's workshop.

"Alice, break this open!" Kady tossed the necklace to the mechanic, who caught it in the air and slammed it on the workbench. "I think there's a tracker in it!"

"Wait!" Larkin yelled, moving to snatch the necklace back. "It's mine, it can't be the tracker!"

With the briefest of apologetic glances, Alice pulled a huge wrench from the side pocket of her tool belt and brought it down hard on the necklace. To Larkin's horror, the pendant popped free of its wire mesh setting with a threatening crack down the middle. Alice swung the wrench again, this time severing the pendant in two, and leaving a small, circular metal disk that blinked red and orange in an alternating pattern, exposed on the workbench. Larkin gasped and stepped back from the table, her hand over her mouth. It couldn't be. It was impossible.

"Smash it!" Kady bellowed, and Alice responded by crushing the necklace to smithereens with repeated smacks with the wrench, destroying the tracker in its entirety. Kady whirled on Larkin, her face full of accusation. "How long have you had that?" she demanded.

"I've had it since I was a child! I've had it since—" Larkin stopped herself.

No. It couldn't be.

"Captain," Kady said into her radio, "we've got a situation down here in the boiler room. It seems I've caught us a spy."

CHAPTER TWENTY-FIVE

Evie's heart pounded in her throat. Larkin? A spy? The only time she'd seen Larkin without that necklace was when she was recovering from her rib replacement, and even then it was never far from her grasp.

"You can't just accuse *everyone* of being a spy," Alice said. "After all, I didn't turn out to be one, even after weeks of you suspecting I was."

"No, but Barnaby certainly did his best to screw us all over," Kady snapped.

"Barnaby wasn't a spy, just a greedy ass," Alice countered.

"What's going on here?" Captain Violet demanded, descending the steps into the boiler room with more poise than Evie thought possible of someone who'd been sure they were all going to die just a few moments ago. "What do you mean, spy?"

Kady pointed at the shrapnel in accusation, her chin jutting out in defiance. "We found the tracker, it was in a pendant Larkin was wearing."

Captain Violet turned to Larkin and inclined her head. "Is this true?"

Larkin nodded, but remained silent.

"She was leading them right to us," Kady said. "Ask Ned, I'm sure he'll say we're losing the fleet now."

"Ned, report," Captain Violet said into the radio. "Tell me what we're looking at."

"Evasive maneuvers seem to be confusing them, and our lead is gaining. However they were tracking us, they aren't now," Ned's voice crackled in response. "A damn good thing, too, I'm not sure how much longer we would have held out if I'm honest."

"See?" Kady hissed. "It was her."

"Vi, I think it's probably important to note that Larkin's had that thing for years. Who the hell knows how long it's had a tracker," Alice offered. "You've had it since you were a kid, yes?" she asked Larkin, who nodded, sullen as a trapped feral cat.

"Who gave this to you?" Captain Violet asked, her voice kinder than Evie had ever heard it when addressing Larkin.

Larkin shook her head and covered her face. Evie knew she was crying, and wanted nothing more than to rush over and wrap the assassin in a hug. Truth be told, she looked just as surprised as the rest of them did, staring down at the remains of the shattered pendant.

"You need to tell us who," Captain Violet pressed gently. "So we can figure out what's going on here."

A long moment passed while Larkin tried in vain to stifle her tears. "My mother."

"Fuck," Alice breathed.

"When?" Captain Violet asked, her voice calm and even.

"When I was a child. Before... before Lionel Cabot."

"There's no chance someone might have switched it? In the prison, maybe?" Kady asked.

"No," Larkin shook her head again, and a tear dripped from her jawline onto the rumpled collar of the black jacket. Evie's heart broke a little bit more, seeing a woman so rock solid and strong become so desperately vulnerable. "No, I made sure to keep it with me, I was afraid they would incinerate it with everything else. I stashed it under my tongue, and they were too stupid to check."

"Never when spending the night with someone?" Kady suggested. "Maybe you unwittingly spent the night with a covert operative?"

Larkin frowned at the invasive question, and crossed her arms in front of her. "No."

"It's possible though, right?" Kady asked again.

"*No.*" Larkin sighed and looked up at the ceiling, tears pooling at her lash line. "I don't... spend the night. Like that. Too familiar. Too intimate.

Dangerous for an assassin, so I always avoided it."

Evie couldn't help but think of the night they'd spent together, curled in each other's arms while they slept the first good sleep they'd had in weeks. She didn't offer up that information, though. She cleared her throat quietly, but fixed her eyes on the floor.

"Alright well, then we're working on the suspicion that what, she's been tracked *this entire time*?" Alice asked, horrified.

Captain Violet sighed and pressed her thumb and forefinger to the bridge of her nose. "It would explain the Blackwall."

"Fuck, I guess it would," Alice said, her voice heavy with the realization.

"No, that's— that's impossible," Larkin stuttered, gripping the edge of the workbench with fists that could punch through solid steel. "We went to Bradach, they'd have found it by now."

Alice shook her head. "Bradach uses tracker scramblers. You would have just gone dark for a while. They'll have seen the approach and exit, but the scramblers work in conjunction with a satellite bounce, too. Your locations there wouldn't have made any sense, and I guarantee they showed up as an anomaly, or an error in the reading."

"But why— why would she— why—" Larkin repeated, her inhales and exhales loud and frantic.

"Alright, let's all just take a breath," Captain Violet said, and wrapped her arms around Larkin's shoulders. The sudden, and frankly, unexpected display of affection broke Larkin, who sagged in the captain's grip, weeping into the epaulets of her crisply tailored jacket. "We can get to the bottom of this, but we have to get some answers first, okay? We have to know how long they've been tracking you, and why."

"I don't understand," Larkin sobbed. "They'll have seen that I was in every location a contract was completed. Sure, they report them as accidental deaths, but someone would have known. Someone would have seen. Why did they let me go? Why arrest me on Skelm? Why?"

Captain Violet and Alice exchanged a look that Evie read as being deeply concerned. Even Kady looked like she felt a little bit sorry for Larkin, despite her initial accusations of spy craft. When the captain released Larkin to reach for her radio, Evie took her place, wrapping her arms around Larkin's waist.

"Ned, how are we looking?" the captain said into the battered old radio, the rusted kinetic hand crank bent from years of heavy use.

"Smooth sailing from here Boss. Though it's probably best to switch on the cloaking shield for a while, until we know for sure they can't track us anymore."

"I agree. Set a course to Skelm, maybe we can dig up some idea of why Larkin was arrested there, and not on any of the rest of her contracts. It's clear that someone was aware of her, someone was watching her all this time, and we need to know why. *She* needs to know why." The captain clipped the radio back to her belt and turned to Kady. "Scramble the ship's data on approach, just in case they were able to latch onto something. I want to be more safe than sorry."

"Already on it, Captain," Kady replied, scribbling notes into a small book. She looked up at Larkin sheepishly, her brows knitted together. "Larkin, I'm... I'm sorry."

"Boss, our ETA on Skelm is two days," the radio crackled. "Provided there are no flightpath blocks we have to skate around."

"Alright, people, you heard the man," Captain Violet said. "We've got two days to figure out where the hell we should even start." The captain turned towards the stairs, but paused to look over her shoulder at Evie, who was still holding Larkin in a tight grip, despite the dull ache in her biceps. "Take her back to her room, and let Hyun know if a sedative is needed. Grab some food tonight for the both of you." The captain's face was troubled, but she tried for an earnest smile. "I hear that there might even be some cake."

* * *

"Are you sure you don't want anything?" Evie asked, even though the food she'd brought from the kitchen had long gone cold. "You should at least try to keep your strength up, Hyun said your body is still healing from the surgery."

Larkin faced the wall, legs curled to her chest, in the same position she'd been in since they got back to the room. She'd refused food, water, and sedatives alike, and had barely moved from her position on the bed, laying on her good side, eyes squeezed shut. Evie had no idea what could be going on in her head, but was desperate to help. Nothing had worked, not even the tempting offer of chocolate cake fresh from the oven, despite the dense, sweet smell wafting down the corridors of the ship, drawing nearly every crew member to the mess hall. With Larkin so upset, Evie didn't partake in dinner or cake, either. Her throat felt swollen, like her tongue was too big for her mouth, awkward and listless. The sip of water she'd taken from the glass on the night stand was tepid, and crashed into her stomach like she'd swallowed seawater. She couldn't imagine how it would feel knowing the last thing your mother gave you before her death was some kind of Coalition tracking device. Evie wasn't close with her own mother, but that was due more to distance than outright selling her information to a fascist government.

"I could heat it up for you," she offered, but still there was no response. She sighed heavily and sat at the edge of the bed, rubbing her thumb across the decorative raised stitching on the blanket folded up beside her. "Just tell me what I can do," she whispered, unsure if it was even loud enough for Larkin to hear. "I just want to help."

Larkin shifted her position, and opened her eyes to look at Evie over her shoulder. She still didn't say anything, she just stared, and Evie was struck again at how pretty those deep brown eyes were, with their flecks of gold that shimmered no matter the light.

"What?" Evie asked, her voice soft.

"You could just... put your arm around me," Larkin whispered. "Just for a minute."

Evie kicked off her boots and crawled across the bed, nestling in the crook of Larkin's knees, and wrapped her scarred, newly healed arms around the assassin, who looked more like a scared, overwhelmed young woman than a cold blooded killer. Larkin grabbed at Evie's fingers to pull the grip tighter around her shoulders, with a small whimper. When she turned back, her dark eyes were searching for answers Evie couldn't give to her. Evie just squeezed her tighter, careful to keep her grip far from Larkin's still healing wounds, and the replacement rib cage that would take a few more weeks to settle into place, according to Hyun. "How's that?"

"Yeah," Larkin said, her voice low and quiet. "I just wanted to feel safe."

The enormity of Larkin's words swept into Evie's heart like a tidal wave, and she settled her head next to the assassin's. "You feel safe here?" she asked.

"I feel safe with *you*," was the reply.

For the first time in a long while, Evie didn't want to be anywhere else.

CHAPTER TWENTY-SIX

Larkin opened her eyes and stared out into the darkness of her room. Light from the bathroom pooled gently under the door and cast a long shadow behind the boot she'd kicked off when she climbed into bed. Seconds ticked by, a slow, languishing rhythm that was more punishing than it was relaxing. Evie breathed deep beside her, fast asleep, her arm still thrown over Larkin's shoulders. There was an uncomfortable comfort in being this close to her; Larkin was equally praying to the shadows for morning, and wishing the night would never end. If she could just get a handle on things, maybe everything else would right itself. She sighed and edged back towards Evie, nestling into the crook of her arm gently, so as not to wake her.

The tuft of unruly hair on Evie's head stuck up in all directions, a quietly endearing quirk that Larkin couldn't help but smile at, despite Evie's rejection only a few days prior. They'd be back on Skelm sooner than she'd hoped, even though that was the most likely place she could find answers to the dozens of questions she had swirling in her head, an angry hornets' nest that buzzed from one thought to the next, and none of them comforting. No matter the reason behind why her own mother had given her the tracker, it didn't change the fact that the Coalition had likely been monitoring her movements for most of her life. It was impossible that whoever had been watching her had missed the correlations between her locations and the mysterious deaths that the Coalition always reported as mundane accidents or illnesses. She needed to know the truth, even if it meant dying for it.

"Hey," Evie said in a groggy, half-asleep voice. Cute. "You okay?"

"Yeah. I'm okay. Go back to sleep."

"Mmkay," Evie sighed, and pulled her in closer, as though she was a child's soft toy, a security blanket against the ills of the world. Larkin didn't mind, and in fact, Evie's warm breath on her neck had a distinctly calming effect, each inhale and exhale even and smooth. Larkin tried to swallow the lump in her throat, and blink back the tears that threatened the borders of her eyes, but they breached, and slid down her cheeks. She choked down a sob, and muffled it with the back of her hand. A tear splashed onto the crisp white bed sheet, darkening a patch that spread slowly.

"Whas wrong?" Evie mumbled, trying to fight off the threat of sleep.

"Nothing, I'm fine," Larkin insisted, wiping her nose with her sleeve. "Allergies."

"You don't have allergies," Evie said, more awake now. "Tell me whatever it was you didn't tell them back there."

"It's complicated."

"Everything is complicated."

Larkin wriggled from Evie's grasp and sat up, her legs dangling over the side of the bed. "I don't know any more than they do," she admitted. "All I know is that the last thing I had of my mother was apparently a Coalition tracking device, designed to spy on me from the time I was twelve years old. I was stupid, I never should have kept it."

"We all have attachments to things," Evie said, resting a palm on Larkin's arm. "You're not stupid."

"So now I'm trying to figure out who was watching me, and why, and how my... mother was somehow wrapped up in all this."

"Mm."

"Eves, it just— it feels like it's all falling apart, you know? I was a mercenary, top of my game for over a decade, no attachments, no snags, no problems. Just get in, do the job, and get out, move on to the next thing. And now suddenly it's prisons, and trackers, and this ship..." she trailed off, and took in the sight of Evie's face, barely illuminated in the dark room, except for a hazy reflection in her deep hazel eyes, and the blurry profile of her face. "And you."

"Are you saying I'm a distraction?" Evie said laughing, but the undercurrent of hurt in her voice was obvious.

"Yes. I've been happy on my own for years, and now suddenly I find myself sleeping curled up next to you as though it was the most natural thing in the world."

"Maybe it is."

Larkin paused, and then gave a husky laugh. "Yeah. Maybe it is." She scrubbed at her wet cheeks with the sleeve of her shirt, and worried how puffy her eyes would be tomorrow. The crew would all be looking for signs that she had been crying, and her tear-stained cheeks and swollen eyes would be a dead giveaway.

"I'm sorry."

"Sorry for what?"

Sorry that I pulled away that night."

"Oh." Larkin froze, her shoulders tense and her hands clenched in her lap.

"I just... I needed to know that things were really over with Holly. I had to know the truth."

Larkin didn't want to hear about Holly, the backstabbing ex-girlfriend, and so remained silent, so as not to encourage any more on the topic. She was frankly sick of hearing about her, and damn tired of ruminating over how she'd stolen Evie's heart immediately with that cherubic face and tactile curves.

"But I really like being with you, in a way I never did with her." Evie shifted behind her, and Larkin resisted the urge to turn and look at her. "You make me laugh, Larkin, and you make me feel like I'm worth something."

"Of course you're worth something," Larkin said, barbs on her tongue like a ripe summer thorn bush. "She was a goddamn... a fucking fetid pool of rancid cat piss for not seeing how smart, and interesting, and beautiful you are."

Evie laughed, and the warm syrupy sound hung in Larkin's ears. "See? You make me laugh."

"I wasn't trying to be funny," Larkin grumbled, but sighed slowly when Evie wrapped her arms around her shoulders, kneeling behind her.

"You don't have to try. And besides, I always feel more like a real person when I'm with you." She rested her chin on Larkin's shoulder, and Larkin relaxed into the pressure. "I never should have doubted that you were better for me than her." She turned her head and kissed Larkin's neck soft and gentle, her breath lingering on the skin.

"Are you trying to distract me from my troubles?" Larkin said, her voice cracking.

"Why, is it working?"

Larkin turned her head and brushed Evie's lips with her own. "Yes."

Evie smirked with satisfaction and pulled her back into the middle of the bed, her arms wrapped around Larkin. "I am sorry though, about that night in the loading bay."

"Shut up," Larkin said, and kissed Evie again, this time with more eagerness. A tightness spread across her hips, and she couldn't recall ever being so hungry for someone as she was in that moment, with Evie looking up at her, her blue hair artfully flopped over one side of her face. Where the hell did this barkeep come from, that she knew the exact way to wheedle her way into Larkin's heart and mind, despite the chaos that surrounded them? She deepened the kiss, and imagined where they'd be if she had stolen her away that first night in the Purple Pig, before they'd both ended up in that Coalition prison. Maybe they'd be safe somewhere, hiding away in a plush bed of pillows and silk sheets.

Larkin traced her fingertips over Evie's skin, resting at her waist first, and then her hips, kissing her all the while. Up until a minute ago, Larkin didn't even think Evie was interested in her at all, not as more than a friendly companion. Given that, she didn't want to push things farther or faster than they should go. Larkin broke away from the kiss, leaning over Evie with her legs straddling her on either side. "Are you sure?" she asked, cautious of ruining the moment by pushing too fast and too soon.

"Of course I'm fucking sure," Evie said, her arms reaching up to pull Larkin back down to her level. "In fact, I've never been more sure of anything in my life." Evie kissed her again, this time exploring Larkin's mouth with her tongue, her lips soft and eager.

The quiet ticking of the clock faded into the background of kisses and shy moans, and the rest of everything dissolved around them. After a month of danger and unexpected consequences, Larkin finally felt at peace, drowning in Evie Anderson. After almost a lifetime of being a transient mercenary, she finally felt like she was home. "What now?" Larkin asked.

"Use your imagination," Evie laughed, and began to unbutton Larkin's shirt. The buttons slid through the buttonholes easily, and before Larkin knew it her shirt was tossed to the floor in a heap, leaving her in a tight fitting cropped top meant to bind her breasts in combat. "Gods, how do you sleep in this?" Evie asked, wrinkling her nose.

"I, uh, usually don't," Larkin answered, unhooking it and tossing it on the floor.

Evie raised an eyebrow and hooked her thumbs through the belt loops on Larkin's trousers. "Okay."

"I usually sleep... without clothes. Naked. In the nude." Even in the darkness, Larkin felt her face heat with embarrassment.

"Lucky me," Evie growled, and tugged at Larkin's pants. "I just want you to be comfortable... sleeping."

Now Larkin laughed, and shifted her weight from one leg to the other to free herself from the tyranny of the fabric. She reached for Evie now, desperate to feel her kisses again, and was surprised to discover she had stripped off her own shirt and trousers in the darkness, her clothes forming a mass of textiles on the rug that stretched from the bed to the door.

Larkin was suddenly very glad that Evie had bolted the door after she closed it hours before. The crew of the Cricket was unlikely to come barging in, but her training and life as an assassin had cultivated seeds of paranoia, especially in the bleak darkness of the night. She reached out and caressed Evie's stomach, stippled with faded stretch marks, the soft texture pleasing under her eager fingertips. Her hands dipped lower, over Evie's wide hips and thighs, and hovered where they met. She was still unsure about pushing too much, too soon.

"What are you waiting for?" Evie demanded, a playful tone dancing at the edges. "I already said yes." It was a surprise when Evie took charge and sidled between Larkin's legs and found her way beneath the black, utilitarian underwear that she wore, but not an unwelcome one. Larkin flinched away from Evie's touch, an old reflex that she'd never managed to drop. Intimacy was tantamount to signing your own death warrant.

"Should I stop?" Evie asked, hesitating, her brow furrowed with concern.

"No, I just... It's hard. For me. When it feels this right, when you feel so right, I can't even imagine a scenario where it's not going to end up hurting me."

Evie shushed her gently. "It's alright. We'll take things as slow as they need to go. I'm in no hurry. Stop sabotaging yourself, Larks. I'm not going anywhere."

"That's good to hear," Larkin murmured, pulling her in for another deep kiss. It was like coming up for air after a lifetime of drowning. It was being seen after over a decade of invisibility, of aliases and occasional one night stands that never left her satisfied, but instead left her crying on her own, her face buried in another mildewed pillow, in another rented room, above another dingy tavern. "Eves?" she whispered.

"Yeah?"

"Will you stay?"

She smoothed the wrinkles from the bed sheets. "Yeah." Her soft hands cupped Larkin's face. "Just *try* to get rid of me now, you fucking grapefruit. You're stuck with me."

Larkin sighed softly as Evie traced the tips of her fingers down her neck and across her collarbone, pausing to plant tiny kisses across Larkin's chest. She was immersed, her body both cautious and craving more. The tightness between her legs bloomed into a heat, a yearning to touch and be touched. Evie gripped her hips tight and pulled her closer, her mouth nuzzled into Larkin's neck. "I've got you," she uttered in a barely-audible voice. "And you've got me."

Evie kissed down across Larkin's stomach and hesitated at that Y-shaped invitation that felt like it was on fire. She cocked an eyebrow.

"Yes," Larkin breathed, entwining her fingers in Evie's short waves of hair. "Yes, I need you." A gasp escaped when tongue met flesh, an explosion of desire and yearning and all the things she'd never felt until that moment. For the first time ever in her life, she allowed herself to lose control, to buck her hips against Evie's eager mouth and cry out as they climbed that final crescendo together. When it was over, and they were both left gasping for air, Larkin laughed.

"What?" Evie asked.

"I'm pretty sure I fucking love you, Evie Anderson."

* * *

When Larkin awoke again, she was nestled against Evie's body, and she felt like she had slept for years. The clock on the wall implied that it had been merely eight hours since she was last awake, but her stomach informed her with a loud growl that she was late for breakfast, and she hoped there would be leftovers.

Breakfast was a casual affair on the Cricket, with some crew members choosing a quick bite of fruit and a black coffee, while others preferred to wake up early in order to prepare something a little more robust. Given Larkin's hunger, the latter was far more appealing. She delicately lifted Evie's arm, and replaced her own body with a pillow, so as not to rouse her from sleep. Larkin dressed in silence, snatching her abandoned clothes from the floor of the room. Without lacing her boots, she eased the door shut as she slid into the hallway.

The midnight activities with Evie felt surreal, encased in the hazy glow of that place just between sleep and consciousness, like a good dream that faded too quickly after waking. It had definitely happened, that much was for certain, but something about it felt like a fairytale, a fabricated story she'd used to ease her own pain and indecisiveness about what was going to happen next, where they'd all end up at the finale of this misadventure.

Back to Skelm, a place she hated above all others. Filled to the brim with Coalition lackeys and people who were lied to, tricked into indentured servitude to earn the greedy Coalition leaders more credits than they could ever spend. The whole thing made her feel sick to her stomach, an impotent rage that had nowhere to go, and no constructive way to change the status quo there.

Fucking Skelm, Larkin thought, pausing in the yellow light of the corridor to loosely tie her boots. Nothing good ever happened on Skelm. A contract that went wrong, getting arrested for jaywalking, though that was now a shitty cover story for something much worse.

Here she was, willingly returning to that pisshole of a settlement so she could try and figure out what the hell had gone wrong at the Armory, and why her mother had given her a device that tracked her location across the Near Systems and fed that information to some Coalition security manager, probably. None of it made any sense, and while she wished she could swallow down the curiosity, it lodged in her throat and made it hard to breathe. She just hoped that finding the answers to all these questions would be quick and painless, and not a drawn out, emotional series of events that would leave her an even more broken woman than she already was.

The noise around the ship was that of a quiet bustle, crew members preparing to land on Skelm in a day or two, some with assignments to trade or purchase spare parts on the grey market there, others working with Kady to improve the efficiency of the cloaking device that the Cricket would use on their approach. Still others busied themselves with the less thrilling, but equally as important day to day tasks of maintaining the ship's functionality. Even in the midst of a wide scale effort by the Coalition to track them all down and likely kill them, the floors still needed to be mopped, and the produce stores still needed looking after.

Larkin found herself in the galley, unsure of where to start. After all, it's not as though learning to cook a nice breakfast was on the agenda for an infamous galactic assassin. She rummaged through drawers looking for cooking implements, and stared at the stove with confusion. How the hell did anyone manage this, anyway? She might as well be trying to decode an ancient dead language for all the good her skills did her in the kitchen. Maybe if some lettuce needed to be assassinated, she'd be able to contribute something to the cause.

"Sneaking out on me, huh?" Evie asked, wandering into the kitchen with a deep yawn, her hair still ruffled from the night before. Larkin's heart swelled in her chest, and felt the rush of happiness people always talked about when they wanted to explain what love felt like. It was warm, comfortable, and completely terrifying.

"I was, uh, going to make you some breakfast," Larkin said with a sheepish tilt of her head, an egg in one hand, and an orange in the other. "But as it turns out, I have no idea what I'm doing."

Evie snorted, edging past her to boil a pot of water. "Well, it's the thought that counts." She reached out and pushed a stray hair from Larkin's face and gave her a broad, endearing smile. "I've got it this time, but don't think you can always rely on me to do the work."

"You can cook?"

"I worked in a tavern, of course I can cook. Who do you think makes all the food, when the cooks call in sick with a hangover, or up and leave on a new expedition because the pay is better?" Evie spooned some vinegar into the heating water, and set to slicing the orange into quarters. "How did you manage to last this long in life without learning how to cook?"

Larkin shrugged. "Taverns. Stealing other people's leftovers."

"Yeah, well, you'd better not steal my leftovers, or we will have words, madam."

"Evie, I— " Larkin started, and then stopped.

"Yes?"

Larkin dropped the volume of her voice to a whisper. "I... enjoyed last night. Earlier. You know."

"I should hope so," Evie chuckled, dropping eggs into the boiling whirlpool she had created and tossing the egg shells into the compost bin in the corner. She turned and brushed Larkin's arm with her fingertips, sending tiny bolts of electricity up her spine. "I did too."

"So what now?" Larkin asked, afraid that the answer would mean Evie returning to her own quarters that night, and pulling away before they reached Skelm.

Evie raised an eyebrow. "Are you saying you want some kind of assurance I'm not going to run away? You, queen of casual friendships that are based entirely on the completion of a contract?"

"I just don't know what this means," Larkin admitted.

"Listen," Evie said, taking Larkin's hands in her own and pulling her closer. "Let's get to Skelm, do whatever needs to be done, and then go from there. You don't even know what your plan is after that, there's no point in asking things of each other that we can't promise with a clear conscience."

Larkin frowned. That's not what she said the night before. "You could come with me on my next contract," she offered, keeping one eye on the boiling pot, which was close to frothing over the lip and spill onto the flame below. "That would be fun."

"Didn't you say that you once spent an entire contract hiding in a cupboard?" Evie shook her head, and then took the pot from the flame, fishing out the poached eggs and laying them artfully over slices of buttered bread. "Just enjoy this now, we'll figure out the rest later." She kissed Larkin on the cheek before handing her the plate. "I'm not going anywhere just yet, and neither are you." She nodded her head towards the table in the far corner, which had become their unofficial spot to eat meals and sometimes, have afternoon coffee while Evie pored over textbooks, scribbling notes into a book with a dull pencil, which had long lost its eraser. It was the best part of her day.

"Thank you for breakfast," Larkin said, trying her best not to sound awkward. "It looks delicious."

"Yeah, well, next time it's your turn, I don't care if it's burnt toast." Evie cut into her egg, allowing the golden yolk to spread over the bread.

"I can probably handle burnt toast."

"I don't know about that," Evie teased, "you looked like a lost lamb when I found you in the kitchen. You might have burned down the whole ship."

"Would have saved us from going to goddamn Skelm," Larkin grumbled. "I'm not looking forward to my unexpected reappearance there. I can only imagine what they might be doing to find me now; I'll bet that fleet chasing us reported right back to whoever's been watching me all this time, now that the tracker is no longer transmitting." She sighed and shoved a forkful of bread and burst yolk into her mouth, savoring the buttery, delicious flavor.

"At least you're not alone," Evie offered, patting Larkin's arm across the table. "You've got me, and the whole of the Cricket."

"I'd take you over the lot of them any day of the week," Larkin said with a wry smile. "No matter how good they are. You're worth your weight in gold, Evie Anderson."

* * *

"I don't know Eves, I don't think it's a good idea," Larkin said, laying face down on her bed while Evie eased the knots out of her muscles. "I really think that you should stay on the ship when we get to Skelm."

"Absolutely not," Evie replied cheerfully, working at a swollen muscle between Larkin's shoulder blades, digging her thumbs into the hard knots. She tried not to focus too much on how soft and smooth Larkin's skin was. "I'm not going to stay here, twiddle my thumbs, and wait for you to come back. That's ludicrous."

"You're not actually a sharpshooter, you know, that was a lie that I made up."

"And you might be an assassin, but you're sporting half a titanium rib cage because this 'not actually a sharpshooter' saved your life on the Blackwall, so pipe down and enjoy this." The oil she used on Larkin's skin smelled of sandalwood, and Evie breathed it deep. It was the most relaxed she'd felt since she first left Bradach.

"I seem to recall that you'd have been ripped to shreds back at the Armory, had I not stayed back with you, so I think we're even now," Larkin said, her voice muffled by the sheets.

Evie stopped the massage, her palms resting flat on Larkin's back. "I'm not staying here, Larks. I'm going to go with the rest of the away team and do whatever I can to make sure you get the answers you're looking for."

"I'd prefer if you stayed here, just in case something happens.

"Of course something is going to happen, something always happens," Evie laughed, resuming the circular patterns with her thumbs and palms, "but it's important that you figure out who was tracking you, and why.

Otherwise you'll spend the rest of your life paranoid that the Coalition is around every corner, waiting to pounce and toss you back into prison, or worse." There was nothing that scared Evie more than the thought of Larkin being thrown back into that hellhole of a prison. The Coalition would have her under constant surveillance, and there'd be no hope of a repeat rescue.

"What do you know about being paranoid?" Larkin scoffed. "You've spent your entire life on a settlement that's invisible to the Coalition."

"I know enough about you to know you'd never stop looking over your shoulder, that's for damn sure," Evie replied.

"You could go back to Bradach tomorrow and forget this ever happened."

Evie playfully poked her in her good side. "I said no future talk, not until this is all over."

"I'm just saying, you have an excellent excuse to not be all that invested in this venture."

"Well you're going to have to get over that, because I *am* invested in this venture. It affects you, it affects others on the ship, and it affects the settlements they help." Evie paused and drizzled a teaspoon of the sandalwood oil into her cupped palm before returning to Larkin's thirsty skin.

"What are you, some kind of rebel now?" Larkin joked. "You gonna steal a transport ship and start making deliveries of your own?"

"I have my own political sympathies, yes," she said, grinding her palm into Larkin's back. "It's true that I was sheltered from a fair amount on Bradach. We knew that the Coalition was bad, and abused their powers, and mistreated people, but it never really hit home until I saw with my own eyes what they were doing. It's disgusting, and I don't want to do anything that would benefit them."

"I just hope we can all get some answers on Skelm," Larkin said. "Then we'll all celebrate with whiskey and cake, and put this whole mess behind us."

"Turn over, I still have to do your legs." Evie wished Larkin would drop it. She wanted to be enveloped in the safety of the moment, not be caught up in thinking about how the ship was hurtling them closer and closer to Skelm, or how once this was all over, having any kind of life with Larkin would be riddled with worry every time she left her sight.

Larkin turned over, and folded her arms behind her head to rest on her interlaced palms. "You don't have to do any of this, Eves."

"Obviously I don't have to," Evie replied, "but I want to." She massaged Larkin's feet, slowly and purposefully easing the tension from the arches of her feet. "Tell me something about yourself, about where you grew up."

Larkin froze, and Evie felt the tension she'd worked so hard to ease out creep back into the assassin's shoulders. "Why do you want to know that?"

Evie frowned at Larkin's resistance."Why not? You know where I grew up. You know that I have two brothers and a mother, who all moved off Bradach years ago and I've not seen them since. You know that I worked as a barkeep at the Purple Pig, and you know that I got screwed over by a woman I was stupid enough to believe." Still, despite Larkin's hesitation, Evie couldn't keep from drinking her in with every glance. Her muscular frame was taut and toned, the result of years of training and athleticism.

"My parents died when I was young, not long after my mother gave me that pendant. I killed Lionel Cabot not long after, and lived the rest of my days as an assassin. That's all there is to it, really."

"No one is born a killer, Larks," Evie said, now working her fingers into Larkin's shapely calves. "Who trained you?"

"You're asking a lot of questions tonight," Larkin said. She stiffened under Evie's touch.

"I just want to know more about you," Evie pouted.

"Alright then," Larkin relented, "I'll tell you three facts about me. I really enjoy mangoes, but only in the morning. The worst contract I ever worked was one where I had to seduce a guy for his security code, he was absolutely vile and I hated every moment of it. In fact, after that I refused any contracts that suggested that kind of *persuasion* was needed."

Evie wrinkled her nose. "And one more?"

"Umm... I can't stand the smell of lavender."

"Lavender? Why?"

Larkin shrugged. "Gives me a headache. Reminds me of funeral parlors and death."

"You're an assassin, aren't you regularly reminded of death?"

"Not my own," Larkin replied. "I try to not think about my own demise. It's morbid."

Evie's hands drifted upward to Larkin's thighs, her movements gentle but effective. "You're really pretty, you know," Evie said.

"Nah."

"No, you are. I know these things, I'm an expert in pretty women, in fact."

Larkin snorted back a laugh. "Well I guess that's true, and I would hate to belie your expertise, my lady." She went quiet for a moment, watching Evie as she worked.

"Yeah, you'd better not," Evie said, her eyes on Larkin's bare breasts. She reached up and caressed them, and then trailed her fingertips back down to where Larkin's thighs met.

"Come here," Larkin growled playfully, flipping Evie over and pinning her to the bed, an eyebrow raised. "It's my turn."

Evie reached up and kissed her. "I can't argue with that." She laughed and buried her face in Larkin's neck. "I don't even *want* to argue with that."

"Good," Larkin said, running her fingertips over Evie's dimpled thighs with a deep inhale. "Then don't."

CHAPTER TWENTY-SEVEN

"Be careful, everyone. Don't take any unnecessary risks," Captain Violet warned the crew of the Cricket. They all stood in the loading bay, each with their respective assignments, ready to disembark from the ship as soon as the loading bay door unlatched and raised up to let them pass. "Remember what we said: gather as much information as you can, but don't put yourselves in any unnecessary danger. We don't know what they're working with here, it could be anything."

Evie fidgeted, the built up anxiety a knot in her guts. She was ready to do whatever she could to take down the Coalition, but on the other hand, she wasn't very enthusiastic about the idea of dying, or of being sent back to the prison for Inspector Allemande to torment. Her assignment was with Larkin, which she was relieved about, because at least this way she'd be able to make sure that Larkin stayed out of trouble. They were to infiltrate the main administration building and steal as much information as they could, including that of Larkin's mother, and any information the Coalition had collected on her through the years, and why.

Kady and Ivy were going to hack into the other building at the other end of the settlement, the one that controlled much of the shift rotations of the Coalition, in order to determine patterns of who was working where, and when. If Evie and Larkin were unable to glean any useful information, it would at least be helpful to have a name to investigate. The entire operation was an incredible long shot, but one that Captain Violet seemed confident they would all accomplish with ease.

"And remember, if we can push our way into a maximum security prison, we can sure as hell do this." Captain Violet gave a dazzling smile right as the loading ramp connected to the dock with a dull thud. It was time. The others filed off the ship, some wearing scarves around their faces to preserve their anonymity in the face of extensive surveillance on Skelm. Evie herself had a green tartan woven scarf looped around her neck, ready to be pulled up over her face to fool the cameras. It was rumored that most of the cameras were just for show, to discourage crime and uprising, but she'd rather be overly cautious than end up back in Allemande's grip again. She gave an involuntary shiver and rubbed her arms gingerly through her shirt.

Captain Violet grabbed Larkin by the shoulder. "I know that we brought you on to help us achieve our goals," she said, her voice low and earnest, "and I was perhaps unfair in the beginning. Go and find out why they were tracking you, if anything, it might help us in the future. Get any information you can." The captain paused a moment, her eyes squeezed shut in concentration. "And if you have to kill anyone to get it, don't hesitate. There are tens of thousands of lives on the line if they have some kind of super weapon they mean to target the settlements with."

Larkin nodded. "Seems you've changed your tune, Captain."

"We live in dark times. Whoever has been tracking you knows our movements, too, and you're connected to all this somehow. I don't want deaths on any of my crews' consciences, but I fear there will be a catastrophic tragedy if we don't succeed in uncovering the Coalition's plans."

"No pressure, then," Larkin said, a wry smirk on her face.

"If anyone can do it, it's the woman who saved me from days of tedious negotiations. Now go. We don't have all day, you know." Captain Violet nodded to Evie, who returned the gesture before pulling the scarf over her face.

"You ready?" Evie said to Larkin, who was pulling a black silk shawl up over her nose and mouth.

"I'm ready."

The walk to the main administration building was quiet, most residents of the settlement being at their workplaces this time of day. The slow ascent up the hill towards the pinnacle of the city made Evie's calves burn after weeks in space on the Cricket. Low gravity was hell on stamina, and she huffed through her face covering. The smog here probably didn't help, either. She checked her pocket watch and grimaced underneath the scarf. They only had a little while longer before the streets would be clogged with people clocking off, a few heading to their luxury high-rise apartments, most trudging back to their Coalition provided tenements.

Skelm's main administration building was huge, spanning the width of the street that dead-ended at its entrance, cloaked in elaborate wrought iron tendrils that snaked from door to window, wrapping themselves around the bluish grey bricks like a cocoon. There were hundreds of windows that dotted the edifice, lined up in orderly rows, each one signifying another office, another Coalition worker they'd have to avoid.

"So, front door?" Evie joked.

"Side door. Follow me," Larkin replied, without a hint of humor.

They edged themselves between the tall concrete fence and the building, a tight squeeze, but manageable. The side door looked like it hadn't been touched in years, covered in rust and grime from the city's thick smog, pumped into the manufactured atmosphere by the many factories there. A large, rusted padlock hung from the door's latch. Larkin knelt down, pulling a lock pick from inside her boot and thrusting it into the lock, before hesitating and sitting back on her haunches.

"What's wrong?" Evie asked, facing out towards the street to keep watch. "Can't pick the lock?"

"Of course I can pick the lock," Larkin snapped. "I'm just worried it's another trap. Why would the Coalition be using old analog locks, when the newer, digital ones are much harder to break into?"

"This door looks like no one has set foot through it in ten years. I bet they just thought no one would know about it."

"Hm. Possible." Larkin knelt and plunged the pick back into the lock again, her face set in concentration. The padlock resisted the intrusion, or at least, the rust did. Larkin broke three picks before the last tumbler of the padlock released, and had to wrench it open, one boot on the door while she yanked mercilessly until it snapped and fell to the ground. "Well, we're in, I guess," she said, easing the door open with her boot, one hand on the belt of knives at her hips. "Be careful. I'm still not convinced this isn't some kind of elaborate set up."

Evie followed her into the building, pulling the door closed behind her and pocketing the padlock. No need to leave any evidence there had been a break in, even if this room looked like it had been abandoned for years, steel boxes covered in inches of thick greasy dust, with layers upon layers of cobwebs draped across the low ceiling. If this was a trap, someone had set it without disturbing the layers of grime that coated the floor, showing vague imprints of the soles of their boots as they traversed the room slowly, disturbing as little as possible.

Larkin frowned. "This room isn't on the official blueprints. It's supposed to lead straight into a hallway."

"How do you know that?"

"I memorized it before we left the Cricket. I don't like being in any place I don't know how to get out of. If this room isn't on that blueprint, it must mean something."

They reached a metal door, thickly insulated and secured with a padlock from the inside.

"Why would the padlock be on the inside?" Larkin wondered aloud, frowning. "What could they be hiding in this mess that they don't want their employees to see?"

"That the Coalition can't afford a cleaning service?" Evie mused.

"It must be something," Larkin said, looking back towards the towers of filing cabinets that spanned the length of the room, lining the walls and cluttering the space. Larkin eased open one of the drawers, cursing the harsh squeak the neglected metal made. It was filled to the brim with immaculately organized files, one right after another. "There could be a million folders in these boxes," Larkin said, crestfallen. "There's no way we would be able to find what we're looking for."

"I don't think this superweapon is going to have a file in here, and I don't see anything that looks like one, not unless someone is planning to bury the rebel settlements in paperwork." Evie nudged at one of the boxes with her boot, scraping a line into the grime with her toe. "What kind of files are they?"

Larkin flipped open one of the cream folders, her brow furrowed. "Medical."

"Why would they be hiding medical information?"

"I don't know, but I think we should take a look." Larkin looked back at the box. "They're alphabetized by last name. I'll start at the end here, you find the beginning."

"Who are we even looking for?" Evie asked, concerned that they were apparently abandoning their mission. "There's so many, and Captain Violet said—"

"I know what she said, just look for files that seem suspicious. Redacted paragraphs, anything like that. Maybe we'll find ourselves a double agent, or someone who's one of the architects of the Coalition. It could be important later."

Evie sighed and examined each box, looking for the start of the alphabet amid what felt like an endless supply of boxes, filled to the brim with endless files. They were wasting time in here, when they should be looking for information on the superweapon, or their plans to attack the rebels, or at the very least, why someone had been tracking Larkin for over a decade. She came across a box labeled *Ca–Cb* and flipped open the lid. Close enough. She poked through some of the files, all of which were woefully ordinary records of Coalition employees' medical checks. A woman with acid reflux. A man who needed a knee replacement, someone else who suffered from repetitive strain injury from sitting at their desk too long. Larkin was poring over records, perched on top of a stack of the steel boxes. "Find anything yet?" Evie asked.

"Maybe. Looks like most of the factory workers have developed chronic respiratory infections, probably due to the toxic fumes." Larkin set one file aside, and picked up another. "I think the Coalition wants to hide their responsibility for the illnesses."

"Larks, that's horrible and all, but doesn't seem like it's going to help the captain."

"Shh. I'm reading."

Evie turned back to her box of files, rankled. Every moment they spent in the building increased the chances they'd be discovered, and if that happens, they were sunk. She picked up another file, but instead of opening it, sighed heavily. "Larkin, this is a waste of time, we need to be looking for information on the superweapon."

"Are you saying the people in those factories don't matter?"

"Of course not, but I'm saying we're risking everything here, and I don't want to end up back with Allemande just because you're too scared to face up to the reason someone was watching you for ten years." She flipped open the file and glared at it.

"Eves, this is important too, I—"

"Oh my gods," Evie breathed.

"What?"

"This is Lionel Cabot's file." Evie looked at Larkin, who appeared to be frozen on the spot.

"What?"

"Lionel Cabot, the Coalition High Council leader you supposedly killed, who has a curiously redacted date of death on this paper."

"*What?*" Larkin jumped from her perch and stalked across the room. "Give me that."

Evie handed over the file, and watched as Larkin's face cycled through disbelief, horror, and then rage.

"He isn't dead," Larkin hissed. "All this time, he's been hiding here in Skelm, in plain sight, with a brand new face he probably stole from one of the poor factory workers who died after inhaling his smog and fumes."

"Larkin, are you sure?"

"I've never been more sure of anything in my life." Larkin snapped the file shut and tucked it into her jacket. "Did you know that the governor here doesn't have an official birth file? I looked, when I was on a job here, the one I got arrested doing. It's like he appeared out of thin air one day. This file suggests Lionel Cabot had experimental surgery, blood transfusions, a long recovery period, and there was top secret clearance for every medical practitioner involved." Her eyes flashed with anger and vengeance, and Evie couldn't help wondering if this was how she always looked on a job, or if this was especially grave, considering the circumstances.

"So what now?"

"I'm going to kill him, *again*," she said, pulling a tiny vial from the heel of her boot, "even if I have to shove the poison down his throat to do it." Larkin stormed to the door and yanked the brittle padlock from the latch. "I have to do this, Eves." Larkin took Evie's hand and kissed it. "You'll be fine, you've saved my ass enough to know how to handle yourself. Head for the east wing, that's where the data centers are. I'll see you back at the ship." She turned and swept through the door.

"Larkin, wait!" Evie hissed, reaching for her. It was too late. Larkin was gone.

* * *

"Fuck!" Evie hissed under her breath, and closed herself back into the file room. Without Larkin, she was more vulnerable, and had no idea where the hell she was going. The stacks of files were amid sparkling clouds of dust, illuminated by the tiny crack of light from the door. For a moment, she hesitated, looking from the door, to the files, and back again. Larkin was sure to be heading straight for Lionel Cabot, surpassing any and all data servers where information about the superweapon was kept in favor of cold, hard revenge.

Evie slid the contents of several folders that held redacted information into her hands, folded them into thick, clumsy squares, and tucked them into her bra, where the points stabbed and prodded her skin. If she was right, they might be useful someday, if not to Captain Violet and her crew, then to someone else in a position to investigate the ills of the Coalition.

Her palms flat against the cool, smooth steel of the door, she pushed out into an empty corridor. Larkin's footsteps had long since faded away, and she could be anywhere in the huge, expansive building. The polished green marble floors were lined with piles of boxes, filled with janitorial equipment. Cracked buckets, worn out mops, and brooms with split, useless bristles were a strange juxtaposition against the impeccably painted walls, with wide crown molding at the ceiling, where huge chandeliers filled with algae hung, casting an odd green glow on the white walls. They were purifying chandeliers, meant to protect the Coalition higher ups from the smog and pollution that plagued the factory workers. Evie felt her stomach burn with the injustice, and had a fleeting urge to smash the chandeliers to pieces.

She edged down the hall, hugging the walls for no other reason than that she felt safer with her back to a solid surface. No one would surprise her from behind then, even though the corridor dead ended into the file room; from the outside the steel door melded perfectly into the wall, so much so that Evie wasn't even sure she could find it again. The administration building was built with two main wings, separated by an atrium with high glass ceilings and water fountains that spurted water into the air. Evie could hear the delicate splash of water against granite far back into the empty corridor.

One wing was where the data servers were held, powered by some of the largest boilers in the Near Systems, with approximately three hundred workers, or so Kady said. The other wing was where some of the higher ups in the Coalition stayed for a time, to meet in secret, or to make a visit to assess the efficiency of the toxic factories that continued to line their pockets with more credits than they could ever spend in a lifetime. Larkin would be in the latter, hunting down a ghost with a new face. Evie, however, would have to make her way into the rooms with the servers, in order to locate and copy the relevant information. She swallowed hard, and felt bile burn at the back of her throat.

The atrium bustled with workers, dressed in crisp tailored garments with silk scarves around their faces, and carrying long umbrellas by ornate, hand carved handles. The rain on Skelm was particularly acidic, and these middle class workers wouldn't take the chance of damaging their expensive clothes. Evie smoothed her shirt and fell into step behind a group of workers headed towards the wing with the data servers. If she was lucky, no one would ask her any questions. She held her breath in her lungs, willing each person who looked her way to find interest somewhere else. The group peeled off down a corridor lined with frosted glass doors, behind which the data servers hummed in a chorus of mechanical engineering.

The last door on the left was quiet, with no murmurs of chatter behind it, only the whir of fans and the gentle burbling of a boiler. Evie pushed the door open, her hands shaking with fear. She'd never been a good liar, but if someone was on the other side of it, her skills in deception would be tested to the maximum limit. The room was mercifully empty, and Evie exhaled the breath she'd been holding for what felt like an eternity. Blood pounded in her ears, her heart racing faster than she thought was possible.

"Okay, Evie, just breathe," she whispered to herself, willing her voice not to quake in fear. "Check the server for information, and get out." She didn't want to think about how the hell she was going to find Larkin just yet; she wanted to try and survive this first. Besides, Larkin was probably fine on her own, or at least, she hoped she would be. Evie's stomach churned.

Data servers here on Skelm were interconnected with immense bundles of wires that ran from one room to the next, so that a worker could input data into one and have it be available across the entire wing. The data was processed with punch cards, but once it was in the system, it was decoded into simple text and line images, and that's what Evie needed to get her hands on. She approached the server, and the door creaked open behind her. Her blood turned to ice in her veins, frozen in fear like a wild animal being hunted for sport. Her hand-me-down boots squeaked as she turned to face the person who was probably about to apprehend her. She shook her head. This was impossible.

"*Tansy*?" she half laughed, half shouted, the name strangled in her throat. "What in the hell—"

"Shh!" Tansy hushed. She was wearing a tight corset over a conservative purple satin dress that fell to the floor and hid her cybernetic leg that she was so proud of. "What are you doing here?" Tansy demanded.

"From the looks of things, the same thing you're doing here," Evie said, eyeing the disk in Tansy's hand. "Superweapon?"

Tansy's eyes grew huge. "A what?"

"Superweapon? Apparently to target rebel camps?"

"No," Tansy breathed. "I was looking for classified medical files, we have a shipment of refugees being smuggled out of Skelm due to arrive on Bradach any day now. We needed information about what they've been exposed to here."

Evie produced the crumpled pages from inside her shirt and held them out to Tansy. "Stole these from some weird room that's not on the blueprints, Larkin found it. Thought they might be important."

Tansy snatched the papers, scanning them one at a time. "It's redacted, but there's enough here to confirm our suspicions. This is exactly what I need." She folded up the papers again, burying them in her ample skirts. "Lets get you some information on this fucking superweapon. I'll watch the door."

Evie nodded, and slid the square disk into the output slot of the server. Light streamed through the floor to ceiling mosaic windows, illuminating every corner of the room. The files were printed on tiny leaves of glass, enlarged by a magnifier for preview before selecting the file to be fetched from the system. Evie spun the wide knob over and over, looking for something that might have information on the superweapon. "I can't find anything," she said, worry lodging itself firmly in her shoulders.

"I doubt they'll have it labeled as a superweapon, Evie," Tansy said. "Where did your friend go, anyway?"

"To kill Lionel Cabot again, apparently."

Tansy's eyebrows almost disappeared into her hair. "Well that's something." Tansy tapped a long, slender finger against her chin. "What if you look at Cabot's files? Just in case? I mean, why go through all the effort of faking your death unless you're up to something big, right?"

"True," Evie said, and scrolled back to the Cs. There were plenty of files on Cabot of course, on his rise to the highest rank in the Coalition military, to becoming one of the High Council, and then of course, his assassination by an unknown terrorist. A botched assassination that he'd had the audacity to survive. "Wait, here's something," Evie said, landing on a file full of jumbled words. "It looks like a code, maybe."

"Take it. And take anything else like it, search any common phrases it uses."

"Four hits."

"I'd say you got yourself some information."

Evie grinned and set the machine to copy the information to the disk, but each file had to be mechanically fetched from the underground database, where the archives were kept, before they could be copied. It would be several minutes of impatient waiting before she'd be able to pocket the information and figure out how she was going to find Larkin.

There was no radio contact with the other groups from the Cricket; the Coalition scanned all non-official frequencies at all times of day. They'd be in the dark until they got back to the ship. The doors along the corridor opened and closed with the flow of workers leaving their posts to head to their pristine, newly built homes, safe behind miles of razor wire fence meant to keep out desperate factory workers and the refugees they'd become once the toxins in their nervous systems were irreversible.

"Didn't expect to find you here," Evie said, glancing at Tansy from the corner of her eye.

"Where do you think I've been the past month? Picking daisies?"

"No," Evie laughed, "but I didn't think you were planning some kind of covert operation, either."

Tansy turned away from the door to face Evie, and raised a perfectly shaped eyebrow. "I did say I missed being out on missions."

"I didn't know these were the kinds of missions you meant. I assumed your glory days with Captain Violet were more about filling your pockets rather than righteous justice."

"With Vi, it's always about justice. She thinks she's some hard ass pirate captain, when she's got a center softer than a marshmallow, especially when it comes to disenfranchised people who need her help. A real hero complex, in spite of any danger."

"It's good to see you, Tansy."

"I'm glad you took my advice! Are you enjoying your time in the sky?"

Evie paused to consider her response, the faint clanking of the machine and bubbling of the boiler punctuating the silence. "I don't know." She pushed a lock of hair out of her face and sighed. "It's complicated. I'm not so sure I'm the right person to be sneaking around incognito, breaking into Coalition administrative buildings and stealing data about some superweapon." The soft shuffle of work boots on marble spilled adrenaline into her muscles, and she leaned to look past Tansy. "Oh, shit."

A petite, tawny-haired woman was standing just inside the doorway in a regulation orange Coalition jumpsuit, mop in hand, an eyebrow raised in suspicion. The janitor's ponytail swooshed from side to side as she appraised them both.

"We're here on a work assignment," Tansy started, her usual easy, steady voice thick with hesitation.

"Tansy, she heard everything I said," Evie muttered under her breath, as though the janitor wouldn't be able to hear her from just a couple of feet away. "If she picks up that radio, we're toast."

"We're here on a work assignment," Tansy began again, her voice steadier now, "transferred from one of the other offices to research... something important. It's classified, actually."

The janitor shifted her weight from one foot to the other, her hand resting on the radio that hung at her waist. "Did you say superweapon?" she asked.

Evie was frozen on the spot, and the air felt too thick to breathe. She gave an almost imperceptible nod, hoping against hope that the janitor was another spy from another ship, or a rebel who had infiltrated the building just as they had. The janitor unclipped the radio from her belt, and Evie's heart leapt into her throat. This was it. They were all going to die. Tansy and Larkin, Kady and Ivy in the other building, they would all end up dead one way or another, it was just a matter of time. The only variable was how much pain they'd be in when they finally kicked the bucket. Evie ran her hands over the raised scars on her arms and swallowed hard.

"Wait, please—" she began, but the sound of the radio crackling with an open channel made her clamp her mouth shut before she finished.

"Erin, there's nobody in data room seven, it's empty here. Tell Mr. Jackson to get his ears checked." The janitor smirked and clipped the radio back onto her belt. "I don't know what y'all are doing here, but you better hurry the hell up. Word's going around that there's some kinda pirate ship in the docks, and security is going to be all over it." She tipped the grey cap she was wearing and sidled back to the door, mop in hand. "Good luck," she said over her shoulder. "You're damn sure gonna need it."

CHAPTER TWENTY-EIGHT

Crouched beneath a stairwell, Larkin took the file from her jacket once more, studying it for some kind of clue. No date of death, mysterious and illegal medical procedures, it all pointed to a living Lionel Cabot, parading around the highest echelons of Coalition society with a stolen face. Rage burned in her gut and made her feel unpredictable, unsteady. Not the way a trained, renowned assassin would want to feel when hunting down one of the most closely guarded men in all the Near Systems. He'd have bodyguards, a security staff, even more controlled and protective than the last time they'd met over a decade before. Lionel Cabot had a lot of nerve turning up alive after she had worked so hard to murder him, fair and square.

She'd only been a child then, but there was the familiar feeling of vengeance that pushed her from under the stairs into the greenish light of the corridor. He'd be in the most lavish office, wherever the largest and most merciless brutes were loitering, waiting to protect their employer from what they assumed was nothing more than Cabot's paranoid delusions. Today, the threat was very real, and Larkin wouldn't be leaving Skelm until she was damn sure he was dead, for once and for all.

Stalking a mark was something that felt familiar, the movements the same as they'd be if she was a stowaway on a ship or gliding through the halls of some noble, aristocratic asshat, but the fury that boiled violently beneath her skin felt alien and dangerous.

Workers streamed from their offices, their claustrophobic cubicles where they were constantly being monitored for efficiency, into the corridors and through the main doors for a chance at relative freedom until their next shift began. It didn't take long for the building to empty, leaving a skeleton crew of janitors and maintenance staff to duck in and out of offices, dumping waste baskets into their wheeled bins and disappearing behind frosted glass doors while they scraped the dirt and grime from the walls, a task that needed to be done every day to keep the yellowing smog at bay.

Lionel Cabot could have any face now. He would be unrecognizable, which is how he had managed to continue his work of destroying families and lives under an assumed name, but Larkin would know him when she saw him. Her last, apparently failed, attempt to take him off the chess board of conniving, greedy snakes would have left a scar on his neck, right across the jugular. How he'd survived that she'd never know, seeing as she had left him bleeding thick, arterial blood into the fabric of a priceless, hand woven tapestry that covered the tile in his spacious office. Larkin had been twelve then, with shaky hands and enough fear to fuel years of nightmares. She was grown now, an assassin who had honed her skills with hundreds of contracts completed, and she knew in her bones that he would die before the night was out.

The vial of poison grew warm in her hands. It was almost time. A janitor gave a long, hacking cough, and Larkin felt a pang of regret that they would probably die twenty years too young. They would fare better than the factory workers, but the harsh cleansing agents used, combined with the punishing smog, would shorten their lifespan considerably. Larkin waited for them to move on, the wheels on the bin squeaking with every rotation. She emerged from the hiding place beneath the stairs and swept across the atrium balcony, to the locked doors that signified where the most important dickheads of the Coalition worked. The locks were digital, and she swore under her breath. She'd have to wing it.

A tall, lanky janitor with a square chin and biceps that threatened to burst out of his orange jumpsuit came through the locked door, whistling a tuneless, irritating pattern. Larkin was perched atop the banister, and he dropped his mop, reaching for his radio.

"Hey!" he shouted, fumbling with the clip, "You can't be in here!" He snatched at Larkin's jacket, a sneer spreading across his face. "Maybe I'll get a promotion if I kill you before security gets here." He abandoned the radio and snapped the wooden mop in half, jabbing at Larkin with the jagged, deadly broken end.

Larkin leapt from the banister and punched him hard in the face. He staggered backward, his mouth in a wordless O, stunned from the force of the impact. Larkin snatched the keycard from his belt and punched him again. He swiped at her with the broom, his steps uncoordinated and clumsy, and lurched backward and over the banister. His body landed on the marble below with a sickening crunch. "Yeah, good luck on that promotion," Larkin mumbled, and swiped his keycard.

The bronze door swung open, leading into a wide hallway with offices on either side. The blueprints showed that the one at the end was the largest and most impressive, with a stunning view that extended beyond the terraformed city into the wilds of the terrain, where sharp, untamed mountains reached high into the sky. Larkin crept from one door to the next, listening through the heavy polished doors for any sign she'd come into trouble. These offices were empty, which was unsurprising. The people that worked in this wing were unlikely to spend even a moment longer than absolutely necessary doing anything other than exactly what they wanted to be doing. They were satisfied with riches, content to do the bare minimum and foist problems onto someone with a lower pay grade. Not Lionel Cabot, though. He was a man who would always work late, because there was nothing in all of the Near Systems he loved more than driving misery and pain into those who least deserved it.

The last time they met, he was swanning around in the capitol of Gamma-3. Skelm was dirty and toxic, but ripe for abuse. It was a capitalist's fantasy. Of course he would be here. If she had paid more attention, she would have recognized the stench of his manipulative rot, a conniving fungus that wove itself through the fabric of the entire Coalition. When he'd died the first time, not much had changed. Another rich, wealthy born Coalition lackey had stepped right into his shoes, and they were a perfect fit. His influence lingered throughout Delta-4, and then all of the Near Systems, and now she knew why. This time, she intended for his expiry to be permanent.

The lack of bodyguards was ominous. He was too smart, too cunning, too paranoid and convinced of threats to leave himself unguarded. She could only hope that he'd grown careless as he aged, but the more likely explanation was that security had been redeployed elsewhere, for some other, more immediate threat. Larkin swallowed hard, thinking of Evie. She never should have left her alone, and that was why she needed to make sure that it was worth it, and succeed in her task to take Lionel Cabot off the board for good.

His door was ornate, gilded with gold leaf and inset with assertive, sharp geometric shapes made from bronze and steel. It was the door of a narcissist, a man who valued himself first and foremost, and she could feel his closed off, predatory energy through the layers of metal. Her own bitterness burned bright inside her titanium rib cage, and gave her the mental fortitude to yank the door open with all the force and resolution of an invading army. The office was circular, with rounded walls made of glass that looked out over the smog that drifted from the city. The floors were covered in vibrant rugs, all laid one on top of the other, deadening the sound of crackling wood from the fireplace across from the desk. And there he was, Lionel Cabot himself, the scar on his neck shining in the firelight, sitting behind a nameplate that read "Governor Ralph Baker."

* * *

When the machine finally completed its task, Evie slipped the disk back into her pocket. Now she just had to make sure that they all got off of Skelm alive. "Tansy, I can handle things from here."

"You're going to go look for her, aren't you?" Tansy asked with a sigh. "I knew there was a girl you were hung up on. I'm just glad that it wasn't the other one."

"I can't leave her on her own."

"I'm sure she can handle herself, you should come back with me. I have my own ship to take care of, and you need to get back to warn Captain Violet and the others. If what that janitor said is true, we don't have much longer before the entirety of the Coalition fleet is crawling up our asses."

"Tansy, please?"

Tansy sighed noisily, rolling her eyes. "Fine. But if you don't make it back alive, you're fired."

"Deal."

As Tansy's footsteps faded down the hall, Evie picked at a scab on her arm, letting the pain focus her thoughts. Larkin had to still be in the building, but if she'd killed Cabot then surely the place would be crawling with security by now. If Evie could just make it to the other wing of the building, maybe she still had time to find Larkin and convince her to go back to the ship before doing something that would land her back in prison or dead.

The hallway was empty now, not even the janitor who had curiously spared their lives was around. Evie inhaled deep through her nose, and exhaled slow and steady through her mouth. They might still make it out of this, if she could just *find Larkin*. She had to find her, because she'd be lost without her now. If she was honest with herself, she'd felt that way since Larkin lied to get her freed from the prison. Evie hurried along, stepping on the balls of her feet to muffle the sound of her boots on the marble. The atrium was dead ahead, the lights dimmed and the skylights dark from the clouds of smog that were rolling in from the factory district. Evie could almost see the other wing, and squinted her eyes to try and read the numbers on the doors, but it was no use.

The last door on the left before the corridor opened into the atrium flew open as Evie passed, and she was pulled inside what looked like a classroom, lined with wooden desks. The door slammed shut behind her, and the lock latched like a death sentence. There was a pristine chalkboard against the opposite wall, not a speck of chalk dust to be seen. At the top, in a threatening, florid script, was written *Introduction to Information Extraction*.

Evie whipped her head around, yanking at her wrist, and came face to face with Inspector Allemande.

* * *

"Well, well. Larkin Flores. I've been expecting you. You look just the same as when we last met."

Larkin flinched at the sound of her real surname, something she hadn't heard in nearly ten years. "Funny, I can't say the same about you." Lionel Cabot sat at the large mahogany desk, his long, spindly fingers steepled in the center. He'd once been a broad, muscular man with a wide smile and bright, burning amber eyes. Now, he was reedy, his lips pressed into a thin, humorless line, his formerly robust, strong shoulders withered to knobbly bones that poked at the seams of his expensive, tailor-made, double breasted jacket. The fiery eyes, however, were the same, and bored into Larkin the same way they had all those years ago.

"Come to finish the job, have you?" he asked. "I'm afraid it won't be as easy this time. I may be a mere specter of the man I once was, but I have plenty more power on my side now. In fact, I'd imagine that every available security officer on this gods-forsaken rock is apprehending your crew mates right about now." He chuckled, and the sound squeezed Larkin's insides. "Curious, though. I never thought I'd see you with a crew. Always more of a lone wolf, weren't you? Even at the start of all this."

The flickering light of the fireplace glinted off something at the corner of his desk. Larkin stifled a gasp. It was identical to the pendant her mother had given her.

"Yes, yes, I knew you'd figure it out sooner or later," he said, catching her glance at the pendant. "Honestly, I never thought it would take you this long. I was under the impression you were smarter than that, Larkin Flores."

"You switched the pendants." Larkin turned the vial of poison over in her hands. "You switched the pendants, and then you killed my parents."

"Yes, well, your parents were getting under my skin, threatening to expose what they saw as corruption. Fools, the lot of them. They couldn't see that progress sometimes requires a body count." He tilted his head to the side, a sneer spreading across his face. "You, however, turned out to be quite the surprise. I never intended for you to kill me, or rather, *try* to kill me and fail, that was not a very good day for me."

"I'm not so sure you'll survive my second attempt," Larkin growled. "You sent all your security to the docks, and left yourself unprotected. That seems unwise, if you know an assassin is coming to correct the one error she ever made."

"Two errors, actually," he said, and produced a bottle of whiskey from a false bottom in the last desk drawer. He poured a generous shot of the dark golden brown liquid into a crystal glass. He drank it and sat back in his chair. "I'm sorry, I'm so rude. Would you like a drink?" When Larkin was silent, he smirked. "Or are you planning on killing me with that vial of poison in your hand? Cyanide, very potent, easily concealed. An excellent first choice for clean, blameless killings. No need to throw yourself off a ravine in order to escape, leading to the authorities pinning the murder on an innocent." He flipped through a file that was spread open on his desk. "What was her name? Magdalena?"

"Keep her name out of your mouth," Larkin said with gritted teeth.

"Ah yes, well I'm not surprised that's still a sore subject. If it makes you feel better, I'm sure she wasn't tortured for too long before they dispatched her to a work camp. From what I read, she lasted several weeks before the toxicity got to her. Nearly a record!" Larkin stepped forward, and he put a hand up. "Now, now, let's not be too hasty now, shall we? You'll get your chance, don't worry."

"You barely even deserve death."

"Death comes for us all, in the end, as you well know." He poured himself another whiskey and set the crystal top back into the matching decanter. "It has been fascinating to observe your achievements, to watch your kills become smoother, slicker, more effortless. It was almost a shame to cut you off from the Coalition payroll, but hard times call for hard decisions."

Larkin stared. "That's..." she started, and then trailed off, her jaw clamped so tightly to her skull that all her teeth might shatter in her mouth.

"Oh, I'm sorry, was that information you hadn't realized yet?" He laughed and swirled the whiskey in his glass. "And here I thought you knew all this time, how silly of me. How else did you think that you always ended up with the most lucrative and high profile contracts? I figured I was obligated to give you some kind of compensation after killing your parents." He smiled and furrowed his brow. "Did you really not know?"

The room felt like it was spinning around her, and she briefly considered that she'd been poisoned. Her lungs felt like they were being crushed by the titanium inside of her, sucking all of the air out of the room. It couldn't be possible. She prayed that it was all a lie. "That's impossible."

"There are very few things in this universe that are impossible, my dear. Sending undercover operatives to present you with contracts is hardly one of them." He ran his little finger around the rim of the glass, coaxing an eerie, hollow ring from the surface. "Why don't you sit down?" he asked, gesturing at one of the chairs against the wall. "We can discuss renewal of your contract. I think you'll find the offer I've drawn up very generous."

The vial of poison grew slick with sweat in her palms, the glass warm from her heated skin. She wanted to leap across that pompous, overpriced desk and pour the poison down his throat, but her limbs refused to move, as though she'd been paralyzed on the spot. All this time, she'd been working for him. Working for the man she'd watched kill her parents, the man who allowed Magdalena to be arrested, even though he knew it was Larkin who'd tried to kill him. If only she had succeeded. Her tongue felt swollen and thick in her mouth, and she swallowed back the lump at the back of her throat that tasted like acid and guilt.

"Don't make this difficult, Larkin," he said, his tone dancing with anger and threat. "I know you're a reasonable girl, and you know a good outcome when you see one. Sign the contract, and you'll be set for life. Keep doing what you've always done, with an account fat with credits. What else could someone like you possibly want out of life? You're a stone cold killer, and a good one, at that. The Council was so impressed that you'd nearly killed me off, that they wanted to put your skills to good use." He straightened the stack of papers in his hands and pushed them across the desk with a gold fountain pen. "Let us help you to continue honing your craft. Sign the papers."

CHAPTER TWENTY-NINE

"I should have known it was you causing problems down by the docks," Inspector Allemande said, her fingers wrapped around Evie's wrist like a vice. "You and your little band of miscreants."

Evie's stomach clenched into a knot, and blood pounded in her brain. This was it. This was how she died, at the hands of the same monster that sliced her skin to ribbons, and who was grinning eerily at the scabs on Evie's arms.

"I'm so *pleased* to be reacquainted, aren't you?" Allemande asked, her free hand dancing around a revolver in a holster at her hip.

"Nope. No, not really."

"Do you know what the reward is for apprehending a most wanted renegade?"

"For your sake, I hope it's a personality," Evie scoffed.

"Foolish reprobates like you are the reason that certain areas of the Coalition fail to thrive. You fill people's heads with dangerous drivel, make them think that they should live a life of leisure instead of a meaningful existence of productivity. It's selfish, irresponsible, and the Near Systems will be a far sight better without you in them."

The pen she'd stolen from Allemande, the one used to slice Evie's arms to ribbons in the prison, was tucked into her breast pocket alongside two pencils and a vial of ink. She never went anywhere without stationery. Evie's eyes darted down to the pen, waiting for the opportunity to use it to get her away from the inspector and back to Larkin. Back to safety.

Allemande's eyes followed Evie's, and she snatched the pen from Evie's pocket with a cold laugh. "Thank you, my dear, I've been looking for this. Here I thought I'd misplaced it, but I should have known a dirty thief had stolen it from me." The inspector ran her fingers over the smooth, unblemished silver, down to the sharpened blade of the nib. "How thoughtful of you to return it to me." She still held Evie's wrist firm, her hand like a clamp, pulling her prisoner further from the door and from rescue.

"You're stronger than you look," Evie grunted, straining against Allemande. "How about we just call this one even? I returned your pen, and now you can release me."

"Fitness takes discipline, something you don't have an ounce of within your fleshy waste of self." Allemande clapped Evie's wrist into a pair of handcuffs that were connected to a wide iron ring on the heavy polished desk. Evie didn't want to know why there were handcuffs in a classroom, but somehow she suspected that the inspector's teaching style matched her interrogation tactics. "Perhaps you'll learn something in one of the work camps before you die." Allemande held the pen up, and the blade glinted in the yellow light. "But I suspect not."

Evie tasted bile in her throat at the sight of the pen back in its owner's hands. "Call the guard, then," she urged. Even a work camp and swift death would be better than enduring the inspector's twisted interrogation methods again.

"Oh, I think we should have a little reunion, don't you?" Allemande asked, pulling a file from her desk and spreading it open, the bladed pen held delicately in her fingers. "I knew I was right to keep your file close at hand. After all, your daring, though ultimately unsuccessful prison escape robbed me of my victory and the chance to move up in the ranks."

"Unsuccessful?" Evie scoffed. "I've been gone for weeks, plundering every Coalition ship I saw, ransacking every last bit of tech I came across."

Anger flashed across Allemande's face. "When I managed to escape that hive of villainy, I knew that someday I'd catch up with you, and you wouldn't be getting away from me again. It seems that fate has rewarded me, by dumping you directly in my lap, the result of your reckless and undisciplined methods." The inspector looked down at Evie, crouched next to the desk, and her sharp green eyes were icy and threatening. "Have you any idea what they'll do to you, once I'm finished? The crimes you've admitted to, well, they're reason enough for a public execution. But a prison breakout, and the ensuing unlawful release of dozens of fellow prisoners? Well, they'll want to make an example out of you, Dear."

"So what do *you* get for dragging me to the local authorities?" Evie asked, her voice smooth and even. "Forgive me for saying so, Inspector, but you don't seem like the kind of woman who would work for free."

"I get a seat at the table, I get influence, I get power and the chance to make the Coalition a better place." A sneer spread across the inspector's face as she leaned forward with the bladed pen. "You're nothing more than excrement on the sole of my boot, Ms. Anderson." She dipped the pen into a well of ink and scratched a note into the file that held Evie's official records. She paused, and knelt down next to Evie, her posture rigid and straight. "Now tell me," she soothed, pressing the flat side of the blade gently against one of Evie's newly healed scars, "where are the rest of your rebel friends?"

"I'd never tell you that," Evie spat. "I'd die screaming before I'd let you have them."

"You'll die screaming either way," the inspector said with contempt. "Brigands like you don't deserve mercy." She twisted the pen in her fingers so the blade was facing Evie's skin. "Or leniency."

The inspector smiled, but it didn't reach her cold, unforgiving eyes. Evie gritted her teeth and head-butted the inspector, her forehead crumpling the soft cartilage in the inspector's nose. Allemande staggered backwards, nose streaming with blood, her hand on her revolver as she struggled to regain her balance. Evie's eyes swam from the impact, and she blinked furiously to clear her vision.

"How dare you!" the inspector shouted, and dropped the pen as she tried to pull the gun from the holster, her hands clumsy and inept. "Guards!" she slurred, but Evie knew that no one would come. The building was curiously empty of the usual security detail. "Guards!" Allemande screamed again, her revolver still strapped into the polished black leather of the holster.

Evie kicked out a leg and snared the pen with the heel of her boot, dragging it close enough to grasp between her feet. She leaned back into the desk and flipped the pen up, where she caught it, blade end first, in her fist. She bit back a yelp when the edge bit into her palm, and watched as blood dripped down her wrist. The pain cleared her thoughts, just for a moment, long enough for Evie to thrust the nib of the pen into the lock on her cuffs. She remembered what Larkin had said - it's all in the wrist - and thrust the pen deep into the lock.

The blade of the pen snapped and rattled within the lock, never a good sign; but to Evie's surprise, the cuffs sprang open, and she lunged forward at the inspector, catching her at the knees. They both went down hard on the pristine tiled floor, and Evie groaned when her knee popped loud and pain streaked across her thigh. She thrust her fist out at Allemande's face, throwing her weight behind the punch. She connected with the inspector's jaw, and Evie's knuckles crunched with the force. Allemande gave an unintelligible bellow of pain, and fury burned in her eyes.

Blood was smeared across the white tiles and the collar of the inspector's impeccable starched collar as Evie struggled with her for the revolver. Allemande freed the gun from the holster and fumbled with the hammer, the barrel pointed at Evie's chest, the graveness of the situation pulling insistently at Evie's clouded thoughts. She'd never survive if that gun went off. She'd never get to find Larkin, make it back to the ship and get the hell off this disgusting planet. She'd never see Tansy or the Purple Pig again if she didn't figure out how to get away from the inspector. The room spun, and Evie's stomach turned. Hyun would be giving her a stern lecture once this was all over for giving herself a concussion with the inspector's skull. Evie summoned up all her strength and grabbed Allemande by the shoulders, lifted her off the ground, and slammed her head into the tiles with a finishing crack so loud, Evie thought the gun had gone off. The inspector lay limp on the floor, her head lolling to one side.

"Fuck you," Evie whispered, pulling herself upright on shaky legs. "And your shitty pen." She took the revolver from Allemande's limp grasp, her fingers slack and lifeless. Evie turned the gun over in her hands, the polished, embellished nickel plating dulled with the smears of her blood. Trembling,

Evie tucked the weapon into the waistband of her trousers, and backed out of the room. It was time to find Larkin and get off this rock.

* * *

Larkin took a step back towards the door. "Never." Her every impulse was screaming at her to run, to get as far away from Skelm and the Coalition as she could. She'd go into hiding, take on a job as a day laborer maybe, adopt another new identity, drink enough to forget any of it had ever happened. "I'll never sign those papers. I'm done being your puppet."

"Don't be ridiculous," he smiled. "You know that if you don't agree to work with me, with us, then we simply can't allow you to live." His expression grew dark, even as he smiled broadly with his ivory teeth, a shark grin in the dim light of the office. "I can't even allow you to leave this office without your full and *enthusiastic* cooperation." The wood of the desk drawer scraped softly, and then he held a small, whirring droid in his hands. "And it seems as though your enthusiasm is already off the table."

"Stay away from me," Larkin said, her voice wavering. She felt small in this man's presence, even as he wore a stranger's face, the imposition, the manipulation and emotional blackmail was the same as it had been ten years ago. Her senses were clouded, her mind a gelatinous pool of fear that she struggled to swim through. She felt like she was underwater, so deep that there was no sunlight, no way to tell which way was up, and drowning was a pressing inevitability.

"Sign the goddamned papers!" he shouted, and picked up the crystal whiskey glass. He threw it into the fireplace where it smashed into a million glittering shards, the last drops of the bootleg swill hissing on the embers. "Sign these papers, or this droid will detonate that black market chip you've got in your arm. He smiled, his eyes flickering with the orange light of the fire. "Or hadn't you realized? I organized that little insurance plan, too." The droid beeped with a menacing tone, and flashed red.

Calm and serene, what needed to be done revealed itself clear as the pools of water on Gamma-3 where Larkin grew up. She bent at the waist, her fingers pulling on the loose threads that concealed a large knife at her thighs. She freed it, pulling the compact hilt through the heavy woven fabric of her trousers. Kady would never let her borrow clothes again after this, Larkin thought, the sound of the knife slicing through the pleasing texture, soft and threatening. The poison vial dropped to the carpet without a sound, and she crushed it beneath the heel of her boot. The time for poison had passed. Now, she needed to take power back into her own hands once and for all.

"What are you doing?" he asked, a tinge of fear to his voice. She was a fearsome opponent, after all. He wouldn't have gone through all the effort of keeping her under his shadowy control if she wasn't. "Put that down, or I'll— " he shouted, holding the droid aloft.

She plunged the knife into her bicep and screamed, blood splattering across the pristine window. The chip was in there somewhere, if she could just get it out, he'd lose. She would probably die from the blood loss, in fact she almost definitely would, but it would be worth it to make him look like a fool who had underestimated her. They'd find her lifeless body bleeding out onto his rug, and he'd have questions to answer. Someone would know who she was. Someone would hold him to account. She dug deeper with the knife, and darkness crept in at the edges of her vision.

She didn't have long before she would pass out from pain, or shock, or blood loss. A beautiful trifecta, she thought, her mind hazy and thick. She hoped Evie would be proud of her. She hoped Evie wouldn't forget her. She hoped Evie would find someone else to protect her from the people who wanted to hurt her for their own gain. Another dig with the point of the knife, and Lionel Cabot, now Ralph Baker, was screaming too. His voice was garbled and thick, unintelligible beyond the slow pound of blood in her ears.

She didn't care what he was screaming. His reckoning was at hand, and he'd be exposed. He had to be. Once the security forces returned from the docks, he'd have to explain why an assassin was dead on his floor. His top secret cover would be blown. He'd become useless to the High Council, and if she was lucky, they'd dump his body and his ugly new face into a ditch somewhere, forgotten by the world. A meaningless existence. At least she'd had Evie, even if only for a few days. That meant something.

Once more she jabbed the knife into her arm, now covered in the dark scarlet sheen of blood. This time, she hit something hard, and she thrust clumsy fingers into the wound and ripped out the chip, bloody and ordinary. The room whirled around her. Ralph Baker continued to roar at her as a blurry figure stepped through the open door.

CHAPTER THIRTY

"Drop the droid!" Evie yelled for the third time, her hands shaking as she gripped the revolver and Larkin continued to bleed out onto the carpet, tearing at the open wound in her arm with clumsy fingers.

"I'm afraid I can't do that," Lionel Cabot said coolly, watching Larkin's struggle with mild interest. "You see, I promised certain people that I could provide top notch, untraceable services to wipe certain other people off the playing field. If she won't join us willingly, then I'm afraid we'll have to abandon the carrot and settle for the stick, instead."

"I'm warning you!" Evie said, and pulled back the hammer, hearing the weapon click with anticipation.

"Leave now, and I might let you live long enough to see her receive medical attention. I'm sure you realize she sorely needs it, she won't last much longer. A pity, really, she was going to be the crowning jewel, my key to ascend back into the High Council."

"You can't have her," Evie said, wrapping her finger around the trigger, "because she's mine." Lionel Cabot's nostrils flared and he reached for the red switch on the droid that would detonate the chip inside Larkin. She'd waited long enough outside the door to hear that, but now wished that she'd burst in much sooner. Maybe then Larkin wouldn't be dazed, watching the thick blood soak into the hand woven fibers. With one last glance at the woman she'd fallen hard for, she squeezed her eyes shut and pulled hard on the trigger. The gun went off, the recoil reverberating from her wrists all the way to her shoulders. The droid flashed on the floor, and Lionel Cabot slumped in his leather chair, a hole where his left eye should be. No one could survive that, not even a man who had spent ten years wearing a stranger's face.

"Larkin. Larkin!" Evie shouted, hauling Larkin to her feet.

"I got it," Larkin mumbled, holding a tiny disk to the light of the fire between trembling fingers.

"Okay Larks, you got it," Evie said, tears springing to her eyes. She'd saved Larkin, but now they had to make it off this gods-forsaken settlement alive, which was going to be one hell of a miracle to pull off, given the number of security forces that were already swarmed around the Cricket and Tansy's ship.

"Is he dead?" Larkin slurred. "Make sure he's dead. He's a ghost."

"He's dead," Evie soothed, tearing a strip of her shirt with her teeth and tying it tight around Larkin's bicep. It was an insufficient tourniquet, but it would have to do until they got back to the ship. "I promise you, he's dead."

"He tricked me, Eves," Larkin sobbed, her face a mess of tears and smears of blood where she'd tried to wipe them away.

"I know Larks, but we have to go now, okay? We have to go."

Larkin nodded, and Evie scooped her up. She was light enough to carry, but Evie wasn't sure how long she could keep it up for. Larkin was fading fast, a dead weight in her arms that made her slower, clumsier. There was no choice. They had to move *now*.

Evie was thanking their lucky stars that Cabot had been foolish enough to send all the security forces to the docks, but they'd still have a hell of a time getting back to the ship, making their way through dozens of patrols. Larkin's bloody bandage and lolling head were too conspicuous for guards to ignore. She was careful on the stairs, her every movement jarring Larkin, who was practically delirious from blood loss. The entryway was just ahead, a shining bronze archway beset with green tinted glass, the foyer lined with more of the purifying algae chandeliers.

"You'll never make it through the city like that," came a soft drawl from the corner. It was the janitor, the one who had let her and Tansy go earlier.

"I don't have much of a choice," Evie said. "She's going to die if I don't get her back to the ship."

"Y'all aren't from round here, are you? Pirates or some such?"

"Something like that."

"Put her in the bin."

"Excuse me?"

The janitor gestured at her wheeled trash can. "I can smuggle her through. No one looks twice at the cleaners."

"How do I know you won't turn us in, instead?"

"Cuz I could have done that already, and I didn't." The janitor wiped her palms on her orange jumpsuit and held her hand out. "I'm Georgie."

Evie shook her hand. "Evie Anderson."

"Pleased to meet ya, Evie. On my gentlewoman's honor, I will get her to the docks." She pulled another orange jumpsuit from inside the bin, crisp and folded. "This one's for you."

"Why would you do this for us?"

"Because, Evie, this place is a goddamned hellhole, and someday soon you're gonna come back for my family, smuggle 'em out, get to some kinda refugee camp. That's the deal."

"What about you?"

"We'll discuss semantics later, put your jumpsuit on and let's get the hell out of here."

Evie set Larkin gently into the wheeled bin, and then zipped herself into the orange jumpsuit. She had no choice other than to trust this stranger. She nodded, and Georgie pushed open the windowed door.

"You'll have an easier time if you pull instead of push," Georgie said, gesturing at the trash can. "Follow me. I know a shortcut that might get us past most of the patrols."

She led them to the back of the Administration building, where a huge fountain spurted jets of water sparking in the scant light that escaped the doorway. Behind it, a wall of ivy that Georgie pushed away to reveal a narrow alley leading away from the building, sloping back down through the city.

They wound their way through the cobbled streets of Skelm, the yellow light of the lamps casting long shadows after them. One tiny, narrow alley after the next, away from the bustle of the main roads and the scrutiny of passers-by or armed militia. Alleys so small, Evie never would have found them on her own. In half the time it had taken to reach the administration center on their way in, Evie could see the docks, and the Cricket, surrounded by Coalition soldiers.

"Shit."

Georgie looked at her sideways from beneath her cap. "I'd say 'shit' is right. I can't get you to the door, not through that blockade."

"You've done enough. If we survive this, I promise, we will come back for your family."

"We're the Paynes. Don't let me down, Evie."

"You have my word. I won't forget this."

"Alright. I have an idea, my friend, but you're gonna have to trust me." Georgie pulled a box of matches from inside her jumpsuit, and snatched a bottle of cleaning solvent from the belt at her waist. "A diversion. Should pull enough of them away to get you through."

Evie caught Georgie's hand. "Please be careful."

"Careful's my middle name," Georgie winked. She tore off down a side street, running back up towards the administration building, her heavy work boots thudding on the pavement, echoing off the red brick walls.

Now, Evie just had to wait for the diversion. She cracked the lid of the bin and peered inside, swallowing a sob at Larkin's lifeless form. Evie's stomach dropped at the makeshift bandage saturated with Larkin's blood, pooling in a corner of the trash can. They didn't have much time. Every second felt like an hour, and Evie found herself praying to long dead gods that the Cricket wouldn't decide to leave without them.

"Hey!" a soldier said, passing by. "What are you doing down here? Get back to work!"

"Just... cleaning the streets?" Evie said hopefully, her heart racing in her ears. "Got reports of... trash."

The soldier rolled his eyes. "You fucking rats, always trying to nose around. Bunch of whiny layabouts."

Evie didn't move. She couldn't leave and risk missing the diversion, her only chance to get back to the Cricket.

"What are you waiting for? Move!" the soldier shouted into her face, his hand drifting towards the baton that hung at his waist.

Her heart pounded so fierce in her chest, she thought it might burst right through her skin. "I—"

Suddenly, a huge explosion from far off, and the sound of dozens of windows shattering with the impact, even this far away. Shards of glass pelted down from the sky, and chaos screamed through the soldiers' ranks. They tore off in all directions, some fleeing from the explosion, and some towards it. This was it. Evie pushed past the bewildered soldier in front of her and ran full pelt towards the Cricket's loading bay ramp, pulling the wheeled bin behind her, lifting it over the lip of the ramp and screaming, "We're here! Go!"

Someone slammed the emergency close lever, and the loading bay doors began to move towards each other, just as shots rang out on the docks from the remaining soldiers there. Evie hugged the bin with fierce protection, shielding it from any oncoming bullets that made it past the doors. The engines were already engaged, the boilers hot and full capacity, and the ship lifted from the ground as soon as the doors were sealed, even as Coalition bullets dented the loading bay doors.

Hyun was already there, fitting a tourniquet around Larkin's arm as Jasper pulled her unconscious body gently from the wheeled bin. He lifted Larkin and carried her off towards the medical bay.

"She'll be alright," Hyun said, and set a hand on Evie's shoulder. "Nothing a few stitches and a transfusion can't fix. If I can make that woman a new rib cage and have her survive it, she will absolutely survive this."

"How in the hell?" Captain Violet asked, her tone equally proud and mystified. "There were dozens of soldiers blockading us. We were about to resort to emergency measures."

"Captain, look," Kady said, standing on the toes of her boots to see out the small porthole window at the side of the loading bay doors. "An explosion at the Administration building."

"Was that you?" Captain Violet asked.

Evie shook her head. "No. A woman, a janitor named Georgie Payne. We'd never have gotten through without her." Tears began to well in Evie's eyes, and she started to lose control. "She helped us, she caught me and—" she paused. "What happened to Tansy?"

"*Captain* Tansy gave us the heads up that you two were about to run into some trouble. Gave us some time to prepare the ship, hope and pray you'd make it back. She left before the blockade formed."

"She said you two used to run together."

Captain Violet coughed. "Something like that. It was a long time ago. Nice to see her back on a ship, she's a fierce woman."

"Yes, a long time ago," Alice piped in, wrapping her arms around the captain's shoulders. "A long, *long* time ago."

"Can I...?" Evie asked.

"Of course, go see her," Captain Violet said warmly. "You've been through a lot together."

* * *

"Eves," Larkin croaked, her throat dry and tight. "Eves, are you there?" Her head was pounding so hard, she didn't even want to open her eyes.

A hand closed over her own. "Of course I'm here."

"Is he dead?"

"He's dead. I'm sure of it."

"I can't do this anymore, Eves. I have to find some other way to live. I can't be an assassin, not knowing all the trouble they went through to control me, to use me to achieve their horrible ends. I can't."

"Shh, it's okay. We'll find something. But first, you have to rest."

"Where's Kady?"

"You know, Larkin, I'm not going to keep lending you clothes if you're just going to bleed all over them," Kady smirked, leaning against the wall.

Larkin gave a weak laugh. "Sorry." When she pried open an eyelid, there they were, all gathered around her bedside. "There was a chip. The black market chip. Had a detonator." She reached into her breast pocket with clumsy fingers and tossed the chip to Kady. "Find some way to deactivate them."

"Fuck," Kady said softly. "I'll have to reach out to my contacts. I wish I could say I'm shocked they did that to you, but..."

"But they're bastards?" Larkin added.

"Heh. Yeah."

"Eves," Larkin coughed, her throat raw, "I'm sorry I didn't stay with you, that we didn't get the data, I just— "

"Shh," Evie shushed again, and pulled a small square disk from her pocket. "I understand. It's alright, I got something." Evie tossed the disk to the captain, who snatched it out of the air with a raised eyebrow.

"Well, Anderson, aren't you a surprise?" Captain Violet said. "What did you find?"

Evie shrugged. "It's encrypted, some kind of code, but maybe you can work on it. At least it's not nothing."

"Hey Boss, there's an incoming radio transmission from Tan— I mean, Captain Tansy," crackled Ned's voice from the radio mounted into the corner.

"Patch her through," Captain Violet said.

"Hello there, Captain Violet and Cricket crew!" chirped Tansy's voice. "A job expertly well done, if I do say so myself. A display of excellent teamwork and a hell of a lot of luck that I hope to recreate again in the future." The radio popped and snapped with the open line. "I've decided to stay on this ship here, I'm *incredibly* taken with the sound of *Captain* Tansy."

"It's a comfort to know you'll be flying these skies with us," Captain Violet said, and even in her dazed stupor, Larkin saw the scowl on Alice's face. "What about your tavern? Are we all destined to unending thirst in Bradach?"

"Hell no," Captain Tansy replied, laughing. "Evie, what do you say to general management and part ownership? If you don't take it, the offer goes to Gabe, and he'll run the place right into the ground. But if you're enjoying life on the run out here, then I'll encourage you to have as many adventures as you want before you lose a limb, too."

Evie sucked in her breath and grasped Larkin's hand, and the warmth was calm and comforting. "What do you think?" Evie asked.

"I'll follow wherever you want to go," Larkin replied, squeezing Evie's hand. "A tavern in Bradach, a ship in the skies, I'm happy to just be near you." She said this as a whisper, a little embarrassed for the whole crew to hear it, but too delirious to care. "Besides, you've saved my ass twice now, my goose is cooked if I try to go it alone from here on out."

"That's an affirmative, Captain Tansy," Evie announced, and then, a bit quieter, "but I'm sorry to be leaving the Cricket. It's been... well, it's changed my life."

"Captain Violet, I'll see you back in Bradach. I hear we have something to celebrate. Captain Tansy out."

"Well, it sounds like you two have a new adventure on the rise," Captain Violet said, a tinge of regret in her voice. "We'll all be sorry to see you go."

Larkin coughed, and took the cup of water that Evie handed her, and took a long drink. "Thanks again for breaking us out of that prison," she rasped, her cracked, dry lips turned up into a smile, "couldn't have done it without you." She reached for her pendant, but found only skin.

"I'm sorry, Larks, that we couldn't get it back for you."

She smiled, and took Evie's hand. "Maybe some things are best left in the past. My future is what's more important to me, now."

Epilogue

"Another round!" Ned shouted, banging his shot glass against the glossy wood of the Purple Pig tavern bar. Gabe struggled to keep up, haphazardly sloshing whiskey and rum into the glasses. "We're celebrating a wedding, after all! To the captain and her wife!" he shouted, lifting his glass in the air.

"To Violet and Alice!" Evie responded, and the others echoed the sentiment. Captain Violet and Alice were celebrating their secret nuptials at long last, both clad in ivory three piece suits, with matching brocade waistcoats and tailored, long tailed jackets. Evie and Larkin had spent hours decking out the Purple Pig with bunches of white daisies tied to every curtain, chair, and hung over every table. It was magical, the perfect reception for a couple so in love.

Evie's mind wandered, despite the raucous cheers from the crew. It had been nearly a month since they'd escaped Skelm, but it felt like years. Her promise to Georgie Payne nagged at her, threatening to drag her back to their apartment where she'd set up a chalkboard the length of the wall, already filled with nebulous plans and ideas on setting up a refugee camp in Bradach. It would be the first of its kind, if she succeeded.

"You alright?" Larkin snaked an arm around her waist and interlaced their fingers.

"Yeah," Evie answered, kissing her on the cheek. "I hope they like the party."

"It looks amazing, Eves," she whispered in her ear as the crew of the Cricket danced and sang. "You're really in your element here."

"They deserved something nice, after all they've been through. After all this time in love."

"Do you think that will be us one day?"

Evie wrinkled her nose. "I don't want some big thing." She turned and kissed Larkin gently. "I just want you."

Later, when the tavern was quiet, and the lights dimmed low, Evie and Larkin danced in the silence, holding each other tight. When they finished, Larkin presented her with her first attempt at cooking: a mostly edible, if slightly burnt, dish of paella.

End of Book 2

Keep reading for a sneak peek into the next novel in the series, **Storm Signal.**

Sign up for my newsletter and get information about convention appearances, book launch parties, new releases, and more! Get bonus content for the Cricket Chronicles series like deleted scenes and extended cuts. You can unsubscribe at any time with no obligation.

http://eepurl.com/gOQBaP

FOLLOW ME

You can follow me on Twitter at @IMRyannFletcher, on Facebook @RyannFletcherWrites, Instagram @RyannFletcherWrites, or email at RyannFletcherBooks@Gmail.com. It's always great to hear from you!

Storm Signal preview

Georgie wrinkled her nose at the full waste bin in the conference room, piled high with half-eaten fruits and used tissues. It never ceased to anger her that Coalition higher ups would waste food when so many here in Skelm were starving. Janitors like her were routinely fired for picking through the trash, as it was deemed *unseemly* by the well-dressed rulers of this rock.

Skelm was dirty, covered in thick layers of grime that settled in your lungs at the first opportunity. The cleaning solvents were harsh, and made Georgie feel like she couldn't get enough air. She wasn't allowed to wear a mask, because that was considered *unseemly* too. She dumped the contents of the overflowing basket into her wheeled bin, and swallowed back a gag at the fruit, not long in the trash, but brown and slimy from the hot sunlight that beat down through the floor to ceiling windows. Whoever designed this building was a mindless fool, and the conference rooms were never anything other than unpleasantly warm.

She tugged at the neck of her orange jumpsuit and felt sweat drip down her back. An unfortunately not unfamiliar feeling for Georgie, who had worked as a janitor in the Skelm administration building for nearly five years. Despite the chemicals that settled at the back of her throat when she scraped away the unending muck that settled on every surface in this settlement, her job was a far sight better than working at one of the many factories on Skelm. That was a death sentence. She thought of her mother, sick and struggling to breathe, and her jaw set firm. Someday she'd get them all off this rock.

It had been nearly two months since she helped the pair of pirates escape the city, and they'd promised to come back for Georgie's family. "We're the Paynes," she'd said, before creating a diversion for them by way of a chemical explosion. Nearly all the windows in the building had shattered, sending shards of glass spiraling through the air and settling on the streets like ice. The windows had been replaced within the week, and already they were covered in Skelm scum.

"Amaranth, honestly, no one can understand you like that!" a flustered man said, rustling papers at the long, oval table. "Why don't you just write it down instead?" The man was a visitor in the city, probably some higher up Coalition manager who wanted to be sure that production was flowing at the factories.

The woman he addressed scribbled furiously on a pad of yellowing paper, splashing ink across the varnished wood. *Great*, Georgie thought to herself, *something else I'll have to clean up later.*

"Amaranth, we're just going to let someone else take point on this one. We understand your predicament and that you've not healed quite yet, but we need someone who can command and train a team of new investigators, and I'm afraid you're not up to the challenge. Don't worry, you'll get your opportunity with the next batch of recruits."

"Uh, she's writing that she's completely capable, and that her jaw will be unwired within the fortnight," said a small man, dressed in a deep green velvet jacket. His voice was squeaky and unsure. "She says that she won't have this posting taken from her on account of not being able to speak, as the most effective interrogation efforts don't require speech."

The first man sighed and rubbed at his temples. "I realize you are very capable at what you do, Amaranth, but we cannot delay these recruits any longer. The Coalition has great need of them! Have you even seen how high the prisoner files are stacked these days? What do you expect me to do, interrogate them all myself?" He paused and gave an exasperated sigh when the woman began scratching at the paper with her pen once more. "No. No, enough. I'm not doing to debate this with you, Amaranth, we have neither the time nor the resources to drag this out any longer." He straightened the papers in front of him and stood up. "We will revisit this when you are better equipped to teach a class. Until then, you will be reassigned to desk duty, where you will review and file completed confessions."

The woman bared her teeth, covered in silver wire, and grunted loudly, something Georgie imagined would sound like "No" if she was able to open her mouth. The woman slammed her fists down on the table and glared at the man. The other participants at the table shrank back in their seats, intimidated by the aggressive display. After all, most of them were here for a visit, not stationed here, and preferred to be much further away from witnessing the violence of an interrogation first hand. Georgie tipped the second wastebasket into the bin and gently pushed down on papers to create more room in her wheeled bin. The delicate crunch of the papers drew the attention of the room.

"Don't you think you could do your job a little *quieter*?" a woman dressed head to toe in vibrant purple silks scoffed. "Surely that's achievable?"

"Yes ma'am," Georgie replied, and plastered a grin across her face. "My sincerest apologies."

"A verbal response was not required," the woman in purple said, her ire palpable. "I shall report this to your supervisor."

"Come now, Rowena, we don't have time for such frivolities. We have to get back to the transport within the hour or we'll have to wait until tomorrow."

"Charles, it would be inappropriate to ignore a breach in etiquette from a member of staff, even in a backwater like this."

The man sighed again and slid his papers into a polished leather briefcase. "Very well, then. But make it quick, I don't want to be late for our next meeting."

Georgie backed against the wall as Rowena passed, the silks of her skirts rustling noisily. She nodded politely, her eyes fixed on the gleaming marble floor, shot through with flecks of gold and sparkling granite. She couldn't risk being written up for any further infractions; if she lost this job, then her family would end up back in the tenement they'd started in. No, she couldn't go back to that. Her mother and sisters deserved better than to be crowded into bunks with hundreds of strangers, all fighting for scraps of clean linen for their beds.

"Amaranth, my decision is final. Stop writing, I won't read it," Charles said, his voice flat and disinterested.

The woman thrust the papers at his face and gestured to her jaw, grunting.

"Absolutely not. It's no longer up for discussion. We will return in six months, and we will reinstate you then, if you are fit for the position. In the meantime, we will have Johnson fill in for you. As I said, we have no time to spare in these matters. We cannot wait for you to be ready to do your job." He strode from the room, briefcase in hand, his footsteps even and sure on the marble.

The woman glared at him as he left, her fists clenched in fury. The small man looked at her apologetically and shuffled to the door, papers in hand.

Georgie moved to the windows and dumped a scoop of the waxy white cleaning beads into a bucket of cold water in preparation to scrub the windows clean and prevent the yellow build up of grease and smog that would thoroughly offend the visiting Coalition management. Georgie began to scrub at the grime, now accustomed to the insistent burning of the cleaning solution as it ran down her arms. Gloves weren't allowed either, as it might make people think the cleaning solution was dangerous.

The angry rustling of papers made Georgie look over her shoulder at the woman, who was shuffling through files looking for something. "Did you need any help?" Georgie asked. It was an infraction to not offer help to someone with seniority and position over her.

The woman stared at Georgie, a closed lipped smile spreading over her face as she dumped the entire well of ink out over the desk, making sure to shake the last drops free. She stood, leaving scraps of paper littered over the desk and floor, and swept out of the room, a silk top hat under her arm.

When the door closed behind the woman, Georgie swore under her breath. The entitlement of these Coalition suits was just breathtaking. She began to mop up the ink, knowing that the longer it sat, the harder it would be to clean. The sticky black ink was already beginning to set, drying into a shiny mess atop the varnished wood. Water dripped from the bristled brush onto the table as she scrubbed. The cleaning agent they used on the windows, walls, and floors would strip the paint from the wood in a heartbeat. She didn't want to think what it was doing to her lungs day in and day out, and whatever harm it was doing wasn't as bad as the emissions from the heavy machinery at the factories. Coal dust filled the air there, a result of the huge boilers that powered the city.

The crumpled page that the woman had thrust at Charles soaked in the water from the brush. The words, "*My name is Inspector Allemande, and you will address me as such*" blurred and disappeared into the soaked paper.

About the Author

First, I have to thank my wife, whose tireless enthusiasm and encouragement are what push me back to writing even on days I feel like I never want to write another word again.

Another huge thanks goes out to all my beta readers, who stuck with me even when Larkin was almost irredeemable. You helped bring this story to life, and for that, I can't thank you enough.

And finally, I want to thank YOU, the reader, for using your precious time to read this book. I hope you will join all of us in book three, Storm Signal.

You can connect with me on:

- https://ryannfletcher.com
- https://twitter.com/IMRyannFletcher
- https://facebook.com/RyannFletcherWrites
- https://instagram.com/RyannFletcherWrites

Subscribe to my newsletter:

- http://eepurl.com/gOQBaP

Also by Ryann Fletcher

Storm Signal: Cricket Chronicles book 3

https://books2read.com/StormSignal

Georgie saved the Cricket crew, but will they come back to fulfill their bargain before all hope is lost? When meteorologist Henry shows up to investigate some anomalies in the storms outside Skelm, she starts to unravel a dangerous secret.

Printed in Great Britain
by Amazon

49822847R00208